Hardening the Steel

Wandering Blacksmith 1

Mark B. Gilgam

Cover Art: Einar Kowalski

Impressum
Mark B. Gilgam
c/o AutorenServices.de
Birkenallee 24
36037 Fulda
Mark.B.Gilgam@AutorenServices.de

Other books by Mark B. Gilgam

Wandering Blacksmith Series:

Wandering Blacksmith 1 Hardening the Steel

Wandering Blacksmith 2 Heavy Metals

Wandering Blacksmith 3 The Bloody Hand

Wandering Blacksmith 4 The Star Song

Wandering Blacksmith 5 Road of Dragons Part I + II

Contents

The Battle of the Blood Swamp

King Tombrok of the Ferys stood in front of his warriors. Every man from fifteen to fifty was there; all the Ferys could bring into the field for years to come.

He missed his wife Idafara, missed her presence, standing behind him as she had in every war. That was the old way, but the old way was dead. Queen Idafara's task was to hold Dokkerhall until his grandsons, Okkilo and Gerbern, were ready to lead. It broke his heart. Both his sons, Kuniwin and Okko, were with him here in Lalland. No spare. Sometimes it was necessary to bring everything. This was such a time.

Tridden Moor was yellow and bare. Few birch trees had grown back since the forest had disappeared into the smelting ovens of Kullen Tor, the bog iron layers run out, the workers left, and the mosses grew and swelled with the rain of the years without summer. Tridden Moor had been deserted until the Kri had come to lair on Kullen Tor.

Tombrok could feel the Kri presence out there by the way his hair stirred on the nape of his neck. He touched his silver amulet in the shape of Donner the Defender's war-hammer.

A tall warrior strode past several paces in front of the Theusten host. With grudging satisfaction, Tombrok marked King Grimwolf. His broad chest and back were armed in iron armour plate, his long hair the colour of reed in winter, was shining pale before he covered it with a steel helmet. Slanting blue eyes expressionless beside the steel nose guard looked towards the Ferys. The red war-hound stalking at his heels also turned his massive head.

"Behold the two vicious wolves going into battle," Kuniwin grumbled.

"Good to see King Grimwolf here," Tombrok agreed. "He returned in time."

Grimwolf passed all other hosts without checking his stride. Tombrok heard Okko's jealous mutter.

"Easy, son," he muttered softly. "This is the time for heroes."

It was as if Grimwolf crossed an invisible line.

5

Men surged forward left and right, their breath white in the cold air. Suddenly the entire northern host began streaming into the frozen Tridden Moor in the wake of the advancing Theusten.

The deep, furious sound of Modi's Urloghorn drowned all words.

The moor sloped upward, black stone ridges jutted through yellow grass and stunted birch trees grew among pools of dark brown water.

The Ferys warriors kept close together, ready to form the shield line at once. Tombrok noticed that the Theusten did the same. The Kri were stealthy like shadows, quick like the wind, and as easy to stop as a storm tide, once they broke into a host.

They passed water-filled ditches where long ago the smelters had dug peat.

There, standing in a single line barring the dry strip of land were the first Kri.

A gasp went up among the northern host. Nobody ever got quite used to the sight of them: tall, strong and fair like Nordheim's war gods of legend.

A furious howling arose from behind.

Black-painted warriors stormed past the Ferys, throwing off their wolf skins and their black shields, naked, yelling and swinging blades in each hand. The Wulfhetnar, the blood-mad warriors of Wutan were in full howling rage. They overtook the Theusten.

The Kri awaited with cold calculation in their light-coloured eyes.

#

The muted noise of clashing shields and shouting receded into the moor like a monstrous tide running out.

With her satchel containing medicines and surgical instruments at her feet, Aslaug stood as far from women of the Vanadis Temple as was possible. Conscious of their ageless faces, she wondered what she looked like to them. Greetings had been exchanged and smiles bridged the distance between those who had remained on Mount Lyfja high above the cycle of love, childbirth and death and the one who had walked down to risk all on love. And lost everything. Aslaug didn't want to answer questions about her man who had followed his liege lord's call to arms. Gutorm hadn't wanted to go and hadn't thought the fight could be won. He never returned. Aslaug

6

was forced to abandon the homestead to flee for safety to the border castle of Tomdam, which turned out not to be safe after the war was lost.

She didn't want to talk about her sons, how she had carried them in her belly, in her arms. She didn't want to talk about how she lost them both, the toddler and the baby, in the fall of Tomdam, ten days ago, and how much her breasts hurt her. She didn't want to talk about who the man was now standing beside her, tall, broad-shouldered, with a red mane of hair ablaze in the rising sun.

She glanced at Eckehart, and he smiled, his blue eyes lighting up, the only smile she had seen that day. She did not respond, knowing it to be graceless of her, and not caring.

#

The sun passed its zenith, the pale-yellow light blinding the eyes, striking glittering reflections from the golden shields and gold studded capes of Svalinir's priests and the high silver crowns of Sinthgunt of the Lands Under the Northern Light.

Aslaug and Eckehart were still standing in the same place.

The judges of Irmin Prono the Lawgiver were still holding their tablets and runestones before their chests as they had done since morning when Svalinir's spear had been cast.

Farther back stood the priests of Nyjord of the Sea and those of the Gentle Twins Levrow Vanadis and Grön Yngvi.

Standing a little to one side were the priests of the Vyndel, Bolapi, Ranen and Sysslas with their wooden statues of the Three-headed Goddess and the White Horse Lord and to the other side were the Loddafafnir, followers of Lopatir the Jester, in their patched cloaks, leather masks hanging around their necks and their faces coated in thick white paint without their habitual sneer, holding talismans of little wire nets in which to capture the fallen Kris' souls.

"I don't believe they can do it."

"I don't understand why they would want to try." No god could want cold souls like these, not even the Tricky Lord.

"They were worse."

Aslaug knew Eckehart referred to the high priests of Fimbultyr, and their plans to bind the Kri to the service of the Allgod of

7

Tyrsland. In their cloaks and crowns of raven feathers, they stood behind the Judges as if nothing had happened to their discredit. Such stupidity, she thought; hadn't they looked at these unnatural killers, hadn't they realised what it was they were seeing? Nobody could use the Kri for anything. Although she hadn't answered, Eckehart seemed to sense her thoughts.

"Sigregin won his point. We can write that on his grave marker."

Although King Sigregin had been murdered, the united northern host had come to Lalland on the Day of the Longest Night to exterminate the Kri before they would have rendered Nordheim defenceless and opened up for the empires.

"Couldn't let them stay, couldn't let them go. Had to come to this one day," Eckehart said.

Of course, he would even miss the killers. He and the other blacksmiths had been enthusiastic about making weapons for these perfect warriors. They were the only ones who the Kri respected and gave freedom among themselves. That was what she couldn't forgive. It made no difference that he had saved her from Jarl Erpen's soldiery and protected her now. It was worthless for he had failed to save her children.

Without the blacksmiths, would it even have come to this? To be just, it probably would have. Men were men, and they would make war with bare hands. However, the damage might have been less. Her children might be alive. Perhaps even Gutorm might still be with her. How had he died, this gentle, wise man? There had been no news.

"It won't matter to us nor to any of them." Eckehart indicated the priests and healers with a sideways inclination of his head, "except Svalinir's Speer bearer if he doesn't drop it quick. Don't be afraid. They never harm those who are unarmed."

Her breath caught. "They'll just kill all our warriors," she said, not trusting her voice. She almost choked with rage. "Then, they'll walk away from their handiwork and leave us to the mercenaries of the empires."

"Our world was already changing," he said carefully, "even before the Kri broke out of the ice of the north, even if Nordheim doesn't become the property of the kings or falls prey to the empires in the south."

She knew with a bleak realisation that he was right, that nothing could bring back the old way of frugal, dangerous, independent living. A hundred thousand men had gone into Tridden Moor to accomplish nothing. All she could do about it was to try to staunch the blood.

"Don't hate me for saying it," Eckehart said.

She didn't. She thought she didn't.

They were the only ones talking. All others were quiet, staring towards the silhouette of Kullen Tor, just barely visible in the distance and the fog, waiting for what would come out of Tridden Moor — waiting what would be their fate.

#

It is over," Eckehart said.

The noise of battle they had heard all day, like waves crashing on a shore, when had it ceased? It left a silence as if nothing was left alive in Tridden Moor, the place where more than a hundred thousand men had fought since morning. Men and women strained to hear something.

A white wall came rolling silently out of the moor, blotting out the afternoon sun. Aslaug found herself alone in the blinding fog, although she knew that Eckehart stood no more than three feet apart from her.

She heard the long-drawn howl of a dog.

Shadows, gigantic shapes, appeared in the mist.

The watchers stood petrified; one Vanadis priestess stifled a whimper.

A distorted figure approached, the outline assuming normal proportions as it became more distinct. A warrior stumbled out of the mist, covered in mud and blood. It was Tombrok, the Ferys king, trailed by four warriors in as bad of shape.

"Is it done?" the First Judge of Irmin Prono demanded. His voice sounded brittle and peremptory and out of place.

The Ferys king staggered past without looking at anyone.

"It is," one of the warriors replied in the king's stead. "We killed

9

them all."

Movement stirred among the crowd; healers surrounded the Ferys king and his men.

Svalinir's priests lit torches and sounded the Audumhorns to guide back the living and the souls of the fallen so that they would not lose their way in the fog and stray into the gates of the Nine Netherworlds opening at the sundown of the Longest Night.

More shadows appeared, turning into exhausted men, badly wounded every one of them.

So few came back.

Aslaug set to work among the remains of the Gauten, Eckehart by her side, the same he had been ever since Tomdam fell. She didn't acknowledge him, accepting his help in setting broken bones and straightening dislocated joints with his blacksmith's hands, as she had accepted all his other help without thanking him once.

"Only one line of shields. With their war bitches behind them," a Gauten spearman sitting on the ground wheezed. Reaching inside him with the senses that had made her a woman of Lyfja Mountain, she knew that a sword thrust had grazed one of his lungs. She wished that he wouldn't talk, but he continued. "Our shield wall was twenty deep, but we couldn't break their one line. They abandoned it to fall upon us. Took a dozen to slay just one of them." The man relapsed into his laboured wheezing.

"These are all the Gauten I have left. The Undead Emperor will have an easy play with Nordheim now." The Gauten leader Rempert winced while Eckehart cut the chin strap of his deformed helmet and the battered mail, whose dents were so deep that they were gauging into the flesh. "I'd have been dead without this mail."

"So you would have," Eckehart agreed. "It's an exceptional mail, Tolosan."

"Tomorrow you'll not be able to rise from your bed, lord," Aslaug warned quietly.

"My men?"

"Much weakened in body and mind."

"But they'll live?"

"If you don't have to fight the next days."

10

Rempert briefly inclined his head. "I hear you, Lady of Lyfja Mountain."

Aslaug didn't dissuade him that she was still of Lyfja Mountain. After all, she knew what to do.

As she worked, she noticed that something was terribly wrong with the men who came out of Tridden Moor. They appeared to be looking beyond fear and hope, resembling terrified survivors of a catastrophe, rather than the victors of the battle. She said so to Eckehart in a breathing moment.

"Like all those who have ever come up against the Kri," he answered soberly. "They break men's spirits. Even in their destruction. When an ordinary man comes up against them, he meets death. Even I, when I worked for them, knew that they were death. I knew they wouldn't attack me; I knew that I was safe. But they, they were like bears, like lions, like killer whales, only with a thinking brain. I don't know if I make any sense."

"Like the Dodlak."

"Exactly. Bless you, woman, there hasn't been a Dodlak seen in generations."

"And that's a good thing, as we shall not see - them - anymore."

The Audumnhorn was still blowing, going on and on, but Tridden Moor gave up no more men. Of the hundred thousand who had marched up to Kullen Tor, less than one in ten had come back down again. The Northern tribes had won the war by a handful of warriors still standing on their feet.

"Tiding of this battle must not spread," Aslaug heard the First Judge of Irmin Prono say in a hard voice nearby. "The women must not mourn, and the singers shall make no songs."

"That can be done." Rempert nodded, his mouth twisting. "This was bad fighting. No honour to be gained. Nothing but nightmare and shame."

"I told you that Svalinir's spear ought not to have been cast over the Kri anymore than over the Man-eaters in the Mist," A raven-clad priest of Fimbultyr interceded.

Aslaug could not hear how the first judge of Irmin Prono

11

responded because the three lowered their voices moving away to where a wary-eyed Master of Horse Herbrand stood among the bloodied remnants of his Nuitonen host.

It was less than an hour from darkness when out of the golden fog of Tridden Moor a great figure came staggering, dragging a huge sword. Exhausted men reached for their weapons again.

"It's a Kri!"

"Hold it!"

"It's Grimwolf!"

Seeing him, Aslaug felt a small bubble of happiness rising inside her. She realised that since her first sight of Grimwolf at the head of his warriors, she had been waiting for him to return. On this day, all her fear had been for him.

The Theusten king was alone, without armour. Blood drops splashed in his footprints; blood plastered his hair to his head. Half of his face was a gory mask.

He stumbled, broke to his knees.

One of the healers went forward and stopped with uncertainty on his face.

Grimwolf looked up; his bloodshot eyes were daring anyone to touch him. His face set in stubborn lines he rose again.

"I killed the last of them, and he killed me." He spoke to no one in particular. "None of my men left to bury me and remember. I shall die here like a dog in a ditch."

"You will die a king," Tombrok said. "Four men are all I have left of my Ferys following. They shall bury us side by side and bring the tide to Theustenland. I have an onion wound," he added. "This good child's brews," he waved a hand in Aslaug's direction "Can't stop up my guts. Won't last much longer than it takes you to bleed to death. Both my sons are dead. It will be a long time until your sons and my grandsons can be at each other's throat again. Sit and drink with me and say your last words."

"Why not. It is a small matter now."

Grimwolf sat down heavily on a black stone.

He drove his red sword into the ground and held on to the hilt. A king on his throne, scarlet with blood from head to foot, near death and indomitable. Wounded men gathered in a half-circle, to gaze upon him.

Grimwolf expected to die of his wounds, Aslaug knew, as she knew that he would not. From the moment that he stumbled out of the fog, she had resolved that she would not let him die.

Aslaug set to staunch the blood running from the king's side, at the same time feeling inside him with her senses. The stab to the chest had touched the sac around the heart and was mortal. It was a matter of heartbeats, maybe a thousand, or ten thousand. She sank her mind into it entirely, felt the fibres knitting. It cost a lot of her strength but she had more to give, and to this king she would have given all.

He allowed her to close the deep cuts on his chest and arms. When she attempted tending the wounds on his head and face, he caught her hand and held it for a while, then released her.

He released the hilt of his sword.

His blue eyes were upon her.

Suddenly, Aslaug was unable to meet this gaze. She set her face towards Tridden Moor as she hastily repacked her satchel.

Her first step was a flight away from Grimwolf.

"Nobody alive back there," Eckehart told her. "Every man I spoke to said so."

"I have to see for myself."

"Of course, you do. I come with you."

She didn't answer him yes or no, but he came all the same.

On the edge of the moor, they found a wounded Theusten lying on his back, holding on to the hilt of a broken sword with his mutilated right hand.

Aslaug bent down to him.

"No! Don't touch me!" he whispered. "Leave me be! I can't live. I came as far as I could. Did not want to lie there, among . . . them. Just don't touch me!"

She did not touch him.

Following the wide trail of the thousands, the stench of shit hit her nose first, the indignity of every battle death. Into it mingled the metallic tang of the blood, nauseous and sad. Catching Eckehart's worried look, she stepped forward.

Crossing the mud churned by thousands of feet, with the Audumnhorns' lost calls still sounding in the roiling whiteness, coming from all directions, they could not feel confident that they were walking towards Kullen Tor.

Their feet sank into the soggy ground. Looking down, Aslaug saw that the woven uppers of her shoes had turned red.

Dark rivulets were snaking downhill, forming red deltas among the yellow grass tufts. Farther on, the first dead emerged from the mists - the black-faced Berserks and the wolf skin-clad Wulfetnar warriors, their frenzied rage met indifferently by the Kri.

"Rabid fools never learn, so they died first," Eckehart commented.

Aslaug thought this a cruel epitaph for these men obsessed with fight and battle, bested so easily and dispatched so coldly.

To see the dead men of the Ferys shield wall was worse. Their broken bodies were so mingled with the earth that it was impossible to count their number.

The ground underfoot was turning into an ankle-high, sloshing swamp. Bloody mud and shit was seeping into her shoes.

Horses lay speared through, where mounted Winiler warriors had failed to break the Kri's line.

The waterholes and bracken were red, and the fog smelled of blood; she was not sure if this was reality or an illusion.

Droplets formed on her skin and ran down her face. The moisture plastering the hair to Eckehart's skull looked pink.

They walked as if parting shrouds, each step revealing a fresh horror.

"They've been blocking the dry stretches, and ours couldn't break their line," Eckehart said; it seemed to Aslaug as if he needed to comment, to give some sense and structure to something that made no sense. "They pushed it back by the sheer weight of their shield walls."

Slowly, very slowly, moving uphill in an agonising progress, trampling their dead under their feet, whole followings ground away. Gauten and Remi replaced the annihilated Ferys and Winiler, with

Vyndel and Ranen closing the gaps.

"How far is it still to Kullen Tor?" she asked with despair in her heart.

"How far? To count the rest of our men," he answered sadly.

No wounded had survived in the heaps of the dead, and all the dead so far had been warriors of the united northern tribes.

The first dead Kri warrior they saw was a woman. Two of the lances that had speared her through and lifted her over the shield wall still impaled her body. She was about six feet tall and powerfully built, and her fair hair was cropped short; yet, she was unmistakably female. Her face had been stamped in by a boot. Shattered bones mingled with mud and brains.

Eckehart bent down to examine her battle dress, the customary leather armour of the Kri, consisting of thick iron-studded straps and a belt with a short skirt consisting mainly of sheaths for blades, empty but for two. He took the sword from her hand, hefted it, and examined the knives.

"She was very young," Aslaug said.

"She was. And armed with iron, every bit. Even a rookie like this one." The tribesmen had been armed with fire-hardened spears, flint arrows, and soapstone clubs and bronze swords; only a few like the Theusten had iron weapons. The Kri had used iron arms exclusively, swords, lances, knives and the strangely shaped throwing blades fashioned for them alone.

"Kri are in love with steel. I could name any price I wanted, no haggling, threw down the gold on the spot, they did, without counting even."

"And you sold it to them."

"I did, and so did Swatgrim, Sonnwind, Wittig and Rudrig. Even Elmar, though they can't have had much joy with his shoddy stuff. Every gold coin of their wages the Kri turned into steel. Iron's been fairly pouring into their camps. Yes, I should know all about it. There must be hoards of steel weapons cashed on top of Kullen Tor." Speaking of this possible steel treasure Eckehart seemed to forget the slashed flesh around him, reminding Aslaug that she did not know

15

this man at all.

"I'm afraid of what I'll find up there," she said, hunching her shoulders.

They came upon another dead Kri warrior- a man- lying beside a heap of dead Langegeri, a big dog's jaw clamped around his throat, half tearing it out. The Kri had slit the dog's belly; he was still holding the knife hilt.

Eckehart also carefully examined him. "From now on, there will be more of them."

All dead Kri they found were young, men and women both, surrounded by dead tribes' warriors and dead dogs, the big war-hounds of the Theusten, Langegeri and Esseni.

"There were more than just one hundred thousand warriors," Eckehart remarked. "I don't think Nordheim would have won this battle without the dogs. And the horses. The Kri kept no animals."

For the tenth time, Aslaug stopped, straining to listen. She heard only the Audumnhorns' hopeless calling. "Nothing lives in this blood-swamp."

The rivulets of blood began running in a stronger stream, pooling in lower places, overflowing, running downhill. The mist was a red haze, and its metallic taste on her tongue sickened Aslaug.

"It's the sunset," Eckehart said with a concerned glance at her pale face.

"It's blood." She refused to be consoled by him.

The dead lay in swathes, tribesmen all of them for three hundred paces.

There had been a second shield line, and the dead Kri they saw there were adult men and women. They lay two by two, each couple the epicentre of a circle of bodies.

"Like swans," Eckehart said. Her uncomprehending look moved him to explain further. "Once a Kri man and woman find each other, they go everywhere together, fighting back to back. They can be hired only in pairs. The young ones might hire out singly, but you can be sure they keep out of the couples' way. Nobody wants to get caught between a Kri and his woman. They wouldn't survive each other either."

16

"I didn't know that," Aslaug said, her voice catching. "That is very– fine- of them."

Eckehart didn't see her painful flush.

There had been a third shield line where the swamp iron diggings had once been, marked by heaps of dead Theusten warriors who buried the Kri beneath their lacerated flesh. The shallow holes left by the smelting ovens had filled up to the rims with blood.

The fourth defence line near the hill summit had been held by old warriors, their short-cropped hair like hoarfrost.

Looking into these deeply-lined faces, at odds with their powerful frames, Aslaug felt a surge of hatred inside her that made her ill.

"How many men will a Kri this old have slain?" Eckehart echoed her thoughts.

This fourth shield wall had been the last Kri defence line just before the summit of Kullen Tor. Up there, among the black rocks, were the children. They lay the same way that Aslaug had found her little sons after the sack of Tomdam: small broken bodies. Like wolf cubs, they had been pulled from the holes and crevices among the black rocks and from beneath the torn-down leather tents.

"Ugly work. Poor bastards," Eckehart said, referring to the men who had reached the summit. He unhooked the flask from his belt, and the sharp smell of plum brandy mingled with the stench of death.

Aslaug shook her head at the proffered flask, regretting at this moment that she had never allowed herself the facile relief of drink.

"Look at the puppy warriors. Well, at least that made it a little easier to kill them."

It took her a while to understand what Eckehart meant and notice that several children held knives and that some of the blades were bloody.

"Razor-sharp. No dolls for these. The old ones taught them."

"Vicious old wretches," she said.

"I know that this," he gestured around him, "had to be done. But all the same . . ."

"Yes," she said. "All the same. That's just it."

"The Kri did countless killings, but never a thing like this."

"They just breached the walls for those who do these things,"

17

Aslaug said, not trusting her voice. "They broke the gates for the murderers, and then turned their backs. They didn't care at all." That was what had happened in Tomdam. She remembered a dispassionate face looking down on her, beautiful and devoid of mercy. "Left the beasts to claw each other up," she said, choking, feeling contaminated by a rage hot enough to dry her tears to bitter salt inside her.

"Now their children are lying here," he said gently.

"And for us, that makes it so much worse," she said. "That is the difference."

Walking among the dead Kri children, Aslaug forced herself to look at each little corpse- always the same small white face, blood-clotted fair hair, half-open blue eyes. It was her sons' dead faces she saw over and over again, the toddler, the baby. When Aslaug reached the summit of Kullen Tor, she had found only dead bodies among the rocks.

With despair in her heart, she saw the field of bodies and mud continue on the other side.

Descending, she came upon the wounded Kri warrior and his dead companion.

"Swans," the word came into her mind unbidden.

They were a man and a woman in their prime lying inside a ring of dead Theusten warriors who piled around the couple in heaps so high that they formed a wall. Standing on the slope, she could see inside that ghastly ring.

Near the Kri lay a big red war dog, his back hewn through, his bloody muzzle set in a snarl: Grimwolf's dog.

She knew at once that this Kri was alive. His face was so white that his short, pale-blond hair and eyebrows stood out in sharp contrast. His blood welled up from many deep wounds.

The woman beside him was dead. Her body was coated in blood, her neck slashed to the spine, her breast gaping red. Her face was calm as if she slept.

At one place, the dead Theusten were strewn wide rather than piled high. Aslaug stepped over the bodies and the dead war-hound.

The dying Kri's eyes opened, light grey and fully aware.

"Don't touch him!" she heard Eckehart shout.

Only then did she notice that he had become separated from her.

He came running down the slope, treading on the dead in a frantic effort to reach her. "Don't go near! Come away from him!"

The Kri raised himself a little so that his shoulders reclined on the dead woman and his head leaned back, offering his bare throat. "Easier," he said, his voice no more than a whisper, yet it held all the arrogance of his race.

"It's a trap!" she heard Eckehart shout. "Don't think of helping him!"

But Aslaug had already seen what the Kri was trying to screen. Instinctively, she went forward.

Between the wounded warrior's torn shoulder and the dead woman lay a naked child, so very still, its light-blue eyes looking directly at her. It was a boy not yet able to walk and unharmed. Not a drop of blood had fallen upon him.

Her hands went out towards the child with a will of their own.

Eckehart stood horrified, not daring to take another step.

He knew that to come this near to a Kri was laying one's life into the hands of uncaring gods. Being a healer did not guarantee Aslaug's safety. The Kri had no healers among their own and didn't accept help from those of other people.

"Don't hurt her, she's no warrior!" he shouted. "You only kill warriors, remember! We haven't seen you! I promise! We'll go back and tell everybody there is nothing left alive on Kullen Tor. I am the blacksmith Eckehart, all Kri have heard of me. And I promise you!"

Aslaug knelt, and Eckehart held his breath while she lifted the child out.

The boy lay still in her arms, looking up to her, and her face softened.

Aslaug straightened up and turned to the agitated smith. "I can't leave the child," she said. "This warrior will be dead by sunset. The wolves and foxes will come in the night, and ours will come in the morning." She turned back to the dying Kri, and their eyes met. "I will take this boy in place of my two sons whom I lost because of

19

your kind, Kri. He will never know about you. He will learn right from wrong and not have to be killed like a raving wolf. Like you."

"Blood," the dying warrior said. "Cannot . . . cheat . . . blood."

"Blood is no excuse for what you did, Kri, for what you are. Blood is no excuse for anything. You chose yourselves. That is the difference between man and animal."

The Kri did not answer.

Pressing the child to her chest, hard, her breasts hurt worse than before.

"What is his name?" she asked with a catch in her voice.

"Kitt," the Kri warrior's voice was almost inaudible.

With a quick scramble, Eckehart was over the ring of dead warriors and stepped between the Kri and Aslaug.

Laying his hand on the blood-caked hilt of the long iron sword, he expected to feel his wrist breaking, the edge to bite into his side at any moment. He knew the Kri, like dead hornets, always had one last sting.

The warrior's right hand moved away from the sword.

"That's right, you want your boy to live," Eckehart said, the strain was audible in his voice. "We're his only chance. You know that." He gripped Aslaug by the arm roughly and pushed her away, keeping between her and the Kri, clutching the sword.

The Kri did not move.

"But woman, do you know what you are doing?" Eckehart hissed when he had her at what he judged to be a safe distance.

"Of course," she replied, casting around for something to wrap the child against the cold and seeing only steel and leather.

"This will cut us off from all our people. We can never go back."

"I don't mind." She took some linen from her medicine satchel and wrapped the boy in that. "It's no concern of yours," she added. "Just keep the promise you gave him. Don't tell anyone about this child. Forget."

"Forget? That? Where do you think you're going?"

Aslaug didn't answer, pressing the child's warm body to her painful breasts. She had not given any thought to that at all.

20

"Isenkliff," Eckehart said. "I will take up Brynnir's Hammer."

Aslaug looked at him with surprise. Every man, woman and child in the Northern Realm knew of Isenkliff, the remote island in the Graumeer, where Brynnir's Smithy stood. Where few had ever dared go, fewer returned. There was always a smith on Isenkliff. Brynnir had been the first in a long succession. There was one there now. If Eckehart offered to take his place, then that blacksmith would be able to leave the island. Not before. And Eckehart could never leave unless another smith offered to take up Brynnir's Hammer.

"But why?" she asked.

"You know why." Eckehart looked hard at her. "Same reason I came here with you."

"Yes, I know," she said, smiling up into his face over the child's fair, fuzzy head that was nuzzling into her dress. "You came for the Kri's iron hoard, blacksmith."

"That also," he admitted. "I have found their store; the whole stack is here in the old mine digs, just as I expected. Tons and tons of forged iron." That was why he had become separated from her when she found the wounded Kri, she thought detached.

"You will always have a second reason, Eckehart, won't you?"

"Maybe I will. Even a third," he said. "I am a blacksmith, and they call us canny, devious. It is all true. You see, it wasn't only for the Kri iron I came, but also for my own. All the way here, I have been looking for my swords, expecting to find them sticking in the guts of our men. I did find a couple." He raised the Kri's sword before his eyes. The straight blade was unusually long and broad, and the grip was wrapped around with leather worn smooth, while the cross-guard was a plain steel bar, and the pommel a steel ball. It was a simple thing of deadly beauty; even Aslaug could see that.

Eckehart's eyes shone at the sight. "This one I didn't forge. I wish I had. Not one notch, not the least bit bent, after all the killing he did with it today." He motioned with his free hand to the ring of corpses and the wounded man in the centre. "And here I am, wishing I could make a thing like that. Yes, Isenkliff is the place for me. As it is for him." Eckehart lowered the sword and touched the small blond head with a finger, "I will teach him my trade. He shall be a blacksmith."

"He shall be a healer," Aslaug retorted. "Not a killer. Nor make tools for killing," she added defiantly in the face of Eckehart's slight smile.

"You heard?" Eckehart turned to address the wounded Kri warrior, who was still watching them. "Now, tell me quickly while you can still speak! Where did you get this sword? Who forged it? One day, your son will want to know."

"He won't," Aslaug interrupted. "Didn't you listen? He shall never know. You will promise me, Eckehart, right here! We take the boy, not the sword. That sword is the last this child needs." Over the child in her arms, they confronted each other, the healer and the blacksmith.

"I give you the promise you demand of me," Eckehart said. "I will play by your rules as I have done since I plucked you out from under Jarl Erpen's thugs. Because if I don't, you'll turn your back on me and walk to your ruin. You needed protection coming here, and you need it much more now. What's more, I will leave all the Kri iron for the other smiths to grab. But I will take this sword. "

"Leave it. Just drop the thing, Eckehart!" Aslaug spoke more softly than she had before. "It is forfeit to the gods as all things Kri are. No smith will care to pick up such accursed metal."

"Like hell, they won't!" Eckehart laughed bitterly. "And don't talk to me about curses. What I take is nothing compared to what you have picked up yourself. No priest's curse can follow me to Brynnir's island. Nor you and him."

Aslaug finally admitted the sense, not by saying as much but by opening her dress, giving in to the urgings of the child's small head. Her breast proved too inflamed to release the milk confined so painfully, and she would almost have cried then. The child did not wail in protest, as any other baby would have. It just looked at her with its blue eyes, snuggling to her like a kitten.

Eckehart had turned back to the Kri warrior, approaching him as far as he dared. "Who forged this sword? Can you still hear me?"

The Kri warrior's grey eyes were open, unfocused; he hardly seemed to breathe anymore.

"What is your name?" Eckehart spoke louder. "Your boy, Kitt, is

22

that a true name? Kitt? Or does it just mean child same as in our language? Who forged this sword? Does the sword have a name?"

The Kri warrior did not answer.

"Too far gone, can't seem to stir him up no more. Can you bring him around long enough to answer me? Not go near him again; only tell me how!" Aslaug shook her head, and the demand in his face changed to contrition. "You see how it is with me, why I'm for Isenkliff."

"Yes, I see," she said, and she even smiled a little.

"Kitt it is then," Eckehart said. "Farewell Kri. I hope you die before ours come back here. For your sake and for theirs."

Aslaug looked into the still face. She was about to leave a man who was bleeding to death beside his dead woman. Nobody would ever know what she had done, except herself and Eckehart. Was there ever a justification for a thing like that, she wondered, and if so, wasn't there a justification for everything?

"Come now! He doesn't expect anybody to hold his hand. I could cut his throat, but frankly I don't dare to do him this favour. Let's get out of here with our loot. Fast."

As he turned to go, his left leg suddenly gave.

He sat down heavily and, with a face of dumb surprise, gazed at the limp foot in his blood-filled leather shoe. "Must have nicked the tendon. Didn't even notice how and when. All that sharp steel lying about."

Bending over him, Aslaug saw a white strand running through his red hair that hadn't been there before. She didn't know yet that her golden hair was now white-streaked.

She bound up his leg tightly; the necessary operation would have to wait. She cast around for something Eckehart could lean on and spotted two broken spear shafts.

The mist thickened so much that she couldn't see the wounded Kri anymore within the circle of his victims.

That made it easier to leave.

She couldn't see which way went up, which down. They just followed the rivulets of blood, Eckehart hobbling on his makeshift crutches, Aslaug carrying the child. Soon her arms hurt but she knew

23

that she wouldn't release him, even for a moment of relief.

They came upon another battle survivor down the slope; it was a big, grey wolf-hound lying on its side, exhausted, its flanks rising and falling. It was a young animal, a year old maybe. There was not a scratch on him.

Since Aslaug would not leave behind this still-living creature, Eckehart fashioned a sack from a bloody tunic and carried the dog on his back.

Brynnir's Forge

First Blood

The boy looked down on the dead Woodstalker lying among the tangerine daisies. He held the bloody knife as if it wasn't his.

Kitt had not been aware of the warrior's presence until the attack.

The deep knife-wound directly above the heart had bled very little. Blue-black hair spread out in a dark halo around his face, which was still fierce, hard and strangely joyful; the black eyes without the whites showing were wide open, almost but not quite looking at Kitt.

The warrior did not seem dead.

Except for two leather bits slung around his hips and through his legs, he was naked. The tanned skin, painted with black swirls and dots, had made him nearly invisible in the under-brush.

The right hand was adorned with wristbands of human skin and hair, brown and curly. The scarred fingers were gripping a short bronze-tipped stabbing-spear. A bronze knife with a bone hilt had fallen beside the body.

Necklaces of animal teeth and claws lay on the now-still chest, bear, wolf and the hand-long, porcelain-white, curved tooth of a Dodlak. This trophy marked the warrior as one who had hunted the Death-Smile Cat of the Murkowydir Wood.

While the boy looked upon his fallen assailant, something changed. The exultation smoothed out, leaving a remote face with the shadow of a smile nesting in the corners of the mouth and the eyes.

Kitt could not say when life began fading, nor at which precise moment the man was gone, becoming only a body.

Suddenly there was a sense of absence, and he stood alone.   The hand not holding the blood-smeared dagger went up to his mouth, like a child who had broken something. For the first time in his life, Kitt had killed a man.

The Woodstalker's blood on his knife was the same as that of any other animal, the bears, wolves and tree cats he had killed in battles fought relentlessly and without resentment. A vague feeling told him that this was not the same, but how it was different, he did not know.

He thought, 'Mother can never know about this.'

That was the difference. The despairing look his mother would give him and which he dreaded.

He knelt to drive the blade into the soil, then rubbed away the last trace of human blood with a handful of grass. If it was not wiped off carefully, there would be rust. Rust of the colour of old blood, as if the bloodstains had become permanent. Then she would see them.

But why should he have that sinking feeling? Would the Woodstalker have felt like this if he had won?

With the grim twisting of his lips, Kitt suddenly appeared far older than his twelve years.

All around the wood, life continued. Leaves rustled in the summer wind, and the clear water of the creek, winding through the little valley, murmured among the boulders; a pirol bird fluted and, somewhere, a woodpecker hammered. Humming bees visited the tangerine daisies beside the still face. Sunlight shining through the emerald leaves of the beech trees wove a green haze among the tall, smooth trunks.

With a feline shriek, a buzzard flew up from its seat, winging its way above the treetops.

Kitt caught sight of a slight movement among the beeches on the far hillside and another on the opposite side of the valley.

He faded into the under-brush growing along the little creek without stirring a leaf.

Where the water had undercut a steep slope, great fallen tree trunks lay. Kitt considered hiding beneath them, keeping still, like a lone wolf cub when a shadow passes the entrance of the cave. He decided against it. The Woodstalkers would not fail to investigate every hiding place.

From the corner of his eye, he glimpsed at naked skin and a feather in a wild rose thicket nearby.

Too near.

Abandoning cover and silence, he broke into a run.

Behind him, the branches stirred violently.

A whistle cut the air.

The trap had almost closed.

Becoming a shadow in the green twilight, the boy ran.

Other dark shadows raced behind him.

Two warriors appeared silently under the beech trees.

They had dark eyes with very little white showing; their naturally light skin was deeply tanned. Both were almost naked except for the leggings fastened to a length of leather wound around their sides.

One warrior was compactly built, he was a-hand-width short of six feet and immensely broad in the shoulder; his hair was adorned with five raven feathers and streaked with grey, although he was not old. A scar ran from his nose across his lower lip to the chin, white seams scarred arms and chest crossed by necklaces and armbands that were studded with wolf fangs and filed human teeth. One hand held a copper-bladed lance, and a wooden sword with edges of hammered copper hung from his side.

The other man was younger and stood half a foot taller, with long blue-black hair held back by a black leather strip. He was armed with a greenstone axe and a long bronze knife; from his wrist hung a bone whistle with three finger holes. As the only adornment, he wore a curved, white, needle-sharp fang, long as a man's hand.

Mangan Sorkera, war leader of the Kra-Tini Sreedok Feen, the Blood-Tree-People, looked down upon his blood brother Agetool A Shushei, the counterpart of his own Graykhol Rere tooth, reposing upon the still chest.

There was only one wound on Agetool, a red slit beside the breast bone; it had bled very little. An admirable thrust that had split the heart. Agetool had died on his feet. A smile still lurked in the corner of his mouth, and Mangan also smiled. A good fight, a good death.

Agetool A Shushei meant Afraid of Rabbit. The man had kept the name given to the toddler, even though he was not afraid of anything anymore.

Like most men, Agetool A Shushei had been content to be a creature of one world only, Nyedasya-Aurayskahan-Ashyalish, the dream world of illusions and lies; he had never aspired to cross the world divide Nedye-Muni into Nyedasya-Dyarve, the real world, to hear his true name, like Mangan Sorkera had.

For Mangan was a man who wandered the real world, where bears sang, horses danced and wolves cried, where all directions led to one place, where one man threw twelve shadows.

Ever since Mangan Sorkera wandered the real world, his blood brother had been nearby in the woods, unseen, unheard, guarding against enemy warriors, watching out that no sorcerers could approach during the days of solitary fasting.

Agetool had stood behind him when he spoke his true name aloud for the first time in the blood-soaked place surrounded by the red trunks of the Tini trees.

Mangan Sorkera.

Some had laughed then because Mangan Sorkera meant Singing Bear. That laughter had long ceased. Singing Bear was now a name spoken with awe around the Feen fires, and with fear and hatred among the inferior tribes of the Sreedok Wood. Even the despicable, crazy, pale-eyed Dshooka, who made war on the Sreedok Wood, to make way for their muddy fields and stinking cattle, even they locked themselves up in their fortified places at the sound of Mangan Sorkera's name.

The war leader had never sought fame; it clung to him like a coat of eagle feathers. Agetool A Shushei had always been beside his blood brother, behind him, unquestioningly accepting his leadership.

Together, they had fought the Graykhol Rere.

The slayer had not taken the Graykhol Rere tooth as a rightful trophy, nor the skin, teeth and hair the way any of the enemy people would have. A Graansha would also have taken the ears and the male member; the Sharog and Amhas took the fingers and the skull, like the Feen themselves did. Perhaps the slayer had not had time. But Mangan Sorkera knew that this could not have been done by any of those enemies. There was not one warrior among the inferior people who could have stood against Agetool A Shushei, let alone bested him.

"Agetool stalk," Brule said, pointing to minor traces in the underbrush by the creek. They both smiled. Agetool could steal upon an enemy like fog.

"Spring, attack."

The enemy, whoever he was, had almost been surprised - almost.

The footmarks in the sand by the creek and the freshly-trampled grass told their story of a long, hard fight, evenly chanced.

#

Kitt stormed up the slope.

Beyond the sheltered valley began the reign of the firs, which grew so thickly that their crowns blotted out the light; in some places, the needled branches reached to the ground, their shadows ink black.

The boy was running with all the power of his long legs, his feet making hardly a noise nor a print on the thick brown needle carpet. He had left his boat in a cave at the foot of the white cliffs of Latunsrigo, the King's Seat. The seashore was more than ten miles away, and he would have to run all of it.

The pipes sounded again, farther back now.

Adornments and weapons marked the man he had killed as a great hunter and warrior, meriting exacting revenge. Maximum pain before death if they caught him alive. He did not allow himself to think about that.

The greater the danger, the less must you think about defeat. Fear helps a man nothing.

Somebody had told him this once, long ago. Kitt had forgotten who, but he had never forgotten the words.

#

A shout and a whistle came from the ridge above the valley. Brule raised his badger's head with a sneer distorting his scarred mouth.

Mangan Sorkera did not stir.

A very young warrior came running to stand before his war leader panting.

"Dshooka. Run past."

The war leader looked silently at the youth who lowered his eyes in shame.

"Kutcher stumble phantom. Again!" Brule said unkindly.

In spring, this same young warrior had been found unconscious near the cliffs of Kadyokanap-Askai. Revived, he had claimed to have fought a Dshooka boy, exceptionally tall and strong, with pale hair and pale eyes. When pressed, he thought the boy had seen no more than twelve summers. This boy had knocked Kutcher out by planting a hammer-like fist between his eyes. The other scouts found

30

no trace of an intruder anywhere among the white rocks and voiced the opinion that Kutcher must have fallen on his head, after stumbling over his own feet. For everybody knew that the Dshooka trampled through the woods like wisent bulls, leaving tracks even easier to follow than those big bovines. None of the despised Dshooka could ever have penetrated so far into Sreedok Feen territory.

The youth had had to listen to much mockery since, and he flushed fiercely at the older warrior's jibe. But he insisted now as he had then.

"Dshooka!"

"Same boy?" Mangan Sorkera asked.

Kutcher nodded, raising miserable eyes.

"Kutcher go Mukine-Kad-Nidyas, call Kra-Tini warriors!"

The young warrior ran off towards the village.

Brule looked keenly at his war leader.

Mangan Sorkera had taken Kutcher aside and had him tell the whole story, three times. Each time the young warrior told the story consistently in every detail.

Then the Jay watch began reporting brief glimpses of light hair and a tall figure that always disappeared from sight before anyone could take up the pursuit, never leaving a trace of his passing. A phantom, the Jays had said.

Mangan did not believe in a phantom, nor in a Dshooka. Something moved through the woods with the elusiveness and certainty of the Mooankayit. No track was leading away from the place of killing, nor was there any trace pointing to the slayer's identity.

He smiled grimly. "Gawthrin Lye."

In the Feen language, Gawthrin Lye meant a fox cub, a clever young animal. By naming him, Mangan Sorkera brought Agetool's killer into the real world of the Feen, thus distinguishing him from the faceless numbers of non-Feen enemy people. With this name, he declared that it was not a Dshooka who had killed Agetool.

With a brief gesture, Brule indicated that he accepted his war leader's decision. "Gawthrin Lye can fight. Can Gawthrin Lye die?"

31

Twin red lights sprang up in the black eyes of the war leader and his warrior.

The youth had a name now, and the Feen would give him the terrible death of a man, with all the honour they gave a brave enemy warrior. From sundown until sunrise, Gawthrin Lye would stand at the stake among the Tini trees, their trunks shining red at sunset, glowing red in the firelight, red before the blackness of night and at sunrise.

The red light filled the eyes and minds of the Feen warriors and their victim with a glowing haze. Life ran from him in red rivulets; the smell of his own burning flesh was in his nostrils. The last his breaking eyes saw would be the still-beating heart ripped from his chest with the stone-knife Nidyas-gooth. Mangan Sorkera would devour Gawthrin Lye's heart and drink his blood from the cup made from his skull, taken while he was still alive.

In the lost, dark Night World of Nyedasya–Lyagum-Olimi Agetool A Shushei's spirit would know that his blood-brother and war leader had avenged his death and honoured his slayer. The drumbeat of Gawthrin Lye's dying heart would open the Ska-Muni Shadow Wall for both of them. Agetool-a-shushei would stand behind his blood-brother and war leader again and watch over the Sreedok Feen forever. Yes, Agetool's killer would have a splendid death, and the Feen would sing of Gawthrin Lye, the Fox Cub, at their fires. Forever.

A sharp whistle sounded from across the hill. The Kra-Tini warriors were in place; the net was cast. The war leader set off in that direction.

Brule stayed back, foregoing the hunt to guard the corpse from scavengers and from the sorcerers of the enemy people, who might try to trap the dead warrior's spirit in Sarkorum-Kotarsup, the black, closed-in place of the dead, where he would be lost in eternal darkness and pain. The enemies hated and feared Agetool A Shushei almost as much as Mangan Sorkera.

Arriving at the hillcrest, the war leader perceived the other warriors of his band spreading out again, which puzzled him.

Shaluwa appeared at the side of his war leader. He was a silent young warrior and the best reader of tracks among the Shakyal-Shakyal, the scouts.

"Shaluwa thinks track go Kadyokanap Askai."

"Shaluwa thinks?" Mangan Sorkera allowed a tone of surprise to seep into his voice.

Eyes downcast, the young warrior shrugged.

"Gawthrin Lye," Mangan said. His smile would have seemed gentle, except for the red light smouldering in the black eyes. "Gawthrin Lye go coast Kadyokanap Askai. Feehafyrin-Fyrin drive Gawthrin Lye Mukine-Kad-Nidyas."

Shaluwa was relieved to hear that the strange boy had a name. No shame fell upon the young warrior now for having missed the track of one with a name like that.

The war leader's bone whistle called on the Feehafyrin-Fyrin, the young Stag warriors.

#

After running seven or eight miles, Kitt had not been able to lose his pursuers from his track. Anticipating every move, the bone whistle kept calling up more warriors ahead of him. They had contrived to subtly, irresistibly herd him away from the straight course to Latunsrigo. There were still at least five miles left to the coast.

Finally, he gave in and took the direction in which they had left him some rope and crossed the winding creek once again.

Fir trees gave way to oaks. He knew that in a clearing ahead at the bottom end of the valley lay a village of the Woodstalker people.

Coming to the killing ground, he thought, as if it concerned somebody else.

A sharp, high whistle-tone pierced the air, piping a complex melody, and answering signals from all across the valley sounded.

Suppressing the urge to continue fleeing headlong, Kitt stopped.

He turned and ran back on his tracks until he almost expected to run into the pursuers, stopped again, and began moving sideways very slowly, deliberately, noiselessly, not the slightest trace betraying his position.

He reached a thicket of oaks and drew himself up to an overhanging bow without the slightest rustle of leaves, walked along a thick ember and sprang into the next tree and another.

Suddenly he froze, pressing his body to the rough bark, not moving, hardly breathing.

A moment later two warriors appeared as if materialised from the oaks, both tall and wiry, black stripes and dots painted on their bodies and faces to make them blend into the wood's pattern of light and shadow, the black deer eyes without the white showing deceptively gentle.

They were naked except for a leather girdle with a strip of leather running between the legs. One wore bracelets of hooked yellow beaks, striped feathers knotted into the long black hair, the other the teeth of a man around his neck and fingerbones braided into the hair.

Each carried two short and one longer spear tipped with flint blades in his hand, bows and quivers filled with arrows on their backs. Stone knives hung in slings from their sides.

Striped Feathers also had a stone axe.

Finger Bones had a wooden club.

From his high perch, Kitt noticed slight movements on the valley slopes all around him. The trap closed while the prey was inside the circle, surrounded like a fleeing elk, except the elk had taken wings and was sitting in a tree.

The two warriors passed beneath Kitt's oak. Finger Bones was scanning the brush ahead of them, as Striped Feathers studied the ground beneath the trees.

The boy felt his hairs rise on his scalp. He deliberately thought of nothing to make his body still.

Striped Feathers looked up briefly.

Then, they disappeared, melting into the oak trees.

Kitt felt very pleased with himself, although he knew that he had only bought a little time. Once the warriors of the village met up with the hunting party, it took them no grand council to figure out Kitt's ruse. He did not kid himself that he could outrun or out-stealth so many warriors for much longer in their own territory. He needed to pin them down.

The one place far and wide where he could hope to accomplish this aim was just nearby.

There is a luck of the brave. There is no such thing as fool's luck.

Somebody had once told him about survival, but he could not remember who and had no idea whether what he was about to attempt was brave or foolish.

The Woodstalker people's village lay in a sparsely wooded ground in a bend of the creek.

Kitt knew well that the perimeter was guarded by boys squatting in the treetops who would give a warning cry that was an accurate imitation of the scolding of jays when they saw something with the least cause for suspicion.

The jay guards failed to notice Kitt slipping by them through the oak trees, just as they had many times before.

He paused, lying on a large ember, watching the village and mapping his next move.

The village consisted of twenty-six dome-shaped houses about twelve feet high and thirty feet in diameter, built from bent oak embers and thatched with a thick grass layer, with an opening for the smoke.

The houses were clustered in a half-moon at the east side of an octagonal place paved with ancient cut stones, about a hundred yards in diameter.

A thirty-foot-high pole was rammed into the exact centre, the smallest stone octagon of the pavement, the reddish wood carved with figures of bears, tree cats, fishes and eagles, and topped by a crown of nine serpents rearing their heads. A second plain pole was rammed into the western half of the place; it was charred, and the stones around were blackened by fire.

At this western end of the octagon stood one single hut, half the size of the others and covered in hides, with a wooden pole the height of a man before the entrance, thin and worn, with a bundle of serpent hides hanging from the crutch-shaped end.   Kitt saw women, children and old men, moving mainly in the space between the carved centre pole and the grass houses; they seemed to be avoiding the place between serpent stake and charred pole, and nobody approached the hut. Kitt knew that daily life was conducted in the space before the houses, even when it rained.   All appeared to

35

be giving only partial attention to their cooking pots, millstones, and stone and wood carving work, from time to time looking in the direction from which the bone whistle called to the warriors.

A naked man crouched on the ground beside one of the houses, bound by the neck to a low pole, peering through a mop of dishevelled red hair.

By another house were two more tethered men, one Woodstalker and a brown-haired Northerner of some kind, whose feet splayed at an angle; his tendons had been cut. From time to time, the captives emitted hesitant barks. Kitt had never seen real dogs in that village, for which he was glad.

He dropped down from his oak and stormed across the village place, past the charred wooden stake. He was spotted immediately, a cacophony of yells and whistles and belated jay warnings filling the air.

Young boys about Kitt's age ran towards him swinging stone-tipped spears and copper knives.

Kitt was at least a head taller than they were and heavier. Where he couldn't outrun them with his long legs, he simply ran them down. His fist connected with heads. Old men hurled spears and arrows, which he avoided with quick turns and twists.

A woman threw a bone and narrowly missed.

Avoiding that missile, Kitt saw a white-haired ancient man emerge from the solitary hut. The next turn showed the old man standing by the serpent pole, frail and upright, the deeply lined waxen face expressionless, watching Kitt run with eyes black, bottomless, ice-cold.

Kitt swerved to pass the charred pole on the far side of that man and hurled himself into the space between the grass dwellings, towards the last row of four houses near the edge of the wood. There he came face to face with an old woman sitting by a cooking fire.

At the sight of the boy running towards her, she rose, lifting a steaming pot from the embers. Before she could scald him with the contents, Kitt dodged past her into a low entrance.

Here, Kitt met the luck of the courageous, for it was empty except for the curtains of dried meat hanging from the wooden poles that were holding up the roof and stacks of baskets of woven grass, finely patterned in colours grey, brown and beige.

He jumped to the opening in the roof above the cold fireplace, gripped a wooden beam and drew himself up, squeezing first one shoulder through the opening, and then bringing the other one through. The wooden beams creaked, gave, and clamped around his ribcage. For an awful moment, Kitt imagined himself stuck with his lower half inside the hut and the old woman coming in with her boiling pot.

The old woman was yelling outside, something that sounded like krafikamme, over and over.

Kitt heaved and kicked, the beams leaving long, white, searing scratches down his sides and back.

He emerged from the smoke hole and lay flat on the hard-packed grass thatch, glaring down at the Woodstalker people rushing in from all directions. All of this had taken much less time than it had felt.

An impassioned discussion ensued below, with the word krafikamme recurring.

Not for the first time, Kitt wished that he could understand the Woodstalker language.

A shout came from inside the hut, and Kitt could hear the space below him filling up with people arguing at the top of their voices. He slid down the tightly bound grass bundles on the backside of the hut, any moment expecting an alarm call, which did not come.

As he faded under the oak trees, he saw that all the guard posts in the nearby trees were abandoned, and this sign of a lack of discipline cheered him considerably.

#

Mangan Sorkera looked at the warriors arriving from the village, and they looked back at him. The trap had closed, and it was empty.

No exclamations, queries or recriminations passed among them. There were more than a hundred Sreedok Feen assembled under the oak trees. Beside the Kra-Tini, other families had come from the farther settlements to celebrate the Sun Sacrifice in the grove of Tini trees not far from the village on the old stone place, Mukine-Kad-

37

Nidyas.

"No track," Shaluwa said, wiggling out of the dense whitethorn underbrush by the creek.

The war leader nodded slightly. "Feehafyrin-Fyrin run Kadyokanap Askai."

No more orders were needed; everyone knew what they were supposed to do. Whatever tricks Gawthrin Lyc pulled, ultimately, he would have to fetch up on the coast. The Feehafyrin-Fyrin, the Stags, were the swiftest among the young warriors; they would race straight ahead to overtake the quarry and lay low while waiting.

The men raised their heads, listening.

A faint noise, as of many people shouting, came from the direction of Mukine-Kad-Nidyas, where the village of the Kra-Tini Feen stood. All broke into a run as one, with the Stags racing ahead.

When the main force came into sight of the dwellings, they saw the Stags slowing and coming to a halt, standing confused.

The village was in an uproar.

The old men held weapons in their hands, some of the women also did. The children darted in and out of the houses, calling out in their high voices, just as they did when hunting a weasel or a fox that slipped in to rob the stores.

There was no enemy in sight.

The call of "Grafya-Gyami!" bounced across the village. Signalling the warriors to surround the place, the war leader strode onto the stone pavement fronting the houses.

He stood by the carved pole in the centre of the square for
several moments, watching the commotion until an old grey-haired warrior noticed him.

"I see Mangan Sorkera," he spoke the customary greeting.

"Mangan stand long Shak Lagat see," the war leader retorted. "Rere Midril, double devil, come steal sense Kra-Tini?" "Viniduneheyul, great scare. Grafya-Gyami, phantom, come Mukine-Kad-Nidyas." Shak Lagat said. "Rere, evil Midril, magic."

"No phantom." Mangan Sorkera said. "Gawthrin Lye. Boy kills men."

Shaluwa appeared beside Mangan, grinning. "No track Gawthrin

Lye leave."

The corners of the war leader's mouth turned down.

The young warrior added hurriedly, "Feehafyrin-Fyrin run ahead Kadyokanap Askai."

"Shakyal-Shakyal, all scouts, find track!" Mangan Sorkera commanded.

He knew there would be a track some short distance from the village, for Gawthrin Lye would be running fast now to use the time his trick had bought him.

The young warrior left in a hurry, his cheeks burning.

Several Feen warriors came into the paved square. Instead of bringing news, they wanted them, as they had seen or heard nothing in the vicinity of the village.

The leaders of the guests approached Mangan Sorkera. After a brief exchange, they agreed to do what the Kra-Tini war leader asked of them and departed to hunt the enemy boy.

A hand like a crow's claw closed around the war leader's arm.

"Grafya-Gyami Karabfrak's house," a raven voice croaked.

Looking at the tough old woman, the war leader thought for a moment that Gawthrin Lye lay in her house, bound and humiliated.

"Grafya-Gyami run house, disappear," old woman Karabfrak explained.

Mangan hesitated. It would be the ultimate daring bordering on utter madness to hide in the village itself. This was just what an enemy of Gawthrin Lye's quality might attempt to trick pursuers very close on his heels. He could hide among the bundles of pelts and food stores that filled up a Feen dwelling, while everybody would be scouring the woods for him.

"Show!"

Mangan Sorkera drew his bronze knife and ducked into the entrance of Karabfrak's house.

Shak Lagat and Kadog Greshano, the stone cutter, were close behind him.

The war leader cautiously approached the back of the house, where the stores lay, and began to pull them down, while the old warriors kept behind, spears ready as they would for a bear sleeping

39

in his cave.

The old woman cackled shrilly, "Not there. Grafya-Gyami disappear."

The war leader rose from his crouching position, and the ancient calmly met his indignant glare. "Karabfrak take hot pot, want burn Grafya-Gyami. Phantom run house. Warriors run house. House empty."

Mangan shrugged, his eyes wandering from the old woman up to the smoke opening. "Karabfrak old, know old trick."

"Shoulders big, big." Karabfrak spread her thin arms wide, in an attempt to outline how big the intruder had been.

A slender young man, not yet a warrior, entered the hut, hovering just at the edge of Mangan's vision.

"Reki speak!" the war leader ordered.

"Grafya-Gyami, phantom, run village. Reki shoot, miss. All arrows, spears, miss."

"Rere!" Shak Lagat nodded grimly. Spears and arrows could not wound Grafya-Gyami. "Grafya-Gyami disappear."

"Gawthrin Lye fool Reki. Fool Shak Lagat. Fool Kra-Tini."

With a slight movement of the head, Mangan Sorkera shooed the boy aside, ducked out of the entrance, and rounded the hut with long strides, surveying the grass roof with quick glances.

Suddenly, he stopped, pulled a broken reed from one of the grass bundles at the backside of the roof, and held it out, with his mouth twitching. "Falcon eyes no more sharp." For 'shak lagat' meant falcon eye. "Shak Lagat new name Gur lagat," the war leader teased remorselessly, 'gur lagat' meaning bleary eye.

The old man pressed his lips together.

All Sreedok Feen left in the village congregated by the carved centre pole. The place thronged with armed old warriors, women and children still clutching their stone knives, and although the commotion had died down, Viniduneheyul, the scare, was still hanging over the village.

One stood alone beside the serpent stake on the other side of the stone octagon, Shangar Shaark Ayen, the Ludoshini, the wise man of the Kra-Tini people of the Sreedok Feen.

The war leader walked over to him across the stone pavement, and they faced each other, both tall men, the ancient gaunt and brittle, the young rangy and lithe, extraordinary strength apparent in every move of the sinewy body. Both had the same luminous dark eyes that penetrated the Asaramuni Dream Wall that hid the real world.

"What happened to this place, Ludoshini?"

"Gita!" Shangar spat the word out like a curse.

Gita! Mangan Sorkera realised that this name, this childhood horror, had lain at the back of his mind all the time. The light hair, the great size, Kutcher talking about eyes the colour of ice. Agetool A Shushei killed in open fight.

Gita!

'Gita' meant fear in the Feen language, a fear inspired in the bravest warriors by overwhelming force such as storms, lightning and landslides. The Gita themselves knew no fear. Thirteen sun squares ago, all Dshooka warriors had united to destroy this race of pale-eyed giants. Mangan Sorkera had often wondered if the Gita had known fear then.

The Ludoshini hadn't spoken the name since the Gita disappeared.

"Many sun squares ago," the Ludoshini raised his right hand four times to show the number of years. "Gita crossed Sreedok. Feen fought. Feen died."

This tale of Shangar's was not one of those repeated over and over again at the fires in the long winter nights accompanied by laughter and play-acting. Just once, on a day when the moon swallowed the sun, and all the world was wrong, Mangan had heard the old warriors tell about the Gita cutting their bloody way through the Sreedok. No trophy had been taken then. Of the warriors contesting their passage, three out of four had died. The Kra-Tini had been unable to stand against these warriors with their iron weapons, who had not diverged one step from their course, crushing every resistance with soul-destroying ease. In fleeing the Gita, the Kra-Tini warriors had abandoned their dead.

Mangan was a boy of four summers when the few surviving warriors came crawling into the village, broken in body and spirit. The dreadful hush that had fallen over the Ancient Stone Place that

41

day was his first memory. The following years had been full of hunger and fear, for there had been very few Kra-Tini warriors left to hunt and protect the village and the enemies of the Feen had become audacious.

Only after Mangan Sorkera had claimed his true name and leadership of his band of young warriors, did the power of the Kra-Tini Feen return with a vengeance. Now nobody hunted in the Sreedok wood at the same time as the Kra-Tini, the way it had been before the march of the Gita. But the war leader would never forget that, once, the Kra-Tini had been almost broken, nor would the Ludoshini forget.

"Gita destroy warrior. Gita kill man dies real world, lies bound Sarkorum-Kotarsup. Pain. Darkness. Forever." Shangar's face was like stone, for he too was remembering the mortal shame of the Kra-Tini.

Recalling the face of his dead blood brother, the smile tucked into the corners of his eyes, Mangan Sorkera shook his head. "No. Agetool A Shushei die good fight. Waits Nyedasya–Lyagum-Olimi, waits. Gawthrin Lye flees Kadyokanap-Askai. Mangan Sorkera follows. Tini trees drink Gawthrin Lye's blood. Agetool crosses Ska-Muni Shadow Wall."

He was about to turn and join the pursuers, but the old Ludoshini held him back, with an emphasis that the ancient had not shown in many suns.

Mangan Sorkera waited impatiently.

"All Feen warriors go Kadyokanap Askai. All Kra-Tini all Feen. Kill Gita poison creature. Gita dies worthless. Sreedok Feen celebrate Sun Sacrifice." Shangar Shaark Ayen's voice was charged with command.

"No!" Again Mangan Sorkera shook his head. "Warriors corner Gawthrin Lye. Mangan Sorkera fight Gawthryn lye alone. With honour. Mangan drinks Gawthryn lye's heart blood. Agetool A Shushei cross Shadow Wall."

This was the first time the young war leader defied a decision of his Ludoshini. Shangar Shaark Ayen looked at Mangan Sorkera fully.

"Mangan Sorkera's shadow long Nyedasya-Aurayskahan-Ashyalish, Dream Shadow World, Mangan Sorkera's shadow long Nyedasya-Dyarve, real world. Many Feen stand Mangan's shadow."

Mangan flushed very slightly at the reminder that he was not a simple warrior, who was free to engage in battles of fame and vengeance as he pleased, and free to risk his life any time. The old man reminded him that there was an older score to settle, an old shame to wash away. It was intolerable that one of the Gita should still be walking the Sreedok.

If Gawthrin Lye really was Gita.

Mangan wondered what Shangar Shaark Ayen had seen in the real world, that made him so sure of that. But there was no time to ask. The allies had departed. Soon Gawthrin Lye would be backed into a corner, and Mangan did not want anyone else to fight this boy, to claim this heart and blood.

"Many warriors hunt down Gita. Corner Gita. Kill, clubs, stones," the Ludoshini repeated his verdict. "All hands kill Gita, break bones, blood run water, scavengers eat flesh. Great pain, no honour. Kill Gita's spirit. Cast Kri Sarkorum-Kotarsup."

Mangan Sorkera was still for a moment, his head lowered. Then he looked up, directly into the Ludoshini's eyes. "Gawthrin Lye die warrior death."

Shangar Shaark Ayen pressed his lips together.

"Mangan Sorkera goes now," the war leader said.

#

Red trees grew resembling the columns of an alien temple; branches began at the height of thirty feet, dark-green thatches formed a thick ceiling.

The air did not move among the vast trunks.

Fallen needles covered the ground with a springy, rust-coloured carpet that did not take the imprint of a foot.

Kitt would have avoided this place, except for the speed and silence it afforded him. Within the grove lay another paved site, with an octagonal stone pillar in the centre, about ten-feet high, blackened by fire and blood, as were the stones in a circle about of two yards around it. He had seen a man die there once, with the Woodstalkers

43

inflicting deeper and deeper gashes with their stone knives, while their victim was laughing into his tormentors' faces and singing out the words of a song, which turned into defiant screams as his skin was stripped from him. A dark circle had spread around the bound man's feet, widening with every heartbeat.

When the fires had died down at dawn, Kitt had still been there, watching as the light of sunrise streamed through a gap in the trees, flaming up over the red bark and the bleeding thing at the pillar that was still alive, still upright, with his own skin lying at his feet.

One Woodstalker had stood out through it all, tall, wiry, with clear-cut features of animal beauty. He wore a Dodlak tooth on a loop of leather around his neck.

This warrior had stepped forward, and, with one slash of a stone knife, opened the chest and tore the heart out, to show it to the dying man at the pillar, as he broke to his knees in the pool of his blood. Making him look upon his own beating heart, as he bit into it, blood spurting over his face.

That had been a year ago.

The shrill tone of a bone whistle sounded very near. His trick in the village had bought Kitt only a little time.

Quickly, he crossed the stone octagon, and the stained pillar seemed to reach out to him with a gaunt arm. He almost slipped in the blood that rains have long washed from the pavement. The smell of rotten blood, imagined or real, was in his nose.

It was like leaving a bloody altar chamber when he left the red trees, running at full speed.

There was very little undergrowth among the firs.

The whistle called again.

Kitt knew that there was a small temporary camp nearby, such as the ones the Woodstalker people made from skins thrown over bent birch saplings, and that there was now one family coming for early mushrooms and strawberries, no more than three warriors.

He veered a little in this course, hoping to avoid them.

A slim figure came bounding through the woods, attempting to cut him off, a youth older than himself, bearing two throwing lances. He hurled one lance while running, which missed, and he stopped to pitch the second.

Kitt increased his speed, storming directly at the young Woodstalker, swerving slightly as the spear left his hand and feeling the rush of the missile at his shoulder.

The youth drew a stone knife.

Kitt did not stop. His fist lashing out, he hit the boy in the chest with enough force to hurl him back with the coughing sigh of the air being driven from his lungs as he hit the ground hard.

Kitt stepped on the knife hand, running on without diminishing his speed.

Behind him, the bone whistle shrilled again in a cadence of tones.

#

The war leader did not waste any time picking up Ushakrat, and merely used his whistle to alert the nearby camp. The young Stag might never become a warrior now. The way he lay there, flung to the ground, showed him broken in several places. And for all his pain, Ushakrat had not so much as slowed down Gawthrin Lye.

The most dangerous fault of youth was a lack of judgment. Gawthrin Lye had no weakness. The speed and silence as he moved through the wood, the uncompromising way he fought, showed the promise of a truly great warrior. The war leader felt the affection of an older brother for the youth he would kill soon. It would not be long now for the hunt to end, but it would have lasted as long as it had to. Then the boy would die as a warrior. The war leader was ready to defy even Shangar Shaark Ayen over the manner of Gawthrin Lye's death.

#

The race for Kitt's blood and heart had begun early in the morning; now, the sun was long past its zenith.

The youth still set his feet without stumbling, broad chest rising and falling evenly, long legs reaching out high and wide as he ran like a deer.

The firs grew sparser, making way for high grass among white rock ridges and whitethorn brush, almost impenetrable thickets along the creeks, except for the game passes threading between trees and rocks, branching into numerous forks in all directions. Bounding along a

45

stone ridge jutting up through the soil and fallen leaves like the spine of a dragon, Kitt spotted a smear of moist earth on a white rock just ahead, a faint trace where someone's foot had slipped. That meant he was surrounded. The Woodstalkers knew where he was headed. Some had overtaken him in a straight run, not bothering with cover, and were lying in wait by the seashore. If they had found his boat-

The sound of a breaking branch and a heavy step told Kitt that the Woodstalkers racing behind him had not gained on him, but neither fallen back.

He sprang onto the white outcrop, doubled back on the rocks for about thirty yards, and stopped to pick up two fist-sized stones, which he hurled in quick succession into the bushes far ahead of him, tearing off leaves and breaking branches.

Then, he crept into one of the game passages in the whitethorn on his hands and knees, carefully avoiding to disturb the numerous animal tracks or making the slightest noise, even though that meant moving slowly when all his instincts told him to scramble into cover.

A stealthy tread sounded, just one.

Kitt froze to immobility, tanned limbs blending into the reddish bark, with his long, flaxen hair becoming indistinguishable from last year's dry grass.

The whitethorn had just finished flowering, and through the first light foliage, he saw his pursuers: six Woodstalkers materialised among the fir trees, silent as shadows.

The warrior leading them wore a Dodlak tooth on a loop of leather around his neck. The last time Kitt had seen this warrior had been in the grove of red trees, as he was biting into a man's still-beating heart, with blood running down his chin and dripping onto his chest.

At that moment, Kitt realised that if they discovered him now, he would fight and kill again. Not only that -he would fight as often, to the very best of his ability, and kill as many warriors as would stand between him and his escape. He would not be tied to that stone pillar.

The leader's eyes searched the whitethorn brush, approaching so near that Kitt could already see the metallic blue reflection of the light in his pupil. The boy stayed motionless, breathing very softly through his mouth and nose, keeping his eyes half-closed, without even blinking.

More Woodstalkers appeared, very little noise was betraying the passage of such a large group of warriors. A youth came running from the opposite direction and addressed the leader who drew away to follow the false track, with another long look at the whitethorn over his shoulder.

When the last tanned back disappeared among the fir trees, Kitt worked his way farther into the game tunnels.

Moving on all fours, he reached the low ground, where another creek was running.

He took two small sips of water, then straightened up from the whitethorn thicket, only to find himself looking right into dark, shocked eyes.

A Woodstalker girl stood on the bank. She had her hands full with moss berries, her mouth purple with juice. Her leather dress was the colour of dried leaves.

She stood stock-still while the boy tried to assume the aspect of a tree trunk. Each knew that the other had already seen.

Kitt gave up all caution about tracks or noise and broke into a full-speed run towards the sea. He had to chance it, boat or no boat. The tide would be coming in just now and with it, his luck of the brave.

Back by the creek, the girl was giving voice like a startled goose, and the deep shouts of the Woodstalker warriors answered.

#

Hearing Moshonalak's yell and turning in mid-bound was one for Mangan Sorkera.

The war leader realised at once what had happened. Setting the Scouts on the track of the Stags meant incredible audacity, and the boy would have brought it off; a quick knock on Moshonalak's head and he would have been away - a stupid little girl with a habit of straying from the other women. She was calling now that the boy was running straight towards Kadyokanap-A-Skai. Sparing her life Gawthrin Lye had made one mistake at last.

Wild shouting sounded from the right. It seemed Gawthrin Lye had changed direction again and was trying to break through to the coast, with the warriors near him going in hot pursuit.

47

The fools would yet lose him! Mangan Sorkera raised the whistle to his lips, issuing a sharp command. Answering whistles came from ahead, telling him that the allies were in position on the shore.
But where was Gawthrin Lye?

Mangan Sorkera caught sight of a tall figure storming up the steep white slopes, fair mane flying. It was the war leader's first sighting of the boy he hunted.

Gawthrin Lye was now heading directly towards the highest point of the Kadyokanap-A-Skai coast, the dread bone place Mark-Nidyas–Rerenejish, where the white rock fell to a sheer drop of more than a hundred feet to the sea.

He saw the Stags running up the cliff, spreading out wide to cut off any chance of doubling back. It was only a matter of a hundred or so wolfish leaps, and the chase would be over.

The war leader raised his whistle to give another command.
"Surround, and hold!" the bone whistle warned. "This heart, this blood belongs to the Singing Bear!"

#

Woodstalkers were closing in from everywhere attempting to intercept Kitt, and there was the whistle again, and another answering to it from the seashore.

Suddenly abandoning the direction he had run in so far, the boy threw himself up to the steep slope of the white cliffs where they were highest, Latunsrigo, the King's Seat, as sailors called it; nobody remembered why.

He heard the Woodstalkers yelling behind; they knew the hunt was at an end.

On reaching the summit, the boy came out on a flat strip of short heather, ending as if cut off with a knife.

With the unchecked speed of his run, Kitt jumped, flying out wide from the top of the cliff with arms outspread.

The flood was in, rising to meet him, and he hurtled down through the salty spray of the waves raging against the cliff. He turned in mid-air, protecting eyes and crotch with his hands. His feet struck the water; the shock travelled up the legs. The sea parted like tearing cloth, and Kitt sank with hardly a splash, feeling a burning sensation on his skin and pain like lightning shooting through his body. The pain lasted only a split moment, and then he sank no deeper, and the coldness of the water smote at his nerves.

Underwater he turned again, sliding through the heavy swell like a pike. His fingertips brushed the sand, and the sting of a sharp edge grazed his hip as the flood drew him towards the rocks he had narrowly cleared.

Too far to the left or right, and the current would have seized his body, smashed him against the rocks and drowned him like a kitten, without all his strength making the least difference. But Kitt knew the sea before Latunsrigo well; the tides, the rocks, and the currents now carrying him safely in their cold, grey-blue hands.

He turned on his back in the water to see the white cliff of the King's Seat soaring above him, rimmed by the silhouettes of the Woodstalker warriors, dark against the sky, looking down on him, knocking their bows.

Dark dots rose in the air and seemed to be hanging above for a moment.

Kitt dived, his legs kicking hard.

A hailstorm of arrows hit the water, and two tips thumped into his back so that it hurt.

Rocks splashed all around.

He came up to gulp air and dived again at once, staying underwater as deep as he could, and only emerging briefly for air at irregular intervals.

No more arrows came down.

It had to be the leader's order, he thought, wanting him alive, wanting his heart.

Kitt swam with the current of the incoming tide until he felt a change in the surge and swell of the water as it washed up against the overhanging cliff.

Just ahead, a cave opened in the white rock wall; the rising flood water was already almost covering its mouth. Rushing in the current drew him inside.

Kitt dived again, swimming underwater, where the tunnel ceiling was hanging down.

A little grey light still filtered in from the narrowing opening behind him. He more sensed than saw the widening surface of the subterranean lake he knew was there.

He swam deeper into the cave, noiselessly coming up for air. His eyes adapted to the darkness enough for some orientation.

He was not heading directly to the place where he had left his boat above the high-water mark, secured to a rock, and instead aimed towards the right side.

The light diminished as the still-rising tide covered the cave mouth; then, the daylight was switched off like a lamp, leaving him swimming in pitch darkness. By then, he reached knee-deep water.

He crawled out quietly, knife in hand, to crouch for a long time, listening for any random noise. Kitt had never seen any sign of Woodstalker presence in the cave, at any time, recent or past, but he took nothing for granted. They had anticipated his flight, but how far?

Steel can correct some miscalculations. Only sort of mistake you are allowed.

Whoever told him in a hard voice a chisel could not cut was right, Kitt knew it, here in this dark wood where the red grove lay like a gory wound.

For a moment, he had a vision of grey eyes, ice-cold with a smile in it, and thought it must have been one of the many warriors who came to Isenkliff for his father's steel.

If Woodstalkers were lurking near his boat, he would fight to kill them in the darkness.

Keeping quiet, heard nothing above the rushing sound of water because outside, the flood was still rising.

Groping about him, he felt a piece of driftwood under his hand and threw it in the direction of the place where he had left his boat.

The noise of wood bouncing from stiff leather over the whalebone told him that it was still there.

As the echo clattered around the stonewalls, he continued listening for furtive movements under cover of the noise but heard nothing. Maybe that only meant whoever lay in wait had excellent nerves.

Never underestimate the enemies. Don't overestimate them either.

Most are inferior to you. Just don't rely on it too much.

Kitt rose and drew another long knife, holding one hilt in each hand.

With every irregularity of the cave floor mapped in his mind, he noiselessly stalked through the darkness.

Reaching out, he touched the walrus-leather stretched double over a whalebone frame. He ran his hand over every inch of it, finding it intact.

By touch, he located a tightly wrapped packet of oiled leather containing flint and tinder.

Then came the moment when he would have light.

This moment between darkness and light was filled with sudden unreasoning images of Woodstalkers standing all around, laughing at him.

The sparks struck from the flint to fall on the tinder were like shooting stars in the cosmic night, lighting up rocks and water.

A steady orange glow appeared, which the boy blew gently into a little yellow flame. Averting his eyes, he fed it dry leaves and twigs from another bundle, then larger pieces of driftwood, until it burned with orange and blue-green flames.

The widening circle of light played over white rock and water, pushing back the darkness into two tunnels running side by side into the mountain. The smoky orange fire shine reached the ceiling to glisten on wet stone draperies, knobs, bulbs and globules.

There was no sign of Woodstalker presence, but Kitt still took nothing for granted, keeping his eyes on the dark openings of the twin tunnels, one hand always holding the long knife, as he took two bundles from the boat. They were in the place where he had stowed them, also well wrapped against the intrusion of seawater, one with dark rye bread and sausage and another containing a three-pint silver water bottle.

Having convinced himself that nothing had been touched, Kitt ate every bit without further delay, washing it down with the water. The food filled a gaping void in his stomach.

From the bag at his belt, he withdrew a scrap of unattractive looking dried venison, which he had snatched from the hut of the old

51

Woodstalker woman. This tasted double good, picturing the Woodstalkers sitting overhead.

His hard mood relaxed a little.

For the first time, he felt that he really was a step ahead of the Woodstalkers -only a small step, but enough. He knew they did not use boats, all their settlements were inland, leaving the coast uninhabited. He knew that it was still some time until the falling tide would lay open the cave mouth again, for him to attempt his getaway. Having grown up on an island, the rhythm of the tides was something natural for Kitt, of which he was aware at all times.

He would have only one chance, with the Woodstalkers waiting for him to attempt just that, as the cliff's height gave their arrows tremendous reach and impact, enough to cut the boat to shreds. What could he use to break the power of their volleys?

He collected all the driftwood in the cave and piled it into the canoe, but he knew it wouldn't be enough. Eyeing the tunnels, he remembered from earlier excursions that the spring tides had carried driftwood far inside; he recalled a large piece of bark.

From his boat, he took a bundle of resinous sticks, lighted one, and entered the left-hand tunnel, silent as his shadow on the rock wall.

#

Gawthrin Lye had disappeared while swimming beneath the cliff overhang.

Mangan Sorkera smiled wryly. The boy could be hiding anywhere in the rock now. There was nowhere he could go, but he had succeeded in forcing the war leader and more than two hundred Feen warriors into idle waiting. The allies set out to guard the Kadyokanap-A-Skai coast on both sides of the cliff, while the Kra-Tini Feen warriors remained on top of the mountain. There was no need to send warriors down the wall to try to pry him out. When the sea Skai subsided, they would pick him up as inevitably as they picked up a day-old gull chicken.

The war leader thought that Gawthrin Lye ought to have made his last stand on the cliff, instead of that jump. If the boy had demanded to die fighting, Mangan Sorkera would have granted that request, as if he was a grown warrior. Maybe Gawthrin Lye was too young to comprehend the warrior's way fully, to acknowledge its end and face death in a manner that did the utmost honour to himself and his enemies.

Mangan Sorkera thought that if the boy planned on escaping by swimming and diving along the shore, he would find that the Kadyokanap-A-Skai coast was very closely watched for a much longer distance than any man could stay mobile in the cold water of the Skai sea. It would be an ignominious capture, to be drawn stiff and weak from the cold waters. If that were Gawthrin Lye's choice, then Mangan Sorkera would soon hear the whistles of the allies announcing the sighting. Deeply dissatisfied, the war leader sat on the white rock, watching the sea and listening for the signal.

It irked Mangan Sorkera that Gawthrin Lye should prove less than perfect after all, as it would have irritated him to see a younger brother show a weakness.

The war leader did not believe in making allowances for youth or anything else. He considered that the boy had some daylight left yet to think about the way all his actions left their trace in the real world and how he wanted his end to be sung at the fires, to draw for himself the conclusion of what he must do. Mangan Sorkera was willing to allow him that time.

The silence of waiting settled on the rocks, all movement ceasing but for that of the sea and the wind.

#

The smoky orange glow of the torchlight tore an enchanted underworld out of the absolute darkness, tunnels and domes dug by churning waters, columns formed by millennia of dripping from the tips of the stalactites onto the stalagmites, meeting, growing together.

The dripping of water was the only sound, overloud.

Deeper and deeper, Kitt wandered into the cave, lured by the gleaming halls he knew were waiting behind every bend. He still had time. He knew that there was one small round cavern deep inside the cave that he had seen only once before, when he had come first to the Murkowydir wood. Then, he had caught just a glimpse, pressed for haste by another Woodstalker pursuit and an outgoing tide. He wanted to see it again now and look his fill.

The tunnel ceiling lowered so deep that he had to crawl through. When he straightened up, he caught his breath, finding himself standing within a druse thickly studded with transparent crystals of the colour of clear water, lilac-pink, a fragile yellow, and deep black with a purple fire glowing inside.

The place was as wondrous as he remembered it. He forgot the tide and the Woodstalkers, and he forgot to look where he set his feet, raising the torch and craning his neck, trying to take in all this beauty at once.

His foot slipped on something round and slick. Directing the light to the floor, he saw the upper part of a skull and that he was standing among bones, thickly coated in an opaque substance, shimmering from pearl-white over bright orange to a dark brown colour. All of them were human bones, all broken, not mingled with the remains of deer and wild pig, as it might be found in a bear's lair. He had not seen this the first time.

The sight of those bones brought him back to reality.

How long had he been wandering about in the cave? Was the tide still in or out already? Still in, his inner sense told him, but could he trust that now? He had used up four of his torches; recalling how long one of them lasted, he calculated with relief that he still had time.

He thought that this time he would collect some of the crystals to bring back to his mother, who smiled so rarely and from whom he couldn't hide anything.

He reached out and touched a rose-coloured crystal; he locked his hand around it. For a moment, he felt loath to destroy the harmony by causing ugly broken surfaces. By giving this crystal to his mother and telling her of the cave, he could avoid telling her about the dead Woodstalker. Anything for distracting her from that, he thought.

He increased the pressure. The crystal broke with a dry crack, and he shoved it in a bag on his belt. He reached for another that shone violet; this time, he did not hesitate to break it.

Suddenly, a deep roaring sound filled the cave, full of fury.

Kitt stood frozen, the violet crystal in his hand like a boy caught stealing apples.

Another roar reverberated from the tunnel walls, sounding with such primal cruelty that it turned his bones to water.

Something big was in possession here.

Do not let unknown danger unnerve you. Analyse as if it had nothing to do with you, but some other person- a not very important person.

Was it one or more? Where was it?

The roaring had seemed to come from all sides, but Kitt noticed himself instinctively backing against the farthest wall away from the direction where his boat lay. If this unconscious feeling was correct, then whatever creature it was must have come out of one of the narrower side tunnels and followed on his track.

A draft of cold air brushed his back; he noticed that he was wet with sweat and that this smell would be carried back.

A low growl came out of the darkness.

Fight or flight?

Find a better place to fight.

The growl came again; it seemed nearer.

Blind now for the splendour dragged out of the darkness by the torchlight, Kitt ran as fast as he dared on the uneven, slippery ground. A strengthening air draft blew in his face, faintly tainted with corruption.

He squeezed through low tunnels, where he would be unable to turn on the menace he felt coming behind him swiftly.

He fought down a moment of panic imagining having lost his way to fetch up at a blank wall or being caught in a maze with the last torch going out and something horrible coming at him in the darkness.

The draft became stronger and smelt of death. A weak grey light filled the tunnel, daylight seeping into the cave from somewhere ahead.

The stench of carrion became overpowering. Kitt saw the source, a shallow recess where more human bones lay intermingled with scraps of leather and bits of wood. These bones were fresh.

At that moment, he felt a burning pain in his hand and dropped the torch; it had burned down enough to singe him. The last piece of it lay on the floor, lighting the nauseating heap in the recess.

Another roar came, sending him on to a headlong flight.

Rounding a sharp bend, he saw that the daylight came from a crack above, too narrow for him to pass. And he had omitted to light a new torch on the flame of the one he'd dropped.

As he rounded yet another bend, there was a bright light at the end of the tunnel.

More luck than sense.

Kitt felt dispassionate contempt for himself. Why had he even run? The crystal cave had been a good place to wait for whatever came.

He emerged into a vast green well, where grass and birch trees were growing in a small world all to themselves, enclosed by vertical rock walls two hundred or more feet high. Swallows were scything the air to land by their nesting places in shelves and crevasses where they sat and chirped, whined and gurgled their song. Hundreds of sparrows added their own chirruping, cheeping noise.

He recognised this place from previous forays into the Woodstalkers' domain but had had no idea that it was another entrance to this cave. That meant, he hadn't known as much as he'd thought, and the reason that the Woodstalkers weren't already there to tell him all about it, was the same reason why they had never been in the cave. And it was coming close behind. In a moment, he would see what it was, and he brushed away the thought that it might be the last he ever saw.

Never do the enemy's work for him.

Forget past mistakes.

Whatever comes at you, face it with all you have.

Kitt dropped the spare torches, drew his knife with his right, picked up a fist-sized stone in his left, and waited.

All the birds fell silent.

A huge paw emerged from the tunnel mouth; a great shaggy shoulder followed, and then a skull from a nightmare, gaunt, triangular, with hand-long curved white fangs protruding from the upper jaw. The pupils of the green slanted eyes narrowed against the light. They were full of malicious intent. It was a Dodlak, the Death-Smile cat.

With fascination, the youth watched the tawny beast coming out entirely; it was as big as a walrus, but of a hungry leanness, and moved towards him like something that had never checked its stride towards meat.

The Dodlak opened its jaws with a grin showing off all the teeth, from the fangs to disembowel and slash the great blood vessels of neck and groin back to the bone-breaking molars.

Then, it crouched leisurely, the tip of its tail twitched, the muscles of the short, powerful hind legs contracted.

Kitt hurled the rock and caught the beast full between the eyes.

The Dodlak shook its head, making a noise between a hiss and a scream.

It sprang.

Kitt jumped high into the air; landing with both feet on the Dodlak's back; it felt as if his feet had struck a log.

The Dodlak twisted lightning-fast, his claw hooked into leather, and the skin below. For a split moment, Kitt felt the terror of being caught by the leg.

He catapulted himself away with all the power in his legs, tearing free from the claw, slitting the leather and the skin of his right calve. His leg burnt like fire; he didn't know how bad it was.

He rolled over in the grass as the big cat whirled around, and hurled himself feet first under the second charge, the knife gripped fast in both hands.

The curved fangs sliced a hair's breadth from his jugular; he smelled the flesh eater's breath. He stabbed upwards, burying his knife into the Dodlak's belly.

The hilt was nearly torn from his hand by the momentum and weight of the animal, but he held on fast, and in a shower of blood and entrails the great predator collapsed upon him, thrashing, writhing, scratching, screaming, and the rocky walls screamed with it.

Mouth, eyes and nose filled with soft fur, Kitt thrust his knife deeper and deeper, searching to split the liver.

The Dodlak was about to rise.

Kitt kicked against its hind legs and punched his free hand into the gaping slit.

The animal slumped above him, pinning him down with his weight.

Kitt's hand pushed through the tissues around the animal's heart. He grabbed and pressed.

The roars ceased, and at last, the Dodlak lay still.

Silence then reigned in the green well.

Kitt dragged himself out from under the furry weight, feeling the warm wetness of blood and entrails sliding over his body.

A robin began to sing in a birch tree, and another fell in.

The wound in his calf burned, bleeding freely, and the skin was torn, but the muscles below were intact. He considered himself lucky that he could still stand on that leg.

Kitt looked into the fading green eyes and stroked the tawny fur; it was a surprise to him that such a great predator should feel this soft.

He touched the point of one of the claws, which instantly hooked into his fingertip. Those claws held what they caught, a very little deeper and they would have caught him for good.

He was aware that the Dodlak's roars must have been heard in the woods around, drawing the attention of all Woodstalkers to this very spot. Yet he could not bring himself to leave the pelt and the teeth.

Keeping his eyes on the rim of the rock well, Kitt broke the tusks and larger teeth from the beast's jaw with his knife. Now he'd have a necklace just like that Woodstalker leader, he thought with sudden glee.

He began skinning the great beast but suddenly sat back on heels, reconsidering.

Quickly, he disembowelled the Dodlak completely and hoisted the carcass up to his shoulders. The mutilated jaw brushed his cheek. The hind paws were dragging; even without the innards, the beast weighed as much as an elk.

He carried the carcass into the cave opening.

Then he came back out again to obfuscate all traces of his re-entry into the cave. He knew that Woodstalkers would see through any hiding attempts at once. Instead, he made sure that tracks were running all over the ground from rock wall to rock wall until meaningful interpretation was made impossible.

In doing this, his eyes fell upon a bone, an old bone, bleached and cracked by the sun, and yet there was still flesh clinging to it, fresh and bloody. It was lying within a cluster of plants-purple blossoms with dark golden centres.

Kitt bent over to look closely. The blossoms were nodding over the bone. Did the dew and raindrops from them conserve the flesh?

Kitt collected the flower heads; there were also dry heads with seed in them, and of these, he also gathered some, stowing them in the bag that already contained the Dodlak teeth and the crystals.

A cracking noise recalled him to the thought of Woodstalkers and the tide and the need for haste.

#

The Skai sea reached its highest level, covering half the height of the Mark-Nidyas–Rerenejish cliff side. Gawthrin Lye had not yet come out of hiding to claim his fight.

None of his Kra-Tini warriors showed any sign of the fervent wish Mangan Sorkera knew they all felt, to run away from this place where the Graykhol Rere laired. They stayed only because they trusted in their war leader's power in both worlds.

Graykhol Rere. He of all predators enjoys his kill, the stalking, the spring, and the struggle as the enemy's strength ebbs, as awareness of defeat comes into his eyes. Graykhol Rere fights with the cunning of a strong warrior. He fights to the death. Always. As did the Sreedok Feen.

Mangan Sorkera had been the only one in many sun squares who had dared to descend into Death Hole, one of the exits of the cave in the Mark-Nidyas–Rerenejish cliff, in search of Tapminyort, the Good Spirit Dalyon's purple blossom of life, which grew only in this place of death.

His blood brother Agetool A Shushei, had been with him on this as on every other quest. He had lured and distracted the Graykhol Rere, again and again, until Mangan Sorkera could finally get in the killing blow. That had been two sun squares ago, and not far from this spot.

It was not entirely correct that Gawthrin Lye had nowhere to go. He did have a choice even now. He could choose between the knives of the Sreedok Feen and the long teeth of the Graykhol Rere pride who laired in the dark guts of Mark-Nidyas–Rerenejish since the beginning of the Sreedok Wood.

Which death would Gawthrin Lye choose?

A sudden roar shook the wood.

All started, spears and knives in a white-knuckled grip.

Two warriors dropped their weapons, for lasting shame.

"Graykhol Rere!"

"Graykhol Rere hunt!"

"Graykhol Rere fight!"

The roaring went on and on, reverberating, growing to a crescendo, and then ending abruptly, as if cut off with a knife.

"Graykhol Rere kill Gawthrin Lye," Shaluwa said.

Mangan Sorkera hesitated. The roaring had come from the direction of the Death Hole. He was reluctant to leave his watch post, as he could not be sure that it really was Gawthrin Lye who the Graykhol Rere had been fighting, but neither could he send his warriors to investigate, being the only warrior who could and who dared to go near the Death Hole.

"Stay! Watch!" he ordered. "Shaluwa stay!" he added to the young warrior who had stepped beside him as a matter of course. The war leader estimated that Shaluwa would grow to be an exceptional warrior, but at fifteen summers, he was too young to face a Graykhol Rere.

"Shaluwa distract Graykhol Rere Mangan kill."

After shaking his head in refusal once, the war leader set out towards the foot of the mountain.

The young warrior followed.

Mangan Sorkera did not rebuke him again, but neither did he acknowledge his presence. Shaluwa would be an exceptional warrior if he lived, the war leader amended his former thought.

The Death Hole opened before their feet so suddenly that Shaluwa expelled his breath in surprise. Without turning around, Mangan knew that the young warrior's face was hot with embarrassment.

He looked down into the Death Hole and straight onto the bright-red signs of the battle that had raged here only moments ago, tangled entrails and thick blood splashes on the flattened grass.

Beside him, Shaluwa was catching his breath. "Gawthrin Lye?"

It seemed clear enough what had happened here. Gawthrin Lye had attempted to cross the line of Feen warriors through the cave hollowing out the Mark-Nidyas–Rerenejish. He found his way through the winding tunnels, but just before he could make his escape, one or more of the Graykhol Rere pride lairing in the cave caught him at the bottom of the Death Hole and dragged him down.

Yet, something snagged at the back of the war leader's mind. It was not a man who had screamed; it was a Graykhol Rere that had roared. There had been a battle, and of the loser, only a shapeless heap of entrails remained. It was impossible to ascertain what the red mess had once been. From up there, no skin nor hair was visible; there was no indication at all that the mangled thing down there had once been human.

"No trace climb," he said thoughtfully, speaking more to himself than to the young warrior beside him.

Shaluwa stared at the implication that Gawthrin Lye should have single-handedly killed a Graykhol Rere. Then, he quickly scanned the walls and surroundings of the Death Hole, dutifully but without expecting to find anything, as indeed he did not. There was not enough left to make up the remains of a whole Graykhol Rere, was that what his revered leader thought?

"Graykhol Rere very small? Cub?"

The corners of the war leader's mouth turned down in the expression of derision, all young warriors dreaded.

Mangan Sorkera set the bone whistle to his lips, blowing the signal calling all warriors near Mark-Nidyas–Rerenejish to close attention at their posts. Then he walked up the steep slope again.

An unhappy Shaluwa trotted at his heels, racking his brains. "Gawthrin Lye kill Graykhol Rere, disembowel Graykhol Rere, hide carcass cave fool Feen think Gawthrin Lye dead," he finally ventured.

"Fool Shaluwa think," Mangan Sorkera retorted.

The young warrior fell back a few paces, his face burning.

The war leader knew now that killing Gawthrin Lye would be his hardest fight, harder than against any of the other enemy people, more hazardous even than against Graykhol Rere. And he knew that it needed to be done quickly. Before that cub grew up.

#

Kitt lit one of the four remaining torches with flint and tinder.

Again he took the weight of the Dodlak on his back and faced the task of retracing the same way he had come in headlong flight.

If he lost his nerve, he'd miss the way, and then he'd be dead, he reminded himself by way of encouragement.

Several times he had to trust his instincts, to be reassured by some stalactite or stalagmite formation which he had noted during his flight through the tunnels.

The padding of huge paws accompanied him; he heard fur brushing against the rock. Nearby sounded a low growling, bone-chilling echoing between the stone walls.

A deep answering growl rose in Kitt's throat, not of his own volition, and he bared his teeth. His reaction surprised him. Then, he thought, yes, come! I'll not run again, and I can do with more Dodlak teeth for a necklace. He was confident that the carcass would shield him against a surprise attack from behind. Anything that came from in front he would give his best to kill.   Another growl rose in his throat by way of confirmation, and although it ended in a high shriek as his voice had become unreliable, deep tones alternating with high, that didn't change anything. He was dead serious.

Although he continued hearing them all around, no Dodlak appeared within the shine of his torch.

He came to the gem cave where he had broken the crystal. After that, he was in familiar territory, where he could hear the beat of the sea against the cliff.

He extinguished the torch a long way before he came near the outer cave.

Grey golden light was scintillating on the water, the upper part of the cave mouth already emerging from the flood. To his eyes, used to the pitch-black darkness of the tunnels, the light was bright enough to see into the last corner.

There was no sign of anybody lying in wait.

The Woodstalkers wouldn't risk coming into a Dodlak cave, he

62

thought. Except for their leader, who wore a Dodlak tooth around his neck.

Kitt watched for some more time before he moved out of the tunnel.

He laid the Dodlak carcass at the bottom of the boat and arranged the driftwood around it along the sides.

The light from the cave mouth was growing brighter as the tidewater rushed out of the cave. Kitt pushed the boat into the water and began rowing with all his might, aiming straight towards the short tunnel, then quickly raised the oars, fixed them back and laid down in the boat on top of the Dodlak. The boat shot through the tunnel and out from the cave with the receding tide. The evening sun was touching the western horizon like a big red disk.

Sand fringes appeared farther up and down on the coast, and little troops of Woodstalkers were struggling in the ebb current, swimming towards the foot of Latunsrigo.

One warrior was crouching on a boulder near the cave; he was the first to see the boat sweep past and shouted the alarm.

A tigerish figure sprang up on the top of the cliff.

Once again, the King's Seat was fringed with dark silhouettes, and a cloud of arrows sped out above the sea, hanging in the air. Kitt threw himself out of his canoe so quickly that it almost capsized, but it straightened up again due to the weight in its bottom, and the boy hid beneath it, grabbing onto the keel, and letting the tidal current carry him out of range. Volley after volley came, hitting the canoe; only very few arrows fell into the water.

When he heard no more arrows thudding, he looked cautiously around the boat up to the cliff - and dived again as an arrow came straight at his face.

The wind freshened, and the waves grew choppy. When Kitt reckoned himself out of range, he clambered into the boat again.

The Dodlak was studded with arrows, keeping the boat's bottom from being shredded. More arrows stuck in the driftwood; only three had penetrated the walrus skin, two through both layers just at the waterline.

Kneeling in the boat, Kitt extracted the arrows, thriftily putting

63

them in a little heap. Most were simply-made missiles with sharpened, fire-hardened ends, but some had tips of leaf-shaped white, green, or grey stone or serrated bone, fastened with pitch. Even eight bronze-tipped shafts had been sent his way. He threw out the driftwood and excised the Dodlak's claws. Then he heaved the carcass over his head, where it flopped and fell apart in his hands, a mass of shredded fur and meat and splintered bones. He threw the bloody, stringy thing out into the water.

He looked after the floating Dodlak with some regret, knowing it to be out of the question to take the pelt home cut to ribbons like this -if his mother saw the savage slashes of the arrow slits, she would at once guess that he had been in a fight and bring out the whole truth with probing questions. He could never tell her about the dead Woodstalker.

After losing the weight of the driftwood and the Dodlak carcass, the boat lay higher in the sea, stopping the water from running in through the arrow holes.

Kitt pushed wool into the holes, caulked them with resin, and bailed out the bloody water using a leather bucket.

Upon the soaring white cliff of the King's Seat, the Woodstalkers stood, watching him work. Standing out among them was the leader. He laid his hands to the mouth and called out with a voice that carried clearly across the water, one word reoccurring over and over again, it sounded like "kottrinelli".

Kitt added another word of their language to his meagre store; he reckoned it was a swear word or a curse.

"Come back here, kottrinelli, come back and fight!" the leader shouted, switching to the language of the Nordmänner.

"Only you and me, kottrinelli! Free passage!"

Kitt shook his head, drawing up the sail.

That kotrinelli word likely meant coward; the thought did sting, not enough for Kitt to pull the boat against the tide and take up the challenge. But it stung a lot.

Kitt raised the double mast and fastened the triangular sail to it.

He was ready for the four-day-long journey to Isenkliff, his home island. Four days to think of explanations why he didn't return with his usual bounty of venison and wild boar meat and spring onions.

The westerly wind pushed an invisible fist into his sail, and soon, the cliffs of the King's Seat were only a white line on the horizon.

#

Gawthrin Lye had a boat hidden inside Mark-nidyas–rerenejish. Mangan Sorkera had not known that. No lookout had ever reported the boat. The boy must have approached the coast with the same care and stealth he showed on land.

The Kra-Tini had been thinking of cutting Gawthrin Lye off from going West or South, to prevent him from losing himself in the great Sreedok wood. They had intended getting him with his back to the Skai sea with nowhere to go- but he went exactly where he wanted to go. Now, he was out of reach, yet plainly visible, on top of the rising waves.

Did he know that the surface of the sea was part of the Ska-Muni shadow wall? Was he fearless of the abyssal Nyedasya–Lyagum-Olimi, the lost, dark, night world lying beneath his feet?

Mangan laughed a short, mirthless bark.

The young warriors laughed too.

"Graansha," Glask said derisively.

The Graansha were fish eaters who even stooped to scraping mussels from the rocks; they were an inferior people to the Kra-Tini. The Graansha had small boats, not the kind which sailed out towards the horizon and could go right beyond the edges of the world. The Kra-Tini had no need for boats. They ruled under the trees; no people hunted there without permission, not even other Feen. So they had never considered building and using a boat.

"Gawthrin Lye coward no Djanadir," Fitcher sneered.

"Glask, Fitcher speak foolishly," the war leader said.

The two young warriors retreated in confusion.

Mangan Sorkera felt drawn between irritation and excitement. Gawthrin Lye had won the race, won every fight, and it was his right to refuse the challenge now. No enemy had ever been able to show contempt to Mangan Sorkera. This would rankle until either Gawthrin Lye or Mangan Sorkera was dead.

White Numbnettle

There is a dark king on Wittewal.
He abides no evil.
Man, judge not,
can you walk across Wittewal,
ask the smith for a sword.

The sky above Isenkliff in the Graumeer -the grey northern sea -was leaden. The constant west wind sang in the gnarled fir trees and caught in the white bush of Eckehart's hair which was streaked with the flame red of his youth.

The Smith of Isenkliff sat on a stone below the towering cliff. Before him lay a heap of reddish-brown lumps, which he was busy breaking up into small pieces the size of his thumbnail with a stone hammer.

He was a tall man and broad-shouldered, the forearms massive and streaked black with soot, the big hands callused hard. His linen trousers and long tunic were held together with a broad leather belt, with pockets and loop holders for tools. His eyes looking out over the restless sea were light-blue.

The blacksmith sorted through the pieces before him, putting the iron ore into a basket, and discarding the empty stones to the side. He carried the basket to a trough hewn into the rock, with water running into it from a channel coming from the mountain, and out another channel down to the sea. As he went, he limped with his left leg, where a dead man's blade had nicked the big tendon -almost cutting it through -in the aftermath of the Battle of the Bloodswamp, twelve years ago.

He looked out to the sea again. His blue eyes narrowed, focusing on a dark dot which had appeared far west. A sailing boat was approaching. He turned back to his work, his face relaxing slightly.

In a shallow hole beside the water-trough, a fire burned low. Eckehart threw thin kindling onto the glowing coals; as the flames caught, he added thick logs. He washed the ore pieces in the trough, sieved them in an iron grid, and then filled the ore into a wide, shallow iron pan to set over the fire, which was by then burning high. The moisture hissed up from the ore in small steam clouds.

The smith straightened up, looking out to the sea again. He could see a figure hauling on the sail, and the boat changed course, coming directly to the landing place below.

He turned to his work again, smiling. Raking the roasting ore through with an iron scraper, now and again, he paused to watch the sea, where the boat was growing bigger very slowly.

Eckehart carried the roasted ore and the coal to a narrow ravine in the cliff, where a chest-high clay cone stood, with walls a foot thick; a coal fire had been burning within it all day. The west wind howled through the opening in the cliff and whistled in the air vents. Beside the smelting-oven lay heaps of limestone and charcoal. The smith filled the hot oven, first with a layer of lime, then coal, then the third layer of dark red ore, singing to himself in a deep muttering voice:

"White stone, black stone, red stone.

Black on white, ashes in the snow.

Red on black, the earth drinks blood.

Black on red, the raven eats.

White on black, the snow hides all.

Red stone, black stone, white stone."

\#

The most convenient access to Isenkliff was in the west-south-west of the island where the mountain was sloping down into a fan-shaped deep bay, open to the west wind but sheltered from the strong winds out of north and north-west by a promontory running into the sea.

This natural harbour was divided by a rock spur the shape of a quay with six great iron rings let into each side and steps leading up, underwater now as the flood was in.

Here landed those who came to Isenkliff for his father's Aurora steel, but now, there was no ship moored.

Standing up in his boat sent a twinge through Kitt's leg, reminding him of the Dodlak and his claws, which were stowed in a pocket on his belt, along with the Dodlak's teeth.

He fastened a rope to one of the inner rings, dragged himself onto the quay, and limped along onto the grass which marked the high-water line above the black pebble shore. The injured leg had stiffened during the four-day sail, and he did not move as smoothly as usual.

Kitt had long spotted his father by the smelting oven and went up through the crack in the cliff.

He helped Eckehart fill the top of the smelting oven with coal and seal it with fresh clay, working quickly, expertly and just as if he had only taken a break from work, and not been away across the sea for almost a month.

Finally, they inserted the bellows into the air nozzles and worked them to blow gusts of air into the oven, until a heart of fire glowed yellow-hot deep inside it.

"Now, let's go and have mother patch you up," Eckehart said.

"It was a Dodlak," Kitt said and extracted the two sharp ivory tusks from his pocket to hold them out as proof.

"A Dodlak, a Death-Smile Cat." The smith shook his head, weighing the teeth, which were longer than his hand. "I thought they were extinct. Which obviously they aren't. Or are they now?"

"There are more in the cliff of Latunsrigo. I don't know how many but three or four at least."

"That's where you've been then, again!" and as the boy shrugged, "Where's the skin, still in the boat? I can't wait to see it."

"I - lost it."

"Lost it?"

"Had to get away quick," the boy muttered.

"Woodstalkers? They're bad, those savages, vicious. Not even sure they're true humans, though no animal could be that bloody-minded. Except for the Dodlak. The one animal that kills for pleasure, so they say. And who knows what else is there in the Murkowydir. It's a dark forest, very dark. But you always go there and look for trouble. This sort of thing had to happen one day." He scowled at the tusks and handed them back to Kitt.

They walked on in a long silence, Eckehart chewing his beard angrily, and Kitt avoiding to look at his father. The great gulls were wheeling above them, crying in the wind.

"He attacked me," Kitt said suddenly, apparently speaking of the former owner of the deadly tusks.

"Bet, he won't do it again."

The boy held out one of the tusks. "You take one, father."

"It was you or him, wasn't it?"

"He was upon me so quickly, I couldn't run. I had to fight. He was strong and fast, and he wanted to kill me."

"It was a fair fight."

"Yes. If he hadn't cornered me, I wouldn't have fought. I always run. There was one who called me kotrinelli, I guess that means a coward. Because I wouldn't come back when he challenged me. That's the second Woodstalker word I ever learned. The first is krafikamme, but I don't know what it means."

"Never mind what it means. Well, I guess who bites first cannot complain about losing his teeth." Eckehart accepted the Dodlak tooth and shoved it into his pocket. "Just keep clear of the Murkowydir from now on. It's a dark, dark land and it does things to men. I need you here. There might have been brave warriors in need of my steel, and then I would have been in work up to my ears, with no help. The Smith of Isenkliff must always be here and ready."

"There hasn't anyone come for months. They won't come for another month."

"The man Neunauge came sniffing."

"You never sell anything to him."

"He brought books, a whole load. They're all on the table, waiting for you. So I gave him a couple of knives."

"New books!" Kitt's face brightened.

The valley was formed by a creek running down to the harbour. Half way up stood a house; it was high as a lord's hall, as long as a ship, built of stones as big as resting sheep. Yet it was dwarfed by the towering rock wall onto which it backed.

On the west side of the house stood a smaller stone building, also built into the rock -the forge.

Towards the east lay a walled garden.

There was a high timber portal on the west side with a smaller door in it. If Kitt had brought venison or had gathered greens, they would have rounded the corner of the house to take everything into the scullery where there were benches and hooks to begin preparation of the foodstuffs. As that was not the case, they entered the house through the door in the portal.

To the right, a staircase was leading to the gallery above the portal and to Kitt's room in the south-west corner of the building.

Five stone steps led down into the big hall with a long table and a big fireplace at the end, where a blue flame was burning almost invisibly.

The hall was flooded by the light streaming from four windows in the upper gallery, a big round window above the portal and a skylight, covered with a glass window composed of twelve thick glass slabs which had been made in the glassworks of Eghaland and brought by ship on the long sea route; these were the only glass windows for several hundred miles.

To the right, there were three closed doors which were mirrored by three doorways to the left leading into store chambers hewn into the rock. A stair led to the upper storey gallery.

Shelves crammed with books covered the walls of both galleries; they had been brought to Isenkliff from all over the world since word had spread to those who lusted for Aurora Steel, that the smith would much rather take books than gold in payment. Books and parchments were lying on every available surface in the hall just as Kitt had left them.

Eckehart threw open the middle door to the right below the stair. The room they entered also had glass windows both facing south onto the garden and a hearth took up the side.

A woman of medium height was sitting in an armchair beneath the right window by the hearth, her head bent over a shirt she was darning. Her golden hair was streaked thickly with white. She looked up with eyes that were blue like a summer lake in the morning and saw everything.

The old grey dog Isegrim raised his head from his mat by the hearth, his tail slapping the floor hard, twice, three times. Then he lay down again. His face was almost white; he had been there as long as Kitt remembered.

It was one of Kitt's shirts that Aslaug was patching. Sharp things often seemed to pass the boy by very near, leaving his clothes in constant tatters, but the skin below was seldom scratched. The shirt she now mended, Kitt would tear as soon as he wore it. Then she would mend it again.

Aslaug liked things to be good and intact. Her hands were always busy, mending and darning, mixing medicines, preparing things good to eat.

To Kitt, it had always seemed that his mother Aslaug had the power to read the truth by just looking at him, that she would somehow gauge the whole story from his injuries, that she could hear murdered men speak through the cries of geese.

"Here's our boy back, at last, mother. Almost in one piece, just some scratches and a bit lame." Eckehart went to the hearth and lifted the lid from a pot. The smell of leek stew wafted through the hall.

Kitt made towards the pot, but Aslaug held him back, and the boy stood patiently as she took a survey of his wounds, lightly touching the big bruise on his hip, fainter marks on upper arms and chest.

"Four days ago that this happened? It's healing well." Aslaug bent down and took off the rough bandage from Kitt's calve.

A mess of crushed purple flowers with yellow centres fell to the floor. The long, slit wound appeared as if it had been inflicted that very day.

"No inflammation," Aslaug remarked. "No scabbing either." She noticed how Kitt looked at his own lacerated flesh as if it was somebody else's. A good trait in a healer, and a warrior. A disturbing one in a boy just turning thirteen years old. She pressed her lips together.

"The seawater stopped the bleeding, but I think the flowers have something to do with it."

"Oh yes." She picked at the sodden plants on the floor. "I haven't seen this for years; it is so rare, and of those who search for it, hardly anyone returns."

"I have more." Kitt rummaged in his belt bag.

Aslaug laid a flaxen cloth on the table.

Kitt spread the entire contents of his bag on it, a handful of half-wilted blossoms, dry flower-heads, two pink and purple crystals, a

71

hand-long white tooth and eight hooked claws of a great cat.

"The Dodlak got me with one of his claws. And then I saw that old bone with living flesh on it. It must have been the dew and rainwater falling from the flowers onto the flesh which kept it fresh. So I put some of those blossoms into the bandage and then wet it," he concluded.

"And where is that place?"

"Latunsrigo," Kitt said and blushed.

"Well for once you have been using those eagle eyes of yours for something worthwhile. This purple blossom is medicine so powerful, that some say it can wake the dead. Which it cannot do. It doesn't even have healing power; it merely conserves, but this it does perfectly. And that is a very good thing because you must always beware of a wound closing too quickly, because it may continue festering into the bone. A cat's scratch this deep must be taken very seriously, for there is poison on their claws. With this flower, you have gained time to treat this as we would a fresh wound. It will leave hardly a scar and no weakness at all. You have healthy blood. Yes, healthy blood."

Aslaug opened a metal box in which silver and golden needles, pairs of pincers and fine blades lay and also pieces of sinew. She took a pair of pincers and a needle and extracted minute specs of dirt from the wound. Her movements were light and quick, but she knew the procedure was excruciating; under it, she had known grown men beg for liquor.

Kitt made no move, nor sound.

Isegrim whined in sympathy.

She opened a bottle of her wound medicine; a smell of burned spirits filled the room, and she swabbed the freshly bleeding wound.

Kitt opened Aslaug's medicine chest. She couldn't see his face now, hid behind the curtain of his fair hair, but still, he said nothing.

Some of Aslaug's medicines came from far-away lands, and those had always held a particular fascination for Kitt.

There was amber from the sunken woods of the north coast, picked up by ragged urchins for a handful of flour, and sold for gold dust in the southern lands.

72

There was Indigo, staining his hands blue, from islands beyond Bharatan.

There were the uncanny black-light stones that had to be kept in leaden wraps because their invisible light had the power to bring on the same incurable illness in the healthy, that it cured in the mortally sick.

A metal casket contained the dried bark and leaves from a tree growing in Kush, of such power, that just by smelling it brought stinging tears to the eyes and reality to dreams of faraway lands.

"If you keep opening that, all the goodness will fly away," Aslaug remarked.

Abashed Kitt closed the casket lid. "In the jungles of Kush grow trees that poison the meat cooked over the fire from their wood, and others that kill those who sleep under them," he ventured. "A sailor from Peleset told me that."

"The things the travellers tell," Eckehart said. "For all we know, they are true."

Aslaug threaded some of the sinews into the golden needle. "Why gold and silver? Why not steel? It holds a sharper point?" Kitt asked. This question was the only sign of impatience -if it even was that.

"Because gold and silver are the unchangeable metals," Aslaug spoke a little louder, to make sure that Eckehart, intent on eating, could hear her. "The master smith has promised me incorruptible steel for my needles, but so far he has wasted his time and skill on swords." As she spoke, she closed the split skin of the calf with stitches of the golden needle, working as quickly as she could.

Eckehart said what he'd said many times before: "Iron is a powerful metal, it can be made so many things; by adding small amounts of different elements it can be made soft or hard, brittle or springy." He waved his spoon about expansively in illustration how many different properties steel could have. "I only need to find the right elements to add, and then I will make steel so sharp you can open a man and sew him up again while he sleeps. And never will a speck of rust mar it. It is almost within the reach of my hands."

"You can never give your steel healing powers, as gold and silver

73

have. It is beneficial to eat and drink from silver and gold, as is to wear golden and silver jewellery. There never will be steel jewellery."

"Very unhealthy, gold, when crossing the course of a longboat full of Nordmänner. Then, steel is the healthier metal," Eckehart chuckled.

"Armour made of incorruptible steel! No more polishing of all those rings and scales!" Kitt said enthusiastically.

"Always thinking of war," Aslaug's voice sounded like broken glass in her own ears. "It is fast and easy to wound, and slow, hard work to heal. That is why you should learn to heal first before you learn to wound. You really made a discovery with the purple blossom, and you drew all the right conclusions. I'm glad about that, so glad. It would be best if you only learned to heal, but that is past wishing for."

"We could make special blades for surgery, with the edge of incorruptible steel, inlaid with gold and silver down to the hardening line," Kitt said. "The gold would not eat this steel, as it does the ordinary kind."

"This remark shows that you have what it takes to become a first-class smith," Eckehart said. "There are many roads open to you, son, always remember that."

Aslaug pressed her lips together, as she always did when she felt discontent. The mood did not reach her hands, working quick and lightly. At last, she finished bandaging Kitt's leg. The boy limped to the table. She knew his wounds hurt far more now than they had before. The pain would last only a little time, and she would have consoled any other patient with those words.

Eckehart cleared another space among the books, parchments, scrolls and stone tablets and filled a bowl with vegetable stew from the pot on the hearth.

Kitt drew the steaming bowl towards him with the keen appetite of a growing boy who had nothing but raw meat and fish during several days on the run through the woods and in a leaking boat. He picked up his silver spoon, looked at it pensively, and began eating with a contented sigh. Spooning with his right, his left hand strayed automatically to one of the new books; he opened it and ate with his eyes glued to the letters. He was reading the account of a Daguilarian merchant who had travelled beyond the Meira Valley to Kush -the fabled realm of the poison trees.

The written word surrounded Kitt all his life. There between the stained covers and tattered pages, he found the whole world. Most of the scriptures brought to the island were written in the slanting Daguilarian letters, the blocky script of Murom, or the involved characters of Cladith Culuris. There even were some brittle scrolls covered in the glyphs of Meira, the rounded letters of Bharatan painted on silk, or the letter garlands of Gülisande. Inked on thin sheets so delicate that a careless movement might tear them, were the ornamental, illegible signs from Luxin Shoo, and the simpler but equally mysterious letters from the Islands under the Rising Sun, the farthest, most mythic of all places, and those intrigued the boy most of all.

Having finished eating the third bowl, he felt sated, at last. His right hand was free to reach for another scroll which seemed to tell about a sky-high column made entirely of iron. Besides the trade script universal to the Meira valley and the White Sea, of which Kitt had a good grasp, there were the rectangular letters like little pictures of birds, plants, feathers and limbs that made no sense to him at all.

Eckehart rose from the table. "Now I have to look to that smelting oven. No, don't you move, Kitt, stay in tonight, so as not to split your seams again."

The boy sank back onto his seat, hiding his face in the book. He was more than a little nervous staying alone with his mother, fearing that she might begin to ask questions now. If she did, she would extract a confession from him in no time. But his mother remained silent. She had turned to the purple blossoms again and picked over the dry flower-heads containing the seed, careful that not a one should get lost.

The Daguilarian manuscript had made just one titillating mention of a cast iron column in the Meira Valley, then went on to describe how the smiths of Kush made charcoal from grass. Kitt supposed it could be done; he thought of the sparse pastures of Isenkliff and that

75

it must take those smiths a long time to gather sufficient fuel to fire just one small smelting oven. Surely not enough for an iron column of that height mentioned.

"I have only a little coal dust left," his mother said.

This coincidence of thought startled the boy terribly; he sat there, staring at her mutely.

"You could grind some if you can spare a moment?"

She didn't seem to have read his mind after all.

Obediently, Kitt laid the books aside and set an iron bowl and pestle on the table. From a basket, he took a handful of coal lumps, mined in the Brynaich mountains on the mainland and brought by ship, and began grinding the coal lumps into the fine fuel his mother used for the preparation of her medicines.

With one blinding moment of illumination, Aslaug realised that all her fears had come true. As if she needed the confirmation.

She watched the rock-hard coal breaking into splinters under Kitt's hands, so easily as if it was but the brittle ice of spring. Some of the bigger lumps he crushed with his fingers first; the cracking sound reminded her of breaking bones. She thought of the children, both dead, and couldn't even picture what the boys she had born would be looking like, now. Except that it would have been nothing like this.

The dying Kri warrior had told her that blood couldn't be cheated - the blood of killers, a long line of killers, generations upon generations, both men and women.

For twelve years their bones had been rotting in the bloody swamp of Tridden Moor, but they were winning. Her hatred of the Kri was a petrified coldness now, as the old ice in the north. She felt her face harden into an expression of revulsion. Intent on his work, the boy did not see it, and by the time he had finished with the coal, she had brought her expression under control.

"I am also out of numbnettle for my wound medicine. But the common purple and yellow blossoms won't serve. It is the white numbnettle which I need, and that doesn't grow on Isenkliff."

"I know a place where they grow. By the stone tables of Wittewal."

If only he wouldn't look at her like an eager puppy. Whenever

Aslaug saw his open smile, she felt warm inside and couldn't go on hating. This had been her weakness from the beginning. "That is the very place, Kitt. So, when you go away in your boat again, you might take a detour there."

"I can go tomorrow morning, mother!"

Always trying to please her.

"But it's too early for numbnettle," she said with a hesitation she did not comprehend herself.

"Numbnettle grow all year around on Wittewal; everything does."

Of course, he knew that. "Not tomorrow. Your leg will be stiff and sore."

"Not a bit of it, mother. You said yourself that I have healthy blood."

"You have." She hardened her resolve. "Oh, yes. It's your blood."

"I go there first light," he promised.

Aslaug smiled; there was a terrible strain in that smile. Kitt didn't see it. He trusted her.

Just then, Eckehart came back in, and they entered into a technical conversation about the smelting oven.

\#

Early the next morning Kitt set out in quest of white numbnettle.

He was limping all the way to his boat, his leg wound hurting him more than on the day when the Dodlak had almost caught him. His mother had said that pain needed to get worse before getting better, so he took the agony as a good sign. His mother knew best. He felt reprieved that he hadn't needed to tell her about the dead Woodstalker.

In the bright light of morning, the smooth back of the island of Wittewal was visible from Isenkliff, lying thirty miles south like a white whale.

The waters around Wittewal were of a milky opaqueness sharply contrasting with the surrounding grey-green waters. In the centre of the island rose a thirty-feet-high, smooth, dome-shaped mound, shining in rosy colours in the early sunlight, turning into blinding white as the sun rose higher.

Kitt rounded the island to sail to the south side. He knew that

77

access was better there, and that there was a colony of albatrosses on the eastern end, and a seal and sea lion colony on the south-east side.

The boat scraped over stone and Kitt drew it up onto the shore over round pebbles crusted white.

On Wittewal, all senses contradicted each other. Ice and cold, his eyes told Kitt, while mild, moist air touched his face and warm springs bubbled out of holes and crevices, running down to the sea. Steam shot whistling out of cracks in the rock, to hang as thick fog in the morning air, smelling of sulphur.

Below the white mound, stood stone tables hewn from black basalt, two upright slabs, with a third polished smooth lying across. There were five such tables, and the white numbnettles grew thickly around them. It was strange to see the dark broad-leafed green apparently growing from ice; a closer look revealed the plants to be rooted in soil blown into the nooks and crannies of the rock, the eyeholes and jaws of skulls, and among ribcages -old bones thickly encrusted in the white gypsum.

Kitt collected the white blossoms by the handful, guarding them in the wooden receptacle he carried with him for that purpose. When it was full, he closed the lid.

As he went back to the boat, he heard a high humming tone.

He turned to see nothing, and about again, unable to locate the source.

The noise rose to an unsupportable pitch. He thought he distinguished one word in it.

"Stupid!"

Something dark rose into the air before Kitt's feet with a nasty whirring noise.

He dropped into a half-crouch, letting go of the container and drawing a knife.

Something resembling a giant dragonfly, flew above his head on two pairs of silky wings, of so deep and dark a blue as to be almost black. It had an elongated body about two hands long, covered in fine scales of the same tint, and no limbs, just fine tentacles floating around it. Did it have a sting?

The flying creature lost a little height and hovered directly before

78

the boy. A tiny face stared at him, delicate and sharply cut, of a mother of pearl paleness, surrounded by a halo of silvery hair. Every single hair resembled a platinum wire embedded in glass. The eyes were huge and shone like quicksilver shimmering through black lace.

Kitt hadn't seen anything like this before, the few times he had landed on the island. No book, no legend, nor his parents had ever mentioned the existence of such a creature.

The high-pitched noise went on, jarring like a snagged nail on sailcloth. "Stupid!"

Kitt straightened up. "Who are you?"

"Stupid, stupid, stupid!"

Kitt couldn't see the creature's tiny slit mouth moving -the noise emanated from the whole black body.

With whirring wings the thing kept hovering in the air, screaming its litany of "Stupid! Spoiled!"

Kitt barely checked the impulse to swipe at it with the knife. It didn't seem to have a sting beside its poisonous tongue.

"You look ridiculous!" As the evil keening went on, he could distinguish more and more words. "All crushed and brown, the numbnettle blossoms. Do you think they are of any use, so crushed and brown? No, they are not of any use like that. Not to anybody."

Kitt opened the receptacle. The white blossoms had already turned into a brown, wilted mess smelling faintly of the corruption of flowers. So, the task was not so easy, after all.

"Stupid, stupid, stupid!" the creature resumed, precisely hitting the whole cadence of tones most loathsome to the human ear. "Stupid, stupid, stupid! Spoilt!"

A headache began drilling into Kitt's head, spreading from his ears, enveloping his brain. "Who are you? What are you?" he asked with a fervent wish to interrupt the torture of that sound.

"Why should I tell you anything, you clumsy brute!" The little creature buzzed an offensive noise and bobbed more and more wildly. "Go back to your iron. Ugh." It shuddered as with profound distaste. "Iron. That's the dirty stuff you are fit to work with your big, crushing hands. Not my delicate flowers."

"Shall I tear out your wings?" Kitt inquired in a forced, reasonable tone.

"Can't catch me!" The creature dived at Kitt, who ducked quickly from a reflex. "Can't catch me, catch me, catch me!" It rose and dived again. "Stupid!" Another swoop at his face, sideways. "Can't catch me! Stupid, stupid, stupid! Oh!"

Kitt's hand shot out like lightning, caught the little creature around the waist, and held it up before his eyes. It buzzed exactly like a trapped wasp, and he needed to apply the same willpower as for holding a real insect.

Securing the abdomen with his little finger, he turned the creature upside down. His impression had been right: it had short, insectile legs with fluttering violet membranes. There was no sting.

Turning the creature back upside, he saw that any resemblance to human features was only superficial. The mouth was like that of a dragonfly, with retracted mandibles. The face was a hard and translucent mask, like a delicate shell. He wondered what he might find beneath it if he were to hitch off that mask with a fingernail.

"What do you gape at me, unnatural monster?" the creature shrilled. "Release me at once! You bruise my wings like you did the numbnettle flowers. Look at the poor things, look at them now and then look at your big, bloody paws!"

Kitt looked regretfully at the wasted flowers, and then at his hands, involuntarily opening them, releasing the little creature.

It soared up with a high pitched whoop of triumph. "Stupid! Yaaah!"

Kitt's left hand shot out and caught the creature by some of the trailing tentacles.

"You misfit!" the creature buzzed like an enraged bee, slewing around at his face. "Slayer, beast, predator! You horror! You hate from olden times!"

Kitt's hand closed about the infuriating little thing. To squeeze the jeering out of it, to twist it into stringy, bloody bits, and tear these strings apart into smaller bits - the impact of the sudden urge hit Kitt so strongly, that the shock of it made him come to his senses immediately.

He found the shoulders of his neck bunched rigidly, his teeth clenched, the fingers stiff.

He breathed deeply in and out and relaxed. "I must hold the numbnettle blossoms carefully. As I hold you," he said very quietly while holding the little creature in both his hands so lightly that not a trailing tentacle was bent. But escape was out of the question. "Wouldn't want you to turn brown and limp like the numbnettle flowers."

"Very, very carefully!" the creature buzzed with a different melody. Suddenly, it felt soft in his hands, velvety, warm and trusting -like a young bee.

"Careful, careful, careful!"

"Yes. Now, no more screeching," Kitt said, opening his hands.

The creature stayed hovering in the same place where Kitt had released it, watching him from silver and black eyes. "Tell me, why didn't you swat little me like a pesky buzz fly, why didn't you crush me in your hands? You are big, and I am little. I annoyed you very much, didn't I? Don't you just hate my voice, doesn't it madden, enrage you? Hey, I know things about you! And I'll tell, I'll tell! All will shun you, hunt you, hate you after I tell on you!" The loathsome tone rose with each word into insupportable shrilling, making the rage bubble up again.

Kitt retreated a step and put his trembling hands behind his back, keeping a deliberate grip on the impulse to tear and rend, just as he did on his hands until his knuckles were white and his nails dug into his flesh that it hurt. He would first break his own fingers before giving in to the creatures malicious taunting.

"You won't lift a hand against me?" the creature inquired with a mild humming.

"You are not my size," Kitt mumbled. Acknowledging defeat, he dumped the spoiled numbnettle flowers on the ground in a brown sodden heap, turned his back on it and began walking down to the shore. Just get away, he thought, before he did something he'd regret.

"Won't do me a favour, won't lose your cool," the little creature hummed. "Won't show any feelings. Simple minds will mistake that for something else entirely. Then they'll get a nasty surprise. Very nasty. You hit hard in your very own time, don't you, Kitt?"

Kitt turned around startled. "You know my name?"

"I am Finsterkuning. I know things." The creature looked at him, expectantly.

Kitt did not feel like asking what it knew.

"Doing no favours to anyone," the creature buzzed. "But I will grant a favour to you. Yes, you are about to receive a favour from Finsterkuning."

"No thanks," Kitt muttered, still retreating.

"You are not properly awed," the creature buzzed in a sharp tone. "I said Finsterkuning. I am he. Surely you know who the ruler on Wittewal is? No?"

Kitt shook his head, thinking that he would gladly have lived on without ever knowing.

"So, you don't know who Finsterkuning is? You thought nobody lived on Wittewal but the albatrosses and the seals? That is strange, very strange. I wonder now. Yes, I wonder very much." The creature bobbed up and down a few times, looking as pensive as a black dragonfly could.

Kitt shrugged, edging away in the direction of the shore.

"I did not say you could leave. You are not done here, are you? You did not do your work yet, did you? Dry, white and perfect, that is how they must be, the numbnettle flowers! That is what you came here for, isn't it? Now, pluck the flowers carefully and then spread them on my tables to dry in the sun. That is the way to collect numbnettle flowers."

Kitt began collecting the white blossoms again and spread them on a stone table. It was slower work this time, as he had already gathered most blooms from the best places at the first failed try. Now he had to make do with those that he had left or overlooked.

At first, his hands were trembling from the aftershock of the terrible rage that had so suddenly seized him. Becoming absorbed in this delicate work, he almost forgot the little creature. When it spoke again, he nearly jumped, bracing himself for another outburst of high-pitched offensiveness.

"Spread them not in heaps, spread them thinly," the creature now hummed in a peaceful tone. "Spread them in a thin layer, for the sun and the air to dry them quickly. Quickness is of the essence here, to keep the numbnettle's potency."

Kitt followed the little creature's advice to the word.

"I am Finsterkuning, I know things," the creature repeated. "I know who you are. I know what you are. But you, do you know? Why do you think that you are made stronger and faster than all other men?"

"I'm nothing of the kind," Kitt objected.

"You are made as you are because you are a born killer. So, have you killed already?"

I'm not, I did not, Kitt was about to say. The image of the dead Woodstalker warrior lying among the tangerine daisies flashed before his eyes. He said nothing.

"Ah." The creature bobbed. "I thought I saw blood on your hands. I see that blood now. Whose blood is it? Is it of someone in the wood? The Great Wood called Murkowydir?"

Kitt tensed, straightening to his full height. "What do you mean?" he said heavily. Did it need a second death, to cover up the first? But he knew already that to kill this creature would only make everything infinitely worse. Locked in a fight for life or death in the Murkowydir wood, he had had no choice. Here on Wittewal, the decision was his.

He bent down to the numbnettles again, not because he wanted more blossoms, but because he needed something to engage his hands, and keep them safe.

The little creature still hovered within arm's reach. "What do I care about the pointless deaths of apes. I don't. Apes that think they are better than the other animals! Think they know things merely because they gape at the stars without comprehension. They know nothing! Nothing at all do they know. I am Finsterkuning, and I do know."

Kitt turned away from the creature to the stone table. Finding the numbnettle blossoms he had collected first to be dry, he quickly began pushing them into his bark container.

"You must leave some blossoms on my table for your medicine to work," Finsterkuning said. "Never forget leaving me my share of blossoms, so that you may always return for my white numbnettle."

83

Kitt closed his container. "Take those that aren't dry yet." Anyway, he wasn't feeling strong enough to wait for the rest of the blossoms to dry. All he wanted was to be away and never come back for anything, eggs, seals or numbnettles.

"Yes, come back often, talk to me. Finsterkuning grants you the freedom of Wittewal. You may bath in my sulphur pools. Very good for you."

These offers held no inducement at all for Kitt. He almost ran towards the shore.

A sudden gust of wind whirled the nettle blossoms on the stone table high into the air. Kitt spun around. From the corner of his eye, he saw Finsterkuning standing above the tables, not a little creature any more. What stood there was a black giant, metallic scales big as soup plates covering its insectile body, purple wings spreading in the wind like dark banners. Merciless quicksilver eyes followed Kitt's every movement. Foot-long mandibles clicked sharply. The forelegs ended in massive claws, grinding together like millstones, capable of crushing a man into a bloody pulp.

As Kitt completed the turn, he was looking at nothing. There only was a dark steam column hissing out of the white mound. His headache had subsided to a dull throbbing memory behind his eyes.

#

When Eckehart returned home for dinner from his smelting oven, he found Aslaug sitting at the kitchen table, staring at a little heap of dry, faultlessly white numbnettle blossoms.

He looked at the blossoms, then at her, then at Kitt, who sat opposite, his eyes fixed on a book.

"Been away again, Kitt? You left early, I didn't even hear you. No holding you at home, is there?"

"I only went as far as Wittewal."

Eckehart looked at Aslaug again. She refused to meet his eyes, pushing the white flowers across the table with her fingertips.

"I bet the Dark King of Wittewal had something to say about that? Finsterkuning is serious about his white numbnettle. Touch them and out he comes, buzzing like a black hornet."

"He did." The boy shuddered. "Wouldn't stop calling me evil

names. I had made a mess of everything. Then he told me how to collect numbnettle properly." He grinned wanly. "I never saw him when I hunted there. He was surprised that I did not know him."

Aslaug's shoulders stiffened.

"Yes, that must have surprised him very much," Eckehart said. "I haven't seen him since . . ." he paused, to continue vaguely "for a long time, and didn't miss him. Of all the obnoxious Swatlings he is the worst! Could goad the Good God Nodun into attempting to slay him. It's a wonder you didn't pluck out his wings."

"I almost did," Kitt muttered. "How can something that black lair in such a white place? He isn't little either."

"Yes, that's him, a black hornet as big as the cliff and in a foul mood. He likes tempting fools into taking a swipe at him, then crush them."

"What is he?"

"He's a Swatelb. They have their own dark world, and they lurk under rocks and in brooks or groves, waiting to punish evildoers. Finsterkuning is a prince among them. No bad man who set foot on Wittewal has ever left it. In the old times, the Judges of Irmin Prono sent those accused of murder to Wittewal. Brought them to the south side in the morning and came to the north side in the evening. If the man was there, still alive and sane, he was judged innocent and restored to his former station. Some ran into the sea rather than wait out the day."

"I saw them." Kitt thought of the bones in their white crusts. "I didn't know."

"There was a smith here once, even before Brynnir," Eckehart continued. "He was the first smith on Isenkliff, and his name is forgotten. He demanded that anyone who wanted a sword first crossed Wittewal on foot. Finsterkuning tells men about themselves, you see."

"How does he speak? He has a face, but his lips don't move."

"He doesn't speak; he can make you hear, using what is in your mind. So the things he tells you are really that which lies within yourself. But as you don't have a single bad bone in your entire body, Finsterkuning got no grip on your mind, and the judges will

85

have no choice but to pronounce you innocent."

Kitt flushed deeply. He felt his mother watching him. If Finsterkuning could see the dead Woodstalker, Aslaug had seen him also.

"Well son, that'll teach you to go roaming about in that boat of yours, shirking an honest day's work," Eckehart said. "From now on, I want you by the smelting ovens and in the smithy, every day, morning to night. That is, if your mother hasn't any more tasks to give you."

"Yes, mother, if you need more?" Kitt said bravely.

"I have all I need." Aslaug gathered together the numbnettle flowers, and guarded them in a white porcelain casket. "You did that well, Kitt," she added, her voice a little unsteady. "Again, you did very well."

"Now go to bed, son! You look all in. Do you have a headache?" "Just tired. I'll go to sleep." Kitt stood up, holding on to the table, favouring his hurt leg.

"Your mother will brew you a tea to make you sleep without pain."

Obediently Kitt drank what Aslaug gave him, it tasted of honey and Narden.

Eckehart listened to Kitt's steps on the stair, and as usual, he heard nothing. He allowed some time because he didn't hear the door of Kitt's room either; he was a very quietly moving boy.

Then he looked at Aslaug directly. She refused to meet his eye.

"You had no right to do what you did behind my back! You had no right!" His voice grew louder; he checked it. "How could you want to do such a thing to my boy!" he whispered. "If ever I had a son of my own, I could not love him more than Kitt. I don't want to think of a life without him."

"It has begun, hasn't it?" Aslaug also spoke in a low voice.

"What has?"

"You saw him yesterday, all bruised and silent. Something has happened, out there in the woods, something he did not tell. Or did he tell it to you?" Now she looked at him fully, her blue eyes bright.

"No, he didn't."

"First blood. He has killed. I always was afraid that he will go their way, despite everything I tried. And now he has taken the first step on their road. I know it, and so do you!"

"I don't know anything of the kind. From what he let fall, he was collecting those purple flowers for you when the Dodlak came upon him. The fight must have drawn the attention of the Woodstalkers, so they attacked him, and he had to cut his way out. I didn't ask. If I had asked him, he would have told me. I only asked him had it been a fair fight, and he said it had. Said he wouldn't have fought if he could have run."

"Eckehart, Eckehart. You never ask the right questions. Why does he go into the dark wood Murkowydir again and again? What is he looking for there? Can you really honestly answer me that?"

"Oh, yes, I can. He is curious. This is a small island for a boy his size and strength. Why shouldn't he go where he wants and look at things that interest him? He's even trying to learn their damn language! Too bad the only language they understand is a good kick in the teeth. Well, it seems they got it. When they have enough, they will leave him in peace. If he had to take out one-"

"Or more than one?"

"What if he killed a hundred of those murderous savages? Should he kneel down to have his throat cut? Or far worse? Doesn't he have the right to defend himself?"

"A very old and tired excuse."

"No Ferys, Theusten or Nordmann would give it a second thought! Why do you expect of Kitt what you wouldn't of anybody else?"

"Because he is not like everybody else. You keep forgetting that, don't you, Eckehart? This first death- first blood- of a human being - for him, it will be different. What it does to him."

"Nothing different. Every young man has to kill for the first time or die on that day. Most have got it over with before their beard grows. It's all in the order of things. So, I accepted the Dodlak tooth," Eckehart drew the long white fang from his pocket and slapped it on the table, "to show him that all was still the same with me. Which it is. And that's how it stays!"

She looked at the Dodlak tooth, hand-long, white, sharp and

shuddered again, thinking of the horrible animal, powerful, malignant, considering that the boy had slain this thing.

"He has never been like other children, didn't toddle, and ran at once. Never fell, never cried. He developed muscles from the age of three. I cried then."

"I remember."

"Do you ever look at him, really look at him? See him move? See the coiled violence within him? He has shaped his body into a weapon. Or maybe it shaped itself. I think of him out in the wild, among the . . . the other beasts of prey. Predator," she sobbed. "Predator."

Eckehart nodded. "He inherited their strength. But not their coldness. He is dangerous. But not evil. I have made swords for so many men, I know what a man is made of, by taking one look at him. I know murderers. Kitt is not one of them."

"No, he is not evil." She dried her eyes. "A tiger also knows no evil. He just doesn't feel guilty for what he does."

"Oh yes he minds, minds terribly. I hate seeing him so downtrodden. And for what?" Eckehart bared his teeth at her. "Do you want a son whose face anybody could slap because his spirit is broken? I don't."

"Even his eyes changed," she said disconsolately. "They were blue when I found him. Now they are grey, like theirs."

"That happens with many animals. Newly born cats have blue eyes, and so do puppies."

"He had such big hands. And such big feet. Yes, just like a puppy." Her lips twitched. "No, not a puppy. More like an ice bear cub. Playfulness and grace that touch something deep inside the heart. You never resisted, Eckehart."

"What for? He's a child."

"Because the cub grows up and his playing becomes too rough for human fragility. When I see the way he walks, the way he looks out of those grey eyes - it shocks me – every day anew."

"So, you sent him to Wittewal because of the colour of his eyes?"

"Because of the life he extinguished."

"And what now? Kitt passed Finsterkuning's test. He hunted on the

88

island before more than once and the Dark King of Wittewal never objected to him. It is said that he abides no evil. Though who he is to judge, I don't know! I haven't seen the dark princeling since the Chaining of the Fenris Hound." He passed the palm of his hand across his eyes and face. "Memories like that are the price for laying my hand on Brynnir's forge. I hope I won't meet the black bug again before Fenris gets loose once more and swallows the world. For if I do see him, I shall throttle the nasty critter before he can screech his first insult. I don't think I'd have passed that test. Could you, Aslaug?"

"Not now."

"You mean, after what you did?"

She nodded, swallowed hard. "When he was so eager to bring me the numbnettle blossoms it hurt me. I . . . I told him to wait a day or two. Then you would have found out and stopped it. But he wouldn't wait. He wanted to go at once." Tears suddenly dropped down on Aslaug's hands in big splashing droplets.

Eckehart came around the table to lay his massive arm around her twitching shoulder. "There now," he muttered. "Our boy is asleep in his bed, and everything is good."

It had been a long time since he had consoled her like that. Eckehart realised that if there ever had been anything between them as a man and his wife, it had withered without him rightly noticing. He had come to Isenkliff for the woman and stayed for the child.

Tempering the Steel

Northwind blows out of Nebelheim, carved on his wings runes from Isenkliff, and the people mutter "The iron folk, they sing again."

Kitt woke long before dawn.

The house was quiet.

Beneath the drowsiness induced by his mother's medicine, he had heard his parents talking long into the night, his father raising his voice and lowering it again, his mother crying.

His fault, Kitt knew. His parent's quarrels were always about him.

On the long pull home from the dark wood Murkowydir across the sea, he had thought up all sorts of convincing stories, and then just had not liked to tell them. But even saying nothing, he had still managed to lie to his father.

His mother knew anyway.

He felt as if a red mark burned on his forehead, telling the tale of shed blood, as in the fable of the jealous brothers. Of course, he knew that killers didn't carry a visible mark; none of the warriors coming to Isenkliff for Eckehart's steel had written the number of their victims on their foreheads. But Finsterkuning of Wittewal had seen it at once, that non-existing mark. The boy rather shied from thinking about the things Finsterkuning had said. No, he didn't want to think about Finsterkuning at all.

For the hundredth time, he thought about the dead Woodstalker. How could he come upon him like that? Either he was very good, or Kitt was not as good as he'd thought. The Woodstalker had been a terrific fighter, as the Dodlak had been.

How perfect everything could have been, his mother pleased with him for once over his finding the purple flower and gathering the white numbnettle. The death of that Woodstalker turned everything into a lie. So, what was the difference between the Dodlak and the Woodstalker?

None. Both wanted to kill you. Both are dead now.

The alien thought had sprung out of nowhere. In the dark of night, there seemed to be a presence near him, watching, judging, saying things like this in a cold, hard voice.

When the birds began singing the boy lay exhausted, staring at the roof beams in the grey predawn light. If his mother asked him, he'd simply tell the truth.

He dawdled over washing in warm water. His room was the cistern room in the south-west corner, where the flue from the kitchen hearth came up. After the cold and wet of the Murkowydir, he enjoyed this luxury very much.

He cleaned his teeth with chalk paste even more elaborately than usual, prolonging the moment when he would have to meet his mother's eye.

A man should meet fate with a clean face. As fate may strike at any time, a man's face should always be clean to meet it. Who had told him that a long time ago, his father, one of the visiting warriors?

Trying to remember when Eckehart had spoken to him about fate, he slowly put on a sleeveless leather tunic and knee-long wide leather trousers, all held together by a tool belt.

Then there was nothing more to do. He had to go down now.

From the polished steel mirror, his grey eyes looked back at him, troubled. There was no mark on his forehead. Of course, there wasn't.

Down in the kitchen, his parents were sitting at the table, both silent. The old dog Isegrim acknowledged the boy's entry by wagging his tail from his mat by the hearth.

His mother poured him lime flower tea, which she kept warm in a pot near the fire and stirred a spoonful of honey into it.

Kitt busied himself with the food on the table, bread and leek soup.

"Not really a meal for smiths," his father broke the silence. "We ate the last sausage in yesterday's soup, and the hens aren't laying."

"If your son only hunts meat unfit to eat, like Dodlaks –then not even bring it home . . . I don't mind eating leek for days on end," Aslaug made it sound a severe threat.

"I'd slaughter one of the yearling bulls if your soft-hearted son hadn't gone and bestowed names on all the cattle. Can't eat an animal with a name," Eckehart said.

"I can hunt goats." Kitt rose. "I go at once."

91

"Anything to shirk an honest day's work," Eckehart grumbled. "Well, I suppose a man must eat meat to hold body and soul together."

In a flash Kitt was by the scullery door where he kept his hunting equipment. One arm in the sleeve of his coat he took down his bow from the wall, it was Kirgis made of many thin horn layers glued together with resin, accurate and long-range, but temperamental.

He also took an ash bow, less aristocratic, and less capricious, which he could leave strung all day, and a short throwing spear with a long thin steel blade.

He escaped outside, blinking into the bright light of the rising sun. The dew-laden grass glittered, and his boots left a dark green trail.

Shining in rose and silver at the lower end of the valley, the sea lay calm, and the air smelled fresh and new. The nightmare shadow of the Dark Wood Murkowydir did not reach across this sea.

Kitt climbed further up the valley to the spring. Soon he found what he was looking for, tracks of cloven hoofs and scattered fresh droppings, pea-sized, black and round, belonging to wild goats. They were called Brynnir's herd, which had remained as a heritage from the previous smiths of Isenkliff.

One after the other, they had left when they could, tired of the hard, long winters and the stony, thin soil that bore a little rye and oats, and the hungry creatures they shared the island with. There remained half-tame cattle and sheep, glad to be milked and shorn and fed in winter by Aslaug and lately, by Kitt, who had given names to every animal.

The goats however, had reverted to be wild, long-haired shaggy sure-footed animals springing from rock to rock, their bright yellow eyes wary of the hunter. There were so many new goats each year that there weren't enough names in the world even had they stood still long enough to be known and named.

Kitt paused a moment to string the ash bow. Just when he was done, a big buck, black with white speckles and a grey belly and short, sharp horns, streaked across the path.

Kitt knocked an arrow and released it in the same movement. Shot through the neck, the buck stumbled and fell.

He arrived where the animal had fallen, feeling his habitual pang of remorse as always when seeing the face of an animal he had killed. But as his father had said, one must eat. And Kitt had left the house without meat, for days, even a month. It was his responsibility to provide.

Kitt reminded himself that the goats gnawed the buds from the young trees and broke into Aslaug's garden to feed on her young plants. Too many goats were not good for an island, he knew. He knelt down beside the fallen buck, drawing the sharp-edged knife he used for opening up his hunting prey.

Suddenly a figure appeared nearby as if grown out of the ground. A Jarnmantsje, hardly four feet tall, but as broad, and everything on him seemed hewn from rock, even the shapeless grey and brown clothes.

He approached to stem short, thick arms upon the dead goat, tilted his head to one side and peered at the boy out of round yellow eyes under beetling brows.

Kitt had known the Jarnmantsjes all his life. They lived underground, mining for ores. Greedy for fresh meat, their short legs and massive bodies made for poor hunters. They were always hungry, and hunger made them angry. Kitt could tell this one was in a terrible mood.

"Good morning, Ungstein," he said.

"I take," the Jarnmantsje declared in a voice like rusty iron.

"You take," Kitt agreed, retrieving his arrow from the goat's neck.

The little man shouldered the goat with ease and scrambled off.

Almost immediately Kitt spotted another buck standing still on the mountain slope, tawny and black; it was nearly invisible against the rock.

It did not move while he strung the Kirgis bow; not even when he drew and sighted, did the goat stir.

It was a very long cast, even with a Kirgis bow, which few hunters would have undertaken, yet Kitt didn't think twice about it. The arrow sped away, the bowstring hit Kitt's leather sleeve with a slap. The goat jumped into the air, hit square into the chest and fell, sliding down the slope faster and faster, until it was met by a row of boulders at the cliff edge.

Instead of stopping the goat's downward slide, the boulder toppled over the edge of the cliff, and the goat fell with it.   Kitt felt disgusted with himself. "Calculate not only what you see, but also what you don't see," he murmured, once more wondering who had told him that?

The ground at the base of the rock had been hollowed out by wind and rain, destabilising it.

Bending over the cliff edge, Kitt saw the body of the goat fifty feet below, caught by a gnarled pine tree growing from a crevice. Farther down, two hundred feet deep, the waves thundered at the foot of the cliff.

Kitt lowered himself over the rim and descended the nearly vertical rock wall. From below came the loud cawing of crows, disputing the goat's eyes it seemed, and Kitt continued climbing carefully to have at least two limbs locked to the rock face at any one time, in case a plucky bird decided to swoop at him. Crows did not care whom they attacked, he knew; he had seen a single crow chasing an indignant eagle, or diving at an outraged lynx.

When he reached the pine tree on its narrow ledge, the goat's glassy round yellow eyes stared into the grey sky peacefully, intact. Nearby the crows whirled and cawed discontent.

Kitt lowered himself onto the ledge to reach for the goat.

Beside the pine tree was an opening in the rock. Out of it shot something dark and hissing, nearly making him lose his hold.

It was a nightmare creature, the size of a dog with grey-black spikes like a hedgehog and a bulgy body on thin legs ending in sharp black claws. The wide-open snout was lined with yellow, triangular, razor-sharp teeth; no eyes were visible, only toothy jaws. It ran to the end of the ledge before its cave.

Kitt held his knife before him, one iron tooth against the many.

The nightmare hedgehog stopped, hissed, turned, and darted back inside the cave.

Kitt kept the knife ready with one hand, with the other he slung the goat over his back.

Twice more the nightmare hedgehog repeated his sallies from his cave, each time shying from the knifepoint. The third time it jumped directly at Kitt's face, the fore claws spread out and the snout open.

Kitt ducked quickly, and as the animal sailed over him, he saw a webbed piece of skin between the fore and hind legs. A gust of wind caught the flying hedgehog and whirled it out to the sea with a last furious hiss.

Cautiously Kitt looked inside the cave. It was shallow and empty, not so much as shit in it.

Surprises of this kind he encountered on Isenkliff and the surrounding islands, over and over. Strange creatures, which he had never seen before; some he had seen only once and never again.

He climbed back up with the salvaged goat, the crows quarrelsome cawing accompanying him to the top. When his head came over the rim of the cliff, he was met with a stare from yellow eyes. To an outsider, it would have seemed the same Jarnmantsje as before, blocky, stunted, grey and ill-tempered. But Kitt could tell them apart, he knew by name all those of the Jarnmantsjes who ventured to the island's surface. Many of them never did. The people of the mainland called them the Lütte Jotun Folk and feared their hunger.

The Jarnmantsje eyed Kitt morosely as he drew himself up, and untied the goat from his back.

"Oh, Vargsot, good morning! You take?" Without waiting for the answer, he walked away from his kill, leaving it by the edge of the cliff.

This little man did not thank him either. He would, in his own time and way. In the cliffs many goats lived; for Kitt who climbed, ran and shot, there always was plenty of meat. He would simply hunt until everybody was satisfied. When the Jarnmantsjes were very hungry, it could be a long day though. But Kitt knew that he couldn't complain, having petted and named the calves and lambs, so that now they could not be slaughtered.

Up and up, he walked the steep slopes of the mountain until he stood on the bare plateau of the highest peak of Isenkliff. Below Kitt, the island lay in the sun. In the centre of the plateau was a big grey boulder, with a dark hole opening at the base.

A Jarnmantsje was sitting beside the rock, grey fur-like hair blending into grey rags, the features coarse as if a very young child had formed them from clay, as a first effort. Round yellow eyes scintillated in the shade.

"Good morning, Gullo," Kitt greeted him.

The Jarnmantsje sniffed.

From here, on a clear day, Kitt could see the mainland of Nordheim as a dark line on the Southern horizon beyond Wittewal.

Far away over the Eastern horizon, he spotted the sail of a big ship, a rare sight in these remote waters in spring, and he followed it with his eyes.

"Not coming to us. Must be going to Abalus. Come off course a lot," he observed.

Both boy and Jarnmantsje regarded the ships' movements like the migrations of birds and whales, the wanderings on the sea.

"Always going somewhere, always wanting something," the Jarnmantsje wheezed with a voice sounding like rusty irons rubbing together.

"No warship, yet," Kitt remarked with distant interest.

A Daguilarian knight had told him that the Immortal Emperor could not die, for shame over the defeat at Aarwood, the second after Kolkris. That he lived for the day when he would send his armies north against the Nuitonen and Theusten again.

"Fools fight for frozen spoils of snow and ice," the Jarnmantsje murmured, closing his eyes again. "That's all he'll get, and then he'll die.   "

"His enemies say that he is a powerful sorcerer who buys himself more life with secret blood sacrifices. Do you think there's truth in that, Gullo?"

"May be, may not be. May be," the Jarnmantsje mumbled. "Oh yes, he'll die for sure. Never fear. One day he'll die and then it won't matter how long he lived. Life always is too short, for you humans."

The wind veered, and a warm breeze hit Kitt's face; it came from faraway lands where it was already spring and summer. Since his earliest youth Kitt had felt the breath of adventure in these warm southern breezes, carrying the wild fragrance of the dreamlands of his imagination.

In the solitude of this island, he had collected fragments of knowledge, trying to fit them into a picture of the world.

Most of what he knew came from books, and from the tales the warriors brought, when they came to Isenkliff for Eckehart's steel.

He knew that far to the South lay the land of Kemitraim in the valley of Meira the magical river, where necromantic priests lived in tombs and worshipped the two Celestial Serpents whose scaly children slithered through the streets of the cities, where the worshippers knelt in their path, waiting who would be chosen for sacrifice. The silver crowned priests of Kemitraim read the knowledge of life and death from the stars and wrote down all their secrets on roles of brittle papyrus in characters depicting little people and animals and celestial bodies, the meaning of which nobody could decipher. Such scrolls had found their way to Isenkliff, and Kitt studied them over and over, but couldn't read a single letter. The Kemitraim warriors wore bronze scale armour and fought with bronze blades shining like sundown. Iron they held in contempt.

"Only one of them has ever come to Isenkliff, and he didn't change his mind."

"What did he want to come here for? We don't want no-one here." The Jarnmantsjes didn't like visitors. They didn't like anyone, not even each other.

The Meira Valley was surrounded by a desert which was so dry that the people living there washed their faces with sand and had their enemies' blood to drink. They lived in black tents and veiled their faces and rode into battle on a humpbacked desert beast that only drank once a month. They never reached the water of the river Meira, for the Serpent Priests of Kemitraim had wrought magic against them.

Kitt's grey eyes were narrowing as if he could almost see the strange coasts.

"Goats," the Jarnmantsje said. "I see goats."

"I'll hunt some more, later," Kitt promised.

"No use waiting. Goats don't wait. No, they don't wait. Run fast, they do. Difficult to catch, very. You go, boy, yes, you go. Gullo waits here. Gullo doesn't mind waiting. Be sure you bring back a fine fat goat. Or two. Two are better than one. Yes, bring back two." He nodded his big shaggy head like one who had just solved a complicated calculation, then sniffed very audibly, for the boy showed no inclination to move, grey eyes still looking out over the sea, far beyond the horizon.

"And south of Kemitraim lies Kush."

Kush was a land which was so hot that all the folk was burned dark and went about attired in nothing but golden beads and bangles. In the steppes of Kush, the animals' herds marched like armies in battle formation; the horses were striped black and yellow like the great jungle cats of Bharatan and just as vicious. The kingdoms of Kush were populated by warriors with ox-hide shields as high as they were tall and fortunes of ostrich plumes on their heads who feasted on the flesh of their slain enemies. Their priests commanded demons and undead things by the power of bones, and phantoms were walking the savannahs not only under the moonlight but even in the bright light of day. They made another magic in caves where painted animals were running over the walls so lifelike that you could hunt them.

"Doesn't work with goats, it doesn't. Must go and hunt goats directly," Gullo pointed out.

But Kitt ignored the hint.

Even farther south there were little people black as jet who rode on big birds as other folks on horses; they shot small darts from blowpipes, the tips they steeped in a poison so powerful that a tiny scratch sufficed to drop a man dead in an instant.

"And in all these lands they forge iron. Except in the Meira Valley." Kitt went on telling the Jarnmantsje what he had read about the smiths of Kush and Edofu, for the Lütte Jotunfolk were skilled smiths.

The Jarnmantsje sniffed again. "Iron and blood. Could tell you all about that but won't. Waste of time, talking to an apprentice. Time to hunt goats. There is no land called Kush."

"Yes, there is. And there are even more lands farther south. Or what do you think the sun shines upon when we have winter? There

98

are many more lands!"

In the lands where the things cast no shadows at noon, steaming jungles sprawled, with trees growing into the clouds, brightly coloured birds sitting on the high branches, screeching curses in dead languages, and wild little furry people threw fruits on the head of the wanderer. Great cats roamed there, venomous fangs lurked, poisonous flowers nodded and killed with dreams, and in the farthest and darkest recesses of the green world slept the long-dead cities of inhuman civilisations. Nobody had ever crossed that great wood to tell if more lands lay behind it.

"And what use are they to anyone," the Jarnmantsje grumbled. "Might be there or might just as well not be there. Too far, no use. What are those lands to you?"

"Everything," Kitt said.

"There aren't any lands under the sunset. There's nothing," the Jarnmantsje muttered.

"Yes, there is. A Tolosan ship has sailed there and returned, it was a big ship with three masts. They tried to keep it a secret, but the Northern Circle ships followed."

"Lies, lies, lies. West lies Ginnungagap, the great howling emptiness, and if you don't watch your step you'll fall into it."

"Oh come, Gullo, you know the world is round. I can't fall off it."

"I don't know anything. You think you know. You think you know everything."

"Alright, then I go east. I know for certain that there are many more lands under the sunrise."

In the east, there were rolling plains and deserts so vast and empty that they made the mind reel. Tribes of savage horse riders, the Karabatyrie, lived there, who mounted their horses at birth and never learned to use their legs. They considered it a sacrilege to tread the earth, and never dismounted at all, changing horses in full run, so that they wouldn't grow fast on their backs. They were the best bowshots in the world, who could hit a lark in the eye and did, for they were vicious people.

Beyond a sky-high range of frosty mountains was the glittering mirage of Bharatan, where the warm sand was mixed with gold dust and spices, where children played with cut diamonds the size of apples and the kings rode on huge animals with two tails.

"Hah, believe everything you read in your books," the Jarnmantsje scoffed. "Any fool can write down anything he wants. Other fools go believing it."

"Once a traveller came from there, and he told me."

"Any fool can say he comes from somewhere. And another fool-"

"His skin was brown like a chestnut, and he couldn't feel warm. Said the northern fog got into his bones."

The brown-skinned man had sat by the fire all day shivering, wrapping more furs over his thin cloak of silk brocade, and gratefully rolling dark eyes at Aslaug, who gave him hot lime flower tea to drink. He had told Kitt of wise men, who forswore food and drink and lived entirely by air and holiness. The god of good fortune had an elephants head and the god of wisdom a monkeys head. The dark iron goddess of death had forty arms, each bearing a different weapon. From time to time, she walked Bharatan to add skulls to her necklace, in her wake a flood of blood and cruelty. The Bharatanian women made love standing on their heads, the man had said in a low voice, winking at the boy.

The Bharatanians spoke and wrote entirely in verses, and the warrior gave the boy a roll of painted silk with the story of the Faithful Lady Savitri. Kitt always liked to look at the tiny figure of the woman, painted red and blue and gold in infinite detail, down to the gold stud in her nostril. Inside the scroll, more pictures were as finely executed. Though Savitri did not stand on her head, and even in the most intimate moments, neither she nor her husband took off their clothes, just bared the relevant bits.

At the Eastern end of the world lay Luxin Shoo, populated by yellow people, who spoke the bird language, and lived in paper houses. The warriors of Luxin Shoo resembled locusts in their lacquer armour, their ring blades were speckled as serpents' backs biting into their own tail, forged by sorcerer smiths. The citizens wore silk, even the peasants, and the nobles wore high hats with little tinkling silver bells on them -the higher the hat and the richer its music, the nobler its wearer. The royal hats had golden bells and were so tall and heavy, that they were carried before the great personage by servants. The women of Luxin Shoo were fashioned from living porcelain by artists who gave them no feet so that they should not run away from the men who were short and ugly. There were warriors with hands of steel who needed no other weapon. One such steel handed man was said to serve as bodyguard to the Immortal Emperor of Daguilaria.

Those were the stories the warriors told; some Kitt believed and some he did not. "One day I'll go see for himself."

"No, you won't," the Jarnmantsje said firmly. "Who is to be the next smith on Isenkliff? Tell me that? You are. There always is a smith at Brynnir's forge. Now don't you take a lot of foolishness into your head and don't you . . ."

"I will be back. You watch me sailing off to the East and return from the West. On my way around the earth, I'll learn the secret of the iron column of Meira and the Serpent Steel of Alkantara and the Rose Ladder Steel of Tammuz and the ring blades of Luxin Shoo. I'll be a better smith for that."

The Jarnmantsje looked unimpressed. "There is no more land under the sunrise any more than there is under the sunset. There are no lands under the sun of noon, only fire, and there is only ice in the north."

"I bet you a broken rasp against all the goats on the mountain, there really are lands under the sunset."

The Jarnmantsje's grey perked up. "All the goats?"

"They are there, all these lands, Kemitraim and Kush, Luxin Shoo and Bharatan and the islands of Zivanga and Zundae in the Sea of Sunrise and the new lands the Tolosans found," Kitt insisted. "I can smell them on the wind."

The Jarnmantsje sniffed vigorously. "I smell cooking goat."

"That will be the goats I gave to Ungstein and Vargsot. Oh Gullo, shame, shame, shame! They'll eat everything and leave nothing for you."

With the speed of an angry badger the Jarnmantsje went down into the tunnel under the big stone, and Kitt found himself alone on the mountaintop.

The wind changed again, bringing the clean, silent smell of snow and emptiness from the north, where the vast ice fields lay, where the days were like white and blue diamonds, and the nights shone with cascades of purple, green and white light. All animals that lived in the ice were white -the white bears who had iron claws to keep them from slipping on the eternal ice, the great white wolves singing their song of winter, the dangerous white snow apes who one day would be people. It was the kingdom of the Isjotun, the Ice Giants, and the Isprinsessans, where the iron hoofs of their snowy steeds struck cold flame from the ice. The white wastes were pressing slowly southward, until one day, far in the future, only the smoking mountaintop of Isenkliff would emerge from the icy embrace.

Grey clouds began drifting across the tops of the cliffs; the sky was no longer blue. Kitt spotted dark dots approaching Isenkliff from the South, still too far to make out exactly; but he was almost sure these were the longboats of the Ferys, who lived on the mainland. They came to Isenkliff to lay broken iron weapons and tools on the promontory rock which they called Brynnir's Anvil because they knew Isenkliff steel to possess a strong virtue that made tools work true and weapons never fail their wielder. He knew that some called it the Devil's Anvil. He stopped and waited, until he could make out the eagle ensign on the first ship's square sail, then went his way without watching further.

King Tombrok's men never ventured beyond the Anvil. So loath were they of even setting foot on the shore of Isenkliff that they timed their approach carefully for flood time when Brynnir's Anvil lay half in the water and could be reached by boat. Even then, they kept to the seaward side of the rock.

Kitt began the descent, choosing a route where he could not be seen by the men in the boats. On the way down, he shot another young buck almost immediately, and this time was not challenged for it.

On his way homewards, plunked down in his path he found a rock the size of a fat kid goat, purple-black, with a slick shimmer and a bubbly surface, like a boiling liquid, suddenly congealed. Kitt knew that if he were to draw a piece of this rock across a parchment, it would give a red line. This was a bloodstone out of the depth of the earth, one of the most excellent iron ores in the world, and weighing thirty pounds at least, a very handsome payment for two goats. A new sword, Kitt decided. He wanted a bigger than the one he had. And this time he would forge it himself.

He took the goat buck into the scullery. Skinning it and cutting up the meat took Kitt very little time, knowing just how every animal was put together.

His mother interrupted her work of preparing medicine to water the kidneys and fry the liver, which in goats was larger than any other animal for their size. Stomach and heart she cut into cubes and cooked them in a stew with vegetables.

Eckehart came in from the forge and sniffed appreciatively.

"I saw King Tombrok's ship coming into the south bay with the flood," Kitt told his father at table.

"Hoes and spades, I expect," Eckehart said. "Maybe sickles and swords. Tombrok is a man who likes to be prepared, be it harvest or raiders. Did they see you?" he asked, casually.

"No, I was careful to keep out of sight. Like you told me."

Eckehart breathed a sigh of relieve.

"Why mustn't they see me? Why did you forbid me the hall when Okkilo came for his sword? Why didn't you let me test him? Now he is the leader of the Ferys shield-wall and famous in the whole of Nordheim. Why couldn't I . . ."

"I told you why. You were then almost six feet tall already, as tall as Okkilo, and stronger than he. But he was twenty years old, and you were eleven. I couldn't let a King's grandson be bested by a blacksmith apprentice in front of his warriors. Wouldn't have done him any good and us neither. The same goes even more for Gerbern, when he comes, which will be soon."

The look Kitt gave him disquieted the smith; it was so sharp and searching.

"But the other warriors who come here from all over the world, they see me, and I test them!"

"And you best them, with the sword or any other weapon they think they're good with, every single time, ever since you were ten.

103

Though you have learned not to let it show too much. And if they realise, they won't tell, to save their pride. But they don't like you any better for it. Anyway, since they are not our neighbours, it doesn't matter so much what they think. Everyone knows that tales grow bigger with distance. The Nordheim people are a different matter, especially the Ferys, living just across the sea from us, and they would not be deceived. Son, I tell you, if they ever see you, they will come here in force to get you." Kitt stared at him uncomprehendingly. "Get me? Why?"

"You will not let Prince Gerbern see you," Aslaug said in a tone that brooked no contradiction and denied explanation.

Kitt looked at her uncertainly. For all her usual exasperation with almost everything he did, she rarely spoke to him like this. "Do you understand?" Her blue eyes held his.

"No," he said slowly. "I don't understand. I don't understand at all."

"But you will do as I say, stay out of the Ferys' and any other Nordheim warrior's sight!"

"Yes," Kitt said.

"Don't mind so much, Kitt," Eckehart consoled. "The Nordheim people want our steel, but they don't want anything to do with us who forge it. The smiths of Isenkliff have the blackest reputation of all. That's really why we're called blacksmith and not because of our dirty hands." He laughed a little self-consciously at his own joke.

"Remember the Kemitraim warrior from the Peleset ship?" Kitt asked.

"I remember him; he really was bound for Rilante but had misunderstood what steel was. Stuck to his bronze sword, wouldn't trade it for one of mine. Wouldn't even touch iron. Very strange." Eckehart looked a little mystified at this change of subject.

"He told me that the smiths of Kush are sorcerers who thrust a newly made iron spear glowing hot into the body of the first man, woman, or child passing the smithy. They say that blades made in this manner strike truer than others because the soul of the victim lives on in the steel, thirsting for blood in blind revenge. Do they make better steel than we do, father?"

"They make good steel," Eckehart conceded. "There are always many ways to achieve the same thing. Knowing the way which was followed in a weapon's making can tell more about the smith, the warrior, and their land than the steel used. If you think closely about what you hear and read you will find that you know a lot about Kush already."

"It's nasty. No matter how good the steel. A warrior who fights with such a blade must be a man unsure of his own strength and courage. Not an honest fighter." As Kitt spoke thus, his eyes were stern, his mouth hard.

"You don't have to go to as far as Kush to find warriors who would rely on such a weapon. We don't work for men such as those. Our way to good steel is through knowledge of the iron, the blade, the warrior. And dedication."

"Yes. We don't use the methods like the smiths of Kush use. So why do the Nordheim people shun us?"

"They think the Lütte Jotun folk work for us. Meaning the Jarnmantsjes. Well, they do mine the mountain for us, for ore, for coal. We could never mine as deep ourselves. And how much steel could you and I turn out even if we worked night and day? Without the Jarnmantsjes there would be no smithy on Isenkliff." Eckehart coughed. "Folks think we trade meat for the Jarnmantsjes help."

"Yes, the goats of Brynnir's Herd." An awful thought struck Kitt. "They think we . . ."

"There wasn't always a good hunter here on Isenkliff."

"The Smiths of Isenkliff fed people to the Jarnmantsjes? Whom? Not customers?"

"In the old times, a smith would take the first out of a party of men to step on Isenkliff. Or the hindmost. Not knowing which made for a bit of a scramble at each disembarking. Or embarking. You know the children's game . . ."

"I don't."

"Of course not. No other children here to play. Well, it was like this." Eckehart sang in a rusty voice:

Going, going, slow
Under the golden bridge, we bow.

The golden bridge is broken
One will be the token
First comes
Next comes
Third is caught
Going, going, slow . . .

"So it went on, until the time Orm was the smith on Isenkliff. He picked on a hero to feed to the Jarnmantsjes, Sigurd the Dragonslayer. That was bad judgement. Sigurd slew Orm, and then he went into the mountain and slew Brynnir. Since then, it was the custom to leave somebody behind. People nobody missed much."

"But that's . . ."

"As bad as the smiths of Kush, yes."

"But we don't . . . we should . . ."

"Put the story straight? If they see you, they will think me in league with the Grote Jotun Folk as well as the Lütte Jotun, and that my boy, would be just too much for them to take."

"Once upon a time there were giants, now, there are no giants anymore," Kitt said weakly.

"Yes, there are. The Grote Jotun folk are hiding from the sight of men even longer than the Jarnmantsjes. Men have always been crazy with fear of them, and killed them on sight whenever they could. The Grote Jotun were never many, as they seldom breed. Now they live far in the north, on the islands near the great ice of Jotunheim. We here on Isenkliff, we also keep our distance, and so we keep safe."

Fear is what makes men dangerous. Not their courage. Never forget to reckon with people's fears.

The thought came so very clear that he wondered if his parents could hear. His mother did regard him strangely.

"Will you stop arguing, boy!" Eckehart said. "Let's go down to Brynnir's Anvil and find out what the King of the Ferys would have of us. Tombrok is usually in a hurry."

"Some say Devil's Anvil. The devils, that's us then?"

"Yes, my son, that's us. Get used to the idea."

Equipped with belts and hooks, they set off to the island's south coast.

Brynnir's Anvil was a long narrow rock promontory running out about two hundred feet into the sea on the south side of Isenkliff, similar to the natural quay on the west side. At flood time, the water reached almost to the flat and smooth surface; at low ebb its foot was dry. Iron rings the widths of two hands were set into the sides.

At the end of Brynnir's Anvil lay a heap of sickles and hoes, all sharpened so often that only the backs remained, a bent plough, three cracked axes, three scythes, six bent lance blades, a broken sword, and what seemed to be at least thirty woven sacks heaped up in a big mound.

"Looks like there's been a raid already. Folks must be getting desperate. Just imagine, assaulting a fortified place like Dokkerhall for the last grains in the larder," Eckehart remarked, lifting the cracked sword blade. "Not one of ours."

"Of course not. Our blades don't crack."

"I wonder who the raiders were?" Eckehart sorted through the pile. "Ah look here, that's no Ferys weapon. It might be Teoden. This far west that would be bad! So, it has begun and will get worse fast. First, there will be more raids, then more and more families will be leaving southwards for the warmer lands. Lean times ahead for us also. The Ferys don't have any food to spare, must make it to the harvest anyhow. Tombrok left us no cheese nor bacon this time, and him such an open-handed man. He seems to have made up for it in charcoal though."

Opening one sack after the other, they found charcoal in eighteen of them, and eighteen more contained bog iron.

"Wonder if he thinks we can also feed on coal like a smelting oven," Eckehart muttered.

"I can hunt enough meat for us."

"No running away from Isenkliff, though. Tombrok's people will be back in ten days or so. I shall need you at the oven and at the forge every day."

#

The two smiths fired the smelting ovens containing the bog iron.

Then it was time for lunch, eagerly anticipated because of the fried

107

goat liver. They returned to the forge, where they had left the tools and weapons to be repaired.

"What will we do first, father, swords or hoes?"

"Oh, hoes, for good luck."

"For luck, a sword would be my choice."

"There you are wrong. When a hoe cuts well into the soil, the woman who uses it will say a little blessing, every time. A warrior never does. He attributes all success to his own prowess, not to the skill of the smith who forged his blade. Therefore we start on the hoes, sickles, and kitchen knives, and we will be putting as much work into them as we do into weapons. For a smith can never have too many blessings said for him."

Kitt eyed his father. Eckehart was not joking.

#

The fire had eaten through the layers of ore, limestone and coal.

The molten ore had wandered down through the flame and changed.

With heavy hammers, the smiths broke the bottom of the three ovens, with iron tongs they took out the hot lump at the bottom, knocked off the slag with hard blows, and had the raw ingots. The slick black Bloodstone was turned a dull dark grey, with little to distinguish it from the humbler bog iron.

Together they hammered, freeing the iron from the impurities spoiling its strength; the sound of the hammers was doubled by the cliffs echo and flew out over the sea.

From a crack in the cliff a little man appeared, as broad as he was tall, carrying a sack on his shoulder, double as large as himself. It was Gullo.

Keeping in the shade of an overhanging rock, the little man put down his burden and opened it, revealing black lumps of the rock-coal which the little folks mined deep under the cliff, which gave a hotter flame than charcoal. The little man closed the sack again and sat on it.

Eckehart left Kitt to go on hammering alone and sat down by Gullo, keeping to the sun, as the Jarnmantsje kept to the shade. The Lütte Jotun Folk disliked the direct sun. They had known each other for a long time, Eckehart and Gullo. Together they sat in companionable silence, watching Kitt hammering the iron.

"A good hunter, Kitt is," the Jarnmantsje remarked after a while. "Never misses a shot, not he. Generous too." He nodded, swinging his short, sturdy legs.

"Yeah," Eckehart said, holding his face into the sun.

"A strong boy, Kitt is," Gullo said. "Never stops working, not he, until he finishes what he has begun."

"Yeaaah," Eckehart said.

Kitt's hammer was still ringing when the birds sang their evening song, and the sunlight turned golden. With the shadow of the cliff growing longer, Gullo moved his coal sack, until he came to sit beside the smelting oven.

When the shadow of the cliff reached the smelting oven, Gullo scrambled down from his coal sack. From the earthen hearth beside the oven he drew the silver bowls, in which the smiths' food was kept warm.

Gullo lifted the lids and helped himself to a generous portion of goat meat and radish which he heaped in one of the bowls which the smiths kept there.

"A good cook, Aslaug is," he sighed, chewing slowly, a ludicrous expression of absolute bliss on his craggy countenance.

Kitt straightened up and wiped the sweat from brow and chest lazily. He nodded to Gullo. Then he looked into all the plates and bowls, finding them cleaned out.

"Time for beating the iron. No time for eating. Choose one or other. Not both," the Jarnmantsje remarked.

"Those who work shall eat," Kitt objected.

"Nonsense. Poppycock," Gullo retorted, settling firmly on his sack.

The iron had been beaten pure, and the west wind freshened up and sang in the air vents of the smelting oven. Kitt and Eckehart wandered to the house in keen anticipation of dinner.

#

Eckehart and Kitt returned to the ovens the next day.

Gullo was waiting for them with another sack of rock coal.

They also had a simple forge by the smelting ovens, and Eckehart filled it with the coal, lit it and then sat down on his stone seat. It went unsaid that this was the better place to work on a new sword for Kitt compared to the forge that was overlooked by the house. Aslaug would disapprove. So much.

In silence, Eckehart and Gullo watched Kitt hammering out the rough shape of a blade, while the iron went from white-hot, to orange and red-hot, then darkened into dusky red.

From time to time the young smith thrust the blade into the forge again, then hammered the heated section, flipping the blade over to work it evenly, just as he had learned from his father. Their roles were reversed for that day, and Eckehart tended to the forge, filling it up with coal again and again, keeping a heart of fire glowing inside.

Frowning with concentration, Kitt formed the sword tip, carefully drawing out all bulges in the thickness of the blade.

"Thing you do in one place pops up in another, it does. Always," remarked Gullo.

While forging the form, Kitt carefully observed the rhythm of heating the whole blade to a cherry red, letting it cool, reheating.

He took the red-hot blade from the forge and thrust it into a long trough filled with water.

All three smiths held their breath, while clouds of steam hissed from the trough.

"Well, it didn't crack," Eckehart observed.

Kitt drew the cooled blade out and critically looked over every inch for fine cracks, finding no sign of a weakness. Proudly the boy put an edge to the blade and handed it to his father.

Eckehart took a grass haulm and drew it along the edge, and the slight force was enough to cut the grass in two. He repeated the same with a goose feather, and it was cut in two, just like the grass. Kitt looked on entranced. This was as in the fables of the famous swords. Now it was one of his blades.

Eckehart took the sword by the tang and drew the edge across the back of his sitting stone.

Grass and feather came into play again.

Now the blade did not cut either.

Kitt felt and looked mortally dismayed.

Eckehart set a foot upon the blade and bent it. When he released the blade, it sprang back, but not completely.

"You wouldn't like a blade like this, son." Eckehart handed Kitt the ruined blade and a rasp.

The boy set to filing the bent blade with a sort of fury, until it was reduced to a heap of iron shavings.

"A good apprentice Kitt is." Gullo nodded. "Asks no stupid questions."

Kitt went down to the seashore to collect the crap and feathers which the wild geese leave behind, and into that noxious mess he mixed the shavings of the ruined blade.

When he returned to the forge, one of the ovens was full of glowing coal. Kitt made a furrow into it to place the stinking conglomerate; then he covered it with glowing coal, and closed the oven.

"Pays attention, he does," Gullo said and grinned, his irregular teeth showing.

"Always remember my son," Eckehart said, "that war and shit are inseparable. The marching armies leave a trail of shit behind. The dying warrior's bowels do him shame on top of his injuries. The bards in the banquet hall sing of valour and honour and heroic death, but they always forget to mention the shit and the stench. But we don't and to make the blade hard, we take a little shit."

#

When Eckehart and Kitt came back to the oven the next day, Gullo was already there.

Again, Kitt hammered the iron into a blade, and when it was finished, he felt a tingling in his hands. Looking at Eckehart thoughtfully, he kneaded the palms of his hands and each finger. Again Eckehart bent the blade, but this time it was not so easy, and in one place the steel cracked. Again Kitt reduced the ruined steel into a little heap of grey particles without complaint.

"What a smith doesn't know, is always more than what he already learned," Gullo said, shaking his shaggy head. "Most important bit of knowledge. Some never learn. This boy knows already."

111

Kitt had made the mixture of iron and goose crap strong, adding shavings of the hoofs and horn of the goats he had hunted in the cliffs. He took out the iron, struck three experimental blows, but instead of forming a blade, he filed the steel down again, to repeat the process with more goose shit.

#

The next day Kitt repeated the process with the iron and the noxious things that would give a blade the hardness he wanted.

"Going to be a good smith. Yes," Gullo finished his thought of several days before.

Finally, Kitt formed the iron bar into a blade again and went on hammering the cooling steel without pause, to bend the grain itself to his will, and make it form a dense, hard surface, that would not allow the blade to be bent again.

He had hunted two goats the evening before and stored their blood in a doubly sewn leather sack. Decomposition had set in and the glutinous liquid he poured into the quench tank was full with dark clots, shot through with bright red spots and streaked with yellow.

Gullo stopped eating to raise a bushy grey brow and smile toothily.

"Now we have all the outer signs of war assembled to make our blade," Eckehart remarked. "Not pretty."

Kitt quenched the sword in the blood. The stink was ghastly.

This time the blade did not bend.

Eckehart took a wetting stone and put an edge to the steel.

The grass blade he laid upon the edge was cut in two by its own light weight. He took a feather to draw it along the edge; the two halves fell on both sides.

"Don't try this one on your seat, Eckehart, no don't, or you'll have to sit on the ground, you will," Gullo coughed, spluttered and wheezed like a blocked-up geyser.

"All according to the legend."

Kitt eyed his father suspiciously.

Eckehart took the blade and struck his sitting stone with the broad side. With a bright crack, the blade splintered into sharp-edged pieces. "Hardness is not all. At times steel must be able to bend, so as not to break. You must teach the steel toughness that it may

112

withstand blunt force; and at the same time, you must teach it hardness, to cut sharp. You must make a sword that can be soft and hard at the same time. Just like a good man."

The broken blade went into the smelting oven again, and the smiths went home hungry again.

#

Early the next morning Eckehart taught the sword to be soft, while Kitt and Gullo looked on. Rumbling a song in his deep voice, Eckehart hammered the hot blade, heated it, hammered it, cooled it, and heated it again.

Gullo also sang with a voice like rusty iron, and when the cycle was repeated a second time, Kitt fell in, his bright boy's voice breaking now and again.

Finally, Eckehart took the blade from the forge for the last time and laid it into a bed of ash from the smelting oven. The evening was falling when they all bent over the finished blade.

Eckehart passed a cloth along the blade drenched in a liquid called the Truth of the Steel.

Under the rubbing cloth, a pattern emerged, fine, delicate, white, bright lines on a dark background.

"Hard and soft, hard and soft, this steel is." Gullo slapped his thick, short thigh.

"There are other ways to achieve this," Eckehart said. "I will show them all to you, son."

"There may be other ways. Easier ways," Gullo rumbled. "But this is Brynnir's way, it is. The only one worthwhile. Who will be the next smith on Isenkliff? He will. Teach him Brynnir's way, yes."

113

True Courage

A Sea Serpent was cutting the waves towards Isenkliff.

The square sail spread out showing a screaming mask painted in red. The rearing prow head was a picture of pure rage, with thin lips drawn far back to reveal long curved teeth; the wide-open eyes stared, and a row of spikes bristled on the curved chest.

In the prow stood prominent a helmeted figure in a long billowing cloak under which silvered armour gleamed.

The smiths heard the men calling out over the north-west wind.

"The first ship is coming from the West. Does it have to be Gamanfar?" Eckehart demanded of the sea at large.

"Harmar Saesorgison of Asringholm?" Kitt looked with interest at the hulking warrior in the bow. The Nordmann's strength, ruthlessness and cunning were infamous along all the coasts down of the Northern Seas. Whatever Harmar Saesorgison wanted he took, ships, villages, even towns, growing wealthy from selling whole captive populations into slavery in the southern ports of the White Sea. The assault onto the prosperous port of Heidapo was his greatest recent success. Completely cold-blooded he had never been bested in battle or play.

"Gamanfar, pleasure ship," Kitt mused.

"Yes, he's the funny man among the sea wolves," Eckehart said, his face grim. "He has his own idea of a good time. Only one to laugh at his own jokes too. Mind, the warriors who come for Isenkliff steel are not generally renowned for their mildness of manners. If I served only decent men, I'd be doing little work. But Harmar Saesorgison is something out of the ordinary."

"I'll better arm."

"Better not. We here, we do not need to fight. Nobody comes to Isenkliff to raid, not even Harmar. What can anyone really take here? Gold? They are welcome to it -a thing of very little account in the long run. But they won't take it. They need us too much, and they know it. Nobody can steal our knowledge. How will they carry that away, tell me?"

"They could attempt carrying away the smith. As King Niyod did with Volund the Alb."

"And we know what happened to King Niyod. So does everyone. That's why those stories get told, over and over, to dissuade folks from doing something short-sighted out of greed or cupidity. Didn't I tell you that smiths had a certain reputation? No, they wouldn't dare."

"Just to be on the safe side!"

"To be armed does not mean to be safe. All to the contrary. You see, Harmar cannot abide any sign of defiance. Beating down all resistance the moment he encountered it has brought him where he is now. Will you think of that, son, when the Gamanfar's crew comes to the shore?"

"Why would I?" Kitt's chin came up stubbornly. "Why should I play by his rules in my own home?"

"Because you don't need to play power games. That's the only demonstration of superiority that means anything." Raising his eyebrows, Eckehart looked at his son.

"Oh, I see." Kitt grinned.

"I thought you would, for the sheer arrogance of the idea. That is your weak spot, my son."

"Maybe it is. But a grand gesture I must be able to afford," Kitt said with a frown. "I'm not sure. He's got forty fighting men at least."

"It would bring him nothing but bother, were he to attack us. Unless he sees a big young man meeting him in arms, then there will be a battle for certain, and it would be a ridiculous mess. So do us all a favour and don't stare into his eye when he comes ashore."

"All right, let's demonstrate superiority without looking anyone in the eye."

Eckehart shot his son a worried glance.

"I'll do as you say," Kitt assured him. "You can trust me."

"I'd like to, son, I'd like to," Eckehart muttered under his breath.

The serpent ship passed by the stone quay and approached the shore. Men were pulling on lines to furled up the big sail.

The stone anchor dropped with a splash. The Gamanfar veered around and came to lie churning with her keel on the pebble shore.

The helmsman called out, and the oars were shipped. Two sailors took down the serpent head.

"Harmar decides to display a remnant of manners," Eckehart remarked.

"We don't mention the delay of it!"

"We needn't. These things have a way of coming back, and around, and back again."

Harmar Saesorgison was the first to jump down to the beach, his booted feet planted on the pebbles broad legged, his right hand just beside the golden hilt of his sword. He moved with a suppleness surprising in such a massive man.

The Nordmann stood well over six feet tall, with shoulders so broad that he seemed almost misshapen, accentuated by the breast and shoulder plates of his armour, which were made of one piece. Contrary to Nordmann custom, Harmar wore his tawny hair and beard cropped short, emphasising an aggressively jutting jaw, on which a tiny muscle was jumping. His green eyes were opaque, those of a man who had seen countless other men dead at his feet.

Four crewmen moored the ship to the boulders on the shore with long ropes; the rest took their place behind him.

Eckehart advanced, Kitt trailing after him with rather ill grace, yet very curious to get a closer look at the infamous ship lord .

"Eckehart of Isenkliff," Harmar Saesorgison said, his voice flat and of medium timbre. "It is said that you are the best smith in the world. Can you forge a sword for the world's best warrior?"

"Show him to me, and I'll see what I can do for him."

The heads of the Nordmänner turned as one towards Eckehart, like a pride of wolves spotting a deer.

Kitt just stopped short of grinning. He must have misunderstood his father, he thought, mild did not mean meek!

Apparently oblivious to the sudden tension, the smith began wandering around the big man, looking him up and down.

Harmar Saesorgison relaxed, clearly putting the most flattering interpretation upon Eckehart's ambiguity.

Kitt's respect of the Nordmann dropped several more notches.

"Take off your armour," Eckehart ordered curtly.

Harmar muttered something, and a boy came forward. He was about Kitt's age but almost a foot less in height and far narrower across the shoulders. He undid the straps of the breast and back plates and the bucklers on arms and legs until Harmar stood there in a mail tunic made of bronze rings.

The boy undid the leather bands, and the tunic slipped down into the sand with a tinkling crash. Kitt estimated the weight of that alone at more than thirty pounds, all of Harmar's armour at about seventy. The sword at his side measured about four feet from the pommel to the tip of the sheath, unusually big even by northern standards. Kitt concluded that Harmar fought in a style similar to himself.

Eckehart measured the circumferences of the massive arms, legs, and chest, pressed the biceps, probed into the hard defined belly, muscular back with the deep central ridge, wide ribcage, all the time asking brief questions.

The big Nordmann answered readily: "Yes, the right is my sword hand, but I fight equally well with my left.

"Yes, I always attack, never wait for my adversary to make the first move.

"I use the sword solely to beat down the other's blade and strike the man behind it, I rarely have to use it for defence.

"I like the blade to go in slowly, to twist it, while I watch the realisation of defeat, humiliation, death come into my enemies' eyes. Not merely death but complete annihilation of body and soul is the fate of those standing against me.

"Age?" Here the great Nordmann frowned. "I don't feel any signs of age - well if you insist, I have seen thirty-five summers come and go, but if you ask me how many fights I won I tell you that I lost count long ago. Can you forge a sword for a warrior of my strength, skill and experience? Can you do it smith of Isenkliff?"

"Oh, yes. Today you and your men rest, eat, and drink, in my hall. Tomorrow I want you to cross a blade with my son Kitt here, so that I may find out exactly where your strength lies, and where your weakness."

Harmar Saesorgison mustered the boy standing before him, his thin lips twisting. "This is your son? How old is he, fourteen years? At

117

that age, I had killed my first enemy in battle, and I was a man already. No, he's younger. Big as he is, he is a child still. I can see his face lacks the hardness of a warrior. You aren't blooded yet, boy, are you?"

Kitt felt himself flush crimson.

"I thought not," the Nordmann sneered and turned his back on him. "For you to assess my strength and skill, master smith Eckehart, I had better pit myself against Sarolf. He's the best of my men." He indicated a dark-bearded warrior who bared white teeth in a snarl. "Trounce you a bit, Sarolf, eh! Not the first time is it! Just to give the good smith an idea what kind of a man to forge the sword for."

"If you want a blade of mine Harmar Saesorgison, my son will test you. That's how I work."

Harmar's green eyes narrowed to glimmering slits. He smiled tightly. "All right. If that is how you want it, smith. You all are witness to that."

"He insisted. We heard it." Sarolf nodded.

The other men also nodded; some laughed without mirth.

Kitt had not moved during the exchange, his face disclosing no reaction, but his light grey eyes missed nothing, and their expression seemed to surprise Harmar Saesorgison for a moment.

The famous warrior shrugged, waving an arm in an expansive gesture. "Bring the gold! You shall find me generous, Smith of Isenkliff."

"Yet more gold," Eckehart muttered under his breath. Aloud he said. "Let's talk about the price tomorrow. Now come to my hall where the lady Aslaug awaits the guests."

"I don't care to wait until tomorrow. I am not a patient man. Let's get everything over with now! The earlier you get to work, the better, smith." He addressed his men sharply. "I said bring the gold. And the scrap iron." Harmar Saesorgison turned to Kitt. "You boy, get ready to test me." His smile didn't touch his eyes.

The servant boy approached Harmar with his mail, and the ship lord clouted him over the head that the bronze tunic fell into the sand again. "Think I need armour? Against this puling boy? Fool!"

The Nordmänner brayed with laughter.

118

With the fervent wish to prick the man's conceit, Kitt went to the smithy to fetch his sword. He reminded himself dutifully that his task was to help Eckehart forging a sword for this warrior, not to pick trouble with a whole crew of Nordmänner.

On the left-hand side, just by the door of the smithy seven swords of different sizes hung on the wall, all the blades Eckehart had ever forged for Kitt. The first was a foot long and fastened four feet above the floor, the uppermost one, the first sword Kitt had forged himself, hung six feet three inches high with a blade measuring three feet six inches.

He never carried a sword inside the house, knowing how much his mother hated to see him learning the way of the sword. This was never spoken about openly. But it was felt all the more.

As he left the smithy sword in hand, he looked over to the house. His mother was nowhere to be seen.

When Kitt returned to the beach, two Nordmänner were setting down a wooden chest, throwing open the lid. Golden arm-rings, neck-chains and silver cups with thick gold bands glittered in the sun. Another man threw down ten swords in a heap, nine bent and cracked and one whole.

Harmar Saesorgison's grin was feral. "Each of these swords belonged to a war leader who opposed me. From them, you shall forge my new sword. My sword shall be made of dead men's iron and be called Dodengel."

Eckehart bent to pull the whole sword from the heap of destroyed blades. "This one I forged for Fastmund of Erteneborg six years ago. A good man."

"Not good enough. I passed Erteneborg on my way here, and Fastmund denied me anchorage. I do not tolerate opposition. You must take that into account when you make my sword. You shall begin at once. Or do you still want me to fight a bout with your boy?"

"Yes, I do. Need to see what you are made of."

"Do you really?" The muscles of his jaw jumped as Harmar Saesorgison drew the sword hanging from his side; it had a one and a half hand hilt and a broad blade about a hand longer than Kitt's

119

sword. "Come, boy, let's give your father what he wants. Are you ready?"

Kitt nodded, his sword hanging carelessly from his hand.

Harmar Saesorgison attacked, coming on like a tidal wave; hitting out with the full strength of the overly broad shoulders behind it.

Kitt's sword was up in an instant, meeting the blow with precisely equal force.

For a split second, Harmar's green, crafty eyes flickered. He attacked again at once, just to be intercepted in mid-strike and thrown back.

The Nordmann was skilled and very strong. But he made mistakes, an opening here, a movement there the fraction of a moment too slow, a hasty judgement, split seconds of surprise and indecision. His reflexes were not that of a young man any longer; there was a lessening of flexibility in his joints. Harmar himself had not yet noticed.

Soon Kitt had teased out all weaknesses and set about to display them. Yes, the infamous warrior would be better off with a sword made by Eckehart, a sword that was explicitly designed to offset his shortcomings. A shorter blade than he wielded now too, Kitt thought with a minute twitch of his mouth.

The Nordmänner had drawn around in a circle, a mutter rising among them as they watched.

Harmar's face contorted and he dealt a crushing blow to split the boy in half.

Kitt danced away.

Lightning-quick Harmar swung around for another blow to miss again.

The blades closed once more. The ship lord fought in all earnest, he fought to kill.

One furious attack after the other Kitt met with just that much more force. He could have stopped any time; Eckehart would already know all he needed to make the sword, but the boy fenced for the sheer pleasure of playing with the enraged Nordmann as if he were a clumsy puppy dog intent on biting.

Now Kitt himself advanced. A little lesson, he felt, would do the man good. With every passage of the blades, the ship lord was forced to cede another step, back, back he went, step by step losing the ground he had gained in all these years. Harmar came to Isenkliff at the height of his strength and fame; now, he was brought down by a mere boy, lower than he had started. Only a few more paces until he was a defeated old man.

The circle of Nordmänner rolled down towards the shore with the fight; they were shouting and laughing, as they passed the heap of broken swords, then the bronze mail tunic, then the plate armour and the high water line. Two more exchanges and Harmar would be standing in the water.

"Stop it, Kitt!" Eckehart called.

Kitt disengaged easily. The way he lowered his sword was the last insult.

Harmar Saesorgison rushed at him, sword poised for the upward thrust through the heart.

Kitt evaded him again with a side-step and turn, not even raising his blade.

"Enough, Harmar!" Eckehart called.

The ship lord did not hear. He spun around, sword flashing in a low arc.

With a short hard blow, Kitt blocked the blade in the centre, that it flew from Harmar's hands.

Blind with snarling fury, the Nordmann sprang after it, drawing a dagger with his left.

"What do you want Harmar?" Eckehart shouted. "Do you want a sword or do you want to kill my boy?"

"That's not a boy!" Harmar roared. "I'll cut this monster whelp's throat!"

"Go!" Eckehart said. "Go, Harmar! Now! You may yet prise many swords from dead men's hands like the scavenger you are. There is no sword here for you. There never was."

Harmar's mouth worked. He raised his blade and made to rush for the smith. That way, he came face to face with Kitt again.

Harmar stopped dead.

Kitt's whole bearing had undergone a subtle but terrifying change.

121

It was his eyes that unnerved the Nordmann, so that he did not dare to make another move, except backwards, all fury draining from him suddenly and completely as from a great gash in his courage.

He dropped the dagger, turned and ran towards the serpent ship past his sword lying on the ground.

His men ran after him, shouting questions and abuse, except for the ones who had also seen Kitt's eyes. Those were silent and pale.

The ship put to sea again with men rowing hard, helped by an eastern breeze that filled the dropped sail.

"I hate these killers!"

Kitt heard his mother's passionate voice and turned to see her standing on the path, her face set in hard lines of distaste.

"No need to fear for me, mother. Harmar is not near as good as he thought. Not even as good as he once was. Way too slow. There wasn't one moment of danger."

"No, he didn't stand the least chance. That is why you should not have provoked him. You take strength for courage. That is a common mistake."

Stunned, Kitt looked at her retreating back, straight and uncompromising. His mother had been more worried about Harmar getting hurt than about her son.

Eckehart said nothing, sorting through the broken steel.

Kitt broke the silence. "He thought he can enforce his own law wherever he comes ashore. I showed him that he can't do it here." His words sounded petulant in his own ears. "It was stupid of me. I forgot myself. And when he was about to attack you . . . if he'd made one more move, I . . . I would have killed him," he said almost inaudibly.

"Might have needed to kill his whole crew also," Eckehart said. "Messy. Imagine what mother would have said to that."

Kitt swallowed hard.

"Harmar Saesorgison is a very sick man now," Eckehart continued. "His men saw the fear in his eyes, and they won't forget that. For him, this couldn't come at a worse time. He is getting old."

"It's not that he is a bad fighter. He's still good. Those men, he can bring them to heel again."

"Not any more, he won't." Eckehart shook his head. "He is finished. Harmar's strength was like steel with an invisible fault inside. It may go unnoticed for a long time until a certain force hitting in a certain way causes it to break at that fault. Then it's scrap metal which cannot be mended again. You showed up that flaw in the man, as you did in his fighting. Harmar Saesorgison's courage lay in the weakness of others. False courage. No matter how strong a warrior might be, at any one time, there is somebody somewhere who is stronger. He forgot that, and you reminded him of it. That is all."

"I shouldn't have let myself be provoked by him. I shouldn't have shown him up before his men."

"Harmar Saesorgison lived by the sword; he'll have to take defeat by it. Don't worry about him too much, son. He wasn't a good man."

"Then I did right after all?"

Eckehart shook his head. "No, my son, what you did was very wrong. Wrong because of yourself, what it did to you. It is bad for a man to fancy himself a judge. It is bad for a man to assume power over life and death. Pain and death must happen; they are a part of life. But cursed are those men through whom they happen."

Kitt nodded.

That he now understood his mother's stern censure was oddly consoling for Kitt. But when he came to where the path diverted to the smelting ovens, his feet took the turn. Walking away from the hall the going was so much easier.

There was nothing to do at the ovens. The Gamanfar's silhouette was on the Western horizon. The sun disappeared behind the cliff.

Kitt was still sitting when the sun, now red and swollen, appeared in the crack where the smelting oven stood, before sinking into the sea.

When the enemy attacks, hit back harder.

The cold voice again. What it said didn't help.

All around Kitt, it became dark and still.

Kitt's first memory was that of a duel between two Nordmänner ship lords. The prows of their ships, one a serpent, the other an eagle, had touched the beach of Isenkliff at the same time, and each ship lord wanted his sword made first. None wanted to wait, none could wait. It was a matter of honour.

The followers of both lords formed a circle. The boy saw nothing but broad leather-clad backs with long, yellow or brown hair spilling down them until a big Nordmann propelled him to the forefront. Never too early for a boy to learn what it takes to be a man, he'd said.

Two wooden shields lay at Kitt's feet, of the serpent lord standing on his side he only saw the back, encased in shining plate mail, the brown mane shot with grey. The eagle lord was a green-eyed warrior with wild red curls, clad in iron-studded leather armour.

The ship lords swung their long swords high, closing in the centre of the circle. The clash of metal on wood reverberated from the cliff walls. A crack as loud sounded when the serpent lord's shield broke. "Luck!" he grinned.

He came to the side where Kitt stood to snatch up one of the shields, and return to the centre, almost running.

The next passage of arms was a long-drawn one, again and again, the eagle lord's blade crashed on the shield with a violence that reverberated from the mountain. The serpent lord barely warded off the blows, staggering with the impact, and at the end of it, his shield broke a second time.

When he came to pick up his last shield, his step was heavy, he was stumbling a little, and sweat was running down his face. As he bent to pick up the shield, his hands were trembling. For a moment, he leant on it heavily. All those around him knew that if he returned to the fight, he would be killed; Kitt had known it too.

The serpent lord went.

The world is crossed by many roads; for this man, but one remained, leading to the place where the stronger warrior waited. Half the men standing around were his followers of many years, but they could not help him. The third shield was also smashed, and the serpent lord was without a shield. He tried a ruse but failed to raise his sword.

The sword of his adversary smashed onto the left shoulder without breaking the mail; the serpent lord was beaten, and as he was still sinking to his knees, the eagle lord's blade described a wide arc and the head flew away with the grey-brown hair trailing. Blood from the severed neck spurted into the air; a splash of it fell across Kitt's face and ran into his mouth, tasting warm and metallic. The head landed with a hard crash and sprang away into the heather.

Soon after the serpent lord's death, Kitt began to learn to fight. He had many teachers.

The first was Liane, a gladiator who fought in the arenas of the big cities of Daguilaria. She used a slender curved blade; hers was the first sword Kitt had ever picked up. Her hands, warm, firm and small, guided his first movements with the weapon; her long dark hair brushed his cheeks.

She smelled sweet, and when they rested, Kitt liked to bury his head in her clothes. He started early in the game, Liane said in her husky voice, caused by a scar beside her throat. She wouldn't explain what game she meant.

When she left Isenkliff before the autumn storms, Kitt had already declared his intention to take her for his wife, at which she laughed, enveloping him in her strong, soft arms and that perfume, promising to take him by his word when he was old enough.

My sister in arms, my lover. You and I against all, against everything. If only I have you, let the whole world go down in blood and fire.

Kitt was forever searching in which of the hundreds of books, scrolls, and parchments he had read these flaming words. Maybe he had dreamed them or heard them spoken by somebody.

Now, that he was thirteen, not three anymore, he knew that was the sort of love he wanted.

He also knew that Liane would never return to marry him. She had died in a marble arena, waiting for the final stroke, helpless from the loss of blood, surrounded by faces greedy for sensation. The victor severed her head and carried it by her long black hair along the seating rows to display to the spectators.

Liane had been the only woman warrior ever to come to Isenkliff; all the other warriors who had prevailed through the lands of

125

Nordheim, or across the stormy northern sea in a quest for Eckehart's steel had been men.

Kemp the old mercenary, who had fought in the vast armies of Daguilaria, Cladith Culuris and Murom, continued Kitt's education. Like all the other warriors, he had come for his father's steel. He had stayed on Isenkliff for more than a year although Aslaug didn't like him.

When she was out of earshot, Kemp told the boy that he had raped so many women in fallen towns, that he had lost count of them, and had no idea how many bastards he might have begotten. He said he would now never teach sword, shield, lance and armour to a son of his own, and wanted to teach what he knew to Kitt. He told him what he knew about the army drill and discipline in all the lands where he had served, about marching, provisioning, camp life, the siege of cities, the hearts and minds of soldiers.

Although Eckehart had presented him with a splendid suit of armour, there had been such a desolate air about Kemp when he mounted the boat to take a ship to Cladith Culuris, where new wars had broken out. Kitt had never heard from him again.

Others had perfected his training with all weapons. While the warriors waited for their swords, battle axes or mail to be made to measure, they showed Kitt the many diverse methods men had developed for killing each other in the perpetual wars of the tribes, cities and nations.

Each time he was in high spirits from having mastered another trick of sharp steel, his mother's look upon him was like a gush of cold water, and his elation died. And now today he had bested a famous warrior, a chieftain like the victorious eagle lord, a bad man. But that was an empty triumph before his mother's sharp disapproval.

Could there be more than one truth, Kitt thought exhausted, opposite, but equally valid? None of his philosophical books seemed to consider that possibility. They were all single-truth books.

Choose one! Stick with it!

An owl cackled madly nearby. The night wind was rustling in the gnarled fir trees.

Kitt saw a dark shadow approaching, his father. Eckehart sat down heavily on the stone seat by the forge. "So, have you thought about what true courage is?"

Kitt nodded, which the smith somehow perceived in the darkness.

"Come to what conclusion? To stand tall in adversity? Bravery and boldness of decision? Never admit defeat?"

"To conquer the fear of pain and death."

"I can guess who taught you that. It's true, but there is still more. True courage is, to be honest, and not to falter in your conviction, and not to give in to the lure of distractions and easy solutions. True courage is the willingness to learn and change your mind. It is the ability to take a long, hard look at yourself. But above all, true courage lies in compassion for your enemy."

"An enemy who has no compassion himself?"

"That doesn't matter. It's about you, not him."

"What if I spare that enemy and he then strikes at somebody else, who can't defend himself as well as I can? Somebody –dear to me?"

Eckehart rubbed his face, sighed. "It may not always seem possible. Not even reasonable. But try, try your best, son, always. You will fail. More than once. Don't give up. Try again. And again. Never resign yourself to evil. That is true courage."

"Yes, father. I understand that."

"I know you do."

Together they walked back down the hill.

Kitt took his sword back to the smithy before entering the kitchen where his mother sat on her seat by the fire.

Kitt knelt down beside her and laid his head on her knees. Her hands fluttered up, hovered, to rest at last on the thick wheat-coloured mane. The boy made a little noise like a contented young animal.

Eckehart averted his eyes from Aslaug's unprotected face.

The Longest Night

The sun rose briefly to describe a short arc above a dusky red horizon. Then, like the black, star-studded coat of eternity, night fell again. It was dark, so dark, and a wind blew out of the darkness, so cold.

The smelting ovens blazed red hot until Eckehart and Kitt closed them.

The only light now shone from the house, steady and warm in the black, freezing sea that was engulfing Isenkliff. Kitt and his father marched towards the golden light.

A sheet of brilliant green flared across the whole sky, waving in the cosmic wind, changing colour into purple and pure white, whispering like icy fire.

Eckehart hurried his pace.

Kitt slowed down. He had seen the aurora sky fires so many times, and could never get enough of it. The white light grew in intensity and then just went out.

#

Aslaug and Eckehart exchanged a glance, and then they both looked at Kitt, who was sitting at the table, his left hand buried in the shock of his fair hair, so that it stood on end. He was holding down an ivory-handled silk scroll covered in spidery script with a muscular forearm. Interspersed among the figures, were paintings of slant-eyed hunters pursuing gazelles and pheasants in a landscape covered with flowering trees. There were eagles with jewelled caps and long-legged spotted cats with silver collars, a black scorpion under a rock, and ornate symbols in black and red ink.

"Time to go to bed," Aslaug said.

Lost in the world painted on the scroll, the youth did not hear.

"Kitt!"

"Yes, mother?" The grey eyes were coming back all the way from Luxin Shoo.

"Time to go to bed," Aslaug said again.

"Already?" Kitt looked surprised.

"It is the Longest Night again," Aslaug said, in a tone as if that explained everything.

Not to Kitt, it didn't, not any more. "The Longest Night. You always send me to bed then, but you never say why."

"It is the night when other darker worlds touch Isenkliff."

"Other worlds!" Kitt said fascinated, just as he would speak the names of faraway lands. "Are the other worlds all dark, and ours is the only light one? How is it when these worlds touch ours, is it like the collision of ships?"

"There are many worlds, light, and dark and our world is one that spins between light and darkness. When the Longest Night comes, the worlds that touch ours are all dark -the hidden worlds of Hollgard Under the Root and the Ice Worlds of Thursheim where the giants came from. All these worlds become one in the Longest Night, allowing beings from those worlds to walk the earth, who are also dark and cold, and some of them are very powerful."

"I'll stand the watch with father."

"Any other night Kitt. Not this one," Eckehart said firmly. "Not a good night to be even awake. For if you don't see the Dark Ones, they cannot see you. But once you have seen them, they also see you. Once they know you, they will find you always. That is why you must go to bed and sleep through it, as you did every year of your life."

Kitt looked from his father to his mother, and they looked back at him. He could see that, this once, they were of one mind.

He yawned demonstratively and laid down the scroll. "Even if I sit all through this night, however long, I'll never make sense of this script. I don't even know which way it runs. So, I'll go and hide under my blanket from the monsters." He grinned, a little insincere. "If something happens, wake me. Goodnight, mother, father." As Kitt stood upright, the shadow of his broad shoulders darkened the room behind him. Then he went up the stairs to his room with his noiseless tread.

"He's way too tame," Eckehart observed.

Aslaug only smiled and began brewing fresh tea.

#

His mother came into Kitt's room to bring him a cup of lime blossom

129

tea sweetened with honey. She put the cup beside his bed and went to the window to close the wooden shutter and hang a steel chain on the fastening, which bore a small iron pendant in the shape of a hammer.

Then she came to collect the empty cup and kissed Kitt's forehead as if he was a small child still. "Now, close your eyes. Whatever you hear, or see, don't open the window; don't leave the room, until you hear the cock crow."

Obediently Kitt closed his eyes, listening to her fastening another iron chain across his door from the outside, then to her light tread down the stair.

He opened his eyes again. This Longest Night his mother's tea would send the floorboards under the bed to sleep.

The night grew darker and quieter as if there would never again be another day. Kitt felt the darkness close in on the house, cluster around, and grow so deep and dense that in another moment, he would hear the wooden beams creak under the pressure.

Darkness weighed upon his chest, like black earth of the grave, on his lids like coins put on the eyes of corpses. The mysterious characters of Luxin Shoo stood before his closed eyes as if written on the inside of his lids with glowing red ink. Finally, he seemed to see a thread of meaning. Trying to grasp it, he woke with a start and the dream clarity receded.

Kitt heard girls' voices laughing and singing outside and thought that he was still dreaming.

He heard it again and listened, trying to understand the words. Their cold sweet music filled his head, vibrated in his body, drew his soul.

He sprang out of bed, unfastened the iron chain and opened the shutters of his window.

The Longest Night was not dark. The white light of the aurora borealis cascaded from the sky like a waterfall and flowed over the snow.

The windows of the smithy were lit by orange fire; the forge was burning. It was from there that the girl's voices came.

Kitt clambered out of his window, remembering his mother's warning, and not stopping.

130

As he approached the smithy he could, at last, understand the words of the cold sweet song:

> "Frost light, ice light,
> glimmer in the night.
> It is a shining from afar,
> And nothing will be as it was.
> Light to frost, ice to fire,
> Nothing is, as it seems.
> Frozen hopes, and lost dreams,
> Steel with flame conspires.
> With fire forge the sword of ice!
> With silver shoe the horses, smith!
> Ice flowers will we give you,
> pay you with frozen kisses."

The orange glow in the smithy grew into a sunset; a rain of sparks flew out of the door, and before it, six transparent figures fled in a spray of tinkling laughter.

They settled on the snow like silver dragonflies, six mailed girls. Their hair was like clouds of spun ice, and they looked at Kitt with enormous, unwinking eyes of the palest blue.

"Young man!" sang the first Ice-maiden.

"Strong man!" sang the second.

"Handsome man!" sighed the third.

"Lost man!" said the fourth with a voice like breaking glass.

The fifth Ice-maiden kissed Kitt on the mouth; her lips were cold, so cold, so sweet.

The sixth took his hand into her white, icy fingers, to lead him away.

"Forfeit, forfeit!" Eckehart's voice boomed from inside the smithy. "Forfeit is the one who takes aught of mine!"

The girl dropped Kitt's hand. She pouted; her mouth resembled rose leaves rimmed with hoarfrost. "Old man, black man, hard man," she sang out. "Forge the ice, forge the quicksilver. I did not take anything of yours."

"See that you don't. The Isprinsessan who takes aught of mine, I will bind to my forge with chains of iron and fire, and I will work the

131

bellows until she melts."

The girl hissed as if already feeling the heat of the forge and pushed away Kitt's hand.

Over the snow six horses came galloping; they were white and had pale blue manes. Their glass hoofs struck blue sparks from the ice, the white bridles and saddles glittered with diamonds.

Kitt helped each girl into the saddle, his fingers sinking deep into their white furs as into a snow dune. Their flesh was translucent, the metal of their mail of frozen quicksilver burned to the touch like fire.

Each girl bent down to kiss him on the mouth. Their kisses hurt like ecstasy, driving icy spikes of pleasure through him, nailing him to the frozen ground.

The sixth Ice-maiden kissed him twice, and her light-blue eyes looked deep into his. "If I kiss you a third time, you will die," she said, and slowly she bent down to kiss him again.

Eckehart appeared on the threshold of his smithy like a dark giant with a hammer in one hand, in the other a blazing torch.

The girl shrank back, and the six Ice-maidens fled like snowflakes driven before the wind.

The door of the hall flew open wide, both wings, and golden light poured out.

Kitt stumbled towards the glowing yellow rectangle.

Through the hoarfrost crusting his eyelashes, he saw his mother Aslaug sitting inside, wrapped in golden rays, green leaves streaming from her hair, and somewhere a bird sang.

"I am so cold," Kitt whispered, clinging to the doorway. He could hardly speak for shivering, and his numb feet would not carry him that one step across the threshold, into the warmth. Helplessly, he sank to his knees.

Aslaug drew him inside.

He clung to her for warmth, and she held her arms around him.

"Who are they, mother?" Kitt asked, his teeth chattering.

"The Isprinsessans. They come over the great ice, to hunt the bird of spring. They can't find him though they hear him sing. It is not yet time for the Snow Queen to take possession." She touched Kitt's face with fingers warm like sun rays, and ice water ran from his lashes like tears. "The bird of spring will fly once more. The Isprinsessans will return in the next Longest Night. The world is turning, and now the time of the ice begins. But the world never stops turning, and spring will come again, and then summer."

"Every year anew," Eckehart muttered from somewhere Kitt could not see him. "Each time when the world turns into the cold, I think that this time it will stand still, frozen for eternity, at last."

"Eternity, eternity," the girls' voices sang. Outside the door, just beyond the circle of golden light, stood the Isprinsessans, glittering in the white luminescence pouring from the sky.

"A time of white has come to Thule," the first Isprinsessan sang.

"A time of white has come to Abalus," the second Isprinsessan sang.

"In the falling snow we wander, we wander over the wide white world," they sang all six.

"Soon, soon our brothers, the Isjotun, come," the sixth Isprinsessan said, and she smiled, a cold, sweet, cruel smile, for Kitt alone.

#

The next morning, Kitt awoke shivering. Outside the wind was howling and keening, doors and windows shook, and it was dark.

"The Isjotun!" Kitt tried to get up. His limbs felt as if ice crystals lodged in his marrow.

"It is just the snowstorm." His mother pressed him down and gave him hot elderberry juice to drink; it was spiced with cloves, which a man from Bharatan had paid for a sword to slay a purple dragon with. Then she heaped fur coverlets over Kitt's bed for more warmth.

"It is the Ice giants, I hear their battle cry!" Kitt insisted, "The Isprinsessan said they would come. The sixths, the one who kissed me twice."

"Dreams are wild in the longest night. Men have been known to wander out into the ice fields in their sleep, and freeze to death, as you nearly did last night if your father hadn't intervened."

"Because you thought that you were too big a boy to heed your mother."

"I heard girls' voices outside." Kitt passed his tongue over the frostbites on his lips, where the Isprinsessans had kissed him.

"Girls' voices, kisses," his father chuckled. "Isenkliff is lonely for a young man and steel is a cold and silent bride."

"I saw them, and I saw you, forging armour of ice and quicksilver for the Isprinsessans," Kitt protested.

"There, you see that you dreamed, my son. How do you imagine any smith could forge armour from ice and quicksilver! You sleep off your fever now, and when you wake up, you'll see what nonsense that is."

In his strangely light mind, Kitt thought that if anyone could forge ice and quicksilver, it would be the Smith of Isenkliff.

The Broken Sword

It was the day of the full moon after Even Light, the beginning of the fruiting season when it should be warm and dry.

In this year, the cold wind whipped around the houses constructed of willow and clay and the wooden King's hall. King Tombrok drew the wine-stained fur cloak around his bent shoulders. Little was left of the warrior who had born arms into Tridden Moor at the head of the Ferys host. His royal advisors and followers, men of the same age, didn't look much better.

Tombrok's two grandsons, armed with iron mail and steel blades, stood before him, their attendants ranging behind bearing their helmets, lances and shields. Both were as tall and blond as King Tombrok had once been before age, injuries and wine had eroded and bent his frame.

Okkilo, the elder by two years, had a clean-shaven chin and a thick blonde moustache while Gerbern let his newly grown beard grow in a golden fuzz all over his face. They looked like brothers, but were cousins; their fathers, King Tombrok's sons, had been slain in the battle of Tridden Moor, which the few survivors called the Bloodswamp -if they talked about it at all.

"Who will go to Isenkliff for me?" Tombrok demanded.

Prince Gerbern sniffed. The old man had been at the wine again, and the sun still in the East. "We have little to give the smith for his work," he objected. "And this little we could use ourselves. Can't our own workmen -?"

"We have always relied on Isenkliff for steel," Prince Okkilo said. "No blacksmith like the Smith of Isenkliff."

"We'll make it up to him, eventually," King Tombrok said. "The Smith of Isenkliff well knows that the last summers have all been cold, and the harvest will be poor again this year. We've always given generously when we had it. Now we don't."

"That's just it." Gerbern's handsome face wore an expression of distaste. "I dislike being beholden to a blacksmith and sorcerer. We don't even know the man. He lives among the Lütte Jotunfolk, and for all we know he is a Jotun himself."

"The master Eckehart is not a Jotun. And her, I know well, the lady Aslaug. She saved my life in the Bloodswamp."

Gerbern was very tired of hearing of the Bloodswamp. "Closed your onion wound; you keep telling us about it." In his cups, he thought bitterly, always in his cups, not making much sense. Aloud he said, "Likely a sorceress herself."

"She was a Vanadis priestess," Okkilo said. "She has the knowledge and the blessing."

"Since you know so much, cousin, why did she leave Mount Lyfja?"

"Don't talk like that, grandson!" Tombrok admonished. "Don't talk at all. One day you will stand before the Smith of Isenkliff, as Okkilo did, and petition him for the sword that you will carry to lead men. The last sword you will ever have because it will be with you for your whole life, be it long or short."

"Maybe I will, maybe I won't," Gerbern retorted.

The old men laughed. "You will, young Gerbern, you will, if you value your place in the succession. No Ferys king who hasn't stood before the holder of Brynnir's Hammer."

"The grain isn't ours to eat in winter until it's in the barn under lock and key," Tombrok continued. "We need the sickles mended, and the blades, or we won't hold out when those traitorous dung beetles the Teoden come back to steal our barley. They spared their forces nicely when they left the fighting in the Bloodswamp to us."

"Sensible," Gerbern muttered.

Tombrok rounded on him, but his grandson did not back off. "Can't the Heerking support us to defend the harvest? Bloodswamp was his battle. He owes you."

"Bloodswamp was Nordheim's battle, and all of Nordheim owes to Heerking Grimwolf who lost the most. You young men always complain that we old men talk about the past too much, but it is clear that you have not listened."

"Young Gerbern has it all the wrong way around, but he has one good point," one of the old men said. "Grimwolf will do you the favour, as one who came out of the Bloodswamp with him. And he will make all the difference."

"So, he will." Tombrok nodded. "And so, he will come. I rely on him more than on my own grandsons."

"I'll go to Isenkliff, grandfather, if Gerbern won't," Okkilo offered. "I've been guest in Brynnir's Hall, and the Smith of Isenkliff gave me my sword. I'll go even though it is my duty as the eldest prince of Dokkerland to slay some more Teoden. I was just warming up. If they feel too comfortable, they'll settle, and then it will be all the harder to roust them out again."

"All right, all right, I'll take my ship Möwe and go to that accursed island," Gerbern conceded. "But I won't set foot beyond Brynnir's Anvil.

"Nobody expects you to," Okkilo said. "All you need do is sail straight there and straight back with the seat of your pants wet, and not from seawater. Oh, and remember to stop shaking long enough for unloading the iron, and do try not to drop it into the sea . . ."

"Very funny!" Gerbern snarled. "Hope you won't make the Teoden laugh! This time they'll be ready for you."

"Good boys." Tombrok turned back to the hall, and a thrall pushed open both wings of the carved portal for him. Vigorous youth tired him, and he really wanted his second cup of mulled wine.

Kitt stood on top of the cliff, looking out for a late flock of geese to fly north to their nesting places.

He saw a brown rectangle of sails coming across the sea from the south, give a wide berth to the dazzling white back of the island Wittewal, refusing the ice-free channel that stretched from there to Isenkliff, and making its way among the ice floes instead.

Idly, Kitt watched the low-built longship, until the lookout standing in the prow of the ship became visible, tall in a large fur coat, with long, fair hair stirring in the wind. He wore a silver breastplate and greaves on arms and legs. It was an imposing figure, a heroic stance, a brave warrior no doubt.

"Not brave enough," Kitt muttered and stepped back out of sight.

He knew all too well what would happen. The visitors would not venture beyond Brynnir's Anvil and hastily leave again. The neighbouring Ferys had visited the hall on Isenkliff just once, on the occasion of Okkilo's, King Tombrok's grandson, investiture with his sword. They would come again when Gerbern, the second grandson, came of age and Kitt would be banished from that ceremony also, to watch from some hiding place. "Mustn't scare men who pride themselves on fearing little," he muttered.

Keeping to the side facing away from the sea, he descended from the cliff, his mood soured.

#

It was a clear day; the wind came from the south, and seen from the ship the island of Isenkliff lay in the sun like a bear warming his grey-brown fur.

The south-easterly wind died down, and the ship Möwe slid alongside the high rock promontory, touching lightly where iron rings were set into the stone.

There was not a speck of rust on those rings, and the Ferys warriors hesitated a little before touching them to make fast the ship.

The sea was calm. The men stood up in the ship and began picking up the bundles of broken iron implements.

The tall man in the wolf-skin cloak set his foot onto Brynnir's Anvil. Walking towards the shore, he didn't turn back towards the men working quickly and silently although he knew their eyes were following him. Grimwolf stepped from Brynnir's Anvil onto on the rocky coast of the island proper, sure-footed in his high leather boots.

The Heerking and King of all the Theusten had entered his forty-fourth year. Although his bones had begun hurting in the morning years ago, he still moved with the same power and authority that he always had. He did not fear the monsters of Isenkliff, which was the last refuge on the fringe of the world for races and beings that had disappeared everywhere else in Nordheim -malignant creatures at home in the darkness and the mists, such as his grandfather Berwolf had destroyed until one poisoned him with a last sting.

When Berwolf died, he had been younger than Grimwolf was now. Monsters had no power over him, not while he stood in the sunshine. He merely avoided the path winding up into the cliff. Any hungry creature, any traps would be lurking there. Surefooted, he climbed the cliff well out of sight from that path. Goats sprang away as he traversed their territory. Brynnir's Herd.

#

"The Ferys ship came," Kitt brought the news to his father Eckehart at the forge. "They didn't see me," he added with a wry grin.

"I hope they didn't. Have they left already?"

"Must have. The wind turned north-west; the flood is going out."

"You didn't watch?"

"Why should I? It's always the same. They dump their stuff and then row to bust their lungs."

"I told you the why of it."

"You did." Kitt shrugged and shouldered the sacks and straps.

Both smiths set out to Brynnir's Anvil on the footpath leading to the south coast of Isenkliff.

#

King Grimwolf didn't need to turn around to know that the Möwe, the ship he had come with were on the sea again, relieved to be heading away fast, helped by a stiff north-westerly wind that had suddenly sprung up after the south-eastern had died. Such good winds were to be distrusted because it seemed that something was watching. Had it seen him? His hand went to the hilt of his sword, and then fell away, as he saw no one.

The men of Nordheim had always hated coming to Isenkliff, yet they kept coming again and again, for the blacksmith residing on Isenkliff was like no other ironworker. Blades, axes and even hoes handled by him held their edge longer, gave much longer use, and did not wear out and tire the way ordinary steel did. Not only did the Smith of Isenkliff imbue any steel he touched with a virtue no other smith could, he also knew the souls of men as well as he knew iron.

That was the reason why Grimwolf, Theustenking and Heerking of all Nordheim, had come to Isenkliff, and why he came alone.

In twelve days' time, the Ferys would return to pick up the repaired weapons and tools -if the Heerking was still alive then, and a free man, he would wait on Brynnir's Anvil and return to the mainland with them.

Looking back from the height of the slope, he could see the Ferys ship passing the white dome of Wittewal, giving a wide berth to the

Island of Judgement.

He reached the top of the cliff and looked down into the valley on the other side beyond which another cliff rose of starkly black stone.

Dwarfed by the sheer rock face, and built partly into it, stood a great hall of wood and stone with crystal windows – Grimwolf knew these to be the only ones for hundreds of miles. This was the hall of the blacksmith on Isenkliff.

To the west side stood another building, also partly built into the rock wall with a stone anvil in front and tools hanging and leaning on the front wall.

The footpath branched before the smithy door, to wind towards the sea shining silver-grey among the lower hill tops of the western side. On the hall's east side were two stable outbuildings with a kitchen garden between them, and an enclosure where chicken scratched the earth. A little stream ran on the bottom of the valley feeding emerald green grass and crossed by a sturdy plank bridge. Twelve grey cows and one huge bull lay there like boulders, chewing the cud. Beyond the outbuildings the garden continued, protected from the eternally blowing wind by a wall of cut stones.

From this high up, Grimwolf could see into the valley as into a basket, fruit trees, vegetable beds covered in thick green, beehives and clusters of summer flowers.

In the garden was a woman dressed like a peasant in a woven skirt, apron, blouse and wooden shoes, carrying a hand basket and a knife. She was of middle height, straight-backed and fair-haired. Grimwolf recognised her at once. For more than thirteen years he had been searching all over Nordheim for the healer who had closed the death wound which he had received in the Bloodswamp. Isenkliff was the only place where he had never looked.

He watched her until she went into the house.

#

Arrived at the rocky promontory, Kitt contemplated the swords and lances with cracked and bent blades, warped arrowheads, and axes with ruined edges; the weapons were outnumbering the hoes, sickles and scythes.

He scanned the horizon, and then his eyes came back to the mound of spoiled iron piled high on the far end of Brynnir's Anvil.

"There was serious fighting."

"Over the barley harvest. Some plough and plant and hoe and water and harvest, and then come those who just wish to eat up everything."

"It seems that so far the Ferys have the longer spoon."

"Long spoons, that's what we deal in." Eckehart chuckled and rummaged through the sacks piled beside the stack of iron. "Charcoal. Charcoal. Charcoal. Bog ore. Bog ore. And once again, charcoal. More than enough to do the work with. No cheese, my son, again. Not so much as a crust of bread Tombrok has sent us. But we'll get cracking all the same. Another flood summer after a hard frost in winter -all that grows now is the moor and no end of the cold misery in sight. We can thank your lady-friends the Isprinsessans for that."

"If they cost me my cheese then they're not my lady-friends," Kitt muttered. He didn't like talking about the Isprinsessans, although he thought and dreamed about them often. He laid down the leather straps and began organising the load striving to transfer the whole into a tightly packed bundle.

"Your old father is still strong enough to carry a little something," Eckehart remarked.

Kitt draped a walrus skin over his head and shoulders, lifted the whole four hundred pounds of iron onto his back and swung onto the path.

"Show off!" Eckehart laughed.

"Nobody here to show off to," Kitt muttered under his load. "The brave warriors run so fast, that I can't even see their sail anymore."

#

Aslaug heard the hall portal open.

Surprised she looked up from the peas she was shelling. She did not expect her men back from Brynnir's Anvil so early, and they would come through the scullery, to leave their dirty boots.

Isegrim growled and rose from his place by the hearth. Aslaug went out into the hall, the old dog stalking at her heels.

A tall, broad-shouldered figure stood on the threshold, fair hair mingled with the fur of a wolf-skin cloak, with mail glinting beneath.

Aslaug recognised the man at once. "King Grimwolf!" It was a cry of despair.

"You know me, lady. As I know you."

The dark timbre of his voice made her want, just a little, to cry. It was like falling, or like flying, she didn't know which. Not peaceful and safe, as with Eckehart, where all the passion had been on his side - and since it cooled, they lived side by side, bound by their secret, considerate of each other. Against this man, Grimwolf, she had no resistance. This was the other thing she had been hiding, ever since the Bloodswamp. How one day could change everything.

The old dog whimpered.

"Quiet, Isegrim!" she admonished. "We did not see your ship coming in," she faltered. "Where are your warriors? Outside?"

"I came with Tombrok's ship Möwe. Stayed behind with the other broken iron." He shrugged. "My men would have come, had I ordered them. I did not. People believe that monsters lair on Isenkliff, but I saw none. Instead, I find the healer who saved my life. And King Tombrok's life. He spoke of you being near, but I did not understand what he meant. He was drunk. He drinks too much."

As he spoke Grimwolf advanced until he stood before her. His eyes were blue, unchanged. A broad white streak marred his blond mane where the head-wound had been streaming blood. The whole left side of his face was deeply scarred.

He caught her hand and held it. "I never thanked you. I have owed you my life for thirteen years."

"Welcome, Lord, to the hall of Isenkliff. "Aslaug tried to hide her turmoil behind formality. "My . . . Eckehart . . . went to . . . Brynnir's Anvil. To fetch the Ferys' iron. Have you not met . . . him?"

"I have not. We brought many broken blades, lady."

"Is there war then?"

"There is. The Teoden have been raiding the Ferys all winter. Every hand is against them, but they are strong." His mouth turned down hard. "All this fighting amongst ourselves . . . foolish and expensive."

Outside a big crash of iron sounded on the stone-floor before the

142

smithy.

"Lord, that is my . . . Eckehart. He will welcome you himself." Aslaug made to run outside, but Grimwolf stood in her way, and he was still holding her hand. "Good. It is the Smith of Isenkliff who I have come to see."

Eckehart's heavy steps sounded on the stone pavement outside, coming to the hall door, surprised to see it open, as there was no ship in the bay.

Without letting go of Aslaug's hand, Grimwolf turned aside to see who came.

Aslaug hoped wildly that Kitt had stayed behind in the smithy, that there would be time to warn him off.

Eckehart entered, and a look of terror sprang into his eyes, mirroring her own.

Kitt came right behind the smith, treading noiselessly as usual. Since the last year, he had grown another four inches and was now as tall as the Theusten king, and his shoulders were almost as wide. Standing in the door, the sun shone on his pale mane.

Grimwolf's eyes lighted upon him, and there was no uncertainty in them. "I am Grimwolf, son of Wolfgang son of Berwolf," the Theusten king said. "Do you know me?"

"I know who you must be," Kitt said. "All in Nordheim know your name, Heerking. And beyond. But I didn't know it was you there in the prow, or I would have watched." He shrugged a little. "It was remiss of me."

No, it wasn't his fault, Aslaug thought resigned, but the catastrophe was there, all the same.

"Who are you? Who is your father?"

"I am Kitt, Eckehart's son. And my mother Aslaug's." A sudden grin lit the boy's face. "I'm no Grote Jotun," he ventured, motioning with his big hands from his face towards his feet. "When I was ten, I just started growing all at once." He shrugged again.

"Your mother saved my life after the battle of Bloodswamp. Did you know that – Kitt?"

"No," Kitt said surprised. "I never . . ."

"We do not mention the Bloodswamp here, my lord," Aslaug said

143

quickly.

"No," Grimwolf said with a world of meaning.

"The warriors of Nordheim are loath to recall the memory. With your exception, lord," she continued, striving hard to maintain her poise. "It was you who led the entire host into Tridden Moor. You first crossed the line of no return. You were the only one who came out of Bloodswamp the same as you went in - a hero."

"No exception." Grimwolf shook his head.

"Welcome King Grimwolf, to the hall of Isenkliff," Eckehart said, his voice sounding unnatural. "I have long waited for you to claim your blade, made for your hands alone!"

"You did not expect me today." The scarred side of his face twisted into a grin. "Had I better return another time for my sword, Smith of Isenkliff?"

"No, Heerking. You need a new sword now."

With another one-sided, crooked grin, the Theusten king let go of Aslaug's hand. "The tales say that the Smith of Isenkliff sees the warrior's heart. They didn't say that you could see through wood and leather." He reached for the hilt of his sword, and half the blade came out of the sheath, about three hand-spans missing. "The king with the broken sword." He laughed roughly. "And I come here, armed with nothing, here where . . ."

"The sword we will forge for you will never notch nor break," Kitt promised.

"You are very forward, boy!"

"Only carried away a little," Eckehart said with forced geniality. "Your fame travels on the winds, King Grimwolf."

"The Song of the Fair Foe," Kitt said. "That is about your battle at Aarwood. The bards at the court of Daguilaria sing it, but the Immortal Emperor does not like this song."

"Come to the fire, lord," Aslaug invited, her eyes pleading. "We need meat to set before our guest, Kitt. You can shoot some geese, maybe," she said in an aside.

Obediently Kitt went to the scullery to fetch his bow.

Grimwolf sat down in the honorary seat by the fireplace of the hall and took the golden beaker with Tolosan wine.

144

Aslaug breathed again. Grimwolf accepted hospitality. If he would accept Kitt's presence on Isenkliff, as the son of Eckehart and Aslaug, then nobody would think of asking questions.

"Have you sent him away for my sake or for his?"

"My lord, he doesn't know – he never knew other than that he is our son."

Grimwolf's head came up. "That isn't right. The Kri – he was a brave warrior. So was she."

"You - saw the child, there?"

"Yes, I saw him. By the time we reached Kullen Tor, only my own band of men, those who served me in Murom, were still on their feet. Halga, Skelt and Rutger fell as we ascended.

"On top of Kullen Tor, we came up against the last Kri, and his woman. I held him in play together with Heerger and Dankward and sent all my other men into his back, Ragnar, Manfrid, Blido, Svidger, Sven, to cut her down, and get him between us.

"Dankward fell at once, Heerger a little later. Then, I saw the boy on the ground between the Kri's feet; he kept still, as they were stepping all around him, killing us and never treading on him. That was excellent fighting.

"I sent Greif in for the child. I had Greif from a puppy. In Tridden Moor he was ten years old and maybe a little slow. The Kri slashed down through Greif's back; when he did that he had to open up, and I ran him through.

"His sword came up from Greif, and he got me in the side, deep. Then he fell.

"She was dead by then, and all my men were dead. She had killed them; never let them get into her man's back. A very fine woman.

"I looked for the boy. He was there between their bodies . . . so still . . . looking me in the eye, a little one like that." Grimwolf shook his head. "I thought . . . that the wolves would take care of it . . . I didn't want . . . so I turned away." He shook his head again. "A king has no right to leave things behind like I did. I was hurting badly. No excuse. I knew the wound was mortal, and if you had not closed it, I would have died.

"This year, Wolfbane, my sword, broke against a Teoden helmet. It

145

must have sustained an inner break there in Tridden Moor. Like I did."

"The Kri wasn't dead," Eckehart said. "Had lost most of his blood, when we found him, but still deadly. One never knows, with a Kri."

"So it was a trap." Grimwolf grinned fiercely. "But for the child, he would have killed me and walked out of Bloodswamp. If your Kitt is his son, and hers, what warrior blood he has in his veins!"

Kri blood, always the Kri blood, Aslaug felt so tired thinking about it.

Grimwolf looked at her. "So, the young Kri is going to be a smith?"

"And a healer," Aslaug said.

"A Kri healer." The king's smile was pure irony.

"Blood is not everything," Eckehart said.

"Remember, Lord, he doesn't know. He mustn't know," Aslaug begged. "I saved your life, you said you owe me, I only beg one thing in return . . . he must never hear."

"He won't hear from me," Grimwolf said, looking dissatisfied. "You must tell him yourself. If you don't want to . . . But it is not right."

"Who took all the Kri iron?" Eckehart blurted out. "The other smiths?"

"The warriors. So many had broken their weapons or lost them."

"There were many more blades than survivors up there?"

"The Theusten women took up arms. Without them we would not have stood against the Teoden and the Empire. Now a new generation of warriors is growing up. But the women won't give up their arms." The Heerking laughed out loud. "This is good for us. Makes the men stronger. Not to mention well-mannered, and polite." He looked at Eckehart sharply. "You are jealous, Smith of Isenkliff, because of the iron. Your kind is. Did you take nothing then from Kullen Tor?"

The hall door opened to Kitt, coming in with two geese, plucked and gutted, ready for the spit. "Got four," he announced. "Left two outside."

"Why, that took you no time at all," Eckehart remarked.

"Just as I stepped out of the door, a flock came flying overhead. They must have heard mother speak." He stuck the geese onto the spit and applied himself to turning it over the flame that came from the inner of the earth. "Will we do the test tomorrow morning?" he asked.

"No test necessary," Eckehart said. "I know the Heerking, and what he is made of."

"But . . .!"

Aslaug shook her head at the boy, touching her lips with a finger.

"What test is that?"

Of course, Grimwolf would ask. Her efforts were doomed from the start. She wondered who she was trying to save from whom.

"The sword match. To find the warrior's strength and weaknesses. I test all the warriors who come for a sword."

Grimwolf looked appraisingly at Kitt once more. "So, you test warriors."

"Not kings," Eckehart lied desperately.

"There was King Amroli of Amiata and Vicini of Croton and . . ."

Eckehart waved both arms. "They were no Heerkings. You're not fourteen years old . . ."

"Old enough, and big enough, to stand in a shield wall," Grimwolf pointed out.

"There you hear it, father! I'm not a boy anymore."

"You are!" Eckehart sounded as exasperated as Aslaug felt herself. "What's more, you are a stupid boy. The Heerking of Nordheim does not need to prove his right to a sword to you!"

"No." Kitt looked surprised. "But how will you forge his sword? It must be adapted to the hand that wields it. Not the other way around. You always say so."

"Stop bothering at once!" Aslaug flared up, "You heard your father. King Grimwolf has no time to play games with you."

"What he says is reasonable," Grimwolf said. "I insist."

That was that. When the geese began to smell appetising, Aslaug realised that she had put herself to shame as a housewife, forgetting to salt the roast.

#

147

The next morning Kitt went to the smithy beside the hall.

His father was already there, and he looked unhappy. "I wish Grimwolf wouldn't insist on this."

"Grimwolf wants us to do the best possible work for him. Such a truly great warrior has to have a sword made to measure!"

"I know it is you who wants it. Be careful of Grimwolf, Kitt. He will try to kill you."

"What?" Kitt looked at his father in astonishment.

"You see, he believes that you are a . . . a Grote Jotun. He insists on the test for an opportunity to attack you."

"A hero will never stoop to do anything without honour."

"Grimwolf is a king." Eckehart sounded tired. "A Heerking. He will do what he considers his duty. If he attempts to kill you, you must not retaliate. Run if you have to. Hide until he has left. Or better to take your boat, go to the Murkowydir even! Promise me that!"

Kitt shrugged. "If he tries to kill me, I run. But he won't."

From the arms kept in the storerooms, he selected a straight Daguilarian blade roughly the same length and weight of the Theusten King's own broken blade. It was no soldier's sword, which were all shorter than Grimwolf's, but one used to fight in the arena. Then he hefted his own sword, the first he had forged entirely by himself, wondering how it would hold up against Grimwolf.

"Getting too big for your boots," Eckehart muttered.

Grimwolf was waiting above the shore, in the place stomped to bare sand and stone by so many warriors, that no blade of grass grew there. The king wore only a leather hose and tunic, the same as Kitt.

Kitt held out the hilt of the Daguilarian sword to Grimwolf, and they touched blades.

Their first passage of arms left Kitt impressed. Grimwolf's fame was deserved. The Heerking was the best swordsman of all who had ever come to Isenkliff. His style was beautiful in its deadly simplicity, relying on the power of his blows, his untiring strength, quick reflexes and instinctive cunning. It was the way of fighting Kitt himself favoured. Harmar Saesorgison had tried to do something like that and not quite succeeded.

As the bout went on, Kitt detected small openings, which an experienced fighter would be able to exploit. It would have to be a very brave adversary to keep his wits before Grimwolf's onslaught. But these fractions of a moment were there, when a quick stab might get through.

Kitt felt delirious to hold his own against the famous warrior king, to have an answer to his every move, realising that he was, in fact, the slightly better fighter.

"Stop it, Kitt!"

Eckehart's call reminded Kitt that he was not fighting for pleasure. He disengaged obediently and lowered his sword.

"Not yet," Grimwolf said.

"We don't need to go on," Kitt said.

"Let's fight for first blood now."

"No blood," Kitt said briefly.

Grimwolf looked him fully in the eye. "You could already have drawn blood twice."

"Yes."

"Why didn't you? Afraid of your mother, boy?"

"Aren't you of yours, Heerking?"

Grimwolf barked a short laugh. "I just can't get angry with you."

Eckehart came at Kitt. "What did you mean by this, son? You can't provoke the king's patience like that!"

Kitt did not contradict. He had been mystified throughout at his parents' obsequiousness towards the Theusten king. Powerful, wealthy nobles had come to Isenkliff and had been treated no better or worse than ordinary warriors. Was it because Grimwolf was the Heerking of Nordheim and could make any amount of trouble for Isenkliff? Yet Grimwolf wasn't that sort of man.

Grimwolf spoke. "He is better than I am. Better than I ever was. Stronger and faster. Cool-headed too." He turned back to Kitt. "If you had taken me up on first blood and killed me, the Immortal Emperor would have been very pleased. He counts me among the worst enemies of Daguilaria, as you know well." He smiled at Kitt's pure amazement. "That thought didn't cross your mind?"

"Attack somebody who comes here to have a sword made?" Kitt

149

looked bewildered.

"The Immortal Emperor is the richest man in the world, and he can grant boons beyond wealth even. He rewards very well those who do him favours. Especially unasked."

"He has nothing I want."

"Does he not? Then he is a poor man, after all." Grimwolf regarded Kitt from narrowed eyes. "Would you follow me into my battles?"

Kitt felt so proud that he was unable to answer. His sparkling grey eyes said it all instead.

Eckehart broke in. "You can't have my son, Heerking. Don't put ideas into his head! I need his work. His mother needs his protection."

"I can give you men to serve you."

"Men don't stay on Isenkliff." The truth Eckehart didn't spell out was that men couldn't stay on Isenkliff, because of the Jarnmantsjes in the mountain. "Kitt is a smith. I need him to help me with the work. To forge all the steel that you need to beat back the Teoden - before the Imperial Army comes again. And come it will. To win this war, you need an endless supply of unbreakable steel, Heerking."

Grimwolf thought briefly, and then gave a curt nod. It was a deal.

Eckehart drew a deep breath of relief.

"See, he didn't try to kill me," Kitt muttered.

"Didn't he? You don't know kings as well as I do," Eckehart retorted.

Kitt thought that a most incomprehensible remark. "There are times when my father can spare me at the forge," he addressed Grimwolf. "My parents never like it when I go into the Dark Wood Murkowydir. So instead I come to you. I'll convince them."

"No, you won't." Grimwolf shook his head. "I was rash to offer you a place in my following. Forget what I said. You must never come to Nordheim. You don't fit."

Kitt's face became very still. "What am I doing wrong? That I may remedy it."

"I have in my following the sons of kings. A blacksmith's son who can outfight all those who deem themselves born warriors - they would never forgive that."

"Remember how many times I told you this same thing, Kitt," Eckehart interjected.

"So, if I took you into my following, I would lose my allies," Grimwolf concluded.

"You'd never lose me." Kitt managed a smile.

"That would be the worst. Stay here. Don't ever leave. Nobody will come for you here. That is the deal." The king nodded briefly and strode away up the path towards the hall.

"Don't look like a puppy dog left behind," Eckehart chided. "Did you really want to abandon us for the service of a king, be he Heerking and even Grimwolf himself?"

His feelings in turmoil, Kitt stared at the Heerking's broad back as he and his father followed him up the path. "I don't like being told that I'm not wanted."

"That's just vanity."

"I think I must be the best swordfighter in the whole of Nordheim." Kitt brightened a little. "Grimwolf himself acknowledged that I am better than he is."

"Which will not make you the better man. It will not even make you a good man."

"What will make me a good man?"

"True courage. You remember?"

"I remember," Kitt muttered.

"Grimwolf has it. You will learn. Now we'll attend to the Heerking's sword."

#

The king laid his broken sword on the hall table.

The hilt was a gold-plated bronzen wolf-head and had once been part of a far older weapon, a bronze sword, as the smiths with their knowledge of weapons could see at once.

The handguard was a newer addition, made of iron inlaid with silver and ending in stylised claws. There were about five spans of the blade left.

Grimwolf shook the sheath and the second part of the blade fell out, two spans long. "Wolfbane belonged to Berwolf, my grandfather. He lost it once, in a battle underground that cost his life.

151

Dead on his feet, he broke the monsters' power and lived long enough to fight one more time. Much later, Wolfbane was found in the man-eater cave and brought back -too late for Berwolf to take onto his last ship."

Eckehart and Kitt both bent over the broken sword, one pointing, the other nodding, understanding each other without speaking. They took the two pieces to the door to look at the break in full daylight. Last they considered the hilt where it was attached to the base of the blade.

Aslaug watched Grimwolf during the examination. The Heerking's eyes were on Kitt. Of the four people in the hall, the boy alone was unaware that he touched the sword that had taken the life of his father, his natural father, his Kri father.

"Nothing wrong with the substance that I can see," Eckehart finally pronounced. "Hit too hard too often, that's all. Good steel; we can use it for the new blade. Leave the old hilt too. It will be the same sword again."

"Except it won't break again, no matter how hard and how often you hit," Kitt added.

"You keep saying that." Grimwolf smiled.

"I don't go back on what I say either."

"You will beg the Heerking's forgiveness for your words!" Eckehart ordered.

"Beg forgiveness for what's the truth?"

"At once!" Aslaug said.

"Not this time, I won't."

"Then, you will accept my challenge." Grimwolf stood up.

"You think if you challenge it puts you back in the right?"

"If I am in the wrong I am ready to pay. With my blood. With my life."

With despair in her heart, Aslaug looked at Grimwolf standing there, firm, and immovable. And at Kitt, who stood at the crossroads of his life, and did not know it, childish, gauche, and dangerous as he was. If no miracle happened now, Grimwolf would die, this very day, by the hand of an enemy believed destroyed thirteen years ago. Never had she felt so powerless, not even at the sack of Tomdam, lying under the rapists' weight.

"I must not fight you," Kitt said in a colourless voice. "So, I must apologise. Whatever satisfies you, I will say it."

Damn the boy again, Aslaug thought almost mechanically. This insolent ambiguity could not be lost on the Heerking.

"You have a strange way of apologising, Kitt," Grimwolf remarked. "But I too must ask forbearance and explain. Taking you into my following would mean to kill you. It is the truth what I said to you, earlier. None would be a match for you one on one. The sons of chieftains could not tolerate a blacksmith being so much better at fighting than they, and they would gang up on you. Attack from behind. Or rouse the rabble against you. Or simply poison your food or drink. I hadn't thought that through when I prematurely spoke."

Hadn't you? Aslaug thought bitterly.

"You don't fit," Grimwolf repeated. "You are too big, too strong, too fast. Too honest. Few men have the greatness to befriend such as you. The worst danger to a brave man is not the enemy's fury, but the fearfulness of those near him."

"It is their fear that makes men dangerous. Not their courage," Kitt said. "I don't know where I heard this."

"I told you so, this very thing, many times," Eckehart said.

"Your father is right. You have much to learn, Kitt -about people. I will make you a promise that I can keep. Nobody will interfere with you here on Isenkliff." Grimwolf hesitated. "If you leave here one day and find too many enemies in Nordheim, say that you are one of mine."

"And you, Grimwolf, call me, if the foes grow too many."

The Heerking smiled grimly. "I will. When I look the Fenris-Hound into the eye."

"Don't make it too easy."

"About that break," Eckehart said.

"Yes!"

The two bent over Wolfbane again.

Aslaug was still shaking inside. Here Kitt and Grimwolf were on the way of becoming fast friends just moments after a duel to the death was averted. Eckehart was pleased because his own evasions

153

dovetailed so neatly with Grimwolf's and he had wrung a guarantee from the Heerking, for a considerable price. It was all very neat, and it was all a lie and she wondered if that was not another ghastly error. Damn the men! Abruptly, she rose and went out of the hall door.

The sun had set, and the glow in the sky was like the banked embers of her inner turmoil. Breathing the sea air and listening to the waves, and the wind in the trees, the tension subsided.

Dew was beginning to fall, and she shivered. She hugged herself, preferring the cold outside to being in the company of the three men she loved.

The hall door opened behind her. Aslaug expected Eckehart to come looking for her, but it was Grimwolf. The sight of his silhouette alone was enough to turn her bones to water.

"Come back inside, lady. There are monsters on this island."

"Oh, yes, there are." Aslaug laughed, high and unnatural.

He caught her to him, kissing her eyes, her mouth, stroking her hair until she quietened, and nestled in his arms.

"I always thought Ungstein and Vargsot were names of Swatelbs in the tales. Now I learn that those are metals."

"Are they being very technical?" she asked, her mouth muffled in his shirt.

"Too much so for a simple-minded warrior. Your young Kri will make an excellent smith."

"I teach him how to heal wounds. He learns quickly and readily. But for him, healing was never enough."

"Useful knowledge, though he won't often need it. Whoever opposes him will be past healing."

It was nice to be held by Grimwolf, but other than that he was no help to her either. Reluctantly Aslaug unwrapped herself from his embrace, already disappointed that he let her go.

He kissed her hand, kept it in his. "You do wrong to deny your boy his heritage. He deserves it. Just now, he acquitted himself very well. If he had taken up my challenge, he would have won. He knew that, he felt in the right . . . and backed down. I can't think of any other youth who could have behaved thus . . . including myself when I was young."

154

"He shouldn't have provoked a challenge in the first place."

"You demand too much of him. He alone doesn't know the truth. He can't understand. Yet, even so, he behaves like a grown man, a good man. This is your teaching, Aslaug. And that of Eckehart," he added as an afterthought.

The night hid their faces from each other, and there seemed an even darker shadow on Grimwolf's. "The Kri, I never asked him his name, didn't tell him mine. I must never speak of his last battle and his death. This has grieved me, all these years."

"We can't go back on our lies, now. What are we to tell Kitt, that he is the last of a race of cold-hearted sell-swords who needed to be hunted down like rabid wolves? That you ordered five of your men to kill his mother . . . that you sent your dog at him as a baby? That I left his father lying in the mud, bleeding to death? Condemned him to be forgotten by his son?"

"Yes, all that."

"No. You promised me, Grimwolf."

"I promised. I respect your right, and the price you paid. You have left your life behind for him. You know I would have asked you to be my queen, don't you?"

I could have been happy, she thought. Just after I lost my husband, mere days after I lost my children, I could have begun to love again. That was the other thing she was running from, ever since she had seen Grimwolf walking at the head of his host. When he had come back out of the mist, wounded unto death, she'd laid her hand on him to staunch the blood of his mortal wound – then turned away to go into Tridden Moor. From there she had fled to Isenkliff.

"When I picked him up, I knew that I would spend my life keeping him safe . . . and keeping others safe from him. I found the last of that terrible race, and all I thought of was to shelter, and protect him. I was weak then, and ever since. I still hold his life in my hands, as I did when he was that child. I am the one who could still stop this menace growing up. But I don't. Somebody has already died, I know. Eckehart says a Woodstalker doesn't matter; he doesn't understand that what matters is the crossing of the line. Many more will die. As you almost did today."

155

She wondered if he understood, or if he even would despise her. That thought was horrible to her, as she couldn't stop blurting out all of this.

He didn't release her hand. "A man's day is fixed. I won't live an instant longer."

"Your name will live forever, even with only half the story told. But for me . . . it's too late now," she said, in the same moment that he said, "It's not too late."

#

Kitt stripped the hilt of Grimwolf's sword from the tang and filed down the pieces. When two thin prods were left of each sword fragment, Kitt mixed the metal shavings with minute amounts of other iron, mineral powders and goat's horn, and then took the mixture to the smelting oven. The filed down sword fragments were heated in the forge, and then Kitt hammered joining them up at the break to form into the inner body of the new sword.

The iron from the smelting oven Kitt hammered into the cutting edges. He and Eckehart fused the sword together, heated it again, quenched and tempered it.

Finally, Kitt fastened the old hilt and handguard. Then, the new old sword lay on the anvil.

Grimwolf's hand hovered over the sword, and touched it lightly. "You made Wolfbane unbreakable?"

"Yes."

"Are you a good smith?"

"I know what I'm doing. My father has kept an eye on this work," Kitt amended. "Let me try out Wolfbane against the blade you had before. If it breaks, you can run me through with that Daguilarian scrap metal."

Eckehart opened his mouth to protest.

"Fair enough," Grimwolf said.

They stepped outside and touched swords for the second time right in front of the hall.

Kitt drove Grimwolf across the open space, slowly, inexorably, again and again beating onto the Daguilarian blade, not sparing the new blade, until the other broke in two.

Kitt raised the reforged Wolfbane, his eyes running along the edges. "Not notched," he announced. "After much use, you will notice a slight jaggedness. Do not attempt to smooth it out. It is designed so, adding to the edge. Rather nasty and efficient." He reversed the new sword, proffering it to Grimwolf across his forearm.

The Theusten king took the hilt and hefted Wolfbane in his hand. He swung the sword left and right from Kitt's face that the boy felt the air draught, and his hair stirring.

"If you don't find the weight matched to a grain, with the wielding improved, you can take off my head," he offered without moving in the least.

Grimwolf lowered the sword. "This is Wolfbane, made whole again -and younger."

Kitt saw his parents standing under the hall portal; both were white-faced.

"See, he didn't kill me!" he called out to them.

"Damn you, Kitt, you're taking awful chances!" Eckehart stormed.

"No, he didn't," Grimwolf said. "Wolfbane has never dealt a cowardly blow, and there is still the blood of a hero on this blade. The fire of your forge didn't burn it away. No fire ever can."

#

After all these years of flight Aslaug couldn't stay away.

She laid her hand on the door of the guest room, couldn't take it away again. She thought she heard a sound from within Eckehart's room. What if he found here here, barefoot in her shift? She opened the door and slipped in.

From the two open windows, fresh air and moonlight streamed in. She smelled the man, leather, metal, sweat, and then his arms were around her from behind, one hand holding a knife.

"Forgive. It is a habit." His deep, husky voice made her shiver violently.

He stepped away to replace the knife in the sheath of his belt, which hung on the peg in the wall. Then he turned around to her, his silhouette huge and dark before the window.

"You must think me very silly," she said in a shaking voice. "I am

157

not young anymore." She made as if to leave, not sure that she could.

One step.

Two.

What if he let her go?

He was by her again, his arms around her. "Nothing can keep us apart, now," he said.

#

Grimwolf watched the smiths working, stripped down to the waist, sweat and charcoal streaking their bodies and faces.

After a while he left them to find Aslaug in the garden, knowing she would be there, under the apple tree that blossomed as it bore fruit.

She told him of the last thirteen years, and he listened. Their conclusions from that were different, diametrically. It made no difference to how they felt about each other. Grimwolf had waited for thirteen years and would wait now until she understood that her time of watch and worry was at an end. It was peaceful under the apple tree, and sometimes they just sat together, hand in hand, until it was time for the preparation of lunch, wolfed down silently by the hungry smiths, and then the same at dinner.

In the nights Grimwolf lay sleepless, listening to the cliff shaking to the rhythm of heavy hammers. Each night Aslaug came to him. She walked across the cold floor, teetering on bare feet as if she expected to be sent away again. He made her stay.

#

On the eleventh day, the hammers were silent.

Grimwolf found Eckehart stacking weapons and tools in front of the smithy. He considered the amount of newly forged arms. "This is not the work of two smiths. What is it that happens here at night?"

"Brynnir's forge working," Eckehart said, looking pained.

All in Nordheim knew of Brynnir's Forge, but they knew nothing about it and knew better than to ask.

Not Grimwolf. "Did you forge all this steel for me, Eckehart?"

"All yours, Heerking," Eckehart answered promptly. "That was the deal we made. Keep your part of it, as I kept mine."

Grimwolf turned his head at Eckehart, fixing him out of blue slanting eyes. Eckehart stared back. He was the first to avert his eyes.

After looking around cautiously, he bent down beside the forge to brush his fingers over what seemed solid stone, and a crack appeared. He raised a rectangular plate out of the floor, five feet long and one wide, and shifted it aside, the muscles of his arms bunching. Inside lay a sword, four feet long, the guard a simple steel bar, the pommel fist-sized with a shape between a perfect sphere and an egg. The smith lifted it out, let the light play on the surface and turned it to sight along the edge. He held the sword out to Grimwolf, who looked at the blade a long time as if trying to see the stains of his own blood upon it.

"I did take something from Kullen Tor. Do you claim this also, Heerking? It is the sword that wounded you."

"I have no claim on this. It is Kitt's heritage."

"Kitt's heritage is Svalinir's Spear. With your guarantee, he will be the next Smith of Isenkliff. That will be best for all. Here, he fits."

"Take up Brynnir's Hammer? Never leave? I like it not at all. I say again, it is not right to deprive him of his heritage. You must give this sword to him."

"I'm surprised at you, Heerking. Or not. An ice-bear cub, that's what Aslaug compares him with. He charmed even you-"

Grimwolf regarded him coldly. "Deadly when grown up? I do not fear him."

"He is dangerous, but he is no murderer. I know men; I see the warrior's heart . . ."

"I do not fear him, as I do not fear death. I want Kitt to have his heritage. The lady Aslaug does not agree."

"I will not lie to you, Grimwolf. Aslaug never was my wife. We just had this common guilty secret . . . Kitt. I don't know her reasons. I know mine . . ."

"Look out!" they heard Kitt's call.

The grey bull was trotting up from the creek to the door of the smithy, his massive head lowered. Kitt overtook the animal in two long strides and gripped his horns. The bull's nostrils dilated and snorted furiously.

The Heerking gripped his sword but didn't advance. He watched

Kitt, his feet driven into the soil, the muscles of his legs, shoulders and arms bunching, turning the bull's head until it faced backwards. Far too much muscle for a boy that age, far too compact, even for a smith's apprentice, with a warrior's symmetry -it was the perfect body for the perfect sword. The gold weight of fighting, to measure every warrior and every weapon against - that was what Eckehart wanted. All he ever wanted, so Aslaug had said. Grimwolf judged that the smith of Isenkliff had achieved that.

Lowing in a disconsolate deep tone the massive animal slewed around and ambled away.

Turning back, Grimwolf saw that the Kri sword had disappeared and no sign was showing of the cash under the stone floor.

Kitt came up to the forge. "Only the three old cows left. The bull knows. I gave names to the calves so they could not be slaughtered. But to the other cows, I gave no names, like you asked, father. And now they are gone. I should have named them. I can hunt enough goats."

"When Kitt was a wee lad, he named the newborn calves, Lise, Suse, Hanne and Ernst," Eckehart explained to the Heerking. "He always was soft-hearted. So now we have three very old cows indeed and a bull who rules all he sees. We pleaded with him not to bestow any more names. But Kitt, for this work even nine cows won't be sufficient payment."

Kitt flushed. "I'll hunt. Make up the price in goats. There was no need . . ."

"You are both trying my patience," the Heerking said. The tone of his voice was quiet, like a sword at the throat.

"I'll tell you what will happen." Kitt ignored Eckehart's frantic signalling behind Grimwolf's back. "Tomorrow morning all the steel will be stacked on Brynnir's Anvil . . . but only if I go hunting now. And if you think of watching in the night, the iron will stay where it is, and you'll have to haul it to Brynnir's Anvil yourself."

Grimwolf frowned. "I will come to the hunt with you. One more smith's riddle and I'll throw you into the sea."

"You want my Kirgis bow?"

"I'll take your spare."

Grimwolf strung the long yew bow with one hand and took a lance.

Kitt led the way west down the valley and then up the path. They passed the smelting ovens, traversed the stand of firs and were on the high plateau, where they shot three goats each in short succession. Placing the animal carcasses beside a crack in the earth, Kitt called a word down into the mountain: "Flees!" Then he turned his back and walked away, signalling to Grimwolf to follow.

They spotted a young goat buck by a rock overhang near the mountain top where a spring bubbled out of the mountainside.

The animal raised its head.

They stopped.

The goat stood perfectly still.

Kitt raised his bow quickly and shot. The buck jumped straight into the air and fell where it had stood.

When the hunters had climbed up the hill, the animal lay still, shot behind the shoulder blade, one yellow glassy eye staring into the sky; the cleft hooves had scraped the sand at the water's edge very little.

"Good shot," Grimwolf said.

"Kirgis bow." Kitt held up his weapon. "Best in the world."

"I said a good shot." Don't go humble on me, you arrogant child, the Theusten king was conveying by his tone. It had been a remarkable shot with any bow, three hundred feet uphill.

"I hit what I aim at because I only aim at what I can hit."

Grimwolf cast back in his mind if he had been like that as a young man. Yes, he had. Kri youth were like all other youths, callow and boastful. Except that Kitt's boast was nothing but the truth, and that was the difference.

"So, you are sorry for cows, but not for goats? Is it because these goats are wild?"

Kitt blushed and shrugged.

"Tell me!" Grimwolf demanded.

"I was little then, and I hadn't thought things through. We must eat. We have obligations." He looked at Grimwolf, and shrugged again. "The things people say about Isenkliff . . . some are true. Some are not true. No giant here, for one thing."

161

"Only you."

"Too big for my boots, father says. Other things were true at some time. Going, going slow . . . you know that song? Father says everyone knows it. But that part is not true, not anymore . . . at a price."

"You think much."

"Too much?"

"There is a time for everything."

"Doubt and die. Doubts cost moments that decide life or death in battle. I don't remember who told me this."

Grimwolf nodded. "True words. For battle. Those warriors who don't think . . . they always follow, never lead."

Kitt retrieved the arrow, without touching the fallen goat.

Grimwolf's eyes went to the crack in the mountain overhang. "As long as I'm looking on, nothing will happen?"

"That's the way of it." Kitt knelt beside the water of the spring to drink from his cupped hand.

Grimwolf remained standing, spear in hand, his eyes on the broad back. Svalinir's spear had been hanging over Kitt's head his whole life, and he didn't know it. He didn't know either that Grimwolf had been the first man of the Nordheim host to swear the oath that no Kri should be left alive. He hadn't kept the oath then, and didn't keep it now. Aloud he said. "You are careless. That way Sigurd Dragonslayer turned his back on his murderer."

"I know the story, King Grimwolf." Kitt rose.

"You must never forego guarding your back against your allies, Kitt. The enemy you meet from in front."

"Ally and enemy is the same man," Kitt quoted. "I sometimes feel . . . as if somebody were standing beside me and telling me things. I don't always like what he says."

"Listen to him! I rather take my chance with the honour of an enemy than the smile of a friend. It wasn't always thus. Once there were men who I could trust. As Heerking, I have no more friends. I have followers, and vassals. The Immortal Emperor, he corrupts souls with his power and wealth . . . but souls are corruptible or not, all for themselves."

162

Grimwolf laid down his spear, knelt down and also drank from the spring. When he looked up again, wiping his mouth, his hand stopped in mid-movement. He stared out to the sea westwards. "Expecting visitors, Kitt?"

A ship was approaching fast with a tower of white sails of Kossean rigging spread fully in the west wind.

It had a prow head of northern design, a sea serpent with the nine dark circles down the bowed neck already clearly visible. The newcomer did not do the spirits of Isenkliff the courtesy of taking down the prow head.

"Mauran Neveokki. The merchant."

"The bastard." Grimwolf's eyes were burning like a real wolf's. "His name is Murolf Neunauge. His mother is a Theusten, to our shame, of a low-rank clan."

"I didn't know that. Then he should know about taking down the prow-head. It is all wrong, too. A Neunauge is not a serpent, but a fish, a parasite. I often catch it latched onto other fishes, eating their flesh and blood, and it doesn't have nine eyes, only two, and eight gills on each side. Tastes good."

"He is a parasite alright. Did you know he is the Immortal Emperor's spy?"

"Merchants always spy for somebody." Kitt's face changed. "Never mattered before. But now, that big stack of your steel!"

"He mustn't learn about you either. Never."

"He's been here several times before, and he knows me."

Grimwolf touched his sword. "Then, I must kill him. Good." Kitt shook his head, calmly meeting the king's glare. "Not good if he disappears on Isenkliff. And mother won't like it."

"I don't ask your participation in this deed. That's what your mother wouldn't like."

"Wait, I have a plan." Kitt knelt down and cut off the goat's head with one slash of his long knife. "The hunt must wait. Take this back to the house. Tell father to send it to me when the smithy has been readied for the visitor. Tell him in those words; he'll understand."

"You are giving me orders?"

"You can trust me, Heerking. As if I was your best enemy."

Kitt drew his shirt over his head, divested himself of shoes and trousers, then dipped his hands into the goat's neck and drew them across his mouth, smearing the congealing blood up into his hair and across his chest and belly.

Grimwolf's stern features broke into a broad smile that transformed the man. "No idea what you plan. But I'll play."

He watched as the boy sprang and ran down the hill.

Kitt paused by the smelting oven to add soot to the blood on his face, hands, hair and chest.

Eckehart received the goat head with no surprise at all.

"Didn't expect Neveokki would come again so soon after our last deal." He chuckled.

"You sold steel to him, Smith of Isenkliff?"

"Just traded two knives against all books, charts and instruments on his ship. A wonder how he made it back."

"No wonder he returns for more," Grimwolf said.

Eckehart evaded the Heerking's accusing look.

They watched the boat fasten to the rock spur and Neveokki-Neunauge climb onto the promontory alone, and they saw Kitt moving downhill. He was like a different creature; even the way he moved had changed; the lithe youth turned feral, stalking almost on all fours.

"Too much cunning," Grimwolf muttered.

Neveokki-Neunauge hadn't yet spotted Kitt. He turned to say something, and the boat cast off.

With great bounds, Kitt loped down to the shore.

The rowers were first to see the beast coming along the rock jetty. They shouted warnings at the amber merchant. Neveokki-Neunauge's eyes widened when he saw what came towards him. He turned around for the boat, but it was already too far out, and the men showed no intention to approach again. If anything, they distanced themselves farther.

He spun back.

The beast boy was before him, eyes and teeth gleaming in the mask of blood and charcoal. Neunauge whipped out a sabre and held out the point. One of the rowers raised a bow and aimed, but somehow the merchant was always in the line of fire.

"Ho, Smith of Isenkliff, Eckehart! Ho, ho, help!" Neunauge's yell came up thinly to where Grimwolf watched; the Theusten king heard the panic in his enemy's voice.

The smith appeared at the head of the path leading down to the shore. "Do you stand still, sir!" he shouted. "As you value your life. On no account move!" He disappeared again.

The merchant stood stock-still. The beast boy fixed him with a steady, unwavering stare out of his clear eyes, bright and mindless in the indescribably grimy face.

Finally, Eckehart appeared again. He came down the path carrying a goat's head which he threw to the beast boy, who caught it, and ambled along the jetty to sit down on the shore like a dog, with a loony smile creasing the blood caked around his mouth.

The way was free for Neunauge to run to Eckehart's side. "You were damn long in coming to the rescue, smith!" he complained. "What creature of Hellheim is this?" it was almost a shriek.

Kitt looked up from the goat's head and growled.

Eckehart's face furrowed. "Don't you recognise him? It is Kitt, my son! Don't mind his antics; he only wants to play. Don't make any sudden movements. And don't look him in the eye; he doesn't like that. I'm used to him, so I don't always consider how he reacts to others."

"Your son? But, but, but . . . I thought . . . you will forgive me . . . I always wondered . . . so is he something else entirely, after all . . .?" the merchant babbled.

"Yes, he changed a bit since you saw him last. Only used to become like this every full moon, and sometimes the new moon. Now it can happen at any time. Must have been your serpent prow that set him off."

"A pox on your barbarian superstition! This has to be some sort of degeneration. And here I brought all those books to trade. Well, he won't want those anymore."

"Books!" Kitt muttered, rising towards the merchant. "Books!"

"Keep him off me!"

"Strangely enough, he now wants the books more than ever. And he means to have them. I don't think he'll let you leave before you haven't handed over every scrap of paper."

"Again."

"Books!" the beast boy growled menacingly."

"Have you at least some steel to trade me? I'll let you have that load of books for even a small knife."

"Not a scrap," Eckehart said with a doleful face. "Come to the smithy and see for yourself that I do not lie to you."

"That won't be necessary," Neveokki Neunauge said in a strangled voice.

But Eckehart moved away, leaving the merchant spy the choice between following or remaining alone with the beast. So he followed, uncomfortably aware of the feral boy close behind him.

It took Kitt an effort to see the iron in front of the smithy. He only saw the stacks because he knew they were there, and was familiar with the workings of Aslaug's runes, which made the eyes slide sideways, and blink, and just not take in things. Zaubar, she called it, and she hadn't yet shown to Kitt how to do any of it. He thought she waited until he had learned all about healing, which was the most important thing for him to learn, she said.

He saw Grimwolf only with the third look, although the Heerking stood planted in full view, favouring Neunauge with an icy glare.

The trader didn't see the Heerking nor the steel, his eyes gliding over the runes painted foot long in white chalk on the iron and the leather of Grimwolf's tunic. Going into the smithy, he almost ran into the Theusten king. "Your forge is cold, Eckehart," he disapproved, looking right at the glowing heap of coal and steel. "Looks like a long time has passed since you worked. Why, there even is dust on your anvil!"

"Without my son to help me, I get no work done at all," Eckehart lied. "You find me at the lowest ebb of my life."

In the storerooms of the smithy, Neunauge saw only empty shelves, overlooking the swords and armour piled high. "Nothing for me here. Well, I will put your son's unfortunate case to the learned doctors of Daguilaria. They may find a way to stop this degeneration, even reverse it. The faster I'm on my way master Eckehart, the sooner I will be back here with help."

"That is most generous of you," Eckehart murmured mournfully. "I thank you already, friend Neveokki."

Together they walked back down to the anchorage, Kitt crowding the spy from one side, as Grimwolf walked unbeknownst at his other side, his hand on Wolfbane's hilt.

"Your son gives me gooseflesh, Eckehart," the merchant-spy complained.

"He does to me also," the smith confessed. The sight of Kitt's light grey eyes shining from the red and black mask, the strong, white teeth bared in that crazy smile, and the predatory way the big youth moved, all that was beginning to tell even on him.

Seeing the books stacked on the shore, the merchant snarled. The men had brought everything, not only a fraction, as he had hoped. The boat was riding at a distance, and the men in it were heavily armed. They made no move to come in further.

Neunauge waded into the water, looking over his shoulder resentfully at Kitt, who was crouching over the books like a lion over a carcass. Some distance the merchant was forced to swim until he was pulled into the boat.

All sails set the ship heaved away with high speed in the wind that had veered east and freshened up.

Eckehart stood on one leg, bent over, convulsed with silent laughter. "Well, that takes care of him," he gasped.

Kitt ran into the sea, ducked under, washing his hair, face and body, and emerged clean.

Grimwolf looked even grimmer, rubbing vigorously at the chalk markings on his leather tunic. "Wind now comes from the east after blowing from the west all day," he remarked. "This is Zaubar."

"Yes, convenient," Eckehart said. "Give Neveokki good speed."

"And the geese, they come when you want to serve a meal to a guest. Convenient also, smith?"

"That is just Kitt. He never misses anything he shoots at."

167

"So he told me."

"Just the thing he would say. Arrogant pup. He's right too. Never saw him like today, though." Eckehart shook his head. "I couldn't stop laughing right now. But it wasn't amusing."

"Wiles of an old warrior -a boy like that. And how he stopped the bull . . ."

"He was showing off to you, Heerking. He hero-worships you. He won't ever serve the Immortal Emperor, or any enemy of yours. And if you ever send for him . . . he will come."

Grimwolf inclined his head.

Kitt had spotted the Ferys ship coming from the south.

Now he trailed behind, feeling surprised that his mother accompanied them to Brynnir's Anvil, which was something she had never done before.

She walked beside Grimwolf on the narrow footpath, her shoulder touching his wolf cloak. Behind them was Eckehart.

Kitt fell back before reaching the top of the cliff and dropped to all fours to watch.

There were men below on Brynnir's Anvil, hurrying, loading the iron into the ship with the naked prow.

"Keep your head down!" Eckehart admonished unnecessarily.

Kitt saw Aslaug and Grimwolf standing etched against the Southern sky, facing each other.

Grimwolf nodded and turned away to walk down the path to the rock promontory. His mother passed where Kitt crouched, her face without expression, eyes unseeing. His father followed her. "You want to think about it," he heard Eckehart say with a sneer. Kitt had never heard him speak in this tone. "You are just the same as me. There is no place like Isenkliff, not anywhere . . ."

"You think that I have been unjust to you. But I know that it isn't out of the love for death and pain, that you forge your famous weapons. I understand your love of the steel, and I know the power that is in a sword; it has its own Zaubar. Even the fascination for the art of fighting, I even understand that . . . a little . . . that you cannot resist the deadly beauty of the perfect union of a man and his steel."

168

"You should. You are in love with a warrior, the Heerking of all the north, no less. You must accept all that he represents. The world is a violent place, so why do you hold it against me and not him . . .?"

Their voices retreated. It sounded like another of those quiet quarrels was beginning, without the voices being raised, and all the more bitter. They just seemed to have waited for the Heerking to leave. Kitt stayed where he was.

One of the men on Brynnir's Anvil looked up, and then they all straightened to watch the Heerking coming down towards them.

Grimwolf moved slowly, to give them time to decide that he was real. When he reached the shore, a tall, young, fair-haired, bearded warrior stepped forward. Kitt thought that this must be Gerbern, the younger Ferys prince. He stopped exactly where the promontory joined the land. Grimwolf was addressing Gerbern, and the young man looked relieved. He half raised his hand as if to point, let it fall self-consciously.

Kitt understood the reason for Gerbern's surprise. Over the last twelve days, the scars marring the left side of Grimwolf's face had receded to being no more than an ornamental badge for a brave warrior. He knew that the bone aches besetting a man of Grimwolf's age had also vanished. His mother could do these things with her Zaubar.

The Heerking stepped into the prow of the serpent ship, and Kitt saw him leave as he had come, tall and proud in his wolf cloak, the wind stirring in the long reed-coloured hair.

The Code of the Red Lily Knights

Over many years, countless swordsmen had set foot upon the shore of Isenkliff.

On a day in late summer, a knight stood there on the stony beach, very tall and upright. His cloak of heavy black silk with a red mark in the shape of a lily on the back flapped in the sea wind like a dark wing splotched with blood, billowing around wiry limbs appearing overly thin in black.

The long, black, straight hair was tied back from his bony face, and shot through with single grey hairs; the thin moustache was black as if drawn there by a piece of charcoal.

A close look revealed many thin lines on the forehead and around the eyes, with arrogance and sarcasm lurking in their fine net. Two deep, cynical lines sprang from the nostrils of the hook nose to the corners of his mouth as if cut in with a knife. The eyes, black and bright, surveyed his surroundings with a slight turn of the head.

His ship, a slim two-master with Kossean rigging, rode at anchor a hundred yards from the shore, the sails furled. A launch had brought him to the jetty, or was it just a rock spur resembling a man-made structure? The boat was returning to the ship, a gantry waiting to draw it up.

The noble knight, Count Diorlin do Consabura et Vesac, Swordmaster of the Order of the Knights of the Red Lily, was not at all sure that he had come to the right place. The sea spray carried by the western wind was cold on his face. He wondered if he would ever get warm again.

Was this remote, bleak island really the legendary Betra Hyerote, the Iron Rock? The ship's captain swore that it was, as sure as he wished to return to his native harbour Tolon, pointing to the jagged double peak of the mountain, the gleaming curve of what he called White Whale Island towards the south, and inviting him to contemplate the towering rock needle on the Eastern horizon.

These were indeed the three sea marks described by the legend, confirmed by the few skippers who had made this journey north. Other than that, he could see no sign that this deserted island was home to the Eternal Smith, the reigning master smith of all the northern lands, who forged the famous Aurora Blades – and other things.

Absurd. Hope always was absurd. If he had come to the northern end of the known world chasing a myth, what a fool he'd look. The thin red lips twisted bitterly, amending, what an old fool he'd look.

Standing beneath the towering black cliffs, the Swordmaster felt that he had indeed reached the end of the world. For him, this was the end of all roads. Was it also the end of the last hope? If he found nothing here, he would go nowhere else. Just stay here, and give the signal for the ship to pull anchor and turn about. Simply let the young knights go back –but back to what? To the tender mercies of Count Hugo and his tame sorcerer Zinnober, to live a hollow form of knightly honour. That or destruction.

And Ramiro -he couldn't bear thinking of Ramiro, whom he had left behind as guarantee of his good faith to Gesalon. King Gesalon, as the man called himself now. Gesalon the Bastard, but Diorlin was in no position to hold that bastardy against him.

Was there anything at all here? Had anyone ever come to this forsaken island, let alone many men at arms, knights among them, even kings -had they all lied about their adventure?

Suddenly he noticed that what had seemed natural ridges in the stony shore were runnels as if trodden by the boots of many men. He conceived the fantastic notion that what seemed a natural inlet had been formed by the keels of ships -many ships, and over a long time. Diorlin's breath caught at this vision.

Above the pebble beach, there was a ring of stones, and inside it, a bare place where the earth was hard-packed and the grass did not grow. "Great Trifold Sky Lord, that is an arena!" he exclaimed aloud.

From the arena, a path led up the valley towards a rock outcrop. A second trail climbed to a gap high in the cliff.   Two men appeared on the higher path, descending, foremost a tall, broad man in a smith's leather apron, with long, white hair stirring in the wind, followed by a tall, fair-haired youth.   The Eternal Smith? Then the other must be the giant who guarded the shore of the Iron Rock, Diorlin thought; the legend had that right, well over six feet tall and

171

built perfectly to proportion. Moved well - damn well. He'd eat his cloak if that weren't a swordfighter.

The two men reached the shore, coming towards Diorlin, who also started walking towards them. The young man passed the older with his longer stride. Was it chance, instinct or intent, the way he was shielding the other man and moving in on the newcomer?

Like the smith the big youth was unarmed, dressed like some serf, but the way he walked, held his head, and his hands, the set of the broad shoulders, told volumes to the experienced eye of the old swordsman. The sleeveless leather tunic revealed muscular arms and a strong corded neck; his back and neck were straight, without the stooping very tall men often showed, and he had the poise and balance of a dancer. The look of the wide-set light coloured eyes was calm, missing nothing.

A weapon, the thought formed in his mind. Diorlin had come for a sword and had found a man, a youth, who was a living weapon -to win a war with. Fanciful thinking; he called himself to order.

The three men met on the verge of the trampled grass. The smith's eyes were startlingly blue, looking shrewd and kind. His white hair and bristling white beard were shot through with strands of bright red, which once had been the original colour and showed his barbarian origin.

Looking into the youth's grey, curious eyes, the swordsman laughed inwardly at his fanciful thoughts. This one was a bit young to be the stuff of legends. No more than fourteen years, even less? All those muscles gave a misleading impression. This was a boy, not an ancient giant in an ageless body of living metal, which was too fantastic an idea.

He bowed formally to the older man. "I am Diorlin do Consabura et Vesac. I have come from Eliberre in the Kingdom of Tolosa to seek the Eternal Smith of the Iron Rock." He wondered whether the smith understood him, what language the inhabitants of this island spoke. "Is this island Betra Hyerote and are you the Eternal Smith?" he asked.

"You are on Isenkliff, and I am a smith. There have always been smiths on Isenkliff. My name is Eckehart." The smith's voice was

172

deep, and he spoke Tolosan slowly and with a strong accent hard to understand.

"Isenkliff means Betra Hyerote, Iron Rock. We have heard of the Swordmaster Diorlin of the School of Knights, one of the true masters of the blade." The boy spoke Tolosan with a minimal accent, in a voice breaking now and again and holding strangely deep overtones.

Diorlin felt tickled by the recognition, awe even, and immediately chided himself a vain, old fool. Think about how he could use this! He gave the boy another appraising look. Enormous potential here, but as yet wholly unconscious -all the better, give them to me when young. Diorlin thought he could bring out all these talents, harness them.

"And you, do you also aspire to become a true master of the sword?" Throwing the spark into the tinder, he could almost see it catching, kindling tiny flames in those grey eyes that did not look so cool anymore. The old Swordmaster had considerable experience in handling young warriors.

"My son Kitt. He is my apprentice," the smith said. "I teach him the way of the steel."

Diorlin seized on the phrase. "The way of the steel and here on the Iron Rock is where it begins. Where it ends?" He shrugged. "Not only have I seen Aurora Blades in Tolosa and the Empire of Daguilaria, but in the hands of fighters from far more distant lands. I am desirous of such a sword, as only comes from the Iron Rock. That is why I came all this way from Tolosa, where good steel abounds, and good craftsmen. Yet I came here."

The smith spoke to his son in a language which Diorlin did not understand. He seemed to ask something, and the youth answered him.

"We will talk about your sword in my hall," Eckehart said. Diorlin bowed again. "I thank you for your gracious invitation."

Kitt looked over to the ship. A figure was visible sitting in the mast, a sailor, and along the railing stood a row of dark figures, black capes billowing in the wind. "Are those your knights? Won't they come ashore?"

"Later. There are things," Diorlin hesitated. "I would speak about to your father alone first."

The master swordsman, the wizard, founder of the legendary School of Red Lily Knights in Eliberre, the most famous fencing school in all the known lands - at first Kitt felt tongue-tied in front of this elegant, seasoned and famous fighting man.

As they walked along the path to the house, Diorlin kept chatting lightly about the long duration of the journey, the ships they had met, and listened politely to Eckehart's slow answers. As Kitt helped hunting for elusive words of Tolosan or translated the more complicated phrases, he began feeling slightly more at his ease.

Diorlin's dark eyes kept straying towards him, assessing, evaluating and Eckehart also turned to his son from time to time, as if seeing him with the eyes of the famous swordmaster. Self-conscious under this double scrutiny, Kitt fell silent again, only speaking when requested.

The sight of the smith's hall surprised the swordmaster.

A fantastic building to find so far from civilisation, he thought, albeit of barbarian architecture.

The smith led the way through a vestibule with rows of pegs on the wall, to throw open another portal into a cavernous room. Diorlin felt as if he was entering the inside of a mountain, and the house was built half into the rock. The roughly shaped stone added to the sense of massive strength, conveyed by the enormous wooden beams of the ceiling, which were more than twenty feet up in the air. Light flooded through glass windows higher up.

The long oaken table and benches were polished, very old, and could seat more than a hundred men, Diorlin thought, maybe had done so.

There were four doors to the right and stairs led to two galleries. To the left four doorways opened, hewn into the rock. Opposite the portal was a great fireplace big as a Tolosan peasant hut. Despite the size of the room and the thickness of the walls, the air was warm. Burning in the cavernous fireplace was no wood, but something that looked like a heap of stones, emitting no smoke. This was the first wondrous thing he saw.

Upon the side gallery, lit by four glass windows, he could see a fair woman bowed over needlework, remote -the lady of the house, of whose face he had retained hardly any impression except paleness and quiet; he could not tell whether she was still young or older. She had acknowledged the guest without speaking, silently motioned to the plates and vessels with bread, smoked meat and wine, which stood on the table as if the guest had been expected. Then she had retreated to her place above.

The big boy named Kitt sat on a wooden box to the side, devouring the bread and meat his mother had heaped on his plate, apparently intent on nothing but his food. He ate neatly enough, plying knife and fork, which was a pleasant surprise.

On the other side of the fireplace sat his host, repeatedly urging food and drink in his broken Tolosan. He filled the wine goblets again, gilded glass from Tarquinia, and then leaned back comfortably as if Diorlin's purpose for coming to Isenkliff had been dinner in his hall. There seemed no hurry, and the Swordmaster found himself putting off broaching the issue which had led him to seek out a craftsman at the end of the world, of whose existence outside the legend he had not even been certain. The reason that Diorlin stalled was that the boy would have to translate. His host's command of Tolosan sufficed to do the honours to his guest and would probably also suffice for ordinary business transactions. Diorlin's request was not quite ordinary. Or maybe it was ordinary enough, the weakness and shame of it. But the reasons for it were not. It was necessary that the smith, and most of all that youth, understood the desperate need behind his request.

"How came you to know about the Order of the Lily Knights here at the end of the world?" he asked, realising at the same moment, that here was the centre of these peoples' lives, and he added: "Forgive me for calling your island the end of the world. We sailed for four months, and it was a dangerous journey."

The smith seemed unoffended. "My son's head is full of minstrel verses of knights and tales of foreign lands."

175

The boy grinned a little self-consciously as he translated.

"Minstrel verses? One hears so much of minstrels' quests to magical lands. Never knew they really went. Though you do have a hall here fit for a king to hold court and listen to minstrels."

"Kings do come to Isenkliff," the smith said comfortably.

"Maybe then you have heard about the struggles for knightly honour, and for the souls of men that have rocked the thrones of Tolosa." Diorlin leaned forward earnestly to look the smith in the eye. How blue these eyes were, and how disconcerting. But it was the grey eyes that he was really speaking to, watching him from the half shadow.

The smith shook his head. "Warriors from many lands come here, also from Tolosa. I make blades for them and armour. They tell me things. But that doesn't mean I know."

Diorlin regarded the smith thoughtfully. Not so naive. Aloud he said with some deprecation: "True, you would hear a different opinion from each Tolosan you happened to meet, as we are an argumentative people. Though there are some bare facts, which almost everybody agrees on. For instance, that it all began with Luvin the Ruthless."

"King Luvin and the Battle of a Thousand Knights," Kitt provided.

"I see you know your history," Diorlin said approvingly. "It took more than one battle to break the power of the old knights' orders of Tolosa, but the Battle of a Thousand Knights will always be remembered as the last stand of knighthood against the kings, and the powers surrounding them."

"I read about it." Kitt rose from the wooden box and went up to the gallery.

Diorlin noted how noiselessly the big youth moved. Only now he saw that from the two galleries up, shelves were covering every inch of the walls, containing books, scrolls and parchments.

When Kitt had found what he sought, a thin book bound in leather with an inlaid bronze falcon, he looked over to his mother, who was sitting on the gallery with her needlework, and he saw that a ball of red wool was lying on the floor.

He moved over to pick it up. Aslaug's hands lay still on her embroidery frame and the woodpecker she had been begun the day before was still colourless without his red marks. She hadn't done a single stitch.

"Is something the matter?" he asked in a whisper.

She looked at him as if she saw an apparition, shook her head. "Nothing. Maybe I slept a little. I know I dreamt. What does he want, this black man?"

"He didn't say yet. Is speaking about the Battle of a Thousand Knights." That was hundreds of years ago. Kitt wondered how long it would take the swordmaster to come to the point.

"He has a grief, this man, filling him all up inside. I can see trouble clouding around him, and trailing behind, just like his black cloak."

They both looked down on the smith's bent head with the white hair on which the earth fire cast a blue tinge, the Swordmaster's hook-nosed profile leaning towards him bathed in the same light.

Kitt returned to the fireplace, holding out the book to the old Swordmaster.

Diorlin was exceedingly well acquainted with this particular tome.

To humour the boy, he opened it at the beginning, and as he looked at the name inscribed on the inside with faded red ink, his formal expression changed to animation. "Sir Vitiza. To think that I would see this name here on this island, written by his own hand. It seems like an omen. Duke Vitiza do Alkotor et Manresa was one of those knights who elected to leave Tolosa, rather than bow to the king's rule, after the Battle of a Thousand Knights was lost."

He leafed through the book which fell open on a page sewn into it, not belonging to the original manuscript. His finger ran down the columns of handwritten names in black and red letters -the missing record of the names of all the knights of the Old Order of Red Lily Knights. What a find! His hands shook slightly. Now he would know much better which families to approach on the quiet. "My own great-grandfather, Diorlin the Fourth Count of Eliberre, for whom I was named, see his name here, he fought on the other side, for the king. That makes it all the stranger that it has fallen to me to restore the

Order of Lily Knights."

"There are more books like this one. Look as if they came at the same time."

The boy went up to the gallery again, and Diorlin noted that he needed no light to locate the nine books he brought back to the table.

"You read them?"

"I read them. Skipped the name lists though. And that book my mother said I must not read yet." He pointed to a darkened slim tome.

"Well, well, well!" The dance of the eyebrows became alarming. "That mangy cur Zinnober would give his collection of pickled babies for this grimoire. Your mother is right; this is not for you to read, nor for any sane man. This one book does not belong to the Knights but to their adversaries. Well, I suppose it is safe enough here on Betra Hyerote." Diorlin's black eyes wandered from Kitt to Eckehart and back. "May I ask how these books came here?"

"I don't know. They were always here as long as I can think. Father?"

"Long before you were born, a Tolosan knight came to the Smith of Isenkliff. But the name he gave was not Vitiza."

"It may well not have been." The red lips under the black moustache twitched cynically. "The hatred of the Tolosan kings reached far; many of the rebel knights died in exile. Their deaths were mysterious and inexplicable." The black eyebrows did another meaningful dance. "Since the Battle of a Thousand Knights, somebody, or maybe I should say something, has been intent on wiping out the last traces of the knightly orders. And even those who submitted, and served the king, did not always escape. These books were believed lost. I realise now that Duke Vitiza has brought them here for safekeeping. Did he say nothing at all to your father?"

The question put to Eckehart, the smith shook his head. "Maybe he did; he told of many things, sitting just where the Swordmaster sits now, but you were not here to translate, Kitt. He was a fine warrior, quick and skilled, but not strong."

The smith spoke as if Vitiza had visited with him, but it had to have been a different smith. Duke Vitiza was dead a hundred years.

Diorlin thought that strange. Perhaps Vitiza had thought it safer leaving all in the belief that no more written records of the Lily Knighthood existed. If providence meant to save the Red Lily Knights, the books would be found -as they had been found now when it was almost too late.

"What is so important about those knights and their Orders?"

"But father!" Kitt exclaimed. To him, it seemed clear.

"Your father asks the right question," the Swordmaster said. "There are other knightly orders, but it is the Red Lily Knights who guard the Way of the Sword, only loyal to the code of knightly honour. The knight's watchword is Purity, Poverty, Mercy. Help, Save, Serve, those are the duties of a Red Lily Knight.

To help without reward, to save regardless of his own life.

To hold his shield over the weak.

To swing his sword in the eternal battle against evil.

He fights fair, fights hard and returns good for ill, forgives the defeated enemy and never dances on his grave.

The Lily Knight serves the Order; thrones and dynasties are as nothing to the Code, and the knight knows no authority except that of the Order, his obedience to the Order is absolute.

This Code is my duty to bring back to Tolosa. Do you understand that, Kitt?" Yes, there was the answering spark, as he had seen so many times in the eyes of young men. He fell silent, looking into the mysterious smokeless fire for a moment, exhausted from speaking so much. Letting his words work.

Kitt's eyes were still on Diorlin's face after he had translated for Eckehart.

After some time, Diorlin resumed: "There are few knights left in Tolosa, most old and broken, or young and unready. It was almost too late when, upon his ascension to the Saddle Throne, Sisebut the Good called me to his court to teach Sisenand, his eldest son, the sword. In a secret audience, King Sisebut imposed upon me the task to restore the ancient order of the Lily Knights. But the king, bless his honest heart, wants to restore too many ancient customs too fast. He issued the decree concerning the New Knightly Order, and closely after that, he issued a proclamation reinstating the old custom

179

of electing the kings." Diorlin had spoken without a pause to translate, and he continued in the same manner without regard for the fact that the smith would not understand. "Sisebut's favour proves useless against the enmity of the nobles and their mages. The king has fallen ill of a strange disease. He has convened the council of nobles to elect his successor according to the old law. It is deliberating as I speak. Queen Teodora has retired to her estates of Talavera, with the two younger royal princes and the infant princess, where the Crown Prince Sisenand has joined her."

At that point of the tale, Diorlin became acutely conscious of the grey eyes' steady look into his face, so direct and scrutinising that it could hardly be considered polite anymore, and the old knight realised that all was in balance now. "You wonder why I left at a time like this? On the surface, Tolosa is at peace. Ever since the decree regarding the restoration of the knightly orders was issued, Red Lily Knights died, went mad and disappeared. To make fast the Order against the attacks and give it the missing Grandmaster, I need time. And my time is running out. The young knights with me, they are the sons of the Lily Knights who died."

Kitt spoke to Eckehart, and Diorlin wondered which points the youth was actually translating, and how.

"Their king is ill and there may be a change of dynasty soon," Kitt said to his father in the language of the north.

"Is there something to concern us?"

"The knights may be under attack."

"Don't they know?"

"They lost knights and they have powerful enemies whose arms reach far."

Eckehart considered that. "How far, that is the question. Did he say anything about the Serpent Steel yet?"

"Not yet," Kitt said, turning to Diorlin, who was watching him.

"My father wants to know about the Serpent Steel of Alkantara. So do I."

"So steel is what interests you most, is it? Forgive me, I should have known better." Diorlin tried hard to hide his disappointment. The fish had not yet taken the bait. Perhaps he had read too much into that youth, perhaps a smith was all he was, like his father. "All the smiths and workshops working the Serpent Steel are in Alkantara. There, every smith is a master of the art and the magic of the steel, for that is the first condition to be allowed setting up shop. I have always used Serpent Steel."

"May we see your sword?" Eckehart asked, bending forward.

The Swordmaster unhitched his sword and laid it into the callused expanse of the smith's hand.

Eckehart drew the slim straight blade from its sheath with something like reverence. The firelight played over the bluish steel, while Eckehart called Kitt's attention to the whorled pattern and the hardening line, faint as water. "The Serpent Steel of Alkantara is famous, with good reason." For Diorlin's benefit, he spoke Tolosan, and the swordmaster noted that about steel the smith spoke fluently, albeit with his thick accent.

"The outer layer of this steel has been folded forty times. It is said that the smiths of Alkantara can make steel consisting of thousands of layers. And yet, solid steel is sufficient for any purpose, if you can smelt the right quality of the steel and know the way to treat it. So why do it, why bother with all of this folding? Because the beauty of the Serpent Steel goes beyond the strength, and hardness of the blade. It is a kind of steel craft that draws merit from itself. It is a thought made into a blade."

Diorlin bent towards Eckehart once more, black eyes intent.

"All you say is true, Master Eckehart. And yet I have come here because my thought requires more than a master smith to forge it into steel. Great as the art of the Masters of Alkantara is, their power has limits. I need a smith without limits; I need more than a magician, even. I need the God of smithcraft himself. That is why I came to you, Smith of Betra Hyerote because I have heard that your smithcraft has no limits."

"So, have you heard that?" Eckehart muttered. "Who told you, I wonder."

"Well, I'll admit it." A humorous light sprang up in the old Swordmaster's eyes. "It was a minstrel, singing about the master greater than all the magician smiths, who lives on the remote island of Betra Hyerote, and forges the wondrous Aurora swords, each to be used in a heroic deed. Did the minstrel tell a lie, smith?"

"They have much to answer for, those minstrels. What is it you need to be made from steel, Swordmaster?"

"What I need is a sword that will nullify old age. I want you to make me a blade that fits my waning strength as well as my waxing knowledge. It must be light enough to allow me the speed and cunning of my thoughts and supple enough to keep my brittle wrists from being shattered when a blade wielded by strong young bones meets it. Say, can you make such a sword for me?"

The old swordsman caught Kitt taking a closer look at him, and with a hot rush of resentment, he knew exactly what the boy saw.

The famous swordsman was considerably older than most people noticed at first sight. Although his frame gave an impression of youthful tautness, the skin on the back of his hands and around the hot, black eyes was paper-thin and yellowish, the black hair lacklustre, and in the fine lines furrowing his face something else besides sarcasm was written -there were the scratches of bitterness and exhaustion.

The old knight's irritation abated when he realised that the grey eyes were purely registering and entirely devoid of judgement.

Kitt sensed the deep sorrow of the old swordmaster, although he did not understand it. In a sort of academic attachment, he thought that one day he too would be old. He tried to imagine it but failed. Of course, Eckehart could forge such a sword as Diorlin asked. His father could do anything with steel. The fact that Diorlin was a master in the art of wielding a blade would make the job so much easier. What Diorlin wanted to be done would need considerable craft, but it was possible.

What made the famous Isenkliff blades so hard, supple and murderously keen began as the smith descended into the dark kingdom of the Lütte Jotun in the mountain to mine ore and coal. With his own hands he mined the ore, smelted it; he then took the raw iron out of the smelting oven, and hammered the impurities out of it with patient strength, and then shaped it, then heated, and cooled it, repeatedly, all the while singing his smith songs for perfect timing. From the moment the smith dug the ore from the earth until he placed the shining weapon into the warrior's hand with a twinge of regret, his hands and eyes and mind never left the iron. This was what Eckehart had taught Kitt. He expected his father to tell Diorlin that this was all the magic there was.

"Your sword hand, Diorlin!" the smith demanded.

The Swordmaster laid his right hand, long, gaunt with knotted joints, into the blackened expanse of the smith's hand, palm up so that the calluses caused by the sword hilt were plainly visible.   The smith examined it meticulously, turning, flexing, pressing each finger, the palm, the wrist. That hurt. It was the cold of this awful clime in his bones -his old bones.

The smith turned the hand around to examine the back, the protruding knuckles. He stood up and extended his examination to shoulders, back and the left arm, while the last traces of youthful pretension left the old swordsman's face. Then the smith sat down again, and looked into the fire.

Diorlin also watched the flames, the blue and green sparks, feeling cold inside, spent and worn. Last chance, it whispered inside his head, last chance. Had there ever been a chance? And the longer the smith said nothing, the more the whispering changed. Too late. Too late already. Should have come earlier. He'll say that in a moment. That I should have come before, that now he can't do anything for me. That'll be his excuse.

The smith sat there, staring into the fire as if he was trying to read there the words suitable to let Diorlin down easily, and he felt irritation that a workman was about to insult him with pity. He curbed that feeling. After all, it wasn't the smith's fault that he had put himself into this position. It was strange really, to find such delicacy here on this island in the cold, barbarian north, in the house of a blacksmith. Diorlin thought that the smith was about his own age, and must know about the agony of a body that could not obey the mind as before, undergoing the transformation into something unknown, unwanted, the infinite sadness of fading strength. But more than that the smith did not know; he could not help himself any more than he could help the old Swordmaster. He was a blacksmith, not a magician, and certainly not the God of Smithcraft.

Grey despair hitting, his mouth and nose became pinched, the eyes became dull, and his shoulders sagged -he seemed a much older man. He felt ashamed of himself, an old man sinking in the river of time, grabbing for a straw, the straw being a song heard in the marketplace of Eliberre, of a magician smith on an island in the northern sea. What a long way to come for a brittle straw and some cheap consolation. Again, he examined his reasons, as he had done often before, whether it was mere vanity behind his wish to put off the inevitable a little bit longer. No, it wasn't that at all, but the feeling of becoming gradually useless, while young Ramiro was fighting against the grinning murderer, count Hugo, who rode through the streets of Eliberre impudently, treading more flowers into the dust after the one, the only rose. He resolved, that if he couldn't have the sword he needed, then he must have the boy.

Except for the crackling of the fire, it was very still in the room. The lady of the house sat silently up on the gallery, candlelight on her fair hair and her hands busy with needlework, appearing to Diorlin's imagination as one of those goddesses who spun the thread of men's lives. Now and again, her blue eyes were on the men by the fire, and more and more Diorlin had the fanciful impression that it was she upon who all depended.

Finally, the smith looked up to the lady, their eyes met, and she spoke. Diorlin did not understand what she said; to him, it sounded like an oracle.

"I wish this man had not come for your steel, Eckehart." Her voice was brittle, and her needle continued flashing with the rhythmic movement of her hand. "But as he did come, he must have his wish granted. The one he says, and the one he craves." With a dry click, Aslaug's scissors cut a thread.

Eckehart nodded and spoke. "You shall have the sword you want," he said in Tolosan, continuing in his own language, leaving it to Kitt to translate. "Strange that in all the time I have worked on Isenkliff, you should be the first to ask me a blade for an old warrior. The young and strong warrior can fight with any blade that comes to hand if it will hold an edge and not break in the heat of battle. It is the old fighter who can profit most from the smith's art. I can make a sword for you that will make you forget the years."

"That is better than I could hope! Much better!" Diorlin looked at Eckehart with evident relief. "I had thought it might be -hopeless."

"It is." Eckehart shook his head. "You know they will come back, the years, and have their tribute, Diorlin. In our age, arm and steel do not grow together to form a unit. They drift apart from the first day."

The old swordsman's face clouded. "I know that a little time of grace is all that I can hope for. It is all I want, all I need. I don't want it for my own sake. When the time comes to pay back capital and interest, and interest on the interest, I'll pay. As I'll pay your price, without any haggling whatsoever. They say your price is very high. Well, just name it, and I'll pay it."

"Oh yes," Eckehart said. "My price is high."

"We have brought gold and gems. You will find it a generous compensation."

"We do not work for gold but for books," Kitt said. "If we make a sword for you, we will want everything on your ship that has a letter written on it -songs and tales, philosophic, historical and medicinal texts and alchemical grimoires. Everything."

Interesting how the boy took over the conversation, and how he looked positively greedy now. "If it is verses you want, you'll have a good bag from us. I have here ten young knights, most of them in love, and therefore cherishing booklets of poetry with dried violets and love-knots between the pages. And I have brought several tomes covering the entire history of Tolosa since Alaron I., which I have attempted to bully them into reading, with lamentably little success. They'll no doubt be only too glad for you to have them."

"Yes, we want all that. And all your maps and charts, and travel accounts," he added rather hastily. "You can make a copy of your sea charts, of course, but we keep the originals."

"I see!"

Diorlin wondered who it really was driving these bargains for books? The father who could barely speak a few words in a civilised language and looked like he had never left his island? Was he the one who wanted maps? Or is it you, my boy? Diorlin thought sardonically. Want to get away, see the big world, is that it? Perfectly natural at your age. Well, you must visit Tolosa!   Aloud he said. "I believe I even saw a map of the mythic Lands Under the Sunset in our captain's cabin, so it's really a wonder he got us here."

"All the maps. Everything."

"In fact, as you said very clearly, everything with anything written on it." A smile curved the thin mouth under the black moustache. "There is a library in the School of Eliberre, of thousands of books, on all topics and spanning centuries, at your disposition, if ever you should visit us."

After that, there was an even longer silence than before.

Then Eckehart spoke again, still looking into the fire.

Instead of translating, Kitt stared at his father, huge surprise written on his face. Then he asked something, and the smith answered, which didn't seem to assuage the boy's doubts at all.

Diorlin broke into the dispute. "Just tell me what your father said."

"My father said that if you want Swordmaster, he can make your wrists and joints of steel so that they will form a unit with your blade as long as you live." He shrugged. "That's what he said. I don't understand it at all. I only translated."

Stunned, Diorlin stared at the smith, who suddenly did a strange little pantomime. He gripped his own left wrist with his right hand, then the elbow and shoulder joint, did the same with his right arm and then each leg, looking back at the startled knight from his blue eyes, which were calm and composed, and ended his performance with a series of determined nods.

Surprise, disbelief, anger, unbelieving hope, awe and scare, all these emotions passed over Diorlin's face in quick succession. He realised that this was what he really had come for, all this way to an island almost mythical. Not for a sword. A miracle. "If I want?" He laughed shakily, gazing at the old smith some more, trying to see if he was making a cruel mockery, such as a man like the magician Zinnober might do. "You do mean it."

"Of course I mean it," Eckehart said in his heavy Tolosan.

"Of course, is it?" Kitt sprang up and walked to the door.

The smith called out peremptorily, and the boy came back, looking furious.

"But how will you go about it?" Diorlin asked. "Will you pull out my bones and replace them with steel? And when you are finished with me, can I take home my own bones in a little bundle, to look at, or will you want them to wreak a spell forcing me to be your slave, or to build a homunculus?"

The boy translated, muttering something at the end.

Eckehart shrugged. "I don't want your bones, Diorlin. I don't work with bones. But once I have them out, you better guard them, guard them well, from others who do work with bones."

The smith was crazy, of course, Diorlin thought. Or a villain. It didn't matter. He couldn't go away now, always wondering to the end of his life. Aloud he said, "I believe you. I need to believe you. What choice do I really have?" He answered the question himself. "None."

"You do have a choice," Kitt said. "Take the sword my father will make for you. You will still be called a wizard of the blade several years hence."

"A few years of grace may not be enough to restore the knightly code to the fabric of Tolosa. There is no one else who can accomplish my task! Oh, you think nobody is irreplaceable? But that is not so in this case, for after me come only those I taught. I am the only one remaining, who has followed the knightly code to the ultimate consequence! All the other true knights have died. Those who still live are those who compromised, defected, resigned. What have they to teach the young?"

After his outburst Diorlin paused, but Kitt did not translate. He sat leaning back against the wall looking from one old man to the other.

"So what price do you want for this, blacksmith? Do you want my soul? Take it, blacksmith, take it."

187

Eckehart shrugged. "Souls are easy to have, Diorlin, this we both know at our age."

"What do you want, smith, quick, say, what do you want? For you do want something?"

"You say that you are the last knight, Diorlin?" Eckehart asked directly in his halting Tolosan.

"The last knight of the code – this sounds like a bad ballad. But it is true all the same, I'm the last, and it falls to me to bring back the ancient order of knights, or the Tolosan realm will be lost to greed, weakness, low-mindedness, and dark sorcery." Diorlin's black eyes burned on Eckehart with devouring fire, remembering the ballad -that the smith of Isenkliff forged swords destined to cut through the knots of destiny. He must convince Eckehart that his cause was worthy of a miracle such as the smith had proposed. And he must convince the youth, sitting in the background so quietly glowering.

Eckehart also bent forward, so that their foreheads nearly touched. "The ancient Knights Code, Diorlin. Say it again!" he demanded.

Surprised, the old swordmaster rallied quickly. With the dizzying possibility before him that he might have both, his youth back and this extraordinary boy, he endeavoured to speak the austere vow of the Red Lily knights most impressively, as at the ceremony of Sword Dedication: The knight's watchword is Purity, Poverty, Mercy.

The knight's duty is to help, save and serve.

The knight's honour is to hold his shield over the weak.

His sword battles evil wherever he finds it.

The knight returns good for ill.

He forgives the defeated enemy and never dances on his grave."

"A good code," Eckehart said slowly. "You teach my son your sword skill and your code, and I will reinforce your old bones with steel."

Before Diorlin could reply, Eckehart spoke to Kitt at length, then motioning him to translate. The old swordmaster could see a multitude of emotions warring on the boy's face.

"My father says that you shall have a sword and metal bones and metal cords for sinews for the sake of that code. He wants you to teach it to me. That is the price he demands. My father said further that it will take three months to do what you desire. The ore has to be mined and smelted, the" here he hesitated for the appropriate word, "the parts have to be formed with precision. It will take one more month to wield the steel to your flesh and bone, then for you to heal up. In the first of those three months, he wants you to teach me all that your hands and eyes and brain know of the blade -every figure, every trick. And every one of the days that you are on this island, he wants you to repeat the code of the knights to me, and teach me all the rules a Knight of the School lives by. That's what my father told me to say to you," Kitt concluded. "I'd deem it a great honour, Sir," he added.

"I dare say you would." Diorlin lifted a sardonic eyebrow. "Ask your father if he really thinks a blacksmith apprentice can learn the courtly art of the blade in three months, where noblemen take three times three years?"

If the youth was taken aback by the sudden attack, he did not show any sign of it. The old Swordmaster wondered if he would translate verbatim. Obviously, he did, for Eckehart chuckled savagely as if about a grim joke only he knew. "Do you think not, Swordmaster? Do you think not?"

Diorlin grinned back at him. Inside the old Swordmaster was singing with unholy glee. All his life, he had taught young men, learned how the young mind was working. All he ever needed was an opportunity to get his hands on a pupil to shape him into whatever he wanted.

His eyes met the smith's light blue ones, watching him, looking right inside, reading him, and almost too late the old Swordmaster remembered the legend, that this smith saw into a warrior's heart. That was nonsense, of course, but he felt compelled to say something to those eyes that was almost the truth. "So many knights have gone through my hands, Master Eckehart. I can tell a young man's promise just from the way he walks, speaks and looks at the world around him. From the very first moment that I laid eyes on your boy, I have seen that he possesses the innate courage of a born swordsman. If teaching your son for three months is your price for the fantastic things which you promise, then it is a minimal price. I'll teach him, smith. With pleasure."

The youth blushed deeply, furiously, as he translated.

"True courage is not a matter of the sword."

The men started, and looked up to Aslaug on her gallery. She continued quietly without waiting for Kitt to translate. The way she bent over her work again, when she had finished, meant final judgement without appeal.

Diorlin saw the boy swallow hard.

When Kitt translated, he spoke hesitating, groping for the right phrases. "My mother says that true courage is what remains when your sword is gone, your strength has deserted you and you are alone. When there is no way out and no end of the pain, if anything then is left of a man, this is true courage. And that no one can teach."

Diorlin inclined his head towards Aslaug, although she was not looking at anyone. "Then I hope I will find enough true courage inside myself, my lady, for I shall need great amounts of it when the master smith draws the bones from my body."

#

Leonin do Almorox et Mohorte was the first of the Red Lily Knights to step onto the pebble beach. His companions were left behind to stew on the ship for yet another dreary day. Well, they weren't missing anything. The towering black cliff, whose double peak outline he had the opportunity to contemplate from the ship's rail, for a whole long day, didn't look the least bit more inviting than from afar. The weather was just as shockingly rough on the shore. He drew his black cloak around him against the drizzle out of the lowering clouds, scrupulously leaving free his right arm and the hilt on his left, and walked up the path he had seen Diorlin take in the company of two barbarians, one old, presumably the smith, one a young giant.

The Hall, as the islanders called the smiths huge, dark dwelling place, was half built into the cliff, and came as something of a surprise. For one thing, it had glass windows, like the Dining Hall in the School in Eliberre, and was big enough to fit the whole School of Knights too; it had a sort of savage and barbarian charm, with those high, massive wooden beams. It was lit and also warmed, by strange fires that seemed to come from fissures in the living rock.

The smith Eckehart looked just like any other old workman, though probably capable enough in his profession, but on the long way here, they must have passed several dozen blacksmiths just like him.

The lady Aslaug, however, well, Leonin was not used to it that any woman, even a barbarian wench, would look through him in quite this manner. He was not vain, but he knew very well that his aspect was considerably more than merely pleasing in the eyes of women, young or old, regardless of their station. He stood just half an inch under six feet, with broad shoulders, slim hips and an easy carriage. It was mainly his face, framed by a shock of curly dark hair with russet lights in them, the dark eyes with long lashes and the quite indescribable shape of his mouth that usually evoked an involuntary gasp from the coldest woman. Leonin possessed a perfect mirror and understood what it told him.

But the lady Aslaug seemed to see right inside him and find nothing much for her to like or dislike. Before the gaze of her blue eyes, Leonin himself was not sure any more that anything much worthwhile was in there. Uncomfortable, so he rather avoided thinking about the lady, even though she was slim in outline and golden-haired. He couldn't guess her age, but she must be somewhat older than appeared if she had an almost grown-up son.

The son of the house, Kitt was his name, if you please -a boy fourteen years old, he already stood three inches over six feet, and seeing the way he carried that unconscionable length, Leonin had realised at once that here was bad trouble indeed.

Just now this boy was facing the swordmaster with a sword at least double as heavy as anything any Tolosan warrior had ever hefted in the long war-like history of that land. Holding it damn casually too. Here was one born to the sword, Leonin thought.

"Ever used a sword?" The Swordmaster inquired with deceptive mildness.

"Yes." The youth nodded. "I cross blade with every warrior who wants a weapon or armour made by my father. To assess weakness and strength." He grinned, a broad, guileless grin.

191

Leonin felt sorry for him.

"Never been bested?"

The youth shook his head.

"So," the swordmaster said. "So. Well, well, well. Let's see. On your guard then."

The old fox. Inviting boastfulness, getting young knights talking too much, and then making them wish they hadn't.

Diorlin raised his sword.

So, did the boy, in a single, fluent movement.

The blades flickered faster than the eye could follow, filling the summer air with a silvery haze, humming like a swarm of hornets, clattering like hail.

The fencers stopped, blades hovering, resembling a pair of dancers, poised and aware of nothing but the song of steel they both heard in their heads.

The tips of their swords connected again. Leonin's breath caught.

Finally, Diorlin stepped back and lowered his blade; the black eyes rested on Kitt, a sudden wistful shadow crossing the thin, bony features which was gone as fast as it had appeared, leaving the usual sardonic smoothness.

He knew it too, Leonin thought. Of course, he did. The guile of an old warrior was what had preserved him from being defeated, ignominiously, on the first day by a blacksmith apprentice. Not only was this youngster far faster than the famous Swordmaster Diorlin, the wizard of the blade, but he also had some fearfully accurate judgement in the place where other people kept their nerves.

Aloud Leonin said. "You really intend to teach that one, Swordmaster? You can't be serious."

Both fighters glared at him. The young knight smiled sweetly. "Well, he's rather raw, but do we really want to change that? He'll only grow into a damned nuisance."

"I won't mind quite as much as you may one day," the Swordmaster grinned. He turned to Kitt again. "You have a lot to learn, boy. You rely on your strength and speed too much. Those are certainly impressive -now. But it is strength and speed that will be the first to desert you and where will you be then? It's all mere

192

instinct with you. Precise knowledge of what exactly it is that you are doing will last you longer. You have talent, but talent is not the same as skill. Not by a very long chalk. Talent turns into skill only after hard, dedicated work, and for this, there are no shortcuts."

The boy nodded quietly. Leonin gave him full marks for that.

"You know hardly any fencing figures, and the ones you do know I don't think much of," Diorlin continued remorselessly. "They're ugly. No style. In fact, you did nothing right. And yet," he suddenly smiled, "you made no mistake either. I admit that I could not take you."

Leonin laughed quietly. Yes, he had seen the Swordmaster make a very good attempt.

"But I could not take you either," the youth said, looking chagrined.

"Ah, no, of course, you couldn't. I can teach you how to try. In three months. But it will take you much longer than that to learn properly. And still much longer for you to become a knight. If ever." Diorlin smiled his tight little smile so feared by his students.

"Then you will teach me?" the boy asked with a hopefulness Leonin thought touching.

"But yes, I'll teach you. Didn't you hear what your father promised me? For that, I'd teach you if you were an armless, legless idiot." Diorlin looked up at the big youth topping his own six feet by three inches. "Fortunately, it's not quite as bad as that. You are neither armless nor legless. You are only a callow, crude barbarian boy without skill or style -just a lot of unnecessary violence. But you may yet learn something if you try hard. Very hard. Beginning now. On your guard!" he snapped, and as the last word was out the blades crossed again.

What did Kitt's father promise? Leonin was doing some furious thinking.

Even without translation, Eckehart had understood what the Swordmaster had said.

The smith contemplated his son. He knew precisely what the Swordmaster saw in the boy. There had been other teachers, seduced by the reward of easy progress in an extraordinarily talented pupil; they had taught Kitt all they knew of the venerable art of killing. But more than he was taught, he seemed to learn by instinct. Already he was a master of all the weapons commonly used, and a good number that were not so common. Kitt's favourite weapon was the sword; this was the one weapon he thought about. And each time when he had learned more about blades and steel, Eckehart had forged a new sword for him. The last one, the one Kitt used now, he had forged all for himself. The young warrior and the steel were growing harder together; the time had come when the steel needed tempering. Could Diorlin administer that tempering? He would provide a warrior code. He even might make it stick if he could stand up to Kitt with the sword. It was already too long that Kitt had found anyone stronger than himself, anyone physically able to set him limitations. Anyone human in any case. Should he warn Diorlin? Or should he trust that the swordmaster realised in time? He was one of the masters, one of those who were called a wizard for their surpassing sword skill, though he was not magical by birth and nature.

Evening found Kitt with a feeling of exhaustion, not so much from the sword practice, as from the critique Swordmaster Diorlin had kept heaping on him all day, culminating in a final irritable outburst. "Three months, indeed! Three years is more like it! If it can be done at all." The old swordsman seemed a blade himself, slim and long and keen, as he regarded his pupil with sardonic disdain. "Go away," he said, "I have quite enough of you for one day."

A feeling which Kitt reciprocated heartily, but he merely saluted, sheathed his blade and turned upon his heel, followed by the old Swordmaster's snort.

Diorlin's style of openings, faints and parades had impressed him; although highly formalised, each figure could lead into almost any other, with infinite possibilities of combination.

Kitt had already decided that he wanted to learn Diorlin's patterns. He only didn't want to see the Swordmaster again until the next day, at the earliest, that was all.

Kitt was hungry, but he did not feel like going into the hall and submit to the double scrutiny of the Swordmaster and his mother. Those two did not seem to agree on anything in this world, except finding fault with Kitt, usually for totally opposite reasons, which made it all very uncomfortable.

The arrival of the smoothly elegant, dark-eyed knight with the endless name from the ship, with his glossy curls, perpetually mocking smile, clipped, supercilious speech and perfect clothes only added to the aggravation.

Seeing the light in the smithy, Kitt headed there.

His father's offer to Diorlin had given him the greatest jolt of all. It so much surpassed the craft of any blacksmith, showing his father in a new, alien light.

He remembered a fever dream of some years before. Then he had dreamed of Eckehart forging armour for the Isprinsessans, from ice and quicksilver he had forged it. Suppose that had not been a dream after all.

Kitt resolved that he would help his father with the work on the steel bones, learn all about it, preferably starting tonight.

As he neared the smithy, he heard voices: Eckehart's quiet, deep rumble and another muttering as pebbles in a stream.

Kitt opened the door without noise, moving in the absolute silence that in the Dark Wood Murkowydir meant the difference between life and death, and had become a habit with him.

He saw the blocky grey shape of Gullo sitting on the coal box. The Jarnmantsje was alternatively biting into a sausage he held in the left and a piece of bread in the right hand with his irregular tusk-like teeth, in-between objecting with his mouth full to something Eckehart said.

Ever since Kitt knew Gullo, the Jarnmantsje had been eating or demanding something to eat.

Fully occupied with eating and quarrelling, Gullo did not notice Kitt although he faced the door directly.

The white-haired smith sat on the bench by the right wall, bright blue eyes intent on the Jarnmantsje, also unaware of his son standing in the door. "I will give the swordmaster Diorlin what he asks," Eckehart said. "The lady Aslaug wants it."

"A great lady, Aslaug is. What the lady wants must be done. Yes, it must. Oh, yes." Gullo spoke through a piece of sausage, nodding his massive, grey head. "A good cook, Aslaug is," he added the usual afterthought.

"Ah! You'll bring me the Royal Ore then," Eckehart said, watching the Jarnmantsje closely.

"Can't." The Jarnmantsje's shaggy grey head rolled from side to side in determined denial.

"Can't?" Eckehart said with exaggerated surprise, reaching for the food basket and setting it on the other side of the forge, out of Gullo's reach.

The Jarnmantsje fidgeted, yellow eyes following the basket with as much anxiety as a cat her kitten. "Is forbidden. Erzkuning won't allow it. No, he won't. Never did, ever, never, for nobody. You know Erzkuning, smith, you know him long."

Eckehart nodded.

Kitt had never seen Erzkuning, nor the mining tunnels, and had never thought of them much, although he did distantly believe in their existence, the same as in he believed in the presence of Erzkuning, Lord over the underground kingdom, ruling from Erzturm, the gaunt rock in the sea three miles east of Isenkliff, who did no favours to anyone, except sometimes to the Smith of Isenkliff. But even Eckehart never knew which those times were. From his castle, the subterraneous tunnels led to all the islands in the Graumeer.

"If you want the Royal Ore, Smith of Isenkliff, you have to mine it yourself. Yes, mine it yourself."

"Then you will tell me where and how."

Gullo shifted uneasily, eyes on the basket. "Long way down, Eckehart, yes a very long way, deep, deep down in the mountain. Dangerous. Very dangerous. Even for you Eckehart, even for such as you. Send the Black One away, yes send him away. Does he want to live forever? He can't. No."

"The lady Aslaug said that it is necessary," Eckehart reminded. "That means it has to be done without fail."

Gullo snuffled unhappily, taking a bite left and right, mournfully contemplating the diminishing length of bread and sausage. "Let the Black One go and mine the ore himself then. Yes, he shall go himself and mine. Do some hard work for once, do him good." Gullo nodded, yellow eyes sparkling with cunning.

Eckehart shook his head and sighed. "That is not possible Gullo, as you very well know. Besides, I already promised. And so, I will have to go and mine the Royal Ore, and you will tell me where and how, or there will be no more sausage. Never, ever, no more."

"I'll go," Kitt said from the door. "I'll mine the ore, father."

Eckehart jumped. "Kitt! Do you want to startle your old father to death? Sneaking in here like a murdering Woodstalker. Shame on you!"

Grinning unabashed, Kitt reached for the food basket standing on the forge, cut himself a piece of bread and sausage, sat down on the bench beside his father, and began eating, first slowly, abstractedly, then eagerly.

Gullo stopped his own chewing to bend an outraged glare upon Kitt.

The youth swallowed quickly. "I've wondered all day. It needs incorruptible steel to do what Diorlin wants, doesn't it, father? But you haven't solved that secret yet. So what are you going to do?"

"Solved it, son, long ago."

"You have? Long ago?" Kitt stared at his father in surprise. "Not so long ago you said that the secret of the incorruptible steel still eluded you?"

"One way of doing it. There exist ores that will yield that steel, and I know how to work those ores. Only, right now, I can't lay my hands on a sufficient supply. And ores are uncertain; there are so many other things in it beside the principle that a smith wants. Now, if I could isolate the principle of each ore and mix them with steel in exactly the right quantities, I should be able to foretell precisely what properties my steel will have. That was what I was talking about."

Kitt looked at Eckehart curiously. Sometimes his father spoke as if he had seen centuries, and what he said then did not always tally with what he had said at other times. "I understood that much. It's just that you never mentioned that Royal Ore."

"Because it is rare, hard to find, dangerous to mine, and tricky to work. I was looking for another way to do it, but as I haven't found it yet, I need the Royal Ore for Diorlin."

"You'll have to tell me about the Royal Ore now because I'll go down into the mountain and mine it," Kitt said, his mouth set firmly. "Bad enough that I don't have the knowledge to pay the price Diorlin wants for teaching me. You do. But I will do all the hard work it involves."

"And I won't be able to keep you out of Erzkuning's Kingdom any more than I've been able to keep you from going to the Dark Wood Murkowydir, is that right?"

"That's right, father."

Eckehart sighed. "Diorlin can teach you something then?"

"Oh, yes." Kitt nodded enthusiastically. "He has a style that is all figures and forms. They make a lot of sense, the higher the speed and force of the battle, the more so."

"And I thought that you knew all there was to know about the blade already."

Kitt winced. "I did think I knew. Until today. Diorlin says that I have no style at all, no skill. And as I could not best him, I suppose he proved his point."

Eckehart chuckled. "So you couldn't get the better of the Swordmaster Diorlin? But he couldn't beat you either, could he?"

"No, he couldn't." Kitt cheered up a little. "It was an impasse."

"Hah!" Eckehart shook with silent laughter. "Yes, I thought so."

Gullo leaned over the forge, reached for the basket and set it on his lap, laying stubby arms over it protectively.

"Well, Gullo?" Eckehart demanded.

"Deep, deep in the mountain," Gullo said and reached into the basket, withdrew another sausage and bread, and began eating hastily, speaking between bites. "Where the mountain is deepest, the red crystals grow, yes grow thickly, but it is not red crystals you want, no, not this time. Green crystals is what you want. The green gems grow where no man can, no man dare go. No man must go. So, you can't have green crystals."

"Is there wood and water down there, Gullo?"

"Is. Take tinder," Gullo muttered with a full mouth. "Take good pickaxe. The ore is hard, yes, hard as steel. Bring goats."

"Goats?" Kitt chuckled. "Always thinking of your belly, you are, Gullo. How many do you want?"

"Goats to feed hellhound," Gullo retorted testily and grappled inside the basket, up-bent and shook it, but as it yielded no more bread or sausage, the Jarnmantsje let it drop to the floor with every sign of disgust and prepared to climb down from his seat.

"Not so fast, Gullo. You've eaten, and now you'll tell Kitt about the hellhound!" Eckehart demanded.

The Jarnmantsje sniffed. "Wasn't much to eat, no. Kitt ate most." He shot the boy a baleful look, another at the smith.

"You see Kitt, Erzkuning has set three hellhounds as guards over the mine tunnels. Their names are Dunkelschrecken, Hässlichertod and Leichengift. Three Jarnmantsjes are their keepers, their names are Neidzwerg, Hintertück and Axtmörder. Dear friends of Gullo's. He's going to tell you all about them."

"You owe a sausage, the one Kitt ate. Was Gullo's sausage, not Kitt's. He ate it."

"Yes, yes, you shall have that damned sausage. After you tell Kitt everything about the hellhounds, Gullo, or there will be no more sausage coming!"

"I'm telling, I'm telling! I tell now. You give the sausage later. Mustn't forget."

"Did we ever have a chance? Now, about the three hellhounds?"

"One. Only one hellhound left now. Once there were three hellhounds. The Undead Emperor sent his alchemist to steal the secret of the incorruptible steel. The alchemist poisoned Dunkelschrecken. Neidzwerg tore the alchemist's arms off and ate them, Neidzwerg tore his legs off and ate them, and last, Neidzwerg ate the head. Said the alchemist tasted sour. Must have been greed that soured his flesh. Yes, greed. Hässlichertod was slain by the Wizard of Thule."

"Hintertück ate the wizard of Thule bit by bit, and last he ate the magic staff, and didn't like it." Kitt grinned.

The Jarnmantsje favoured Kitt with another dirty look.

"Precocious, this boy is," he muttered. "Yes, precocious. Know the tale of the precocious brat, Kitt? He came to a sticky end. Very sticky. Yes. Not pretty."

"So the last hellhound left is Leichengift -poor lonely doggie. Worried that I'll twist his tail, are you? Is that why you never told me about the Royal Ore?"

"Ha!" Gullo clambered down from the coal box. "Ha!" He repeated and shuffled off through the back door that led into the mountain. "Ha!" they heard it echoing hollowly from the tunnel.

The back door closed with a bang, sounding like a coffin lid.

Kitt looked rueful. "I annoyed him. He's easily annoyed, Gullo is."

Eckehart frowned. "Gullo was in a strange mood tonight. So are you, son. What's got into you, I wonder? That was quite the wrong time to tease Gullo. Now he may play you a trick, and Jarnmantsje's tricks are no laughing matter, least of all deep inside the mountain."

"I'm not doing much right today. Diorlin told me that I lacked both skill and manners. Looks like he's right."

"Don't mind Diorlin now. Think about mining the Royal Ore. And there we're off to a bad start. I've known the Lütte Jotun, the Jarnmantsjes that is, a long time. What you must understand about them, my son, is that they live almost forever, and so the duration of a short human life holds very little significance to them. Gullo has seen many smiths here on Isenkliff, and he expects to see many more. Whether you die tomorrow, or in a hundred years, Gullo is going to preserve you a fond memory for all the goats and eggs you've given him. Understand?"

"A good hunter Kitt was. Generous. Yes. But precocious. Came to a sticky end. Not pretty. No. Mended his manners for him that did."

Eckehart nodded. "You understand. So if you come down to the Royal Ore vein, and it turns out there is no wood or water . . . I don't expect a lie this base, but you never know . . . however it may happen that you will want something stronger to help you break the rockface or . . . any other obstacle you may unexpectedly encounter down there." Eckehart unlocked a small massive iron chest from which he drew a wooden container, which he opened; it contained black powder, a mixture of saltpetre, sulphur and coal -firedust.

Kitt had seen what firedust could do and did not much relish the idea of invoking its uncertain power deep inside the mountain.

"I needn't remind you to use this only in an emergency." Eckehart rubbed his chin unhappily. "Jarnmantsjes don't like the use of firedust in their mountain. They don't like it at all. As for Erzkuning, I hate thinking what he'll do if he ever suspects the presence of a grain of the stuff in his domain. But when there is no other choice, don't hesitate using it! Blast your way free, if you must!"

"Right. And when I come back, I shall want answers, father."

The next morning a launch from the ship brought the remaining nine young knights of the School.

They walked along the rock jetty in a single file, all dark-haired, dark-eyed, slim, with serious, passionate faces, the red lily on the back of their long, wide, black cloaks, each armed with a sword with golden, bejewelled hilts. In the wake of the knights, eleven valets came carrying baggage, and then the ship's crew disembarked, stocky Tolonian seamen in striped cotton blouses and wide trousers.

Leonin awaited them on the shore with orders from Diorlin regarding deportment.

"Is this the end of the world? What does the Swordmaster want to come to this forsaken place for anyway?" a tall, thin knight with a small, carefully trimmed goatee inquired in a petulant voice.

"You heard the Swordmaster, he wants a sword made. This is the fabled smithy where the famous Aurora Blades come from. The cream of the fighters, which you naturally wouldn't know anything about, consider Aurora Blades as a mark of excellence, and only the cream of the fighters can afford them. I might add that a second-hand Aurora is easily worth anything between a thousand and three thousand pieces of gold."

"You sound like a damned second-hand salesman, Leonin!" another knight exclaimed; he was thin as a reed and had a narrow face with the dark eyes standing very close together. "Three thousand for a used? That buys a villa in Lutetia right beside the royal palace. How much is a new one then?"

"Couldn't tell you that, as you can't buy them new in a shop. You can't just come here wanting one either. You see, this smith, he doesn't sell his blades like an ordinary tinkerer from Alkantara. First, he sizes you up, then turns you inside out, then decides whether to make a sword for you or not. If he does decide that you are worthy of his steel, then you'll get a blade that has no equal, you'll pay the earth for it, and anyone who wants it has to prise it from your dying hand. As only the best get them anyway, even second-hand ones are rare in the market."

"If you say so, Leonin. And we must address this smith as a lord? Oh well." The thin knight shrugged. "Suppose this is another of the Swordmaster's famous lessons?"

"I haven't paid for my last two mail tunics, but I wouldn't dream of calling my armourer a lord any more than my dressmaker," a tall knight with saturnine features and long straight hair remarked. "Just one name, like a peasant, so how can we be expected to call him a lord?"

"If master Diorlin wanted you to call this smith an emperor, you would do just that, Sintilian."

"Emperor! Well, I suppose I would," the saturnine knight drawled. "But lord what? Lord Dirtyhands do Charcoal et Smoke?"

"Lord Eckehart, Smith of Isenkliff," Leonin said.

"Really like a King's name?"

"And right smartly."

"What's Isenkliff?"

"Betra Hyerote, the Iron Rock, the very island you're planting your flat feet upon right now. Isenkliff is the name the natives of these uncouth lands call it, in their own clumsy language, which I suppose they have a right to do."

"Betra Hyerote at the End of the World? It exists? Where's the giant? No giant, no Betra Hyerote, and I won't give you a discount on that."

Leonin laughed. "Just you wait."

When they had come halfway to the house, Leonin had the knights stop to erect the white linen pavilion which bore the scarlet lily of the School of Knights on each of the six sides.

"Can't we build that tent a bit farther into that valley? Nice high

202

rock walls for shelter from this beastly sea wind," another knight objected to Leonin's irritation.

"No, we can't go any too near the hall, which is just up there, as Diorlin said explicitly that we're not to incommode the lord Eckehart and his lady Aslaug by sight or sound."

"We all share the master's passion for good steel, but to leave Eliberre in these times, with Hugo running wild, and nobody knowing what the king plans? Or who is rightfully the king, for that matter?" the thin knight complained.

"You go and ask the old volcano yourself, Erevin."

"Hasn't he told you anything, Leonin?" the thin knight insisted.

"Just that he wants an Aurora blade." Leonin shrugged carelessly. "What does it matter? Where master Diorlin tells us to go, we go and be it to the end of the world."

"Well, this is it," the saturnine knight called Sintilian said.

"And what the hell is that? See it up there, quickly!" One of the knights stared at the slope above them, where he had caught sight of a tall, leather-clad figure, carrying bow and spear. Although he was coming towards them, he did not acknowledge anyone. Leonin was sure that he saw them, counted and analysed. Only a born knight could convey this level of indifference, the beautiful knight had always fondly imagined. "You mean, who the hell is that! Why can't you say what you mean? Grammar, sir knight, grammar! That - is an apprentice blacksmith. His name is Kitt; he is the son of the house."

"Kitt? What a name! For a dog or a slave rather than a man."

"Will you look at the size of that brute!" a slim, rather short knight exclaimed.

"Six foot three, fourteen years old and still growing. Living proof that life is unjust, gentlemen!"

"Long as we don't have to call that big lug lord also," the knight with the goatee said.

"The presence of a giant on this island is conclusive proof that we have indeed reached the end of the world," a slender green-eyed knight with a mischievous face remarked. "Once in a tavern I heard some drunk northern mercenaries singing gloomy songs of the end of the world, where the giants live, and they should know."

"I say, does anyone know some language in which to hail this barbarian giant to lend a hand with the tent?" Sintilian inquired. "Look at us struggling with it in this infernal western gale."

"Barbarians have no proper language, which is why they're called ba-ba-ba-barbarians. Try sign language," the green-eyed knight said wisely.

"That one can serve as the tent pole," the short knight suggested.

"And you can serve as a peg, Wallia," Leonin snapped. "Lend a hand, instead of standing around with your arms crossed."

"There he goes," Sintilian observed. "Excellent timing. How did he know which exact moment to make himself scarce?"

Ten young knights looked after the tall figure striding away on the footpath leading up to the cliff.

"It's an instinct all servants and workmen possess," Gundemar, the youngest knight, gave his opinion. "Melt away the precise moment when they're needed."

"We'll call him Sir yet. You'll see."

"What is that blithering nonsense you spout, Leonin?" the knight with the goatee laughed.

"Have you got eyes in your head or dull coins out of circulation? Will you watch him move, the animal! That is a fighting man, a damn fine one, and you better be very polite to him, or it'll hurt you."

"What, did Diorlin say that?"

"No, but I do."

"Oh you, Leonin, you always try to assume authority, but you have it not. You are not even the oldest. Sigerian is."

"Senior Pupil does mean anything to you?"

"Just that you are with Diorlin longest."

"Sir knight apprentice blacksmith," the knight with the goatee laughed.

Leonin spun round to him.

"Ten gold pieces on it, Viterin," he offered.

"You haven't got ten of anything to your name. Isn't that why you came on this end-of-the-world-mission, to escape your creditors? All right, all right." Viterin stepped back before the dark blaze of Leonin's eyes. "Ten gold pieces. Just as you like. When you lose, I'll take your sword in payment, and you can fence with a wooden stick, see if I care."

"You're all positively scintillating with wit today, you make my head ache. Well, you can't say I didn't warn you. Now come along to the hall, and step as if you were in the court of Eliberre."

After entering the hall Leonin greeted Eckehart formally, bowing deeply as if he had not seen him just this morning, and as if the smith were wearing a state robe, not an extremely stained linen smock. The young knights followed his example obediently, valiantly suppressing the surprise written on more than one face.

"Mylord, allow me to present to you these Red Lily Knights. Sigerian do Lallin et Arosa, Wallia do Galera et Orce, Erevin do Alkotor et Belver, Amaris do Frades et Osuna, Viterin do Grullos et Luque, Sintilian do Caspe et Fraga, Tulga do Arosa et Manresa, Terence do Rasqera et Sousel, and our youngest, Gundemar do Esmoric et Ilaskas."

The smith merely nodded at each name. The look of the light-blue eyes made the young men uncomfortable.

"Weighed, measured and found wanting," Sigerian murmured. "For the second time."

#

Kitt adjusted the load on his back -a pickaxe, a leather-bag for the ore, ropes, a bundle of torches, in another sack the two goat carcasses which he had hunted that very day.

Evening was falling; the blazing ball of the sun stood low above the horizon. Where Kitt was about to go, the lack of light didn't matter.

His father handed him a lit torch and a heavy pickaxe of a peculiar shape, with a double spur. "Listen to the mountain, to the air in the tunnels, to the water. Don't trust anyone you meet. I haven't seen Erzkuning for a long time. He never was a comfortable potentate to deal with . . . doesn't hesitate to bring down the mountain on anyone who irritates him. And he's very irritable. Should you happen to meet a big bad-tempered man with a black beard and thick black brows down there, throw this pickaxe between his eyes as quick and hard as you can. He knows my pickaxe."

Kitt passed through the doorway opening by the forge, and entered the rock-hewn chamber behind it, dimly lit by hissing flames from fissures in the walls, that were lighting shelves cut into the rock, which contained iron bars -tons of iron and steel; big boxes on the floor contained ores.

From there, he went through another doorway into another chamber that was lit in the same way as the store; there stood a colossal stone anvil, and above it, silently loomed a great beam with a hammerhead, and in the back, barely visible, was the outline of a great wheel.

This was as far in the mountain as Kitt had ever been allowed to go- but he knew what lay ahead, having looked against his father's prohibition. The youth passed through another passage and into a tunnel, following it deep into the heart of the mountain, until he came to a high cave filled with firelight and the sound of hammers. Such was the smoke and hissing and clattering that at first, it seemed to him that there were hundreds of Jarnmantsjes smelting, forging, welding and pouring liquid metal, but in truth, there were only twelve.

In the centre of the cave stood a big iron anvil, with a half-finished sword on it, and the tools lying about as if the smith working here had just stepped out for a moment. Kitt had never seen who it was who worked on this anvil, the four or five times he had ever entered this cave against his father's wishes, buying the Jarnmantsjes' discretion with goat meat. Even so, they had never told him that there was a way deeper into the earth.

The Jarnmantsje nearest to the entrance was Gullo, who hardly looked up from the sword hilt he was working on, polishing a pair of fighting gryphons, one golden, one silver, inlaid into the iron. "Go down. Always down. Down, down. Or go back. Yes, better, go back. Better for you," Gullo rumbled.

"I'll go down," Kitt said.

Gullo jerked his blocky grey head into the direction of a tunnel entrance. That was all the help he was going to give. The Jarnmantsje was still cross with the precocious boy who had eaten a sausage.

From then onwards, Kitt entered unknown territory. He went down into the tunnel hewn from the rock by the Jarnmantsjes long ago, and each time when the tunnel forked, he chose the way that led down, down into the mountain. The air became closer and hotter, and the torch burned lower, the yellow flame changing to a dusky red. The air he was breathing felt curiously unsatisfactory, empty.

Kitt lost his sense of time, wondering if he was still on Isenkliff, or if he was already walking beneath the sea. He came into a corridor, where the cave floor was strewn with human bones so thickly, that he was forced to tread on them; they crunched and rustled under his feet.

Some of the bones were old, partly petrified, and some skulls had extraordinarily broad brows and strong jaws; there were arm and leg bones with sharp spikes, and something that vaguely resembled the skull of a great serpent, but with the eyes sitting higher on the head and closer together. All the bones showed signs of corrosion as if an acid had dripped on them.

Suddenly, a reek of stale corruption welled through the tunnel, like the smoke rising from the embalmed corpse of a king, who was being burned by his successor so that his soul might be lost forever. Quickly, Kitt strove not to be distracted by this weird association of thought. He heard a scraping and wheezing noise approaching.

A long toothy snout appeared around a bend in the tunnel, followed by a barrel-like body that was encased in sharp black and purple scales from which a yellow phosphorous liquid dripped. That yellow liquid was poisonous, as Kitt knew instinctively just by looking at the sickly luminescence of the nauseous slime. Red spines protruded from the slick back, looking as if smeared with clotting blood, and the thing had straight, black claws, and long, thin, curved fangs, white as frog's bones. The hellhound did not resemble a dog in the least.

Leaving a glistening trail of slime, Leichengift approached the youth with abrupt, crablike movements, the claws scraping on the cave floor. The long snout opened wide, and a wheezing sound came from it as if the creature was short of breath. Its eyes were milky white. Against appearances the hellhound Leichengift was not blind,

207

not out of breath -the cumbersome gait, though ungainly, was speedy and blocked the passage effectively as it swayed from side to side.

Kitt stuffed the first goat's carcass into the gaping maw, which closed on it with cracking of bones. As he used the moment to slip by, the sharp scales rose with a snap, bristling like a hedgehog's. Still holding one hind leg of the goat, Kitt tugged forcefully, dragging the snout around for a surprise moment and causing the barrel-like body to slew a little, so that the poisoned scales missed him by a fraction.

A speckle of the poison had fallen on the sleeve of Kitt's leather tunic, leaving a smoking stain. Behind him, the sound of cracking of bones and rupturing meat continued, and Kitt wondered if the hellhound would pursue, once it had finished the goat's carcass. Maybe it wouldn't, it would perhaps forget? That was another thing he ought to have asked Gullo, instead of wisecracking, he thought, straining to hear the scraping of claws, the wheezing sound.

The hellhound was not following into the next tunnel, which descended steeply, and was so low that Kitt had to bend his neck. The walls closed in brushing his shoulders, and he had to drag the equipment behind.

At the next fork in the tunnel, he hesitated at first to squeeze into yet another black opening but reminded himself that a Jarnmantsje could go upright here. As the tunnel was winding down endlessly, becoming lower and narrower, Kitt had to go down on hands and knees. The torch was only a glowing ember now as if squeezed by the weight of the whole mountain, the same weight that pressed together Kitt's chest, descending slowly, burying him alive. Sweat began running over his face, and his heart began to flutter like a bird caught in a black fist.

Panic if you like. But it won't help you. Fear has never helped a man.

A cold, detached voice was speaking somewhere, the same voice he heard in moments of great danger.

Suddenly, a little yellow flame leapt up from the torch, kindled by a draft of dank air that came from somewhere, and Kitt emerged into a cave where he could stand upright. He couldn't see how big that cave was as the black walls were swallowing the torchlight.

Somewhere, water was murmuring. White points glimmered like the eyes of small, vicious creatures.

Kitt knew that red crystals would shine white in the crimson torchlight. Iron gems! Their presence announced the iron ore of the best quality, and here the walls were crusted with them.

But were there green gems too? Or would he have to go still deeper, on knees and belly into the narrow tunnels opening from this cave? From a little bag, Kitt took a small portion of the fire dust, and dropped them on the glowing torch. Golden star-shaped sparks sprang up like a meteor shower, bringing the gems in the cave to blazing red life, shining into the last recesses. In one of the niches, crystals gleamed green.

The golden meteor light showed a pile of dry wood and glittered on the water running into a basin from a crack in the tunnel wall. As it faded, the cave sank back into the red darkness.

Kitt was relieved that Gullo had spoken the truth about the wood and the water, and that he would not need to let loose the power of the firedust, which would eat up the thin air and awake the masses of stone above with a bang and roar, goading them to come down upon the intruder, or worse, just block the tunnel and trap him down here like a rat.

Kitt thought of the hellhound, still feeling the vile aroma clinging to his nose and the back of his mouth. Again, he strained his ears for the shuffling and wheezing of the creature but heard only the running water and the hissing of steam from a crack somewhere.

Kitt raised the pickaxe which seemed to weigh as much as the whole mountain, and hacked against the rock wall breaking out pieces of ore and crystal. Each movement made the sweat break out anew, and his chest heaved for air.

When the wall yielded no more ore to the pickaxe, he piled dry wood into the newly formed niche, and lighted the wood with the torch. The flames of the fire were dusky red, and burned low for lack of air, giving only a little more light than the torch. The air became still closer, and emptier, the more wood Kitt put onto the fire. His father had warned him about the invisible death that was now beginning to fill the cave from bottom to top. He reckoned that some of the gas would sink into the tunnel that led further down, but not being able to see made this a difficult time to hold out.

He filled the leather sack with water from the basin, and as soon as he dared, he flung the water against the wall.

White steam billowed out, and among the hissing noise, Kitt heard a faint cracking sound. When he took the pickaxe to the wall again, walnut-sized pieces of ore rained down.

Kitt risked repeating the process once more. Then he picked up the ore from the floor holding his breath, until the leather sack was filled. The green crystals were easy to mine, and he put them on top of the ore. Now he had all that he wanted and was ready to go back the way he had come.

Kitt toyed with the thought of leaving behind the pickaxe. It could have little further use, as he wasn't allowed to kill the hellhound, and his hands were full with about two hundred pounds of ore, the second goat's carcass and the torches. Of course, if there should be a rock-fall or Erzkuning should appear . . . He thought with detachment that wanting to leave behind his father's tool just showed that his strength was impaired.

Retracing his steps, the closeness and lack of air did not affect him as badly as it had on the way down into the unknown, although he had to drag his own body weight in ore behind him.

When he stepped into the wider tunnel and was able to go upright again, Kitt thought that, so far, there had been little difficulty about his task. All he had to do was to keep his nerves.

Just as he thought that, a rock began moving, arms and legs appeared and bright eyes. Another and another stone came to live - Jarnmantsjes! He had never known that there were so many Lütte Jotun in the mountain. They blocked Kitt's way across the width of the tunnel, as a slow avalanche of large, grey animate boulders.

"I smell, smell, smell, food, food, food!" the voices grated and rumbled.

"Goat!"

"Meat!"

"Mine!"

The Jarnmantsjes advanced on Kitt in a shuffling, growling,

creaking line, with gnashing tusks and rolling eyes. So deep in the mountain, there was nothing for it, but to surrender the goat, leaving Kitt without meat to stuff the hellhound's maw with on the way back. Now he was glad that he still had the pickaxe, just in case that nothing better occurred to him yet.

The Jarnmantsjes drew around the carcass; those behind them mounted their shoulders and then toppled inside the ring. Kitt sidled past the heaving, snarling mound, wary of their slow, robust greed. He had always known the Jarnmantsjes only in the line of mining and metalworking, had seen them as beings much like himself beneath their grey, stony appearance, who inhabited a similar world as he did, just smaller, narrower and darker. He had given them a lot of goat meat in exchange for ore and coal but had never seen them devour it raw, and he had never known that there were so many of them underground.

It's a mistake to assume familiarity. Take nothing for granted. Never expect allies.

Get away fast; so that you may learn from the mistakes you survived, Kitt completed the thought, picking his way by the tunnel wall until the Jarnmantsjes snuffling and rumbling faded behind.

An idea came to him, and he paused a moment, to stuff the ore bag into the now empty sack that had held the goats' carcasses and smelt of the animals and raw meat. Just as he finished his preparation, he heard another sound; it was the sound he had strained his ears for - long claws scraping on the ground, sharp scales gauging the tunnel walls.

A sickly glimmer appeared in the darkness before him. Suddenly there was that smell again, coming at Kitt in waves, and seeming worse than it had the first time. The hellhound approached, its scaly head wagging from side to side. The milky white eyes looked at Kitt with primitive cunning.

Leichengift stopped, its jaws opening wide to display the needle-sharp, dripping teeth; it raised all its scales at once, which clicked on the walls, blocking the tunnel with poisoned sharp edges.

From behind Kitt heard a shuffling. Looking over his shoulder, he saw a rough, blocky, grey shape shambling nearer, recognising the general form of a Jarnmantsje, but such as he had never seen on the surface. It held an axe in both hands with a broad, heavy, grey iron blade, the flaring edge glittering -Axtmörder, coming to the aid of his pet.

Holding up the full ore sack before him, Kitt ran towards Leichengift, who opened his maw even wider. Kitt stuffed the bag into it, and then, as he felt the teeth locking into the leather, he pulled back as forcefully as he could. The milky white eyes blinked for a moment in surprise, as the hellhound was dragged over the floor. Then it stemmed in its legs, and with the steel muscles of its thick neck, it pulled back, just like a dog not wanting to let go a piece of meat, at the same time lowering its scales. Kitt used the drag to run up the tunnel wall and over the hellhound, holding on to the sack, thereby pulling the hound's head backwards, that it sat down on its hind legs. At that moment, Kitt adjusted his hands to let slip the outer sack. The hellhound shook the leather over his eyes.

Never rely on the same trick twice, Kitt thought, trying to remember if it had been his father's advice. His knees shook a little, and he felt a strange lassitude in his muscles, due to the hellhound stench and lack of air.

When Kitt came into the vast cave again, filled by the metallic clatter of the hammers, only Gullo looked up from his anvil. "Mined the Royal ore, then."

Kitt plunked down his booty before the Jarnmantsje, opened the sack, and held out a piece of black-green ore studded thickly with green crystals.

"Humpf," Gullo said.

"Met your folks down there. Hungry too. They took the second goat, which I had saved for you."

Something like animation came over Gullo, grey lids disclosed the outraged glare of round yellow eyes. "No folk of Gullo's, no. Thrymthralli. Bad, bad, bad. Stupid. Always eat, eat, eat."

"What do they eat, down there?" Kitt asked, mystified.

"Eat too much. Gullo doesn't like them. Mustn't give Thrymthralli goats. Goats must be given to Gullo."

"Well, I didn't know about them. You didn't warn me."

The Jarnmantsje hissed like steam from a geyser about to break out.

Kitt remembered not to tease the Jarnmantsje too much. "Tomorrow I'll hunt," he promised. "The very first goat shall be yours."

Gullo revealed grey tusks in an anticipatory smile.

#

When Kitt emerged from the mountain, it was another sunset, golden light flooding the sky.

He stood drinking in the greens and blues of the grass and the sea, revelling in the feeling of space, with the odious after-taste of the hellhound smell still clinging to his lungs and nose and the back of his mouth.

As he opened the door of the hall three faces turned towards him from where they sat by the fire, three pairs of eyes were directed at him, two blue and sleepless, and one black and curious.

Kitt nodded politely to Diorlin, grinned at Eckehart and dropped a small cluster of translucent, green, perfect gems into Aslaug's lap. With a strained smile, she laid the gems on the table and rose to go to the kitchen.

"Green crystals -we have the ore for the work, Swordmaster," Eckehart said, picking up the gem cluster. "Was it dangerous?" he asked Kitt in a casual tone, but the look he directed at the youth was anxious.

"Just way too little space down there for the smell of Axtmörder's pet Leichengift." Feeling drenched with that stink, Kitt thought that everybody must smell it on him. The bread and the ham, which his mother brought him, tasted of the hellhound smell, and he soon stopped eating; all he wished for was to soak in a bath for a few days and maybe burn his clothes.

#

On the following morning, Eckehart and Kitt began smelting the Royal ore. After closing the smelting oven, Kitt walked down to the place where Diorlin was supervising the sword practice of his knights.

213

When Kitt presented himself to the old swordmaster, the young knights shot sideways glances at his big, blackened hands and sniggered. The smirks slid from their faces like melting snow from a steep roof, once their Swordmaster and the blacksmith apprentice crossed blades. There were a few muttered curses.

Only Leonin smiled, raising both hands with spread fingers towards the knight Viterin, twice. "Twenty, I should have bet you twenty. Anyone take me for thirty? Forty?"

Viterin scowled while the other knights looked blank.

Diorlin shook his head after the first passage of arms with Kitt. "Hopeless. Quite hopeless," he said. "Strength, speed and stamina, which you so richly possess, they do not suffice to make a swordsman. Not by a very long chalk. The deciding factor is skill. And beyond skill is mastery. Mastery means discipline, precision, strategy -all of which you lack, and that is why you are just a barbarian brute. A very gifted barbarian brute, admittedly, but your parents have more to do with that than you have. It's no better than living on your inheritance."

Kitt expected the knights to laugh at this dressing down, as they had at his blacksmith's hands, but they didn't so much as smirk.

"Fifty anyone? A hundred? Two hundred?" Leonin offered.

"Come on comrades, two hundred to one against? I'm taking all bets, any amount by your note of hand!"

His fellow knights shook their heads.

#

After opening the smelting oven, Kitt barely waited for the steel lump to cool; he turned the twenty-pound mass in his hands, weighed, and even tasted it. Then he carried the raw metal down to the smithy, laid it on the forge and worked the bellows, watching it turn red-hot, yellow, and white-hot, and then struck the glowing iron for the first time.

Eckehart chuckled at the surprise on his son's face.

Kitt rubbed his arm. "It kicks."

"That is the price the smith pays for incorruptible steel, son. Your strength comes in very handy for this work."

"I'm glad that it is good for something," Kitt grumbled, thinking of

214

Diorlin's sarcastic comments.

He hammered the glowing bar, gradually increasing the strength of his blows, then stuck it into the forge again, wiping the sweat from his brow. "Makes little difference for the working whether this steel is red hot or white-hot," he observed.

"That, my son, is precisely the crux with this steel. Hit it too little, you make no effect, hit too hard, it'll crack. And what's more, you can't reheat it, as the incorruptible principle will boil out of it easily. The bar you stuck back into the forge just now, we'll use it for something else. With incorruptible steel, you have just one chance. This job has to be done well, and it has to be done fast."

Under his father's direction, Kitt forged the tubes and spheres that would replace bones and joints in Diorlin's body.

Eckehart took over at sunset. "You go to bed."

But Kitt did not go; he stayed, not wishing to miss any little detail concerning the working of this steel, and watched Eckehart polishing every piece until it shone like a mirror.

Hammering the incorruptible steel all day had taxed even Kitt's strength, and also his mind, and come midnight he was fast asleep on his feet.

#

Every day, the place before the house turned into the School of Knights. Diorlin's pupils squared off in five pairs while Diorlin personally taught Kitt the art of knightly battle, whenever Eckehart released the youth from work.

The work with the incorruptible steel took six days of steady hammering, and by the seventh day, Kitt had forged the last pieces for legs and feet.

He had fallen asleep by the door of the smithy, and woke before sundown, to see Eckehart standing before the workbench on which he had all the parts of the steel skeleton laid out on in the right order, as they would replace the bones of the living man. The metal hands and feet were present, all the joints, and the pieces that would reinforce the spinal column and the skull, the ribs, and the arm and leg bones. The thin metal cords to strengthen ligaments and muscles coiled about them.

215

Kitt asked the question that had been going around his head since the day of Diorlin's arrival. "How are you going to get this inside him?"

At the sound of Kitt's voice, Eckehart jumped. "Not asleep, son? You did the work of three men; you ought to be dog-tired and asleep for days."

"How will you weld his flesh to your steel? That will need a major act of butchery?" And as Eckehart did not reply at once, "You are not going to keep me out of this?"

"There is other work I need you for. The sword Diorlin asked, I want you to have the entire making of it."

"What? Me?"

"But yes! By now you have crossed enough blades with Diorlin to know better than anyone, what sword the old master needs."

"But all will be changed after you are -finished with him."

"Use your judgement and your skill. Diorlin's bones will be reinforced with steel, and his sinews will never slack, but where sheer power is concerned, they will still be the muscles of an old fighter. So make the sword as light as you can without impairing the balance. Remember all you learned so far, and put it into this sword."

"And then you'll teach me the welding of steel to living flesh and bone?"

"Of course I could teach you that too. But it is far less accurate an art than plain working the iron. You see, on the whole, I have always found it best to leave nature to run her courses, youth and age, the eternal change of the generations. I haven't done such work for" here he paused "many years. There was no good reason for it, and many good reasons against."

"I always thought you would teach me all about iron."   "Listen my son, I'm teaching you all I know. The welding of living flesh and steel is not smith-craft, it is -an art that takes as much time again to learn, a time that you may come to regard as wasted in the end, because it deviates you from your ironwork and then you'll reproach me why I did not dissuade you . . ."

"Hardly. I don't expect you to make up my mind for me, for or against."

"Fair enough. Of course, if you insist, and don't I know how good you are at insisting, maybe you will bully me into teaching it to you, but it will be against my better judgement."

"So, if I insist, you will teach it to me?"

"Didn't I just say so? But how about first forging Diorlin's sword from the Royal Ore? See what bargain you can strike with this steel, how far you can solve the insoluble contradiction of edge or strength! At least, with this kind of work, if it doesn't work out, we can always throw it on the scrap heap and start all over again."

Kitt made a wry face, thinking how many of his metallurgic efforts had already landed on that scrap heap.

"Now stop arguing with me, son. I see the Swordmaster coming here."

Diorlin pushed open the door. His eyes fell on the workbench at once, and he drew nearer. Fascination and revulsion warring on his face, he regarded the metal skeleton, its obscene likeness to humanity. Touching the metal ligaments, which trembled and twitched as if alive, his face turned paper-white.

"Ready, Diorlin?" Eckehart asked in his broken Tolosan. "You still want this?" He indicated the metal skeleton. "This, much work, much danger. I see you are afraid? No shame. If you change your mind, I don't mind. Kitt doesn't mind. We make the sword for you, the best, to take years off you."

The old sword fighter's head jerked up, his features were haggard.

#

"Buying me off with this task of making the sword -but he won't," Kitt muttered.

Sword building seemed mundane now compared with the art of which he had glimpsed tantalising details. This feeling of an opportunity missed for acquiring more knowledge would not go away. Kitt had let himself be persuaded but superficially, headed off for the time being, because Eckehart had been so very clear in his wishes. His first thought was to check Eckehart's tools to see which the smith had with him in the mountain. Everything was in its place. Nothing was missing.

Kitt picked up his bow and wandered up to the smelting ovens, thinking alternately about what was going on inside the mountain, how to make the sword for Diorlin, whether a goat would venture near so that he could fulfil his promise to Gullo.

A flight of ten geese passed over the cliff. Kitt raised, notched and released the bow, all in one movement, and had brought down two geese before the others began wheeling away; before they fled out of range, Kitt shot two more, and a fifth he caught with a long shot. Goats did not appear; since the knights had come ashore, the animals had withdrawn higher and higher up the mountain. He hoped that Gullo would be content with geese.

He opened up the smelting oven and took out the cake of molten steel, still hot and riddled with the slag.

The knights looked with interest as Kitt strode past with his brace of geese. Ignoring them, the youth went into the smithy, closing the door firmly behind him. He entered the storeroom behind the forge, dimly lit by flames from fissures in the wall.

From there, he went through to the anvil chamber in the mountain. He removed the covering from the chimney that led up the wall, and the room was lit by fire glow, throwing a stark red light onto hammer-beam and hammerhead, stone anvil and the front of the big wheel.

Kitt opened several vents, and the inside of the chimney began glowing orange, then yellow. He thrust the bar of raw iron onto the fire.

When the iron glowed yellow, he went to open a shutter. Water rushed onto the wheel and disappeared again in a vertical shaft. The wheel began moving; the iron teeth of a horizontal cogwheel gripped into the corresponding notches, and the big hammer rose and then smashed down onto the anvil. He showed the raw iron under the hammer. The sound changed to a dull clanging.

Kitt picked up the geese, and went further into the mountain, leaving the hammer to thunder behind. When he came to the big rock dome, Gullo was there by his anvil as if the Jarnmantsje had never moved. "For the sausage," Kitt said brightly. "I'll still get you a goat."

At the sight of the five geese, Gullo's round yellow eyes shone like

218

those of an owl. "Is a good boy Kitt is, keeps promises." Adding, "Precocious though. Yes, precocious."

From the rock dome, tunnels opened leading to the smithy, the hall and down into the mountain. Kitt took the passage leading to the store-rooms in the back of the hall. He entered the rock-hewn part of the house, moving in the dark without hesitation, making no noise at all.

He was in the corridor leading to the storerooms. Behind those, there was another dome hewn out of the rock. The door leading into it was made of thick ironbound planks, and it was open a crack.

Light streamed out, a warm shine, and a bird was singing. Water bubbled and there was the scent of roses. It was all as he remembered it from the longest night, when this warmth light had saved him from freezing.

He looked through the crack and saw the water well in the centre of the dome and opposite, the big cold fireplace with the cauldron hanging inside. The room was empty; his mother, father and the Swordmaster were nowhere to be seen. But he heard Diorlin talking endlessly as if in a dream.

"Sonnica was a flower, sweet and precious and fragile. I watched her grow up and bloom. Like a flower, she was broken. One night she was a rose between the white teeth of a smiling, attractive rogue. The next day, she lay in the gutter. I don't know how he had managed to get to her, how he had deceived her. It must be the sorcerer Zinnober's work! He served Hugo even then. Sonnica never spoke. She gave birth to her son, Ramiro. Then Sonnica lay pale and still. There was nothing I could do against the laughing rogue. Not even king Sisebut could do anything against Hugo, and then I realised how weak he was. As Ramiro grew up, I became a power in the land myself. I won the allegiance of many young Tolosans from noble families. I earned a gold-heavy war-chest in Daguilaria. Imagine my bitterness, when I noticed old age overtaking me remorselessly, that I would be too old to restore the ancient order of the knights, and have to leave Ramiro to fight alone against the devil Hugo!"

"Love changes the path of life," Aslaug said.

"As can a child," Eckehart said. "A child changes everything."

Their voices were so near that it gave Kitt a start. And still he couldn't see anyone, and the dome remained empty. He retreated, dissatisfied, and as carefully as if he had to fox the leader of the Woodstalkers.

When he reached the mountain passage, he moved more rapidly. From the Jarnmantsjes hall came a mutter and the smell of burning feathers and roasting goose meat. The Lütte Jotun did not seem to notice his passing and Kitt avoided watching them feed.

Baulked, and wondering more furiously than ever, Kitt returned to the water hammer. He took the iron block, which had been hammered into a shapeless lump and put it back into the earth-fire, to hammer it roughly into a long, thin bar, which he left there among the other iron.

When he finished that work and passed through the storeroom again, he saw that the steel bones were laid out on the work-table as if they had never been moved. Had there no welding of steel to living flesh taken place at all?

Eckehart was in the hall. "Have you and Gullo made up?" his father inquired, his blue eyes twinkling. "Diorlin changed his mind. He cannot be blamed. Mother will do her best for him, and so must you. I will not go back on my word. You have the forging of Diorlin's blade." He did not seem to notice Kitt's discomfiture.

#

The last of the Royal Ore was smelting in the oven, and Kitt sat on Eckehart's stone seat, recapitulating everything his father had ever taught him about steel, and step by step laying out a plan for the forging of the blade. He knew that he had one chance only.

The steel had to be light, there was the old dilemma of hardness versus suppleness, and now the steel should also be incorruptible. For the first time, Kitt thought how much easier it was to make a heavy blade for young, strong muscles and bones.

The next days Kitt spent in the smithy, heating, hammering, twisting, shaping and welding. His father kept his word and was leaving the entire work on Diorlin's sword to him.

Going back and forth between smelting oven and forge Kitt passed the knights with long strides. They were going through their exercises half-heartedly, confusion at the disappearance of their master written plainly on their faces. Some even seemed about to direct their questions at Kitt, but the young blacksmith had no time for them. The intricacy and difficulty of the work his father had entrusted him with banned all other thoughts from his mind.

###

Kitt laid the finished sword before his father, still disassembled in blade, pommel, crossguard and hilt.

The old smith slowly scrutinised the blade, observing the thin, brilliant edge contrasting with a slim body of darker steel, and then laid his hand on the youth's broad shoulder. "Those welding seams are going to hold up; I can see that with my bare eye. You are a fine smith; you have the knowledge of steel that comes from the love of it, from the understanding of its very soul."

"I can't show this to mother," Kitt said, giving words to the nagging thought that had been at the back of his mind since he knew that his work would be good, and that he would succeed in finishing his first sword all by himself. "Do you think it is better to make a sword than living by it?" he asked. "Or is it just as bad?"

"A smith makes weapons for men. He does not make their choices," Eckehart answered and was suddenly aware of a quick searching look. "You think that is nothing but a lame excuse, my son? Well, find out for yourself, then make your decision, master smith or master swordsman, pick one, stick with it. You can do whatever you want."

"Both, father, I want to be both," Kitt said eagerly. "And I want to be a healer, as mother wants me to be. Why should I have to choose one?"

"Because everybody must choose in the end, my son. Now, this is the first blade of yours that will leave your hands and go out into the world, because it is perfect."

Kitt shrugged, too happy to say anything.

"You know that all smiths sign their work for it to be recognised as theirs. What shall your signature be, Kitt?

"I never thought about signatures."

"How about this?" Eckehart took a piece of charcoal and painted seven dots on the anvil. "You can punch it in at the base of your blades."

Kitt recognised the most brilliant star constellation of the skies. "The Southern King," he said. "A bit grand."

He took the charcoal from Eckehart's hand, and also drew seven dots, but in a different alignment. "The wagon of the north is good enough for an apprentice smith. My humble hay-wagon." Kitt smiled a sort of lunatic grin. "A hay-wagon I know about. Kings, less so."

"Did you know the fiercest arrogance lies in humility? Well, well, a smith of your quality can have any signature he wants." Eckehart ruffled his son's fair hair. "Punch in your hay-wagon, and then let's fasten the hilt." He raised an eyebrow at the pommel, crossguard and grip lying on the anvil. "Gold inlay all over. You know the grip leather will cover much of these bands of the lilies you worked on so hard. And yet you did right because the Gods of battle will see them. And that is what matters."

"I'm still wondering, did you ever mean to teach me about the incorruptible steel?"

"I would have told you about the Royal Ore eventually, but I knew the moment I did that, you would be off into the mountain to mine it, no matter what I said. As you did. I am searching for a way to make incorruptible steel, to cook it up like one of mother's stews, without depending on the Royal Ore. Now that you have seen for yourself Erzkuning's kingdom, you should understand the why of it. But I haven't succeeded yet."

"So you say."

"Don't take that tone with me!"

"It's true, though."

"Excuse me, my lord Eckehart, Sir!" Leonin's cultured, clipped voice said from the door. "I'm here on the Swordmaster's behalf."

Eckehart threw a cloth over the new sword before he turned to the beautiful knight. "The swordmaster has consulted with my lady Aslaug. He is undergoing the treatment she prescribed. He must not be disturbed. Has he not said?"

"He has my lord, and furthermore left the specific order for me to put this raw novice," here Leonin nodded very slightly towards Kitt, "through his paces in the meantime, so that the Swordmaster will not have to teach him everything all over again, because he's forgotten at dinner all he learned before lunch."

"Put me through my paces?" Kitt surveyed the young knight from the glossy black hair to the shining black boots. "You can have a try."

Leonin raised both hands. "I merely convey the swordmaster's own words. I thought you knew his style by now."

"We better get moving," Kitt muttered.

"Precisely. I'm glad you take it in this spirit. Neither you nor I want to hear what he'll say about it if we don't."

Walking side by side, Kitt noticed yet again the graceful way Leonin moved, and the watchful look of the brown velvet eyes. An arrogant elegant, but dangerous, was his judgement of the young nobleman.

The Senior Pupil made polite conversation. "Did Diorlin tell you that you are easily the most gifted pupil he ever had?"

"No."

"No, of course, he wouldn't tell you that. But you are. And I agree with him of course, because I've never seen a fighter like you. You know Kitt; I told our knights some time ago, that we would call you sir yet."

"I heard you."

"Yes, I realised that you speak Tolosan very well, without much of a noticeable accent even. Read and write it too, don't you?"

"It is a major language."

"Just so. Yet somehow my fellow knights still labour under the misapprehension that you speak hardly at all, and understand less. You know, I suspect you of making a little game out of keeping people in the dark about your intellectual abilities. Why? One wonders about your motives. Not to mention that it's hardly good manners, you know. I hope you don't take offence, as I just mention it in case you want to thoroughly revise your behaviour at a later date."

223

"You'll tell them now."

"But I will not! I like the mischief of it. In any case, they wouldn't believe me. Just for my own information, how many languages do you speak, Kitt?"

"Fluently? Five, no, six. But I can understand the phrase *will you look at the size of that brute* in about twelve or thirteen idioms."

"Sarcasm!" Leonin sighed plaintively. "So much for simple barbarians. You've just wrecked another very dear prejudice of mine. Not a kind thing to do, and frequently resented."

"You talk a lot. A lot of nonsense."

"Why, of course." Leonin looked surprised. "You don't expect me to talk sense, do you? I'm a nobleman, not a peasant, nor a craftsman like your own capable self. As for talking a lot, I've been assuming your part of the conversation, since you seem to prefer striking the attitude of silent, strong man. Wasn't that considerate of me? Now, shall we?"

They had arrived at the arena, and before the last word ended, the young Tolosan had whipped out his sword.

Kitt turned his head very slightly, feeling the air draught of the slim blade hissing past his face. His sword was out at the same time, blocking Leonin's with a hard hit that made sparks flash and the knight wince.

"Damn, damn and damn," Leonin smiled into Kitt's eyes over the crossed blades, "You got fiendish reflexes. And a devilish temper. I think I may have broken my wrist. Whatever for do you want to learn Diorlin's faints and repartees; you can just break your adversaries arm."

Leonin's wrist was not broken, as he proved by executing a disengaging movement followed by another slash, which Kitt blocked even harder.

"Brutish strength showing off, I think the Swordmaster called this sort of behaviour. I call it distinctly unfriendly manners."

"Talk to me about manners," Kitt growled. "What about saying *on your guard*?"

"Well maybe not quite according to decorum." Leonin's grin was unrepentant. "However, the means were hallowed by the object, which was to draw just a little blood from you. Why, that would have been better than taking a maiden flower! Alas, it didn't come off. Oh, oh, I see you've drawn that steely look again. That icy glare of yours is quite something! In the Royal armoury of Lutetia, they'd stick it on the inventory. Freeze, one, killers, for the use of."

"Let's simply fight now," Kitt said, measuring Leonin's face for the cut.

#

Diorlin made his re-appearance in the evening of the twelfth day.

He looked straight and fresh and full of new strength and power. The knights surrounded their master with questions, to which he gave brief, impatient answers. "Yes, a slight indisposition. Now I am better than I ever was. Twelve days? Seemed like two hundred days to me."

Kitt stood well apart. He was surprised. What had his mother done? The Swordmaster seemed a new man, taught, sizzling with energy and oddly elated.

Diorlin's eyes met Kitt's over the heads of the knights. "You were right, I had another option," he said cryptically.

Leonin, the left side of his beautiful face marked by three bright red scabs, concluded his report. "So everything has been done exactly as you ordered, Swordmaster."

"Been in the wars, have you?" The black eyes were on the scabs. "That must hurt quite a bit. Somebody at last wiped that impudent smile from your face?"

"Not at all, sir. Merely a slight accident. Fell into a bramble bush. Some fearful brambles on this island."

"I think I know that particular bramble bush. I should strongly advise you to stay well clear of it in the future, my dear boy. You don't have the sort of thorns it takes."

"Nobody that I know does, Sir."

"Just so. Well, well, step right here Kitt, smartly now. Does that thick skull of yours remember the rules of knighthood?"   "Purity, Poverty, Mercy. To help, save and serve. To battle evil and return good for bad."

"Very pat! Excellent! I'm sure a parrot couldn't have repeated better. But do you know what these words mean? Or have you learned almost nothing at all of what I laboured to teach you for a month? A knight, Kitt, must never permit his actions to be determined by others."

"I'd like to see anyone try."

"Indeed?" Diorlin's black, sardonic eyes twinkled. "Would you even notice if anyone was doing it to you? I have a shrewd idea that Leonin got away with just that. Did he, or did he not, succeed in needling you into engaging in a childish dogfight?"

A deep dusky flush flamed across Kitt's face.

"Let me explain, sir!" Leonin endeavoured.

"Excuse me, sir knight, this concerns you but indirectly. I'll deal with you later. Now, Kitt, I suppose you are very proud of your handy-work. And why shouldn't you be? Three fine lines, evenly spaced, just below the eye -precision work, indeed. Do you think that's what a knight does, the same as every other bully, just more skilfully? Let me tell you that it is not. After an entire month of training, you are still just a crude, adolescent show-off." Diorlin laid his head to one side quizzically, bright black eyes regarding the big youth motionlessly standing before him. "Well? Aren't you going to explain how entirely justified you were?"

Kitt shrugged.

"No? That's a relief." The Swordmaster smiled. "Now you listen and learn it by heart! Whatever you do at any time of your life must be your own considered decision. Sometimes you have only a fraction of a moment to make that decision, just the same as in battle when you decide on a particular fencing manoeuvre. That is why you need principles. Principles are essentially the same as figures in fencing, serving to help you make a decision that is both fast and precise. That is what makes a knight, principles and skill. In that order. Understand?"

"Yes."

"Well, well." Diorlin said, appraising the big youth, "This calls for punishment. I will see you here on this very spot tomorrow at sunrise to take it." The old Swordmaster's black eyes rested on the youth's face, white with humiliation. "Or you needn't come before my eyes again. As a killer, there is nothing more I can teach you. As a knight, you leave entirely too much to desire."

Black eyes and grey eyes stared into each other, while the knights stood around silently.

"Swordmaster!"

All heads turned around towards the house, where Eckehart waved from the door of the hall. "Come Diorlin, come and see your sword!"

"Coming lord Eckehart!" Diorlin cried. "Well, well, something agreeable to the day, after all. Come gentlemen and celebrate my new blade with a beaker of wine, or even two or three! Leonin, make yourself useful and see that somebody brings up a casket of Jara wine."

Followed by the subdued knights, Diorlin marched to the hall, with Kitt trailing behind them. Entering the hall last, he hovered by the door. From there, lying on the table, he could see the sword he had made.

Diorlin walked down the six stone steps into the hall and advanced. His fingers inserted into the basket and locked around the hilt. He raised the sword, with his face bathed in a sudden light that was almost religious.

It was a sword with a thin blade, little more than an inch wide, but four feet and four inches long;, the hilt was enclosed in an iron and gold basket.

"Just as you promised, Eckehart." Diorlin's voice caught with emotion. "A perfect balance, just perfect. This is a blade that will be joined to my arm for many years to come." He executed a complicated fencing figure, repeating it with ever-higher speed until the air whistled, and the blade moved too fast for the eye to follow, while he continued speaking: "The legend has proved true, and more than that. It is usually the fighter, who has to adapt to a weapon, however suitable, because the fighter can change, while the weapon is constant. But not so with this sword which has been fitted to me in a way I never dreamed possible. We thought we had come to the end of the world, but where steel is concerned Isenkliff is the centre." He went into another fencing figure, executing this also with increasing speed. "I have seen the best steel in the world, and it's all mere tinsel compared to this blade. This is a masterpiece, and you are the master of all smiths!"

The blade came to a stop. Realising that Eckehart could not understand his torrent of Tolosan, Diorlin saluted the smith with his new blade. "You, Eckehart, are the master smith!"

Eckehart chuckled. "I deserve no praise. My son Kitt made this sword for you, Diorlin. It is the masterpiece that shall count to make him a master blacksmith." Eckehart pointed at Kitt, who was still standing by the door, then to the seven punched dots at the base of the blade. "This is his signature. His steel will be marked thus."

Although he spoke the Tolosan with a strong accent and mixed with the northern language, the knights seemed to understand him correctly. All crowded around to look at the blade. Then, they turned around as one, to look at Kitt.

"The basket may make you slower on the draw at first," Kitt broke his silence. "But you will notice that the hand slips in very easily once you have acquired the knack. You'll find that this sword cannot be knocked from your hand by some brainless brute with no skill beyond a big swing."

"Ah, I'm pleased to hear you quote my very words. For sometimes I'm not sure if you are listening to me at all," Diorlin hissed from the corner of his mouth, his eyes never wavering from his new blade.

Kitt continued, "And however hard that hypothetical brute should hit the blade, it won't break, although it is very slim. I made the blade in this manner because you prefer to thrust rather than to swing. That is the most efficient technique for a man of your built."

"I'm glad you approve of my technique."

"This is my judgement as a smith first, and a swordsman second," Kitt retorted, and there was an air of authority on him that was new to the knights, the authority of the workman who knows precisely what he is talking about. If he did not add that of smith-craft, he considered himself a better judge than Diorlin, it was clearly implied.

"Ah, but my dear boy, a swordsman must always be a swordsman first and foremost," Diorlin confined himself to remarking mildly.

"Should you happen to hit armour with it, this blade will always spring back. Neither will it rust, as the outer layer is the same "incorruptible steel that was," Kitt checked himself, before saying too much in front of the young knights, "made from a specially mined ore," he concluded quickly.

"What, incorruptible?" Clutching the sword in his hand Diorlin eyed the big youth, smiling thinly. "My sincerest congratulations to your masterpiece, Kitt! Ah, and here is the Jara wine to celebrate this excellent new Aurora-Blade." He nodded to the sailor who set two baskets onto the table, knuckled his forehead and hurried out with a nervous look around the hall.

Leonin extracted a dozen glass bottles from one basket, as Sigerian added red glass goblets.

Diorlin took his usual chair by the fire, and the knights sat down around. Then all rose again, as Aslaug came into the room dressed in black brocade, which made startling the fairness of her hair, gold shot with silver. Without a word, she looked at the sword lying on the table.

Leonin sat down near Kitt, raising his glass. "How about coming with us to Tolosa, Kitt? A talent like yours is wasted here at the end of the world. You'd be an asset to the School, and in due time we'll make a really smooth knight of you yet. And the ladies of Eliberre just love a huge brute. I promise you!" The last he muttered under his breath, in deference to the lady Aslaug.

"Leonin is precipitous as usual. I beg pardon of the lord Eckehart and the lady Aslaug." Diorlin bowed to Eckehart and Aslaug, who looked at Kitt, their faces very still. "It is true that your son is an accomplished swordfighter and that, with more training, he could become the best. However, he has on several occasions expressed that he considers himself a smith. He certainly made an excellent blade for me. Maybe he should stick to blacksmithing and forget about the knightly arts and the knightly code."

A wave of red flamed across Kitt's cheekbones, and ebbed away, leaving his face deathly pale. "I should. I consider blacksmith the better calling."

Derisive laughter sprang up among the knights, and there were outraged mutters about craftsmen forgetting their station.

"More productive," Kitt explained. "I still have to see one of you do a day of useful work."

"We have drunk the new sword," Diorlin said. "Now we drink the new master smith!"

All the knights followed suit, which surprised Kitt.

"Master Kitt is right," Diorlin pursued. "I keep telling you that every knight should have more than one thing he does exceedingly well." He smirked. "I exempt Leonin, who is the perfect elegant, which counts."

"Not as easy as you might think," Leonin chipped in. "Dressing well is a science."

"Just as I was saying. Pray don't interrupt sir! But Kitt, what you must understand is that being a knight is being ready. Ready at all times to spring into action in any condition, and then make no mistake. I admit that to the uneducated eye, this being ready might look like being lazy. That is an error, as many an evildoer and monster found to his cost. The most challenging virtue, however, is to keep to the knightly code even in the most dangerous situation, and make no mistake there also, for no victory is worth breaking the code for, as the examples of both Gozon the Dragon Slayer and Moyeros the Rebel Knight show us.

"The honour of the knights is no mere outer garment, to be donned and doffed at convenience just like your Lily cloaks, or even to be bought and sold in the marketplace.

"That is the Code I have brought back to Tolosa, and I will uphold it, even if all of you desert me." He glared at each of his knights in turn, who all earnestly protested their allegiance to him. "Even if I have to do it alone until the hidden enemies kill me," Diorlin concluded as if he hadn't heard them. "I'll see you all in the morning."

He rose, and that was the sign for the young knights to also take their leave.

"Father!" Kitt said when the hall door had closed after the last knight. "Can you truly declare me a master? I have read that in other lands the decision lies with the guilds."

"There are things not written in your books, my son. The Smith of Isenkliff is such a one. When I laid my hand on Brynnir's forge, all the knowledge of every other Smith of Isenkliff became mine."

"All the knowledge?"

"And all the memories, back to Brynnir himself. You see that I have every right to declare a master blacksmith, with the authority vested in me of all the smiths before me. My right holds wherever iron is being forged. When, if, when you lay your hand on Brynnir's forge, then that knowledge will become yours. Including all of mine. Including the one you asked me, to forge steel to living flesh."

"But then, you would not be Smith of Isenkliff anymore?"

"No. I will be dead. Or gone away."

"Then, I don't want that knowledge," Kitt said.

#

The sun had risen already and it was a beautiful day, mild with a soft wind. On one side of the arena stood the knights, all ten of them, in uneasy silence, on the other was Kitt, his face pale, and his eyes burning. Only Diorlin was still missing.

At last the old swordmaster appeared on the path, the black cloak hanging from his shoulder in straight folds. "So you have come. Very good," he addressed Kitt. "I wasn't sure, after yesterday's little rebellion. Now let's see if my pupils between them can't cut you down to a more reasonable size."

At Diorlin's command, four of the pupils took position around Kitt. There was the swishing sound of blades whipping from their sheaths; the four young knights closed in on Kitt, who instantly became the centre of a storm of sharp steel.

For a while, Diorlin looked on fascinated, and then he signalled another of the pupils to join the fight, one after the other.

Already before the fifth knight entered the circle around him, Kitt realised that even the best fighter could only resist the concerted attack of a certain number of men, particularly skilled swordsmen, as were the young Tolosans. Survival depended on the ability to draw out the field so that he would never be engaged by more than two or at most three fighters at a time.

Soon the place was a milling melee of knights trying to corner a single blacksmith apprentice, who did not stand still for a moment, running, dodging, jumping, high in the air above the men's head one moment, down on the ground the next, using every opening for a feigned slash or stab.

Leonin was the last to still stand aside. "Oh, that was a good one!" he applauded as Wallia leapt after his errant sword.

"Care to get some of your own back, now he's a little distracted?" Diorlin enquired.

"Not near distracted enough, Swordmaster."

"You did take him on alone, didn't you? And now you hesitate to go in as the tenth?"

"You want me to take a hand, Swordmaster?"

"I do. Hair of the dog, my dear boy, hair of the dog."

Leonin drew philosophically and winked at Kitt, who was turning slowly, keeping in sight all his adversaries.

"One of us is in deep trouble," he said. "But frankly, I don't know who."

"You talk too damn much, you crybaby."

"Of course, I had to tell everybody. It was too good a jest. For a joke, I'd betray my best friend, and I don't even like you."

"Come on in, jest some more now!"

"Be witty with your blades, gentlemen!" Diorlin snapped. "On your guard now!"

A blade flew high while Viterin clutched his wrist, cursing.

Kitt snatched the hilt from the air and continued fighting with both swords.

Hands stemmed on his bony hips, Diorlin laughed his shrill laughter. "Ten skilled swordsmen! And they can't hold him! Five would be dead already! Ho Gundemar, you can come away now, because you've been dead twice over! Did you see that lord Eckehart?" he shouted.

Kitt was laughing with the pleasure of the swordplay, but the knights were exhausted, and there were pale faces and wide eyes.

The clashing of the swords and the shouting were like the sounds of a battle.

The commotion had drawn Eckehart and Aslaug down to the arena.

"That is what you wanted all the time," Aslaug said in a voice husky with bitterness. "For that, you have drawn the most capable killers to the island to be Kitt's teachers, and now he is as you wanted him, the perfect hand for your perfect blade."

"I want Kitt to learn all there is about steel. Steel is all he has."

"He knows too much about it already."

"I want him to learn the virtues that make the difference between a knight and a killer. I want him to be fair and courageous, with bravery tempered by dedication and compassion."

"Fairness, bravery!" Aslaug spit out the words like needles. "Words, those are just words! Do you see the terror on their faces, Eckehart? Do you remember this same terror on the faces of other men? That there is a perfect killer, and no fine words can make him anything else."

"That there is our son. If we turn from him, he will be alone in the world."

Without answering, Aslaug went back up the path.

Declared dead one after the other by Diorlin, the knights left the contest, some laughing shakily, some grinning sourly, three looking very afraid.

Leonin was the last fighter left, but not for long, as his sword was struck from his hand and broke, the two pieces rising high into the air.

All eyes watched the fragments turn over and over, glittering in the morning sun until they struck the ground with a thud.

Leonin shrugged. "This had to happen." Just in time, he thought. His sword-arm ached.

"Anybody hurt?" Diorlin inquired.

The knights shook their heads, surprised that none of them had sustained so much as a scratch.

"Nothing hurt, except our pride," Leonin said cheerfully.

"No, not a scratch," one knight murmured. "But even so, for a moment I felt as if certain death stood before me, and I tell you, it is a strange feeling."

The others nodded at these words that so accurately described the one terrible moment each of them had encountered in their battle against the blacksmith.

"Why," Leonin said, "I had fully expected to have my other cheek carved up. You weren't the only one scheduled for a lesson today, Kitt. Diorlin was as mad with me as he was with you. Don't bite off more than you can chew, was my lesson. Mind you, it wasn't really necessary, for I knew that all along. I suppose it was sheer perversity that made me challenge you. Plus, it didn't matter much that I lost. It's no shame to lose against a force of nature. For that's what you are."

"Kitt is one of a kind," Little Wallia said. "Or that's what we all hope. I'd feel a lot safer if he did limit himself to blacksmithing, but I suppose there's no more chance of that now."

Diorlin cleared his throat, and as usual, the knights fell silent at his first word.

"I'm sure you have come to regard me as the most cantankerous old crank ever getting on a young swordfighter's nerves." he began.

"Not at all, Swordmaster." Kitt grinned like a maniac. "Just over on Wittewal lives one who is an even greater master of the art of insult." He laid the stress on the numeral which provoked a snort from some young knights, "He is only this long," he indicated about a hand long, for it was Finsterkuning the Swatelb, dark lord of the island Wittewal, he had in mind "so he beats you where aggravation value per inch is concerned. But even he couldn't make me bend so much as a wispy hair on his ugly little head. I am really very patient."

His hands stemmed on his lean black-clad hips, Diorlin fixed Kitt out of black eyes. "Are you're quite finished exercising your barbarian wit? Yes? Then let me tell you that it is as crude as your fencing. As I was about to remark, when you so rudely interrupted me, I may not suffer fools gladly, but until now everyone, down to the most conceited beginner that ever wasted my time, and frayed my patience, has had to admit that I have never yet been mistaken in my estimate of a fighting man." He gave each of the knights a piercing look before which only Leonin managed to maintain his easy manner.

Diorlin smiled. "And this my unfailing sense for justice requires me to declare that you, Kitt, have acquitted yourself of all tests with

234

exceptional distinction. As you gentlemen all are aware, because I keep reminding you at least once a day, the Red Lily Knighthood is an honour that cannot merely be conferred by birth but must be earned."

There was a surprised mutter from the knights in reaction to this announcement.

Leonin grinned, extending his open palm to Viterin.

That youth shook his head. "I don't believe he'll do that. I just don't."

Leonin shrugged. "Fine. I am perfectly willing to wait for my winnings until you hear it spelt out."

"As the Order of the Red Lily still lacks its Grandmaster, I exercise my special prerogative as the Swordmaster of the School of Eliberre, to invest you with the Red Lily and salute you as a knight of the order." Diorlin drew his new sword and saluted. "Sir Kitt."

Leonin followed suit immediately with the inevitable smile, and so, one after the other did the other knights, after ever so slight a hesitation.

Diorlin sheathed his sword. "The captain tells me, that the weather will change soon. We will get ready to leave." The Swordmaster turned on his heel that the black cloak with the red lily flared out wide, and walked away, leaving nine young knights standing to stare after him.

"I claim the privilege," Leonin announced, as if anxious that another knight might get in before him, taking the heavy black silken cloak with the red lily from his shoulder. "You Sir Kitt are entitled now to wear the red lilies, and I'd take it as an honour if you'd consent to wear mine. Besides, you brought me ten pieces of gold on a small side bet so I can afford the gesture. I always have my cloaks made a bit longer than fashion prescribes, so it might just be acceptable." He threw the mantle on Kitt's shoulder and stepped back to view the effect. "Still looks short on you. Quite ludicrous, in fact. Those unconscionably wide shoulders of yours spoil what's really an elegant cut. Well, it is the intention that counts. Maybe if you'd ask your mother to let out the seam?"

"I don't mean to be pedantic, particularly as it's the Swordmaster's decision, but I do seem to remember that noble birth, albeit no guarantee for admission into the Red Lily Knights, is nevertheless a necessary precondition for an application to join the Order." In fact Viterin was very sure of his ground because he was the one knight who had studied the regulations carefully from the first to the last article.

"If you think you can wriggle out of your bet on a petty technicality, let me tell you that I consider that low!" Leonin said hotly.

"If you consider the order's regulations petty, then I would be interested to hear what you do attach importance to?" Viterin retorted.

"Why, here's one important question that really might keep me awake nights. Are you looking forward to telling everybody how a mere blacksmith had ten Red Lily Knights hopping at the point of his sword? That he's not an apprentice anymore, but a fully-fledged master smith doesn't make it any less embarrassing, not to me. Oh and he's fourteen if he's a day."

It was not only Viterin's face that was a study.

Leonin grinned. "Thought so. And me he bested twice. So, I, for one, am fully prepared to consider that conclusive proof of birth, and I will challenge any knight foolish enough to deny this. Before he does. As a favour to you idiots."

Viterin looked mulish. "I can show you the passage in the regulations of the Order."

"Go and show it to Diorlin. Oh, and as well leave your cloak here, for the swordmaster is sure to rip it off your back and demote you to mucking out stables. I can use the material to make Sir Kitt's a proper fit! That, or pay up now!"

With a sour expression, Viterin began digging coins from a purse on his belt, one by one, which Leonin cheerfully transferred into his own pocket.

Kitt took off the ill-fitting cloak and dropped it. "I'm a smith, son of a smith. There is no better calling, and I challenge anyone to dispute this."

"Don't mind them, Sir Kitt," Leonin said. "They are just an

illustration of one of Diorlin's favourite remarks, which is that nobility of birth alone isn't what makes a knight. True nobility shows itself in battle. Where you outrank all of us."

"I don't mind them. I just don't have time for this. Unless someone wants an iron job done. We smiths of Isenkliff specialise in fitting blades to a warrior's own hand, to make the best of what strength he possesses, and compensate for his weaknesses. I know every weakness of each of you. Any who wants a blade fit to make him a better swordfighter can come to the smithy and see me about it."

He turned his back on them and walked away, up the valley.

"Ouch. Only a true knight can be this beastly rude without using any actual swear words," Sigerian remarked.

"Stay, Sir Kitt!" Leonin called out peremptorily.

Kitt rounded on him. "Don't you sir me, Sir! I don't consider that a compliment."

"Oh, I hope that's not your last word! Diorlin wants you, and therefore, we all want you. Don't we, gentlemen?" And hissing out of the corner of his mouth: "Make the right noises now, or take the consequences."

"We'd be silly fools if we didn't accept the one swordsman who can lick the lot of us. When I go into battle, I want him somewhere near me and not on the opposite side either."

"That's the second time you've spoken in one day Sir Sigerian, so you seem to feel about this as strongly as I do."

"I do. Never heard such praise for anyone from the old black scorpion."

"As we can't beat him, make him join us. The only sensible thing to do," Amaris chipped in.

The knights muttered something affirmative, nodding vigorously. "Well, Sir Viterin?"

"The regulations cannot be disregarded," Viterin began.

"He is right," Kitt said. "You have to abide by your own regulations. I'm not going to rat to Diorlin, so that's your chief worry taken care of. Just tell him I refused."

"If you will allow me!" Viterin raised a hand. "I was not finished yet laying out my legal argument. The question of birth refers to the admissibility of an application. However, Sir Kitt did not apply for admission into the Red Lily Knights, as he has made clear repeatedly before witnesses. There is no pre-requisition of birth concerning the conferral of a Red Lily knighthood by the Swordmaster's decision. Subject to approval by the Grandmaster of course, once the Order has one."

"Well that applies to all of us, doesn't it?" Leonin said. "So everything is according to the regulations after all, as you could trust the Swordmaster for it to be, and I don't understand why you kept fogging the issue, Viterin. Unless it was on account of your lousy ten gold, which I call plain mean and unworthy. Now Sir Kitt, about your cloak . . ."

"I haven't accepted. And now I have work to do."

Kitt walked away, but he couldn't shake off Leonin. "Here, will you take that cloak to your mother, or shall I?"

"Why do you insist this much?"

"Didn't you hear what I said? Sheer vanity. I simply refuse to have been ignominiously whipped by a barbarian blacksmith boy."

"I heard you. What's the real reason?"

"Damn, you marked my face! I'll bear those scars all my life! Give a rakish air to my handsome countenance, and the ladies will simply love it. Naturally, I mean to make out that they were given to me by the first and foremost of all the Red Lily Knights. As a sort of badge of honour, don't you see."

Kitt just kept walking.

"Oh, you mean the genuine reason. Well, I think by now you've gathered that Diorlin is working up to an all-out battle for the soul of Tolosa? I fear he's bitten off more than the lot of us can chew. And for all that he is the Swordmaster of Eliberre, he is an old man. Even if your mother drew old age out of his body with her medicines, even if your father replaced all his bones and sinews with his famous steel . . ."

"What are you talking about?" Kitt demanded, confronting the knight.

"Oh, don't take on so. I know perfectly well that it's all a fantastic legend. But you see, I do suspect Diorlin is nourishing the most preposterous hopes. I don't mean any disrespect, but not even your formidable parents can change what we are, flesh and bone, fragile and mortal. The only thing we found on this island that really is out of any common human framework is you, Kitt. You can take it from me that there are very few warriors, if any, remotely a match for you in the entire known world. And you are still growing. So naturally, the most sensible thing for us to do is secure your alliance."

"You may be exaggerating the danger."

"Afraid not. My brothers in arms are a bunch of blockheaded young fools, except for Sigerian, who thinks a lot more than he talks. All they know is that once we get back to Eliberre, there will be a most unholy upheaval, with us in the very centre of it, and they are even looking forward to it, and dreaming of knightly glory in restoring ancient ideals, the babies. What they don't realise yet is what we are up against. I don't know what it is myself, except that it is something too big and bad to fit into any frame of ordinary politics, let alone knightly rules and swordplay. Whatever it is, for some time now, it has been picking us off one by one. Oh, it all seemed natural enough, here an unnecessary accident, there a silly duel, or a harmless wound turning suddenly into gangrene. Some knights have simply disappeared, vanished without a trace after getting into trouble with gambling or unsuitable attachments. Everything that could go wrong went wrong. Call me fanciful, but I don't believe in that many unhappy coincidences. That's why I came on this hare-brained journey to the world's end because I was too scared to be left behind! Whatever it is, we have nothing to put up against it. So I want you to come with us and save our asses. Maybe our souls."

"I as your wonder weapon?" Kitt shook his head. "You overestimate me."

"Maybe I do," Leonin shrugged, "what with you beating the stuffing out of me in every encounter, I naturally hope you will bestow the same favour on our enemies. Besides, the final genuine reason is that for some perverse reason I like you."

"I like the other reasons better," Kitt retorted, entering the smithy and firmly closing the door behind him, leaving the beautiful knight standing outside.

"Well, well, running after him like a mother hen after her one chick," Wallia sneered.

"Damn you, fools!" Leonin retorted. "You keep providing him with reasons to wash his hands of us."

"Rather dirty hands," Wallia said. "His fingernails are a fright, and no pumice can ever rub away those calluses. I still can't see why you and Diorlin are so crazy about him."

"No? I thought he demonstrated the why of it to you quite clearly mere minutes ago. You can't possibly have forgotten already."

"He doesn't fight like a knight, he fights like a savage."

"Oh, he does fight like a knight, albeit at a rather higher level of force and speed. It's just too fast for your eyes to follow and too hard for you to meet. And now his cloak must get done, or there will be serious trouble. I want all spares in the pavilion this minute, and then you ladies sit down and sew the thing together."

The knights had never seen their Senior Pupil so angry, and they sprang to do his bidding, even Viterin.

#

Diorlin came to the Hall with Leonin, who carried the finished Lily cloak.

Without further ado, Leonin threw the garment around Kitt's shoulders. "There, it fits."

The swordmaster looked Kitt up and down. "You are a Red Lily knight now. You must remember that at all times! I'm not so sure if adherence to knightly principles may not put you at a disadvantage in a world that has forgotten honour." Suddenly, Diorlin sounded forlorn. "Sometimes, I feel that I'm trying to resurrect something that is hopelessly outdated. This is not an easy time to wear the Red Lily."

"If I am as strong and skilled as you say, I can carry it off." Diorlin spread his hands in an expansive gesture.

"I see you know exactly what you want."

"I still want the same thing as before. I am a smith." Kitt made as if to take down the cloak.

Leonin stayed his hand and pinned the cloak with a silver fibula.

240

"You don't understand these things, Kitt. There was an acclamation."

"It is an honour that does mean something," Eckehart remarked, setting four goblets on the table. As Aslaug came in late from her garden these days, he went out to fetch her.

Kitt looked resigned. "What about obedience? I'm not good at serving."

"Oh as for that, baby steps," Diorlin cut in. "We start with the books Kitt, the ancient records of the Lily Knights. I will have to take them with me."

"Nobody takes any books away from Isenkliff. You can have a copy made, but the books stay here," Kitt said, and added deliberately: "Another Swordmaster may need them."

"So that's what you think, is it?"

"In case you lose your war," Kitt elaborated.

"I quite understood what you meant. You may be convinced of my mental capacity to appreciate your crude innuendo. You must get used to the thought, my dear boy, that you are one of us now. You are a knight, Sir Kitt."

"Right. I'll keep your books safe, here on Isenkliff."

"Never saw a smith who was so set on keeping his library intact." Leonin burst into a snigger. "The Swordmaster keeps telling us not to neglect letters over the sword. And here again, Sir Kitt sets an example to the other knights."

"He does not set an example in obedience," Diorlin said sourly. "I will tell you, Sir Kitt, why the original books must return to Tolosa. Books like that confer their authority upon those who possess them. The originals have this power to a much higher degree than any copy. There is a good reason for that. Copies can be subtly altered, and very often are. People kid themselves that they know what the first writer's meaning really was, taking it upon themselves to clarify the points which they feel strongly about."

"That means you'll have to watch Viterin closely when he copies the book," Leonin said mischievously.

"So I don't end up with the order's regulations instead of the code," Kitt put in.

"Exactly," Diorlin smiled. "I am glad you are at least considering to let me take the originals, but it will hold us up, copying the books for you. If only I weren't in such a hurry to return to Tolosa."

"Well the more of your knights are capable of writing, the faster you'll be. And in the meantime, you can show me another trick or two." Kitt spoke pleasantly enough, but there was a steely undertone. "Everything you thought of keeping back."

"Keeping back?" Diorlin said in some surprise.

"Of course. You too have been keeping something from me, I'm sure. But I want it all."

"But my dear boy, I have taught you all. In fact, I taught you more than any of my knights, simply because you learn more in any given time than any pupil I've had so far."

"You said I needed more training," Kitt said stubbornly.

"Who's been keeping things from you, Kitt?" Leonin asked curiously.

"Everybody," Kitt said savagely. "All I want to know is just everything of at least one thing. You can shovel in as many admonitions as you like, quote the code back and forward, I don't mind. I just want to know."

"All right," Diorlin said and shrugged. "In fact, I commend you on that attitude and will accede to all your demands, however rough your way of putting them. I have thought from the very first moment that I saw you, that swordsmanship is the natural science for you and have striven to teach you everything I know."

"Everything?"

"To the point that you can become a better swordsman than I ever was. That's how I taught you from the very beginning. If I prove to you that I have shown you all, and that I left out nothing in your tuition, then you let me take the originals of the code and the lists? For I have proof. And something you may want." From his black jacket, he drew a slim tome.

"For the original code, I'll give you this one in exchange."

There was black lettering on the cover, Tolosan but hard to read, archaic and rubbed away as it was. Kitt identified the words sword, art and Anjel Montoja. He opened it, and on thin transparent pages, he saw drawings of fighting men in different stances, of swords, of

242

armour.

"This book has been in my family for two hundred years. It saved my father's life." Diorlin fingered the nick in it. "I made this by accident when I was still as clumsy as you never were. Go over these drawings one by one, and then tell me if I taught you all. I meant to give this to Ramiro, my nephew, but I see that the knighthood doesn't make as much difference to you as it should. Yet. To get something of value to me, I must give something of value to you."

"I keep this," Kitt said, clutching the small book. "Take your code, Swordmaster!" He added: "I have read it through. More than once."

#

The day for the Red Lily Knights to leave had come, a good day for sailing, with clear skies, and the wind veered to the East.

The swordmaster stood before the hall, expostulating with Eckehart. He looked much younger and fitter than when he had come. "I wish you would concede to take the gold I offered you, Eckehart. That's what I brought it for. I didn't come here looking for a bargain."

"Then stop bargaining with me, Diorlin," Eckehart said, folding his arms in a final gesture. "I don't want your gold. I wanted you to teach my son the knightly code and the knightly sword. You paid my price in full."

"But I feel as if I paid nothing and took everything. It was pure pleasure to teach your son if teaching it can be called. I merely honed what is an excellent, natural fighting talent. And Kitt didn't really need my teaching. That terrible strength, lightning speed and uncanny instinct would see him through anywhere. Naturally, I didn't tell him so, never does any good to tell a young man this sort of thing. But it's the truth nevertheless."

"You taught him something more important than skill; you taught him principles."

Diorlin's hands flew out wide. "Again, I did not teach him anything. This young blacksmith has a keener sense of honour than many a noble. And more than that," he suddenly smiled. "For all his potential deadliness as a warrior, Kitt is a sweet boy."

Of all the compliments the famous Tolosan swordmaster had

made, the last seemed to gladden the old smith most. "Yes, he is a good boy. Isn't that so, Aslaug?"

Almost reluctantly, she nodded.

The sailors were waiting in the boats made fast to the rings of the rock quay. The young knights were waiting for Diorlin on the shore. Viterin carried Count Vitiza's books.

Kitt was also there, beside Leonin, which surprised the knights, who had the suspicion that the young blacksmith did not think much of them. He certainly wasn't bidding goodbye to any but the Senior Pupil and to Sir Sigerian.

"It was an education to meet you, Sir Kitt," Sigerian said.

Leonin touched the three red lines on his cheek. "I have something to remember you by."

"Here's something else." Kitt unhooked a sword from his belt. "It is one of mine."

"Lord of the Host! You've snubbed all my offers of friendship every day, just to present me with an Aurora blade now? And one of your own too!" Leonin drew the blade and swung it. "Never thought I'd be able to even lift a sword of the mighty Sir Kitt! Why, that's just the right weight and reach for me!"

"I found it too light and short last year. Made myself a bigger one."

"Ah, a gift like a blow in the face. For a moment there, I thought you were unbending. My error entirely."

Kitt grinned. "This won't break like yours did. A king hit it with all he had, and it did not get notched. He was a strong man and very angry. My lack of courtly manners, again."

"What became of him?" Leonin asked, fascinated.

"Left in a hurry. My father gave him no sword. Probably will be back someday to have it out with me."

"More fool, if he does."

"Oh, it won't come to anything. My parents don't let me do any real fighting. Not because they're afraid for me. Always worried that the other man might get hurt. Even if he tries to kill me."

"Really?" The Tolosan knight laughed at Kitt's wistful face. "I wish I had known about that earlier, would have pulled your leg

244

more. Why would they be afraid for you? Wouldn't occur to me either."

"There's a thing like bad luck. I might stumble, or slip."

"Never seen you do it. In fact, the one thing I don't believe you can do. Well, touch wood." Leonin performed the rite on a bow of driftwood.

"And what is that for then?"

"Don't know. Diorlin would say that a knight has no business to stumble or slip, and that bad luck is usually nothing but bad judgement and lack of wind."

"He's half right there. As usual."

"I'll tell him you said that. He'll be charmed. Aggravation value per inch, indeed! We're all still laughing about that wisecrack. There he comes. Mind your manners now!"

With a little toss of the head, Leonin set foot on the mole.

Kitt looked after the eleven black-clad knights marching along the jetty in single file. The red lily on their coats resembled fresh wounds in their backs.

Death by Moonlight

The Birlinn Yehan was leaving, and her three steel masts turned to catch the favourable eastern breeze, which always gave good speed to ships departing Isenkliff.

Had the wind not been favourable, this ship could have forced a passage into any adverse wind by the power of its steam kettle. The vessel also had a steel skeleton beneath her wooden hull, and a steel plate enforced bottom. Her keel was two hundred and eighty feet long with another thirty-six feet for her beam and she had a hundred and fifty-foot hollow mainmast also made of steel.

Her captain Lodemar, by his own account, had found this amazing vessel washed up on the shore of Rilante, but by what tide, not even the legends told. He had taken it to Isenkliff for advice, and Kitt had been all over it for the last month. He was still reeling with the impression of all the novel mechanics he had seen.

He closed the smelting oven and fired it. The metal ship had left behind a lot of corroded iron, and rust by the handfuls. Kitt hoped to see it again. There was so much iron in it to warrant constant attention. The Birlinn Yehan's topsails disappeared over the rim of the world and Kitt wandered down the path.

As the eastern died down, and the regular western wind sprang up again, a tower of white sails appeared above the grey horizon. By the time Kitt took the path towards the bay, he saw a tall battered Tolonian two-master with the characteristic strongly-curved belly, and the rigging that required many hands; men were climbing along the forest of spars and taking in the sails.

Kitt smelled vanilla, cinnamon and nutmeg on the wind. It was a Spice Island trader, one who hadn't come to Isenkliff before, or he would know that the time of the year was dangerously late for sailing. Soon the autumn storms would begin.

If he came for Aurora blades, he would be disappointed, like so many before him. Eckehart never sold to traders. But ever hopeful, the adventurous merchants would claw their way up the Rilante coast, wary of the swift Nordmänner serpent ships, passing the treacherous Scattered Islands, were sandbanks might deliver them and their wares into the hands of hard-living, cold-eyed island dwellers, or the Woodstalkers of the dark wood Murkowydir on the mainland. Kitt wondered whether too few made it back, to tell the others that Isenkliff steel was no ordinary merchandise with a price that could be settled by bargaining.

The ship dropped anchor, and a boat was let into the water, to bring to the shore a thin man of middle height and indeterminate colouring, with eyes set close together and an aggressive beak nose, under which hung a long moustache and goatee. His clothes had been luxurious once, green and brown brocade embroidered with silver, but now they were wrinkled as if he had slept in them many nights. When he caught sight of Kitt, his mouth dropped open.

"Have I come to the right island?" he demanded in Imperial, the language of Daguilaria. "You are not the famous smith, are you?"

"My father doesn't sell to merchants," Kitt answered him in the same language, which he spoke fluently, albeit with an accent.

"I haven't come to buy. I sell." The merchant stepped from the boat with a black bag in his hand, and from that, with a wary expression, he drew a long bundle, which he unrolled. From about ten feet of fabric emerged a two-handed sword, with a three-foot-long blade sheathed in black, which he thrust at Kitt like a piece of hot iron.

"What would your father give me for that?"

The sheath was a double one, made for two swords of equal length. There was only one hilt, a foot and a half, almost long enough to serve two-handed even for Kitt's big hands, and it was wrapped in rough, grainy, gleaming leather the kind of which he hadn't seen before. Was it fish? It was held in place with crisscrossing braids of worn silk that had been black once.

The sheath was wooden, lacquered black and silver, and also wrapped in silk, chafed in places. The owner wore it with armour at least occasionally, Kitt thought. The handguard was a burnished steel disk just wide enough to protect the knuckles, and it had no pommel.

The slim, curved blade slid out of the sheath easily. Kitt surveyed the grainy pattern of the steel, the hardening line rolling in a white wave along the edge, the grey-blue back. He tested weight and balance, and puzzled briefly over the three signs etched at the base, two letters of an unknown alphabet, and a sickle-moon.

At the same time, he taxed the merchant's frame that had never born the weight of iron, the uneasy face, the small fidgeting hands, and the ferret eyes straying over his shoulder constantly.

"For this, you can ask anything," he said slowly. "Even an Aurora blade."

"I want gold. A whole lot."

"Just that?"

The merchant looked at Kitt narrowly. "With the prices your father takes for his weapons, he must be rich. He can't be spending much of it here, can he?"

"You mean gold?"

"Of course I mean gold," the man retorted, considering the youth as if he was a halfwit.

Kitt nodded and turned to lead the way with long strides, keeping the sword in his hand, forcing the merchant to run after him.

"You are getting the gold, right? Until my price is met, the merchandise remains in my possession!"

Kitt nodded without slowing his stride up the path. There was no way he'd hand that sword back to the trader he heard panting after him. The western breeze died among the rocks of the cliff, and the step of the merchant's boots on the gravel sounded loud in the sudden stillness. Kitt walked soundlessly as a leopard.

"Have you ever been to Daguilaria?" the merchant asked, as if to break the silence with his voice.

Kitt shook his head.

"Know anybody at the imperial court?"

Kitt shook his head again. Among the many warriors who had come to Isenkliff, there had been several Daguilarian knights, and he knew at least one imperial spy. He did not bother to explain that.

"Thought so. Good. Perfect. What a howling wilderness."

They rounded the rocky outcrop, and before them lay the big weather-beaten hall at the foot of the cliff.

"That your barn? This blade came very dear. I want much gold for it," the trader said. "A whole lot!"

"I heard you."

248

Kitt threw open the door of the hall. His father and mother were there, in expectation of the guest. Kitt had stopped wondering how his mother always knew.

"A sword has come, father."

"Welcome. And also welcome to the man who brings it. You didn't ask our guest's name? Well, well."

"I am Roguier, arms supplier to the imperial court of Daguilaria," the merchant announced, his eyes scurrying into every corner of the room.

"You have come a long way, you must be tired." Eckehart also spoke Daguilarian, with a heavier accent than his son. "Sit down, warm yourself!"

Aslaug came over with a goblet of hot spiced wine.
Roguier waved her away impatiently. "I'm never too tired to do business."

Without a word, Aslaug returned to the fireplace and hung a kettle over the earth flames.

Kitt leaned against a wooden beam, watching the merchant with attention and dislike.

"How much is this worth to you?" Roguier waved at the black and silver sheath Kitt was holding.

Kitt slid the sword out of the sheath. "Seems Luxinian work. You can see it never was his." He spoke in their language of the north.

"Luxinian?" Eckehart asked, reaching for the blade.

"Luxin Shoo, got it in one," the merchant seized on the one word he understood. "From the hidden City of Idols, where the ancient masters of steel offer human sacrifices to iron statues descended from the sky at an eclipse of the sun." The glib tone of genial merchant praising his wares sounded forced.

Eckehart looked the blade over, weighed it in his hands, tapped on it with a fingernail, he even tasted it.

"Want it, or not?" Roguier demanded. "Are you people always so slow?"

Eckehart looked up from the blade to survey Roguier instead, and his blue eyes looked him over and through. "We have time. It seems that you don't."

"I am in a great hurry!" Roguier snapped, baring his teeth. "Time is money."

"Time is the stuff life is made out of," Eckehart said.

"Thank you for this gem of rustic wit! Makes no difference to my price."

"You have lots of time. There is a storm brewing, and it's going to blow a few days."

"Then, he can tell us how this sword came into his hands." Kitt smiled; the smile did not reach his eyes. "Tell us why a court supplier came all the way here to sell one blade. Was there not enough gold in the Dominant City to buy it?"

"Want it, or not? I can throw it in the sea." Roguier shot a crafty look from one smith to the other.

Kitt knew that his own face showed just the same expression he could see on his father's. There would be no haggling.

Eckehart shrugged. "If your life is money, then come."

Kitt lit a lantern. He led the way to the third doorway hewn into the rock, and from there to a windowless room. He threw open the door and held the lantern inside for its light to fall on a rock floor strewn with gold, laying there as if Eckehart had just opened the door to throw in handfuls of coins each time he was paid for a blade. That was indeed what he did. Roguier gasped audibly.

"Take as much as you can carry," Eckehart invited.

Roguier immediately spread out his coat and fell on his knees amidst the gold, to scrape and shovel the coins with both hands. He seemed to have forgotten his hurry, forgotten to look over his shoulder, and forgotten the smiths looking down on him.

A coin sprang from his twitching hands, and he hunted after it across other coins. It was as if he could not bring himself to stop heaping more gold on the coat, and in doing so, some of the other gold pieces slid away again, and he tried to stuff them back, cursing.

"Watch what gold can do," Eckehart said in their northern idiom. "Iron can only kill a man, but gold can slay his soul."

"Only those born with one," Kitt said.

Finally, Roguier knotted the ends of his coat and straightened to take up the swollen bundle; it seemed as if nailed to the floor. He heaved, but it would not move. His eyes, wild with gold, lit upon Kitt. "Hey you there, big boy, lend me a hand here!"

"Take as much as you can carry. Not as much as I can carry," Kitt said and laughed.

"Help him!" Eckehart said quietly.

Kitt lifted the bundle, estimating Roguier had managed to pack about hundred and forty pounds of gold, making not much of a dent in the hoard, as the storeroom was only the foremost of six more. A small price for that sword, he thought, as he carried the gold out of the hall, again without checking his stride, the merchant panting after him. The seams of the coat creaked.

Out of the valley, the wind was blowing stiffly from the West, and white foam topped the wave crests. The rowers' faces were anxious. Kitt dropped the gold among them, and the men exclaimed as a stream of coins flowed over the bottom.

Rogier scrambled into the rocking boat, and Kitt gave a shove which freed the boat-hook from the iron ring.

The rowers moved the oars, straining against the pressure of the wind, which began veering sharply, first to the north and then north-east, making the water of the harbour foam.

As Roguier looked back at Kitt, a joyless grin distorted his mouth, moving the long moustache in an odd angle. "Good luck, big boy!" He shouted, the wind blowing away every second word. ". . . despise me . . . I laugh . . . in the moonlight . . . death . . . coming . . . better you than me . . . Luxin Shoo . . . you think you know ha, ha, ha . . .! Row!" The last was directed at the rowers.

A wave rose and lifted the boat to eye level with Kitt, flowed back, and the boat shot out into the open sea.

Kitt was back in the hall even before Roguier could have reached his ship. He laid the sword before him on the table on its black wrapping, which was velvet, tightly woven, with long slits in it, as if the blade had been taken out carelessly.

He slid the blade from the sheath again. "This hardening line . . . like water in the moonlight. Roguier shouted something about moonlight. Salesman's prose, but true. Don't know why he bothered though, he'd made the sale."

251

"I don't think he meant the hardening line." Eckehart shook his head. "He is in a great hurry, and not because of the storm. Because he is scared. And tonight is a full moon. So, he did shout something about the moon?"

Kitt laughed. "He was afraid of his own shadow."

"No," Eckehart pulled his beard. "He was afraid of something else."

"Or someone. If he stole that sword from the man it belonged to, then he's right to be afraid."

"From what you say, he reckons that now that we have the sword, we are in trouble."

"That is possible. But where will the danger come from?" Kitt rose to hunt in the book shelves for the two scrolls in the collection reputed to have come from Luxin Shoo. "Let me see if I can find the letters etched on the blade."

For the rest of the evening, Kitt studied the square black signs of the first scroll, one by one, his eyes straying to the sword.

Outside the wind keened. The water kettle was boiling, steaming, and lifting the lid. His mother didn't take it off the fire. "They have foundered," Aslaug suddenly said.

"Too much hurry," Eckehart answered. "Now he has no more time or gold."

Kitt looked up briefly, having already forgotten about Roguier. He started on the second scroll, and when he came to the final line, his head hurt and he had found no letter corresponding precisely to those on the blade. He identified a couple of similar signs, and copied the words onto a sheet of papyrus which had been the gift of a warrior from Kemitraim.

#

That night Kitt slept lightly, to wake in the middle of the night with a strong sense of danger, coupled with the urge to feel a sword hilt in his hand.

His sword was in the smithy, in deference to his mother's feelings regarding weapons of war. He could reach the smithy through the rock passageway without having to go outside. That meant crossing the hall, where the Luxin Shoo sword was lying on the table. The thought of passing that blade unarmed made him realise the origin of his disquiet.

He took two hunting knives, conscious of how puny they were against that weapon. But who could have arrived in the night and broken into the hall to wield it?

He opened the door of his room onto the landing, and saw a bright silvery light at the foot of the stairs, running under the hall door like floodwater.

He tiptoed down the stairs into the vestibule and took one knife blade in his mouth to throw open the hall door, to see - nothing. The hall was dark. Outside the clouds raced before the full moon, driven by the storm, that out on the sea had already taken two-master, moustache and gold. His mother had said so, and she knew these things. Kitt stood on the threshold, waiting and listening, a knife in each hand.

Outside came a break in the clouds, and the light of the full moon flooded through the glass windows, lighting the room and striking a blinding reflection from the naked blade lying on the table. The reflected moonlight congealed into the spectre of a woman fashioned of silver and ivory, tall and svelte, standing on top of the hall table.

Like a flower her head turned slowly above the high-necked silver brocade of her dress, the thick silver tress woven through with white pearls the size of cherries snaking down her straight slim back. Her long black almond eyes looked around the hall, glittering with fury and cold malice as they lighted upon Kitt, standing lost in admiration of her rosy mother of pearl skin.

The sword began rattling; it rose and danced within the white beam of light containing the image of the girl. She became diffuse, turning into a silvery whirl of steel and moonlight, she rushed towards Kitt. He suddenly found himself fighting for his life, fending off the sword with nothing but the hunting knives. The storm of silver light and steel drove him back and back to the opposite wall, and above it, the midnight eyes were mocking him.

Suddenly the light was blotted out as storm clouds passed before the face of the moon. The sword clattered to the floor at Kitt's feet.

He pounced on it, grabbed the hilt, and felt his way through the sudden darkness to the table, to sheath the blade and wrap it into the length of the black velvet cloth, all ten feet of it.

Remembering the slits in the fabric, he doubled the fabric top and bottom, to keep the sword from sliding out not so accidentally.

To undo the bars of the hall door with that sword in his back was out of the question. Kitt hurried to the first doorway and crossed the stone corridor to the smithy to arm himself with a sword and a mail shirt.

When he returned, the hall was awash with moonlight again. The sword was rattling on the table inside the wrapping.

Kitt pounced to hold down the jumping bundle, feeling the vibration through the velvet, like a steel hornet against the weight of his hand.

Another cloud passed and the blade lay still again.

Kitt used the moment of quiet to wrap a length of chain around the dangerous bundle.

Whenever the moon shone, the sword moved, while Kitt watched wide awake, his hand never leaving the hilt of his sword. More death to follow, so the merchant had said, and Kitt was ready for it to arrive.

The moon paled in the first morning light, and the sword lay on the table, inert.

A sudden blow on the hall door broke a plank. The second blow broke another hole, and then, with a crash, the bar splintered, and the debris flew inside.

A stranger stood in the door, a golden warrior. He had long dark almond eyes in an oval face, golden-hued, with high cheekbones and full lips, and his bronze-coloured hair was braided in a long tress that lay over his shoulder, the end tucked into his gold-studded girdle. The stranger's clothes were made of stiff gold brocade, yet he moved within them like a tiger, as he stepped through the ruined door into the vestibule and crossed into the hall.

Kitt was just something in his way. The golden warrior made an abrupt movement with his left arm, as a man walking in the jungle might do to brush away a plant, lightning-fast, hard as falling rock, and aimed at the heart.

254

Kitt deflected the blow with an equally fast and hard hit of his bare hand, and also the second blow that followed immediately. A third and a fourth blow whistled through the air, and were deflected. Both fighters spun away from each other. Out of elongated, dark eyes, the golden stranger watched Kitt, still between him and the table, where the sword lay.

"It was you I've been sitting up for," Kitt said in Daguilarian.

"This sword is mine!" the golden warrior said in a voice that tolled like a bronze bell. He stretched out his hand, and the sword jumped across the room, leaving the wrapping, chain and sheath behind on the table. Pressing the naked blade close to his chest, the golden warrior turned towards the door.

Kitt could not let him go. He grabbed one of the scrolls from Luxin Shoo from the hall table and with a long stride, he was between the stranger and the exit and pushed the paper cylinder towards his face. "Can you read this for me?"

The golden warrior stopped, his hand moving an inch and holding still. The long, dark almond eyes rested on the manuscript and then on Kitt.

"This sword is mine."

"Yes. Nothing could be clearer. Now, can you or can't you read this scroll?" In his eagerness, Kitt stepped from one foot to the other like an impatient puppy.

The golden warrior's perfect countenance wavered into a smile that did not reach the infinitely sad almond eyes. He thrust the sword into his girdle and used both hands to unroll the scroll covered in the spidery black glyphs. He began to read in a language unknown to Kitt, and then he switched to Daguilarian, which he spoke with an accent even thicker than Kitt's. "The title is *Remarks of king Limang of Arletoxo to his son Lizu, the duke of Zenxun concerning the art of using eagles and cheetahs for the hunt.* He says: The actions of animals and also humans are often governed by habit rather than reason. Therefore consider well, that a scorpion will always be a scorpion that will, if he finds nought else, sting a stone."

"That king, is he the ruler of Luxin Shoo?"

"Limang was the thirtieth king of Arleto, one of seven kingdoms in the land western barbarians call Luxin Shoo. He died a thousand years ago, and his remarks to his son the duke of Zenxun are cited often, for their wisdom."

"A thousand years! How old everything must be in Luxin Shoo!"

Steps sounded, it was Aslaug descending into the kitchen from her room.

"Breakfast," Kitt said. "Let's eat first and then translate the rest of the manuscript." He blushed. "If you will do me the favour. My name is Kitt."

"What land is this?"

"Isenkliff."

"Isenkliff? Is that the island also called Betra Hyerote in the language of Tolosa or Eisenberg in that of Daguilaria?"

"Yes."

The golden warrior's shoulders slumped as if exhausted. "At last. The Dark Gods must be asleep to allow me to reach here. My name is Malan Jian. I will repair your door and read your book."

"There are two scrolls," Kitt said. "Don't worry about the door."

The storm had blown itself out over the sea.

Kitt surveyed the boat with the one tattered sail on a cracked mast. "You came in that thing? If you had missed your course, the storm would have driven you into the ice of Jotunheim."

Malan Jian smiled one of his melancholy smiles. "I could not miss this island, even in a storm, because my sword was on it. It is like a beacon for me. You don't believe me?"

"You are here. I believe you. This was the first storm. Sailing stops now. Will you stay the winter?"

"I won't go anywhere from here." Malan Jian smiled a melancholy smile.

That very day Kitt repaired the broken hall door with Malan Jian's help, who patiently answered his many questions as they worked.

Yes, man-eating cats hunted in the steaming forests of Luxin Shoo, striped black and yellow like hornets.

Yes, the waterlilies had floating leaves big enough to carry whole families, though not to build houses on them.

It was true that the cereal grew in the water, and that the people ate frogs, lizards and snails and dogs -everything that had a little meat.

No, the peasants did not wear silk, but a cotton fabric that was finer than the flaxen clothes of the north. Silk was made by worms that would eat only one kind of tree leaves, and the trading of it was a prerogative of the Emperor. No, the Emperors of Luxin Shoo were not immortal; they would not pay the price.

No, the women there did have feet, only prostitute slaves did not, as at childhood their feet were shaped into the form of the golden lotus in a protracted, painful process that bore its own reward of beauty.

Yes, there were holy monks, who had foresworn weapons and defended themselves with bare hands against all attacks, and it was this method Malan Jian had used to break down the door.

Aslaug opened the repaired hall door to see Kitt and the Golden Warrior Malan Jian circling each other, as if listening to the old melody of a deadly dance, their hands whistling through the air so fast that she couldn't discern a single movement. She watched with the familiar mixture of fascination and dread, and the contradictory love she never failed to feel at the sight of the boy's pale golden hair and quick smile. She felt Eckehart come up behind her and look out over her head.

"He doesn't even need steel to fight," she said. "Do you remember how I said that his body is shaping itself into a weapon?"

"I remember."

"It is as if he knows in his blood."

"But with him, all takes on a strange innocence," Eckehart said. "So, what will you do about it? Where can you send him after he returned from Wittewal? Who will kill him from behind, as Grimwolf wouldn't do it?"

She whipped around. "I feared for him as much as you did!"

"For whom, Kitt or Grimwolf?"

"Both," she said honestly. "But then, Grimwolf is so much more generous to his enemy than I can ever be to his son."

"That he is. But I would have liked to have a child with you, Aslaug."

"You have the son you wanted."

"That's true. I'm just jealous. I'm a man."

"You are a smith first of all." Aslaug turned to him and smiled. "I always liked that about you, the consequence of it."

"But you love Grimwolf, and you are with his child."

"I have always loved him."

The second scroll was *The Golden Medicine of Wandi Kounelun*, also written on bamboo paper.

Both scrolls were deciphered and translated word by word and sign by sign, and the contents of Aslaug's chest compared to the recipes of the *Golden Medicine* and the strange and extensive weaponry of Luxin Shoo to the simpler northern ways of fighting. Kitt learned the knack of breaking down a door with his bare hands.

They went hunting in the cliffs together, challenging each other with difficult shots, Kitt with his Kirgis bow and Malan Jian with a double bent bow made from horn and lacquer.

Whenever Kitt was working his steel, Malan Jian would sit there, telling of the many smiths he had encountered, and what he had seen of their secretive methods, having taken an extraordinary interest in the forging, tempering and hardening of steel. Kitt experimented with leaves, feathers, mud, and worse, forming the result into a blade, hardening it, polishing it, tempering the hardness in the fire of the forge, until the edges took on golden, bronze, and blue hues. Then he reduced the whole to a heap of grey shavings with a rasp to start again.

Finally, Kitt was content with the shape and handling of his new sword, which was slightly curved just like Malan Jian's, but with a blade almost four feet long. Now, there remained to achieve the hardening line, like white water.

Twenty-six days passed in this way and all this time the sea remained calm after the first autumn storm.

Yet Malan Jian showed no inclination to leave Isenkliff. After the

258

first day, Kitt had never asked about the woman in the sword. "Moon almost full," he remarked tentatively at breakfast.

Malan Jian smiled. "Any moonlight is enough to bring her. But she is strongest on the three days of the fullest moon."

"She almost killed me."

"You are the first who fought her, and lived."

"Roguier?"

"He only escaped, barely."

"Does she affect the handling of your sword?"

"Yes."

Kitt mulled over that, while they were drinking lime flower tea.

"Once in the market of Loyuyank I saw a beautiful woman," Malan Jian began to speak. "She was being sold as a slave to pay the debts of her family. Niluba. I bought her, and I loved her, with a love that I knew was forever.

"And she loved me also. But she could never believe that my love, the love of a man, could last longer than her youth.

"We came to Anjank, the City of Idols because Niluba wanted to go there, and what she wanted, I wanted.

"I should have woken when she rose in the night, and went to the temple of the Fallen Star. I slept, when her life and soul were made into a sword, this sword. Because I loved her, I should have known the moment when her living heart went into the steel.

"But I did not wake until the morning, and when I didn't find her beside me, I didn't know where she could have gone. I looked for her all over the City of Idols, and I passed the Temple of the Fallen Star where a ceremony was being held, a sword dedication. I didn't know then which sword. In the evening they brought it to me.

"That night a full moon shone, and I couldn't sleep. If only I had not slept the night before. As the moonlight fell upon the blade, I saw her. She was the same as she had been when she left me, so beautiful. Only her raven hair had turned into silver. I saw her, but I couldn't touch her, couldn't feel her touch. I went to the Temple of the Fallen Star, but the priests only mocked my pain. I killed them all, with this sword. Since then, I wander the world, with her, searching for the secret of banning a soul into a sword."

"That's how you know so much about steel," Kitt said, suddenly enlightened.

"Yes." Malan Jian smiled his melancholy smile. "In Bharatan, I found many secrets of steel, but not the one I sought. There I saved the merchant Roguier from robbers, and came to Daguilaria on one of his ships. He presented me to the Immortal Emperor, who was impressed with my skill at arms, and kept me by him. I thought Roguier was my friend. Somehow, he must have seen her in the moonlight, and wanted her." Malan Jian's lips twitched in mirthless humour. "He had no joy of his nights anymore."

"So Roguier really was a far-travelled merchant. I thought he was just a common thief. It must have been fear making him into a rat, fear of you, and of her in the sword. That fear made him sail directly into the storm. He didn't survive it."

"I care not, if he lives," Malan Jian said, caressing the sword.

Kitt wondered if ever he would find a woman who would stand side by side with him to fight the world, and love him enough to sacrifice everything for him, as he would give everything for her.

My sister in arms, my lover. You and I against all, against everything. If only I have you, let the whole world go down in blood and fire.

"I wish for such a love as yours, Malan Jian," he said suddenly, passionately.

Malan Jian clasped a hand over Kitt's mouth. "You don't know what it is you ask. Grant mercy that the Dark Gods have not heard you now. I feel them watching me, even here at the end of the world, forever mocking me with the rotting grin of their slain priests."

That day Kitt saw Malan Jian talking to Eckehart, who was standing in the door of the smithy, shaking his head.

The Golden Warrior went away, passing Kitt but seemed not to see him, and Eckehart went into the smithy, banging the door behind him.

"What does Malan Jian want from you, father?"

Putting an edge to a blade, Eckehart's expression and whole bearing were still one of absolute denial. "You know already, son, that his sword has a soul. A human soul banished into the iron."

"She is so beautiful!" Kitt's eyes shone. "And dangerous! What she did was for love of him."

"Malan Jian fears that when he dies, she will be left alone. He wants to bring the same sacrifice for her, join her in the steel. He wants to be able to touch her again. I keep telling him, I don't do this kind of Zaubar."

"But you could? You can weld steel to living flesh. You forge quicksilver and ice."

"I can do many things. That does not mean that I will do them." Eckehart laid a hand on Kitt's shoulder. "You don't want that kind of knowledge, my son. Trust me on this."

"I don't ask you to teach me, father. I ask that you help Malan Jian."

"To ban a soul into steel, it must become steel itself, or it will evaporate in the smelter. A lifetime of hardship may forge a soul, hammering it by the forces that just are, grinding it to nothing by the pettiness of men, and quench all the fire in heartbreak. What is left then is steel. But to do it to a human being in one single day . . ." Eckehart's voice trailed off. "Even the gods shy away from that, all but the darkest."

#

Kitt found Malan Jian on the mountain slope above the smelting ovens.

He refused to return to the smith's hall until Eckehart agreed to do as he asked. Kitt's warning about the Jarnmantsjes made no difference to his resolve and he would take no weapons but the sword. Kitt helped him widen the rock recess on the southern promontory of the cliff, where the moonlight would meet no obstacle.

When he came down, he saw an iron plate placed onto the access of the path with runes scratched into the surface. No Jotun would pass this. His father at least did this much.

From then on, Malan Jian sat in his rock place completely motionless except for the hands caressing his sword. His hair grew down his back, and his thin beard fell on his chest.

261

Kitt brought him food and tried to coax him into the house, but Malan Jian always refused, and he hardly ate anything.

Sometimes at a full moon, Kitt saw the woman of the sword from afar.

###

One day when the red light of the setting sun struck the ledge in the cliff, Kitt didn't see the golden figure there.

He climbed up the steep path, and found that the cave was empty. Only the curved sword lay on the ground, and the food Kitt had brought, untouched. A shred of seaweed clung to the rock. A giant wave must have plucked Malan Jian from the ledge at flood-time, Kitt thought.

Warily Kitt waited for the silver light of the full moon to come into the cave and strike the blade. He had his sword but did not draw it. He hoped that he would be fast enough.

Then she was there, the lady of the sword, pale, so pale in the moonlight. For a moment the almond eyes rested on Kitt, and then they strayed out to the sea. "How?" Kitt asked.

The moonlight girl shook her head slightly, still looking out to the sea. He could see that she was waiting.

There was no way Kitt could pick up that sword. He left it in the recess.

Ice Giants

The Longest Night was near, and the unbroken ice field that stretched all the way to Jotunheim, lay blinding white in the sun.

Kitt smelt smoke. Keeping carefully hidden, he looked over the edge of the northern high-shore. Tracks from the north-east showed that something had come across to Isenkliff. Kitt at once thought of Isprinsessans and Isjotuns, but the Cold Folk needed no fire.

The fire was down on the frozen beach. An old man was sitting there; he was feeding little pieces of driftwood to the red flames. A sheet of leather hanging from two sticks dispersed the smoke, but Kitt had smelt it. By the fire lay three long-snouted pikes, gutted and cleaned. The old man wore thick clothing made of seal fur and leather so light in colour as to be almost white; it was embroidered with little pieces of ivory, and he wore slinky necklaces of fish bones. His face was deeply lined, and he had long white hair. This was not an Ice Giant, but only an Ice Rim Hunter.

Kitt knew about the Ice Rim Hunters from Nordmänner tales, that they lived on fish and seal meat on the Frozen Islands far to the north, where no trees grew. He walked down to the fire openly, keeping his hands away from his weapons, but not too far away.

"Good day, grandfather," Kitt greeted in the language of the Nordmänner.

The old seal hunter looked Kitt up and down out of his dark-green eyes without the whites showing, quietly taking in every little detail: the tall, broad-shouldered figure, the fair hair and grey eyes, the fur-lined leather clothing, warm, yet leaving the boy to move freely, the sword hilt over his shoulder, the Kirgis bow, a full quiver and the iron lance.

The old man stuck the pikes on a spit and hung them above the flames. "Sit down! Eat!" he said in the same language.

Kitt sat down by the fire, his back to the direction from where he had come. "Come far?" he asked.

The old man pointed north-east.

"Come far?" the old man asked in turn.

Kitt shook his head. "I live here."

263

The old man took the spit down and held it out to Kitt, who took a fish, charred coal black. Its heat was very pleasant to feel through the leather glove. He broke the fish open with both hands; inside the flesh was steaming and white. The old man appeared relieved at seeing him eat.

Kitt opened his bag of provisions and offered the old man bread and goats cheese. The seal hunter sniffed both with a sceptical face and handed it back. "Not know, not eat," he declared, pointing to the fish. "Good."

They sat for some time in silence, watching the red and green fireworms crawling through the ashes of the fire; it was the salt in the wood that made the colourful sparks.

Kitt rose to more collect driftwood. When he straightened up with an armful of frost-dried boughs, he saw a dark dot approaching from the north-west over the ice, and another, smaller from the other side. The dots came nearer; one was a sledge, drawn by six huge white dogs each. The smaller dot was a walking Ice Rim Hunter. The old hunter saw them too and began feeding the fire and cutting spits.

The sledge arrived first, carrying two seal carcasses. The hunter broke one open there on the frozen beach and fed the innards to the sledge dogs; their thick grey and black fur made them look enormous.

The second Ice Rim Hunters reached the shore, and they came both to the fire. As they pushed back their fur hoods, Kitt saw that they too had bone-white hair, although they were young men.

They spoke to the old man in a language that Kitt did not understand, and stuck pieces of meat onto the spits which the old man had cut from driftwood, not betraying any curiosity towards Kitt.

Kitt noticed their spears, which had iron tips. Cold forged iron, he could see. "You make steel?" he asked, using the Nordmänner language.

One of the hunters pointed to the sky.

"Chimrie," he said. "Eld chimrie."

"Sky. Fire," the old man said in the Nordmänner language. "Burning iron."

One of the young men made an arching gesture with his right arm, accompanied by a whining noise ending in a hiss. "Fire fall from sky," the old man explained.

When they had eaten, the Ice Rim Hunters laid down to sleep among their dogs.

Kitt sat by the fire, from time to time feeding it with driftwood, watching the colourful sparks.

A white aurora flamed over the sky and was reflected from the ice in a silvery light, that made rocks and gnarled trees on top of the cliff standing out clearly visible and yet unreal. A tension was in the air. The dogs whimpered, their big, rough paws twitched. The sleepers stirred, and Kitt saw that the old man's eyes were open. He shoved the driftwood deeper into the fire, feeling oddly comforted by the warmth and reality of the red flames.

Kitt woke with a start, surprised that he had slept.

The fire had burned down, and in the flickering light of the aurora he saw something coming over the ice, thirteen great forms in a long, drawn-out line, like wandering mountains.

The Isjotun, Ice giants.

Kitt threw driftwood onto the fire.

An ember caught, and the flames leapt high.

The first Isjotun neared Isenkliff. He had to be standing twelve feet high. Kitt clearly saw scales of transparent ice, icy eyes rimmed with lashes of hoarfrost, a thick beard of icicles. His white hands gripped the hilt of a glittering sword made from a ten-foot-long sharpened icicle.

Kitt held the blade of his sword into the flames.

The seal hunters scrambled to hitch the dogs to the sledge. They jumped into it and drove over the heaving ice sheet northwards.

The first Isjotun was just about to set his ice boots onto the shore. Kitt ran down the beach and in under the long ice sword, aiming the hot blade at the right knee of the giant. It went in sizzling and was stuck before it could cut through.

Kitt released the hilt, ducked away under the massive Isjotun's arm and slid onto the ice; he fell, and was unable to get up again, his hands and feet sliding over the slick ice without hold. Raising his ice sword high in an arc, the Isjotun turned, and his right knee broke with a loud crack. He crashed down headlong and broke into glittering shards of ice.

The second Isjotun was nearing the coast. Kitt still found no hold on the ice sheet, which was inclined a little upwards towards the shore. He drew his knife, and hacked it into the ice, to drag himself along. From the corner of his eye, he saw the second Isjotun coming nearer like a siege tower, ice legs rising and descending like pistons that would crush him into the ice in a matter of a few more steps.

Something flew over the sky in a glowing arch, a red-hot, fist-sized object drawing a shower of sparks behind. A hammer? It crashed into the ice before the feet of the second Isjotun.
Steam hissed up, and cracks appeared in the ice like a spider net, turning dark with the water welling up.

The Isjotun sank into the breaking ice, first to the knee, then to the waist, and then up to the chest, his cold eyes looking over to Isenkliff. The water swallowed him, and a moment later, his head bobbed up with a wave to swim on the dark water as an iceberg.

Kitt, at last, managed to drive his knife into the pebble beach and drew himself up to the shore.

Another glowing, sparking hammer sailed through the sky and crashed into the ice before the third Isjotun. He too sank, to re-emerge as an iceberg among the floes of the breaking ice sheet.

Seven more Isjotun stopped their march on the rim of the dark channel that was widening before Isenkliff. Long, deep cracks ran over the ice, and the Isjotun sank one after the other, all but the one standing farthest away.

Far out on the ice, the black dot of the sledge was on its run north. The sun came up rosy in the east, and a thundering noise was coming from the sea. The ice field continued breaking around Isenkliff; the freed sea was lapping at the shore, and softness was in the air.

Among the thick ice piled up on the shore by the waves, Kitt spotted his sword encased in ice, and two more ice-floes with dark enclosures. Each had embedded a fist-sized lump of iron, without any similarity to a hammerhead.

266

Coming home, Kitt saw smoke billowing from the chimney of the smithy. Inside his father's shadow was standing huge and dark before the fire. "We wondered where you were," Eckehart grumbled. "Always running about. Should know better with the Longest Night coming."

"I met Ice Rim Hunters on the north side, and spent the night at their fire. They have iron weapons, made from iron they said fell from the sky. They left in a hurry when the ice broke in the middle of the night." Kitt glanced over Eckehart's tools. The hammers were all there, none missing. "I must have dreamt."

Smiling into his red-streaked white beard, the smith looked kindly at his son from his light blue eyes. "Isprinsessans again?"

"Isjotuns. And iron hammers." Kitt held out the two fist-sized iron pieces from the ice-floe.

The smith took them and turned the iron over in his hand. "With the Longest Night near, those who are born under strange stars can have strange luck. And strange dreams also come with the ice. Isjotun, indeed."

"Is that good iron, father? The books say it is."

"The best you can hope to find. If you know how to work it. It is always a matter of knowing how to work it, as with any steel, and the question of what it can be and what it cannot."

"This time you don't appear the worse for your recklessness," Aslaug remarked, a smile belying her stern words, when Kitt came into the hall. She was stirring a bubbling kettle hanging above the hearth fire.

"This time our son took on the Isjotuns," Eckehart informed.

"I tried," Kitt said ruefully. "They were just too big. Iron from the sky broke the ice just in time. And the warm wind drove it apart and away from the shore."

Aslaug took the kettle from the fire and set it down beside the hearth. "The Winter Child is a warm wind comes this time of year, every year."

"And just at the right moment," Eckehart chuckled.

#

The next morning was still and cold, and thick hoarfrost rimmed twigs and reeds, smoothed sharp edges and wrapped every surface in white velvet strewn with diamonds. The ice-coated branches of the weeping willow by the door tinkled.

Kitt wondered how stout his mother was growing. He began feeling worried because it took her more and more effort to move with her swelling belly. His father also was concerned, Kitt saw him looking at his mother when she didn't notice. Aslaug denied that she was ill, and indeed she looked young despite her cumbersomeness; the gold of her hair shone, and the silver strands had disappeared.

Aslaug bore her daughter in the fourth moon after New Light and named her Swantje. Swantje was a quiet child with a fuzzy blonde head and a broad, toothless smile. She mostly slept with the determination of a little animal.

Kitt was beside himself with joy at having a little sister.

Little Killers

The sun was standing high in the south, but the land still lay under a white shroud for the seventh month.

The earth was frozen hard as if in a death paroxysm, never to wake up again. There had been a brief thaw in the time of the birth of Kitt's little sister Swantje. After that, it grew cold again, and snow kept falling in big, white, soft flakes from the low grey clouds.

Then one morning, the white curtain was thinning, the clouds began to dissolve, leaving a blue sky spanning over the white waste. The sun poured through the window and made Aslaug's hair gleam like gold, as she sat at the table, plucking green leaves from parsley plants that grew in a little pot, and sprinkling them over the plates of soup, in which the yellow cubes of turnips swam, and not much else.

The wooden beams of the store-room beside the hall that in autumn were hardly visible behind onion braids and beef sides, now stood bare with their spindly hooks outstretched like thin fingers. Baskets were emptied of the last apples and nuts, and only a few wilted turnips were left in the sand-filled boxes.

Kitt was stirring his soup, and crumbling his bread, eating very little. Although he was hungry, he was tired of the endless turnips, particularly as the ham that makes turnip soup a tasty dish had long vanished. Kitt was hungry for a piece of fresh meat, it was the hunger of a predator, and he even imagined that his teeth were growing longer and sharper. "It's stopped snowing," he remarked. "Today, I'll go out to hunt. A goose would be good." The word alone conjured up the juicy roast with yellow fat under the brown, crisp skin, and he swallowed. "But they have gone far south this year. It will have to be a wild goat again, if I can find one. They seem to have disappeared."

"A boy doesn't grow to your size on a diet of turnips," Eckehart said, looking depressed.

"It's worse for Isegrim. He needs meat."

At the mention of his name, the old dog lying by the hearth wagged his tail. His face was almost white.

"The soup was very good," Kitt said loyally. "Especially the green bits," he added with longing.

His mother always managed to have at least some green leaves to add to the food. She grew them in little pots on the windowsills; all the space was taken up. The southern sun stood already high, shining warmly through the glass, making the green plants thrive. Without them, the turnip time would have been much harder to bear.

"I wish I could give you more of that," Aslaug said. "But we must leave some seedlings for the planting seasons, when it comes, to make up for the lost time.

"If spring ever comes and with it another planting season," Eckehart said.

"It will come, a few more times."

Kitt rose from his place at the table, and went to the window to open it and strew bread crumbs on the sill. Winter thrust its fist through the crack immediately, as if to strangle all the warmth inside. He rapidly closed the window.

Kitt went out into the scullery and donned his fur-lined cloak and gloves, and gripped spear and bow. Before he could open the door, he had to clear away the rags and cushions his mother had placed to keep the cold air from seeping through the tiniest cracks.

He fastened snowshoes under his feet, wooden frames over which leather straps were spanned, and opened the door, to close his eyes immediately from the blinding reflection of the sun on the snow. Winter shouldered into the house like a troop of soldiers.

Driven by the wind, the snow had piled up waist-deep behind the door. Kitt clambered over it.

The valley before the house was filled up with snow, a white expanse, from which the gaunt grey cliff jutted. Looking over the brilliant still landscape, Kitt could see no end to the winter in sight, and the east wind hit his face, cold and stiff. He trudged past the empty stables and through the vegetable garden that was buried in the snow and his snowshoes left a broad spoor behind him. Snow lay as little white caps on the tree buds waiting for the spring. Kitt saw three owls sitting huddled side by side, brown feather bundles with big round yellow eyes. By the time he came to the stone wall overgrown with bare rose thorns, he was feeling hot.

Outside the wall surrounding the garden, he found the snow

disturbed and speckled red. Bones lay strewn about, and he found shreds of skin and hair which showed him that it had been a wild goat, fallen near the garden the night before, seeking out the human dwelling. This the animals frequently did in a long hard winter, when the burrowing for the brown grass in the deep snow took away more strength than it gave.

From the tracks, Kitt saw that the usual guests had been there, foxes, crows, weasels. Then, he found clumps of fox-hair and the black wings and beaks of a crow. This surprised him. Usually, the succession for feeding at a carcass was regulated merely by size and snarls and sudden darts at competitors. But here a bitter fight for precedence seemed to have taken place.

There were other tracks, which by their depth he thought at first might be a tree cat, but on looking closer, decided that these were too oblong, and the furrows in the snow showed that they had been made by very hairy paws. Kitt paused to look at the unfamiliar tracks carefully, memorising them.

Pushing on through the snow, he soon came upon another track, a deep trench in the snow, where a goat had ploughed its way through the white blanket. At the end of the trench, the animal was a dark speck stuck in the white. He caught up with the goat, a pitifully thin and exhausted female, the black and tan hair crusted with icicles. It looked at him in dumb suffering from a yellow glassy eye, in which the boy could see mirrored his own miniature picture.

Kitt lowered the spear and took off a glove to burrow in his pockets for a piece of bread, which he held under the goat's frost rimmed nostrils. The animal sniffed and took the food with its soft mobile mouth, chewing slowly, painfully. It dropped the crust, half-chewed and stood with a hanging head. Kitt picked up the bread, crumpled it into smaller bits, and held it out again. The animal nibbled a little more.

Near the goat Kitt saw more of the strange tracks; he estimated five or six of whatever animal it was, and thought of the bloody scraps he had seen in the snow a little while before. With both hands, he reached under the belly of the helpless animal, lifted it clear, and loaded it on his shoulder.

"You can have my turnips. I'm sick of them," he muttered.

Retracing his own tracks, Kitt came past a boulder jutting from the snow; now an animal was sitting on it such as he had never seen before. It was snow-white, except for a coal-black spot under its chin and at the end of the flowing bushy tail. A least two feet long without the flowing tail, which was as long again, the strange animal had the lithe, powerful body of a marten and the keen face of an ermine, framed by a thick long fur collar. Comic tufts of white fur sat at the end of the triangular ears, and around the paws, which Kitt immediately recognised as the cause of the puzzling tracks. Out of green eyes with long white lashes, the animal contemplated the spectacle of the boy carrying a live goat. Kitt couldn't help smiling despite his gloomy thoughts about turnips.

"You don't look hungry," he said conversationally, slowly approaching the strange animal; he was surprised that it did not run, even at the sound of his voice. As if it knew that he was too encumbered to move fast. "Where do you hunt, you furry rogue, that you can look so sleek in these starvation times?" He approached another three steps. When only ten feet separated him from the animal, it became restless, and the bushy tail quivered. "Are you the one whose messy leftovers I found? I'm sure you are."

At this accusation, the white animal increased the distance by jumping to another stone, where it sat down on its hind legs, furry forepaws in the air, its pale blue nose twitching.

"You wanted this goat, didn't you? You can't have it."

Finally, the animal seemed to have enough of human conversation and took off across the snowfield, the tufts of white fur on the paws functioning as small snowshoes, keeping them from sinking in.

Kitt looked after the white stranger, as it stalked away easily over the deep snow, white bushy tail erect. Once, it turned back the furry head to give the youth a very green look from its emerald eyes.

Back in the garden, Kitt stopped to scoop up the three owls. They wouldn't have a chance with the new strange animal about. He set the brown birds on his left arm one by one and then picked up the goat again. The owls didn't even flap.

Kitt slammed the door shut in the face of winter. After the

272

brilliantly light snow-world, it was dark in the hall, and warm. In the hearth roared the underground fire, and beside it sat his parents, looking with mild surprise at their son, and the animals he brought in.

Kitt set down the goat and placed the owls upon the beam above the door. He freed his feet from the snowshoes and peeled out of his coat. A puddle of thawing snow formed around his boots and under the goat.

His eyes adjusted to the dimness, Kitt saw another figure squatting beside the fireplace, a thickset gnarled, little grey man dangling short legs. The Jarnmantsje's deep-set, yellow eyes almost disappeared under beetling brows, his long thin lips pursed below a hook nose. He was sewn into goat's skins, but it was difficult to ascertain where the pelt of his attire ended, and his own began.

"Oh Gullo, the disappointment!" Eckehart laughed. "My son comes home from hunting empty-handed. Unless you count the owls."

"Snowblind you must be, smith," the Jarnmantsje said, sniffing loudly. "Goat is right behind Kitt, I see."

"Thin goat is behind me, Gullo. Too thin to slaughter," Kitt said. "I brought in another eater, instead of something to eat."

He went into the second doorway leading into a storeroom, took a handful of grain from a sack by the door and brought it to the goat. The animal took up the grains from Kitt's hands and mumbled, impervious to being inside a house with more humans, not to mention a hungry Jarnmantsje.

"Humph!" Gullo said morosely and climbed down from his seat. "Wake me up then when the goat is fat enough to eat. Humph!"

He shuffled through the door that led directly into the mountain.

"They sleep?" Kitt asked.

Eckehart nodded.

The Jarnmantsjes slept when food was exhausted, then they lay in their caves like stones, warmed by the heat of the inner earth. They could sleep long in this way, just like bears, and when they woke in spring, they were as gaunt and hungry and dangerous.

After he had laid another handful of grain before the goat, Kitt came to the fire and sat down on the place the Jarnmantsje had vacated. "I found this goat stuck in the snow, and I just couldn't kill it for the little meat it has left on its bones." He lifted the lid of the pot hanging over the fire for the evening meal, making a face at the overly familiar smell. "Not as long as there are turnips," he said heroically. "I'll hunt seals. If I can find any, as there is no open water."

"What difference does it make, whether you kill this animal or the seal, whether you kill the goat now, or in summer?" Aslaug asked.

Kitt paused to think. "Seals don't mind the cold, they are sleek and cunning. In summer, there is an equal chance for the goat to get away and me staying hungry," he finally said.

"An equal chance, is there really?" A peculiar expression crossed Aslaug's face. "The seals, do they stand a chance? When was the last time your arrow or your spear missed a deer or a goat or a goose you shot at? Where is the equal chance in that?"

Kitt shrugged helplessly. The questions his mother asked were always so difficult, and he felt miserable for giving the wrong answer.

"So, why did you not kill this goat? Why did you give it your bread and carried it home on your back?" Eckehart asked.

His father's questions Kitt could always answer.

"In summer, when I see them from afar I just shoot and hit, and when I come near they are dead, and I'm a little sorry, and then I break them up, and there is meat. This time was different. I came so near it. I could see that it was suffering. I couldn't . . ." He looked at his mother, helplessly. "I don't know."

"Think about it!" Aslaug said. "It's important."

"There is one out there who has no scruples. None. I envy him." Kitt told of his meeting with the strange white animal, describing it minutely. "I thought I knew all the animals here, but I have never seen any like these, not even in the great wood called Murkowydir."

"What you saw was a Witlyn, a snow marten," Eckehart said. "They live in Jotunheim, and must have come over the ice."

"First the Isprinsessans, then the Isjotun, and now white fur balls. Maybe Jotunheim has run out of bad things." Kitt laughed.

A shadow passed above in the darkness beneath the rafters of the hall, wings beat soft and dark, and a mouse squeaked.

"That won't nibble any more of our grain," Eckehart said. "Things are evened out. Don't worry about it, my son."

He carried the warmed up pot to the kitchen table, and by then the youth was so hungry that he began eating his soup, slowly, trying not to breathe in the turnip smell, and making the crust of bread last as long as it could. He wouldn't ask for another one, having just brought in an additional eater. Even so, Aslaug cut another slice of bread for Kitt, and after a little hesitation, he ate it.

Suddenly a white, furry face appeared at the window, looking inside with shining green eyes.

"There it is!" Kitt pointed to the window with his spoon.

"A Witlyn indeed," Eckehart said.

"It's beautiful. I wonder if I could tame it."

The furry animal sat on its haunches, as if to see better the humans inside, the pale blue nose twitching. A titmouse about to land on the windowsill saw the white animal and sheered away with a frightened chirp. The smooth white body shot into the air vertically. Blue feathers floated in the air.

"Oh!" Kitt exclaimed.

The white predator devoured the bird right on the spot, and then sat calmly on the sill again, cleaning a blood speck from its pelt with a fastidious blue tongue.

"No more putting out crumbs on that ledge," Eckehart said.

#

The next day, the icicles hanging from the roof were dripping, and a bird sang loud and clear.

Spring came to Isenkliff at last and arriving so late it came like an explosion. Kitt could almost watch the grass push through the wet soil and unfurl millions of narrow green leaves, from one day to another, wrapping the earth in a green cloak, studded with the little, bright-yellow discs of the buttercups. Buds swelled and burst into flowers, white and pink, and unfolded the improbably luminous green of young leaves.

The owls stayed in the hall, and built their nest in the rafters. Their shadow wings flapped under the roof as they hunted the mice.

275

The rescued goat also stayed, and soon, two little goats were staggering before the door of the hall. But one day, they had disappeared without a trace, and Aslaug milked the goat to relieve the pain the milk caused. There was goat's cheese now, which Kitt would have enjoyed much more if the loss of the kids hadn't nagged at the back of his mind.

Everywhere Kitt came upon the snow martens; he thought them the most graceful animals he had ever seen. They were now very conspicuous with their white pelt. Unlike weasel and ermine, their fur did not change to a darker colour but stayed as white and thick as in winter.

Once in the middle of the green valley, Kitt saw a snow marten sitting, like a patch of the last snow in the grass, and from the cover of a clump of willows, he watched the little sleepy feline face turned to the sun, the sun-soaked white pelt warm and fluffy.

Suddenly, the snow marten sprang high into the air, a furry paw lashing out, and a lark fluttered in the curved hooks of its claws. Brown feathers floated down.

Just then, an eagle shot down onto the conspicuous white fur as if to righten the balance of nature. Instantly, the snow marten jumped again, and turned on its back in mid-air, to drive all four clawed paws into the breast feathers before the eagle's talons could get hold. The eagle screeched and tried to reach the snow marten with its great, yellow beak, but the needle-sharp teeth had already fastened in its neck. The broad wings beat the air, but the eagle was unable to rise, its feathers turned red, and the wings spasmed.

Kitt swore softly under his breath.

The snow marten took the eagle by a wing to drag it away; it walked proudly like a victorious warrior, and looked back at Kitt in a way that he felt glad that this beast was only the size of a small fox.

Kitt did not have much time to watch the snow martens. Aslaug was busy as the rest of nature, and she deprived Eckehart of his assistant, employing Kitt to dig the garden from early till late, and prepare the seedbeds for buckwheat, radish, onions, peas and carrots; the soil had to be extra fine and crumbling for flax and ironherb, foxglove, chamomile and poppy.

Once, Kitt paused in his digging. "I hear no birdsong," he said. "Mother, there are no more birds."

Without answering him, Aslaug bent over the young cabbage plants which she had cultivated in boxes in the house.

A white furry head poked out of the hole in the old apple tree at the far end of the garden, where the robin used to build its nest.

"Snow marten," Kitt answered his own question. "They look like fluff, but they are the best hunters I ever saw, faster than any other animal, and cannier. Soon there will be no more birds, no more small animals! There are about twenty of them; what if they have young - how many young can one female have in a year? If they are like weasels or tree cats, it could be six, or more, if they have young twice, and what will those eat?"

"When winter comes, they will spring onto the ice floes."

Kitt looked at his mother with worry. "The other islands. And then to Dokkerland and the Murkowydir wood. It will be a sheer massacre." He shook his head. "They are such beautiful animals."

That evening, Isegrim whined, wanting to be let out, and did not come back in.

Kitt searched for him all over the island, and couldn't find any trace of the old dog. What he found were Witlyns everywhere. The snow martens had young, between three and six a pair. The soft, white fur balls were just leaving the nest to scamper and tumble about, warming Kitt's heart in his loss of Isegrim – until a horrible suspicion assailed him.

The silence spread on Isenkliff. The cliffs that had held the colonies of seagulls, albatrosses and geese were mute and snowed over with feathers and broken eggshells.

Baby rabbits were wholly absent, as were lizards and squirrels.

Kitt spent days hunting in the cliffs, without seeing a wild goat, and when he came upon a herd, there were more than a hundred animals as if banding together against anger. The nanny goats led very few young.

The snow marten cubs were growing up, and the silent summer was roaring in Kitt's hears.

One day, he spotted an adult Witlyn sitting in the garden, in the exact spot beneath the cherry tree where his mother was accustomed to lay down little Swantje when she worked in her vegetable beds.

From then on, Kitt carried a bow whenever he left the house.

The next Witlyn he came across sprang away like lightning, but the arrow was faster. It entered the back of the neck, and the red tip protruded from the chest; blood ran out of the furry snout staining the sharp white teeth.

It was one of the adolescent Witlyns who grew very fast. "I don't know what else I can do," Kitt told the dead animal. "You are just too good at killing."

He divested the stone marten of its pelt. The meat had a pungent smell, inedible like a fox's, or a tree cat's, and so he left it. When he saw another spot of white in a tree, he loosed an arrow at once. In the evening, seven snow marten pelts were hanging outside of the scullery door.

"I feel like a murderer. But I can't not do anything either."
Kitt's hand ran over the thick white fur.

"I know," Eckehart said. "Let's suppose for a moment that you don't do anything. How can it end?"

They both pictured an Isenkliff where only snow martens lived, sitting in the trees, their luminous emerald eyes looking out over the sea, hungrily.

"Any way you think it through; there are only two possible answers to this question. They or us."

"Why should it be us?"

"No good reason. No right or wrong either way. Just survival."

"What does mother think?"

Aslaug was in the garden, a basket with radish on her arm, her face unsmiling. Kitt thought that thus the judges must look, who sat before the gates of the cities in the south, where hard laws were inscribed in stone with sharp chisels, and of whom he had read in his books.

"Beautiful, and deadly," his mother said. "The earth cannot carry them. There is only one creature on Isenkliff who is a match for the snow marten, and that is you, Kitt."

###

All summer long, Kitt hunted the Witlyn with bow and arrow.

He did not come upon them as often as before, but having watched them long enough to know their habits, and knowing the island well, he couldn't fail to find all their hiding places. Once he spotted them, their conspicuous white fur made them a sure mark for his arrows. The animals were fast as white lightning, but Kitt's eyes and hands were quicker.

His success awarded Kitt no satisfaction; pitting his strength and cunning against that of the animal held no thrill for him. Every day, he had to remind himself of the coming winter, the ice sheet reaching the mainland, and the fate of the eagle. And Isegrim's. He missed the old dog so much, and it hurt him to think about how his old friend must have died.

Every night Kitt dreamed of the Witlyns.

He was running through the Murkowydir wood. Hundreds of snow martens were sitting in every tree, their brilliant green eyes following him. They knew who he was. They knew that he was their deadly enemy. The tree growth became denser, and his shoulders were brushing the branches where the Witlyns sat. There was a white surge of fur and teeth.

He woke.

Every night he dreamed this dream. One night he did not wake when the white surge came.

The white surge of the snow martens engulfed him, and he fought for his life, rending and tearing with rage and hatred. The bodies lay all around him, white fur mussed with blood.

He woke at last, with the feeling of being tainted beyond redemption.

#

The hedge roses and rowan-berry bore their red fruit, and the elderberry tree bore black fruit, and the sunlight mellowed into late summer.

The bellies of the female snow martens were swelling again. When Kitt saw that and realised that the snow marten had a second season,

279

he almost cried. There was only one way he could see.

Sick to the stomach from killing the pregnant females he didn't eat any more and slept little, afraid of the dreams. Every day he rose in the first light of the morning, to come home after dark with three or four white pelts. He sat down to prepare the skins, and didn't speak a word after the first greeting.

"Maybe you should leave it be," Eckehart one day said, tentatively.

Kitt shook his head furiously. He couldn't stop what he was doing for the simple reason that he had begun it. If he did stop before the task was completed, then all the killing he had done so far would be in vain, and that thought he could not bear, as he could not stand any doubts. That was what he would have said to his father if the words had not stuck in his throat, because he felt more and more alone, cut off from his parents by what he did every day.

#

"It is too hard a task for the boy," Eckehart said.

He was sitting in his seat before the fireplace, his big blackened hands idle, his blue eyes worried. "He has now brought home seventy-four snow marten skins. I am afraid that his soul may become . . ." here Eckehart paused to search for the word "tainted."

Aslaug looked up from her book, her face expressionless. "Then, he will be lost. And there is nothing you or I could do about it."

"You have been reading this same page all evening," Eckehart accused.

"Have I? Well, don't ask me what's written on it because I don't remember a single word." Shutting the book with an angry bang, she rose to hang a pot on the pothook over the fire. "He'll be here soon."

"He won't eat anything." Eckehart shook his head. "Hasn't eaten for days. Just shoves the food about on his plate, pretending. He is getting gaunt."

"I have noticed it."

She laid the end of the hall table with a clatter, cut bread, chopped green beans.

"Better not give him meat of any kind."

"Of course not!" Aslaug fetched goat cheese and butter from the larder, pushed everything in position on the table once or twice, and when she had run out of routine movements to keep herself from thinking, she sat down again at the table, opening the book she wasn't reading.

"It cannot be the killing as such, that is upsetting him so," Eckehart pursued. "He hunts, and though he knows regret, he has accepted taking life, as every man has, so that we may eat. He wasn't bothered by slaying the Dodlak when it attacked him. This snow marten killing is also self-defence. Survival. He sees that. And yet it is different . . ." Frowning he began walking up and down before the fireplace. "But what exactly is different? We must find out because he is going to pieces before our eyes."

"You keep telling me that Kitt is not a murderer, but now he feels like one. And yet he doesn't stop."

"That's it! He knows why it must be done, but as a reason for cold-blooded killing, this is all too abstract. He has no hatred anywhere inside him to answer all questions, quell all doubts." Eckehart paused in his tramping, and sat down on his seat again. "There is nothing to make things easier for him. Those snow martens only follow their instincts. And sometimes I think that we all do just that."

"Innocent killers." Aslaug's eyes took on a faraway look. "That is what I have often thought. To survive yourself, you have no other choice but to kill them. And then, when they are gone, you are left alone with your judgment."

Eckehart looked at Aslaug, sharply. "You feel that too? I never even thought you did. Imagine what a terrible burden that is to place on a boy. The snow marten is an animal that he would normally never kill. They are beautiful. On the one hand, their grace and skill at hunting fascinate him, and on the other hand, he feels sorry for the robins, and finches and larks. Anything small and defenceless can count on his sympathy. But deadly as the snow marten are against birds and other little creatures, the wounded and the weak, they have no chance at all against a hunter like Kitt.

"Just imagine, to go out each day with the aim to extinguish. To know the fight can end only one way. To kill where he would like to caress. And so, he has to make this decision daily and tell himself, over and over again, the reasons why he must do it. It is a sterile sort of killing. And it's too much for him."

"Those snow marten, in their own way they are like . . ." Aslaug hesitated, her eyes on the table. "Like the Kri, aren't they?"

And then one day in autumn, Kitt brought no snow marten pelt home, and he looked like a convict whose punishment had been suspended.

The same happened the next day, and Kitt said the first words in weeks, without being asked.

"I haven't seen any more Witlyns for days. And yet, I know somewhere there are still one or two of them left because I keep finding the remains of their prey."

"Come and eat!" Aslaug invited. "I made pancakes, of sorts, for I had no eggs, but you can have them with honey."

"I can't eat, mother. I have to finish this first."

#

After days of careful tracking, Kitt finally came upon a pair of snow martens, high in the cliff.

They had seen him also but were oddly reluctant to flee. It was easy for Kitt to shoot them.

He stood on the ledge, looking out to the north, at his feet what he hoped were the last snow martens. Below him was the little beach where the ice-floes had piled up the winter before. There was already a smell of snow in the air.

He passed his hand over the female's belly, feeling the swollen teats in the thick white fur that was rumpled and untidy. The snow martens had had their second cubs.

He scanned the cliffside, and it was not long until he saw a tiny white head protruding from a small cave where rock-swallows had once lived.

Kitt climbed up and reached into the nest. His fingers found a soft fur ball, closed around it, and tightened.

Sweat broke out on his face.

He withdrew his hand and laid the little limp body aside, to reach in a second time, and a third.

He retched.

282

The fourth time, his hand found nothing, but he knew that there was another cub, because he heard it hissing and spitting.

For a moment, he leant his forehead against the cliff face.

Then his hand began searching again, and he found the last cub, hidden in a recess under a flat stone, which was so small that at first Kitt could not get his entire hand in. He had to widen the opening by clearing away clay, and smaller stones, all the time imagining the last snow marten cub, huddled in the farthest corner to evade the searching fingers.

Finally, the opening was big enough so that he could reach in.

The cub clawed his hand with fine claws and bit him with little pointy teeth not yet long enough to pierce his skin. Kitt felt the wild heartbeat, and his fingers just would not close for the fourth time.

Then, he looked at the white ball of fluff lying on the broad expanse on his hand, quiet now. He stroked it with a finger and put it in his shirt.

#

The kitchen door opened to admit Kitt, his face pale and his long fair hair dark with sweat.

Stepping to the table, he drew something from his shirt, a snuffling and wriggling ball of white fur. All three looked at the little snow marten's uncertain dither across the table.

"But Kitt!" Aslaug said, "You can't keep it!"

"This is the last one. It can't . . . it won't . . ." the boy's voice was unsteady. "I killed the other three cubs, but . . . I just couldn't squeeze the life out of this one. I couldn't." He shook his head, not looking at Aslaug or Eckehart. "You do it!"

The cub reached Aslaug and pushed its nose into her hand. She sighed, slopped a little goat's milk into a bowl and dipped her finger into it. The cub licked with a tiny, rough, blue tongue.

She dipped her finger into the milk again and again, until the little snow marten curled up in her hand with a belly slightly swollen with milk, and went to sleep.

"It is just too hard to kill the young," she murmured. "Sometimes a soft heart is the worst obstacle to doing the things that have to be done."

"But without a good heart, everything would be worse," Eckehart muttered. "Far worse. So, let's let him live! As he's the last one."

The Snow Queen

The sun shone pale, coloured leaves were falling, the fog rose over the moor. The autumn storms came howling from the west, blowing brown leaves before them, clearing the way for the snow.

Flocks of grey geese and swans passed over Isenkliff, calling to each other on their way south, and Kitt followed them with his eyes, thinking of the warmer lands, where the birds would pass the winter. Often the grey geese landed in the little bays of Isenkliff to rest. In the years before, Kitt had laid out bread on the shore, with entirely ulterior motives. But this year, he did not shoot any geese, nor did he hunt goats, feeling that never again could he bear even the sight of blood. Sometimes he remembered that his parents might like a roasted goose, but they said they didn't.

One day Kitt saw a blackbird busily scratching in the fallen leaves beneath the walnut tree. It was the first blackbird Kitt saw after the silent summer, and the sight made him deliriously happy.

A flash of white lightning shot past him. The blackbird had no time for one squeak.

"Let go, you little assassin!" With one mighty jump, Kitt reached the triumphant little snow marten; his hand shot out to grab the white bushy tail. "Let go, or I'll make you sing in spring!"

All Kitt caught were a few long white hairs; growling the Witlyn streaked away with the boy in hot pursuit. The little animal saved itself to where Aslaug was harvesting the late apples.

"Give!" she said sternly.

Abashed, the Witlyn spat the blackbird into her hand.

"Don't do it again!"

The young animal trod from one furry paw to the other in a show of embarrassment.

Kitt looked sadly upon the crumpled heap of black feathers which lay in his mother's hand, the yellow lids shut and the little beak open.

Aslaug breathed on the blackbird, and the wings twitched, the round eyes with the orange iris flew open, the orange beak shut, opened and shut again, and then the blackbird whirred into the air.

The Witlyn's luminous green eyes followed the bird until it

disappeared in the blue autumn sky. After a baleful look at Kitt, it stalked away with the bushy tail erect.

"Did you see that dirty look? Little beast!" a cloud passed over Kitt's face. "It knows that I killed all of its kind. If at least we could have eaten them. But their meat is rank like that of a fox. The snow marten hunted to eat, and to live, just like I do. And all I wanted was their absence."

"We. Not you alone, Kitt. Eckehart and I wanted their absence. We just did not have the . . . the skill." Aslaug swallowed hard, "But this little predator doesn't know any of that. It suspects you of wanting to eat the bird yourself. That is all."

"But I didn't take it, you did," Kitt objected. "Anyway, it flew away."

"Believe me, Kitt, all it really knows is that it is I who feeds it scraps in the kitchen. So it won't cross me, and takes it out on you instead."

"I also feed it. Whenever I eat, it sits beside me and stares. If I don't hand over a share fast enough it pats my leg. Even claws me." Kitt had to smile. "But it never heeds me in the slightest."

"Because it thinks it owns you, and you owe it tribute. He reckons you rank lowest here, you see." Aslaug laughed. "I'm the cook, and I'm always there, so I'm the one who matters. You go away to hunt, or to work at the smelting oven all day, so you are just an extra, to be managed at will. That is the difference. That is the way an animal thinks, Kitt. And many humans, for that matter."

Kitt did not seem to listen. "I heard of holy men who live in bowers suspended from the earth, so that they may not tread on any living beings; they hardly breathe for fear of swallowing a fly, and they never eat meat. Sometimes I wish I could be like they are. But I'm not. I'm just the opposite. Sometimes I think why can't I just be like a wolf, and not think at all? Sometimes I think just give everybody enough room -but how far can I give way? I have thought and thought." The words came tumbling out after the long silence.

"What will you use the Witlyn furs for?" Aslaug asked.

"The furs?" Kitt stared at her. "I did take and prepare them, as it didn't seem right to let them rot, but. . ." he stopped helplessly. "You

286

cannot want them, mother?"

"Why not? The snow marten has a wonderful pelt, winter and summer, more precious than ermine. What I would like is a cloak made of snow marten pelts. It will annoy the Isprinsessans very much. For the Isprinsessans and me, we have a longstanding feud. The snow martens are their pets, and they have sent them against Isenkliff to eat my blackbirds and robins and finches and nightingales and my hares and red katteikers and even the goats, so that we should starve in winter. Didn't you realise that it is all the Isprinsessans' doing? They want to bring down another Gate of Spring and extend their icy rule from here all over the world. The Isprinsessans don't care about the death of their pets, not as you do. They are so very cold themselves."

"Then they ought to come themselves. One should always do one's own killing. Everything else is cowardice." Kitt's face was stern, seeming far older than his fourteen years.

Aslaug winced. "That's just it. Once you begin to fight and kill you have to do it again and again. It was a mistake."

Kitt's head jerked up, his eyes burning. "A mistake?"

"You bought us time," she said hastily. "But the price was too high -too high for you."

"If the snow martens come over the ice again, I'll be waiting for them on the shore," Kitt said, haunted grey eyes looking out towards the next winter. "I wish the Isjotun will come instead. I prefer fighting ice giants."

That very evening Aslaug began working on the Witlyn cloak.

The thick white furs covered the hall table like a warm snow dune, startlingly set off by the black of the throats and tail spots.

For a while, the young snow marten chased the bushy tails, which Aslaug used to decorate the hems; then it curled up in the middle of the heap, and went to sleep.

The cloak half-finished Aslaug sat with her hands idle. "A mistake," she breathed, sighed and resumed her stitching.

Outside, the autumn winds blew, stripping the trees of the last brown leaves. The next day, the first snowflakes fell and covered the ravaged island under a white blanket.

Kitt dreamed of the snow martens often; in this dream, he had to kill the cubs all over again.

He killed the three cubs all over again with his bare hands, only to realise that there were hundreds more, and he had to kill them too. For if he did not, all the deaths he had dealt would be in vain. So he crushed them, while they fastened their little white teeth and claws into his hands, more and more of them until he was sitting alone among thousands of small soft cadavers.

Then, he woke.

The winter came in earnest, with white ice-packs swimming in a leaden sea and piling up on the shore, and a numbing wind blew out of Jotunheim. Undisturbed by the hunter, the geese were long gone south.

It was the day of the Longest Night again; the sun made only a brief appearance over the Southern horizon, and her pale rays briefly gilded the ice floes which were floating in the quicksilver-grey sea.

The channel of open water before Isenkliff steadily narrowed each year until it had closed the winter before for the first time in a thousand years. Then the Isjotun had come, followed by the Witlyn, the snow martens.

Eckehart and Kitt opened the smelting oven. Heat welled out, turning the snow into slush. Little rivulets of meltwater ran to all sides, and the earth became dark mud that began freezing again immediately, locking the imprints of Kitt's and Eckehart's boots.

The iron cake hissed in the snow. Waiting for it to cool the smiths stamped their feet.

Two zile birds picked nearby. They watched the small birds with the steel blue backs, yellow throats, and black spots on both sides of the head. Kitt smiled; it was a twisted little twitch of his mouth.

They took the iron down to the forge, and by the time the water-driven hammer had hammered the impurities out of it, the sun sank into a dusky red horizon.

Night fell, like the black, star-studded coat of eternity. It was dark, so dark, and a wind blew out of the darkness, ice-cold. The forge blazed red-hot in the freezing night.

When Eckehart and Kitt scraped the glowing coal together and covered it, only one light shone from the house, steady and warm, the only light and warmth in a sea of cold engulfing Isenkliff.
Kitt and Eckehart marched towards it.

After they had eaten their dinner Kitt went purposefully to the book shelve, and took down two bamboo paper scrolls; these were the same which he had attempted deciphering the year before. To it, he added several brittle sheets painted with letters in black and purple ink. They had been among the books the merchant-spy Neveokki had brought, wedged into a travel account to the island Magatama. He settled down at the table with an air of scholarly intent to accomplish a lengthy and complicated task.

They sat quietly, Kitt studying and both his parents making a pretence of sewing and mending work. Curled into Kitt's lap slept the little snow marten.

Outside it grew darker, and the darkness began pressing against the house.

"The way of the sword," Kitt muttered. It had taken him a long time to figure out this one line, but now he was quite sure that the script ran in columns from top right to bottom left. He took up the other bits of similar writing to see if he could translate further.

Aslaug prompted Eckehart with a look and an energetic nod, and the smith coughed.

"It's late," he said. "Time for bed."

"Oh no, it isn't. Not when I'm just beginning to make sense of this." Kitt unrolled the scroll further. "Remember when Neveokki brought these? Finally, I have time to see . . . in Luxin Shoo they fashion books out of ground straw, and it seems they do too in Magatama. But these are not exactly the same kind of letters."

"I won't forget that in a hurry," Eckehart said. "You scared Neveokki so much, and he didn't get a single scrap of metal for his books -I doubt we'll ever see him again, which is a good thing. Glad you find this interesting."

With a reproachful look at Eckehart, Aslaug sighed wearily. "We should not treat you like a child any more Kitt, but..."

"That's right. You won't send me to bed tonight."

"But the Isprinsessans almost killed you."

"They won't do it this time. They can never again have power over me. Never again be beautiful to me." Gently he stroked the little snow marten, who stretched white furry paws and continued sleeping.

Aslaug quailed at the sight of Kitt's face, it was so hard and still. "This Longest Night will be worse than before. Tonight the Snow Queen herself may come," she warned.

"Let her come!"

"You should not try to face this," Eckehart said. "When the Graumeer freezes over entirely, all the way to Dokkerland and the great wood Murkowydir, then the Isjotun will sail forth in their ice-ships with sails of hoarfrost, on a voyage to conquer the world. There will be nothing you can do about that."

"Old legends. Are you telling me they are true?"

"You know that they are."

"The ice is growing each year that much is true. But it's always done that."

"Said the day-old chicken. Once there was a great warm current running along the mainland, as a separate river in the ocean, coming up all the way from the warm seas in the south. A branch of that warm river washed around the Kings Seat Latunsrigo to Isenkliff, around Wittewal and to Abalus. Then grain grew in Scatenauge, wine climbed the brick walls of Burgenland, and there was ice only on the mountain tops in winter. The borders of Jotunheim lay much farther in the North. It happened then that the Snow Queen sent her army of Isjotun to attack the land of Thule, far in the Cold Waters of the Western Ocean."

"So Thule really existed!"

"Aren't I telling you! Of course, it existed. Thule was famous for its learning and Zaubar power, but the foundation of their riches was the Blue-tongue cattle grazing on the meadows of the southern part of the land, giving them milk so fat that it was yellow, and the most exquisite leather. They may have understood the very fabric of the universe, but I can tell you that they were also accomplished at physicking cattle, though they didn't advertise this fact so much.

"But when the Isjotuns' ice ships anchored before the South coast of Thule, the grass stayed frozen in the fruit month, the blue-tongue cattle starved, and the white bears came down with the mountain glacier and broke into the stables.

"Then, the wizards of Thule raised the Scattered Islands from the seafloor, and so the whole stream of the warm current was directed towards Thule, and the Isjotun were driven back."

"Thule was saved? Where is it now?"

"It was saved from the ice, and its grass grew greener than before, and it is now called Blauochsland. Yes, that name, you know. Because another land also came into the benefit of the warm current which now runs up far north -Asringholm. And their king was Ragnar Roi."

Kitt had heard of Ragnar Roi, everybody had.

"The Nordmänner had been abandoning their land for years, taking their serpent ships far south. But with the warmth, they waxed numerous on Asringholm. They needed land, and this time, they did not go south -they invaded Thule. The wizards slew many with their craft, but the more Nordmänner died in the assault, the more ferocious they became. That is how the men from Asringholm are, grim fighters all, who respect only those who beat them decisively. Like you did Harmar Saesorgison."

Kitt nodded.

"Well I guess you can't defend a land with milkmaids and in the end, there were too few wizards and too many Nordmänner," Eckehart pursued. "They graze their cattle in Thule now. Since then, the ice has been growing in Jotunheim, where the warm current reaches no more. That was the real purpose of the Snow Queen's attack on Thule. You see now how cunning she is, and on what scales she sways the world? Now the only obstacle barring her way south is Isenkliff."

"And me."

Eckehart shook his head. "You have never met anything too strong for you, Kitt, have you? You don't know how it is when elemental powers catch you in their grip and shake you like a puppy. But with

291

the Isjotun you came close and if the ice had not broken when it did. .
."

"Too late," Aslaug interrupted. She reached for her snow marten pelt, throwing it around her shoulders.

Outside, the night lit up; the white Northern Fire washed around the house like floodwater, rising and rising outside the window. The Isprinsessans were there, their outlines blurred in the frosted window glass, swaying and silent.

Kitt looked out at them, the white light in the sky reflected in his grey eyes, which appeared almost white and still and frozen.

Eckehart shuddered.

The snow martens of Aslaug's cloak raised their heads, opened wide emerald eyes and showed sharp, white teeth.

The living Witlyn woke and scratched at the door furiously until Kitt opened it a crack, and the little animal shot out like white lightning.

Before Kitt could close the door again, outside, just beyond it, stood the Snow Queen herself. Three white flames flickered over the snow beside her, pale and wan, the Isprinsessans, eclipsed by their glittering queen.

The Snow Queen's slow smile was terrible. "I know what you want, you bright-eyed child. You want to read in my books of ice where all the knowledge of the world is written. That is what you want, all the knowledge of the world. And it is all right here. You will never have to search, never need doubt again. Think! What sense does all your seeking for bits of knowledge make, when you know there exist books where it is all written down. So futile."

"How can all the knowledge in the world be written in your books? There are warm places where you have never been."

"There are no such places, child. None. Not in all the world. Not in all the universe, for I am the oldest of anything there is. Look at my books and see the truth underlying everything." Suddenly, her hands were full of shining ice tablets. "Look, child, look. You don't have to come out to me. Just read."

Sharp-edged characters were cut into the ice tablets. Kitt's lips moved as he deciphered formulas of crystal clear sense, simple, logical and final.

"And that is all there is," the Snow Queen said. "All there ever was, all there ever will be."

Without even remembering that he had crossed the threshold, Kitt found himself on his hands and knees in the deep snow, scrambling for the tablets, striving to put them into a logical order. He found two, three that were fitting together; their razor-sharp edges cut his hands, and his blood froze onto the ice. Some fragments also fitted, and he found the missing link, right at the bottom of the heap that seemed mountain high.

"The pattern of life is simple," the Snow Queen's clear voice murmured. She stood close to Kitt, radiating an excruciating cold. "As simple as a snowflake or an ice crystal or a diamond -but not as beautiful. A decaying smear on the surface of perfection, that is what life sums up to. Fleeting moments of beauty are just a dream for feeble minds too weak to endure reality. Foolish and fragile. You are strong, the strongest of your kind. But not strong enough. You must realise that there is no such thing as love either, and it is that which breaks your heart. Yes, it kills you. I can see how it does. You want this pain to stop, don't you? I will kiss you, and then you won't mind anymore. Your heart will become still and your mind clear, and that will be so much better." The Snow Queen bent over Kitt, her coldness piercing him through.

A fiery light sprang up very near, growing and growing into a fireball, drenching the ice tablets with an orange glow in which the letters grew diffuse and disappeared.

Kitt felt as if he was thrown into hot water. He heard a furious shriek, far out on the ice.

"Hands off my son!" Eckehart's voice rumbled like thunder. "Your time has not come around yet. How often do I have to tell you Cold Folks to await your time!"

Kitt woke in his room with no idea how he had got there, feeling frozen to the marrow. The snowstorm was screaming outside the window. Many candles shone; the air in the room was warm and full of the smell of beeswax and cloves, and his mother was there with a steaming cup, and his father.

Kitt struggled to sit up and reach for the hot cup. His hands were bandaged. "It's not true, is it?" he whispered, his teeth chattering.

"What isn't, Kitt?" Aslaug asked. But she knew exactly what he meant. "No, it is not true." Being an honest woman, she added. "There is a way of lying by telling one particular part of the truth. And that, to my mind, is the worst type of lie there is. Now drink your elderberry juice, with lots and lots of honey so you can sleep. And here, to warm you and remind you, how you have thwarted her attack on our home." She spread the snow marten cloak over his bed. "It was for this that she came herself, the Cold Queen, because she is furious, furious about the failure of her attacks on Isenkliff."

"Will she return next winter, and the Isprinsessans and Isjotun, and the winters after that?"

"Yes, they will."

"Can't you loose the earth fire against the ice, father? Undo what the wizards of Thule did?"

"These lands are ancient, their fires long burned out. The fire of Isenkliff is just sufficient to heat the forge or melt the Snow Queen's frozen gown a bit." Eckehart chuckled. "Not enough to keep her away when the time of the ice returns."

"So the ice will come, no matter how hard we fight."

"Yes. The glaciers will bury Isenkliff three thousand feet high and weigh heavy enough to drive it down into the sea."

"Why do we fight then?"

"The ice comes, the ice goes. It is all a cycle, like a wheel, it will turn around once more, and when it does, we will lose a little ground, win some, lose some, win again, every time. We mustn't weaken, hit back, push, and shove as at a pendulum to make it go through the dead point. Only when it stops, this up and down, only then will we have lost."

"True courage."

"That's it, son. Over and over again, never gets better, never stops. But now you can sleep in peace -until next winter."

Kitt drank a second cup of elderberry juice, looked suspiciously at the snow marten furs lying there innocently, and then dropped off to sleep.

A noise of furious scratching woke him; he heard the door below open, and his father's voice. "So you are back, are you, you faithless little rogue! Better for you, for your blood is warm, and for that, the Cold Queen can never love you. But we, we do. Though for the life of me I don't know why, you ungrateful, murderous little piece of fluff. We're the only ones in the whole world who can ever love you. Don't you forget it."

The door of Kitt's room opened a crack, and a white furry body wormed in and sprang onto his bed, to push an ice-cold blue nose into his face.

"I thought you had gone with the Snow Queen," Kitt murmured. "She is too, too beautiful! But cold, so cold. And it was all lies she told. Her books also are all a lie."

The sun rose in the sky, higher, hotter, and all inhabitants of Isenkliff turned their faces up to follow it's run like flowers did.

The icicle curtains hanging from the roof were dripping.

The thaw came quickly, and the water ran into the sea, first in murmuring rivulets, rimmed by violets cased in thin ice, then in rushing streams running through the thick green and yellow cushions of Springstar flowers.

One day a blackbird was singing loud and clear, the next there was a chorus, joined by the call of the cuckoo.

Far from a slow recovery, it was as if somebody had told the birds of the death of the white predators, the snow martens, and called them to the empty nesting places. All the goats dropped twins and even triplets.

Kitt climbed down the cliff teeming with birds. Halfway, he came upon several seagulls nests, and appropriated fourteen eggs, taking only one from each nest.

Acting on experience, he distributed the eggs into several bags hanging around his neck, three in one container which he left outside, the other two with four and seven eggs, respectively, he tugged into his shirt.

When his head came over the cliff edge again, he saw a pair of sturdy legs in rough goat skin trousers. "Hello Gullo, not sleeping anymore?" Kitt pulled himself up and relinquished the visible bag with the eggs.

The Jarnmantsje continued staring at Kitt. "I knew a wise boy once, yes I did," he said in a grating voice. "Took a bad end with him, bad, bad, bad." He sniffed vigorously.

With all signs of reluctance, Kitt withdrew the bag with the four eggs. "Nothing edible escapes you, Gullo."

The Jarnmantsje looked into the bag, then at Kitt, and snuffled suspiciously after the boy striding down the cliff with long steps.

The first Ferys ship had been and gone. Kitt and Eckehart were smelting the bog iron using the charcoal King Tombrok had also sent. "They can't have much left to keep warm themselves after this winter," Eckehart remarked.

As they closed the ovens with clay, a grey form shambled out of a hole in the cliffside and sniffed over their lunch basket.

"So much for lunch," Eckehart said. "Hello Gullo, find something you like?"

"The sausage is good, yes it is. A good cook, Aslaug is," the Jarnmantsje's voice rumbled like boulders in a landslide. "Eggs?" He pulled a silver dish from the basket and seemed put out to find only two boiled eggs inside it. "Three and four are seven, and seven more are fourteen. You think Gullo can't count," the Jarnmantsje grumbled. "Three and four and two are not fourteen. Gullo can count, don't you think he can't."

"Maybe fourteen is the wrong number?" Kitt suggested.

The Jarnmantsje glared at him.

"Yes, quite the wrong number," Kitt said. "Makes no sense. Not when the cliff is three hundred feet high. Fourteen for you and none for me who climbed that high cliff. Who'll risk such a climb, if fourteen is the number?"

"Three and four are seven, and two more are nine. Five are missing. Gullo can count."

"It was a long hard winter," Eckehart said gently, blinking into the warm sun.

The Jarnmantsje withdrew farther into the shade of the cliff; he did not like the sun, and he glared at the two smiths from deep-set yellow eyes.

"All right, all right. It was just a try. I thought nine for you and five for us was sort of fair sharing, Gullo, but you disagree. So I owe you five eggs. I'll go down that cliff again today," he promised. "But hunt I won't," he breathed to himself. "Never again."

Gullo shuffled into the tunnel. "Gullo can count," his hollow voice could be heard muttering, and then it was quiet.

Kitt held his face into the warm sun. "It is all as it ever was before, isn't it father?"

"It is, son, and it is not," Eckehart muttered lazily. "It's always been like that. So ultimately, yes, I suppose it is all the same as before once more."

When Kitt came home from work that day, he found the little snow marten curled up on his bed in a stiff, cold hoop. Its furry white belly had inflamed inside, and its death showed its kind to be close to that of ferrets, which die in pain if they cannot mate.

Just when it happened that little Swantje ceased to be something attached to her mother and got hold of Kitt, making him her thrall, Aslaug never knew, and she was sure Kitt didn't either.

Maybe it was when Swantje began throwing her comforter out of her cradle, to point at it imperiously for her brother to retrieve. He started bringing things for her, an apple, a pine cone, a piece of polished wood, all of which she received with glee and then threw out of her cradle, and he never lost patience and fetched the same thing for the tenth time.

Kitt called his little sister Birla because of her thick golden hair like a pelt and the way she rolled around waving short, sturdy limbs, making skirling noises like a newborn bear cub.

The name stuck; Grimwolf adopted it at once when he came to Isenkliff that spring. The Theusten king brought a puppy for Swantje, an ugly and endearing animal, spotted red, white and black, with big paws, a direct descendant from his war dog Greif, he said.

Grimwolf made Kitt come to the hunt again for the first time since the Witlyn invasion. What Kitt told him about that and what Grimwolf said to him, Aslaug never found out.

Poison Trees

The Birlinn Yehan called on Isenkliff, and Kitt was excited to see the big metal ship again.

He waited on the shore, watching the four boats make fast to the iron rings of the jetty. The first to come along the rock spur was a lithe man of middle height in his thirties, with blond hair cropped short, and the beardless face of a scholar. He wore breeches, a dark-green shirt with a leather vest and a brown cloth waistcoat and over-knee leather boots. Nothing in this simple attire indicated that Captain Lodemar was one of the most successful sea raiders, a pirate or a privateer, depending on the political situation.

He clasped Kitt's hand. "This time, I come for a sword. You think your father will award me one? And I'll want your opinion on something we captured."

The sailors filing onto the jetty after Lodemar were rejects from many countries, one even was a Woodstalker, and Kitt was glad to see him. He had many questions.

The device Captain Lodemar had captured turned out to be an oversized fire-lance.

Kitt could lay his hand on several treatises in his library on the functioning of such a weapon, including recipes for fire-dust and its use in warfare.

"Do you ever think, Kitt?" His mother scolded.

He had never seen her so mad. Her hands were dancing with irritation as she more threw than set dinner upon the table.

#

After sleeping badly, Kitt left the house early without breakfast.

He and Gweronell, the Birlinn Yehan's tame Woodstalker, went to hunt wild goats together. A great amount of steel was required for repairs on the Birlinn Yehan, and Lodemar was always in a hurry. The Jarnmantsjes in the mountain needed to be bribed with meat to help work the large components.

Gweronell was thought to be an Amhas, who were tamed Woodstalkers. He had told Kitt the truth, that he was a Kra-Tini

Feen, and that his real name was Dukas Raden which translated into Black Lizard. He told him things which Kitt hadn't known of the Dark Wood Murkowydir which he called Sreedok, about the people of the seven ancient races, each a survival from lost worlds.

Kitt knew the Kra-Tini Feen, Gweronell's own people who had ousted him. Why, the Woodstalker never told of his own volition, and Kitt didn't ask.

He told Kitt about the war leader Singing Bear, Mangan Sorkera in his own Feen Woodstalker language, of the Wise Man of the Feen, the Ludoshini, Shangar Shaark Ayen. And he told him what the name meant, that Kitt had thought to be an insult -Gawthrin Lye, fox cub, clever child. Gweronell said it was a compliment because the Feen just called everybody not a Feen a Dshooka, which meant bad, stupid people, and to them, all Dshooka were the same.

The hunt was difficult. Brynnir's herd had been reduced by the snow marten the year before, and there were no yearlings. The ewes were leading many kids, but this year it was challenging to shoot the seven bucks required to satisfy the Jarnmantsje, and the hunt took the whole day.

For themselves, the hunters cooked a goose over a fire.

The hall was not far, just around the southern promontory, but Kitt was loath to go home, remembering how wild his mother had been about the fire-lance. Although she hadn't said much, her disapproval was so palpable that it was likely she'd say more at dinner. Gweronell was also content to stay outside; he was a quiet, unsociable man.

The moon rose and on the seaside of the cliff appeared a white light, high up -the Silver Lady of the Sword, looking out to the sea, and waiting.

Kitt found himself telling Gweronell about the Golden Warrior Malan Jian and his woman whose souls were bound together, his and hers, by a band of steel. How the sea had taken him, and she was waiting. "Even in death, they can't meet. If only I could help them." He didn't expect Gweronell to comment, and only spoke to relieve his heavy heart.

"They are on different sides of the Ska-Muni shadow wall,"

Gweronell said, unexpectedly. "This woman is a warrior who died a good death full of pain. She left Nyedasya-Aurayskahan-Ashyalish, the dream world of illusions and lies and crossed the world divide Nedye-Muni into Nyedasya-Dyarve, the real world, the world behind the fire. The man you speak of could not follow her there. He just slipped off the rock and so he is in Nyedasya–Lyagum-Olimi, the lost dark night world."

"He was a brave man. He tried to join her in death." And had been denied the excruciating rite it took to banish a living soul into steel, by his father, Kitt explained.

"A man needs as much strength to inflict pain as he does to bear it well," Gweronell commented. "Perhaps your father had not enough regard for this warrior."

Kitt tried to understand that remark, and wasn't sure that he succeeded.

"Nyedasya–Lyagum-Olimi, the lost dark night world, is there." Gweronell pursued and gestured towards the sea. "To fall into the sea is to cross the Ska-Muni shadow wall. That is why the Kra-Tini have no boats. Kra-Tini are afraid to cross the shadow wall by accident. Dukas Raden was afraid. Gweronell – is a different man. He sails the Skai sea."

The Woodstalker fell silent. The sky was cloudless, and the third quarter moon lit up the sea. The silver-light in the cliff shone so brightly that Kitt could see the Silver-Woman clearly now. But even when he couldn't see her, he had always been aware of her presence on Isenkliff, and of her loneliness, ever since Malan Jian sat down on the rock ledge, where the wave finally took him.

"Couldn't one or the other cross those shadow walls and world divides, so that they can be together?"

"There is an ancient power, Kaulra Gooth, a stone blade -the tooth that can open both the Ska-Muni shadow wall and the Nedye-Muni world divide."

"Where can I find this tooth blade?"

"I don't know. Shangar Shaark Ayen, the Ludoshini of the Kra-Tini Feen, he knows. He is wise as Nine Serpents, knows everything." Gweronell shuddered. "You don't want to ask him."

301

Following Gweronell's advice, Kitt put his boat into the mouth of a nameless river, and steered under the overhanging dome of a willow.

There he took off all his clothes, except for a pair of short trousers. Of his weapons, he took only his sword, fastening it on his back, and a knife, and let himself down into the dark water.
When he came to the opposite shore, he dug above the waterline, until he had a handful of wet clay, with which he painted lines and patches on his naked skin. Thus camouflaged, he traversed the wood until the sun sank and night fell.

The thin sickle of the waning moon did nothing to light the way, leaving the Murkowydir wood pitch dark, except for those who could see in the night, wildcats, cave bears, wolves, the long-toothed Death-Smile Cat, Woodstalkers and Kitt. He moved through the wood silently, himself a part of the shadows and the faint moonlight.

Near the Feen village he spotted the first Jay guard sitting absolutely motionless in the little clump of young willow trees. The young Woodstalker had washed his body in a poultice of bark and leaves to hide his scent, but even so, Kitt knew precisely where he was. A society of recently initiated warriors, the Jays took on all guard duties. Kitt had never known them to do anything really cunning, but he kept in mind that the Singing Bear had also been a Jay once. Becoming the shadow of a tree, a bush, a rock, making as much noise as they, Kitt passed the first Jay.

Concentrating on the places awarding the best cover as well as the best outlook, Kitt saw the next Jay sitting in an oak astride a thick ember. He could even smell the dried meat the young warrior was munching. Easy. Kitt smiled grimly.

The next Jay lay hidden under the low branches of a fir, a good hiding place, but he waved at a gnat, and Kitt spotted the movement.

A fourth Jay stood motionless like a tree trunk in a copse on the edge of the clearing where the village was; Kitt passed him with equal ease as the others.

The grass houses of the Feen village were grouped around a circular, stone-paved place, with a tall pole carved with bears and birds in the centre of it, and a plain one half the distance between it and a hut standing alone. Only from that one hut came flickering firelight, which played on a pole carved in the image of serpents writhing around each other. Without counting, Kitt knew that there were nine. This was the dwelling of Shangar Shaark Ayen, Wise as Nine Serpents, the Ludoshini, the Old Man of the Feen, the one who Kitt wanted to consult.

He was about to approach the hut, when he saw a movement on the other side of the place where a long slim pole stood, from which skulls and bones of wolves and bears were suspended, and a Dodlak skull without the upper canines, showing the house to be that of Mangan Sorkera, Singing Bear, the war leader.

Swinging in the light wind, the bones clacked together from time to time with a dry hollow sound, their monotonous rhythm suddenly altered. Something was tied to the pole, which now got up on all four fitfully, a dog, a human dog, a captive, in the darkness Kitt could not see to which rival people the watchdog belonged.

Kitt waited until the wretch cowered down again before he approached Shangar Shaark Ayen's hut like a shadow, and pushed aside the skin that hung in the doorway, briefly wondering which animal the rough and long hair had once belonged to.

Shangar Shaark Ayen was sitting before the fire in the centre of the room. Long white hair lay on broad, gaunt shoulders; his face was seamed with many lines, yet it was ageless, and the old back was still straight. The Ludoshini seemed not to realise the intruder towering above him, but Kitt had not the least doubt that the old man had noticed his entrance.

"Gawthrin lye wants Mirril, magic. Ban man iron," Kitt said slowly in the Feen language which he had learned from Gweronell.

"Kra-Tini Ludoshini no Mirril Gita," Shangar Shaark Ayen replied. He had not yet looked up to acknowledge Kitt's presence.

Kitt didn't know what Gita meant; it was not a word Gweronell had taught him.

"Gawthrin lye gift." He lowered himself on one knee in front of the Ludoshini and with both hands, he held out four claws of the Dodlak, the Death-Smile Cat. The Feen called this animal Graykhol Rere.

Hooded lids rose a little, and a pair of Feen eyes, coal-black without the whites showing, looked first at the Dodlak tooth on Kitt's chest, and then down on the curved yellow talons, which lay on the broad expanse of a pair of hands capable of breaking the old man's neck with a touch.

Shangar Shaark Ayen looked at the Graykhol Rere tooth that hung on the Gita's chest, hairless, a boy's, broader than the strongest warrior.

No threat lay in the deferential manner befitting a young man towards an elder. Except for the gift of the Graykhol Rere claws, that gift was a clear threat. Only the best warriors dared attempt such a hunt, only the very best survived, and those who emerged victorious were the most dangerous of all. Among the Feen had been only three warriors who survived an encounter with the Graykhol Rere, and two who had brought home the teeth and claws.

Shangar Shaark Ayen nodded, stretching out a bony hand to put logs on the fire. "Teeth," he said. "Black stone tooth eat Sreedok, eat wood heart. Kaulra Gooth." The flames leapt high and threw the shadows of the two men on the reed walls, Kitt's broad shoulders darkening the firelight that the room behind him remained in shadow. Shangar Shaark Ayen's shadow did not resemble that of a man - behind him, a knot of serpents danced on the wall. "Gree Meder, spoiler, cut heart wood, cut heart man," the Ludoshini continued, putting more wood on the fire. "Gawthrin Lye find Gree Meder take Kaulra Gooth."

The air in the hut became stifling hot, and Shangar's shadow grew on the wall behind him as he bent forward again to put still more wood on the fire.

"Kaulra Gooth. Black stone tooth. Black stone knife. Where?" Kitt asked with a stumbling tongue, his mind reeling.

"Surgu. Shakro-Shork," Shangar Shaark Ayen said.

"Thorns, black thorn tree?" asked Kitt.

Shangar nodded, putting still more wood on the fire.

Suddenly Kitt saw another shadow on the south-western wall, that of a great thorn tree, Shakro-Shork, flames of greenish light dancing between the spiky branches.

"Souls of men," Shangar Shaark Ayen said, pointing at the green lights.

Kitt wanted to rise but found that he couldn't.

"Gawthrin Lye weak." Shangar smiled a fine, wise, derisive smile.

"The logs," Kitt said faintly, mixing up northern and Feen words. "Kush. I did not know."

Shangar chuckled a dry old man's chuckle. "No Dshooka knows all trees grow Sreedok." He rose and came to the paralysed Kitt, stroked his flaxen hair, looked into the grey eyes. "Gita," he said softly. "Did you not know that you must die?"

Kitt wondered lazily why the smoke did not affect the old man and thought that maybe these things were different with serpents, and that seemed an entirely plausible idea. He stopped worrying about that, as it was much too hard work to think.

Suddenly the hut was full of men. Kitt had not seen or heard them come. They bound him hand and foot, while he could not move, could not even speak, as they dragged him out of Shangar Shaark Ayen's hut and across the stone-flagged village place. He was left to lie on the stones by the plain stake.

Kitt felt feet padding around him, but all he saw before his eyes were images of black, thorny bows, specks of green light playing between them, and a night-black stone knife with rainbow edges.

For a long time, Kitt was lying on the ground. Now and again somebody gave him a vicious kick in the ribs, each time saying the same words, "Agetool A Shushei". That meant afraid of a rabbit. Kitt was too tired to care. "I'm not afraid of you, shushei mong, foolish rabbit," he said sleepily.

Somebody kicked him again. The kicks did not hurt him much, and he would have slept if it had not been for a voice speaking angrily nearby. It was Mangan Sorkera, the Feen war leader, his old enemy, and Kitt wondered idly, why the Singing Bear was shouting so. The long chase was over at last, and Kitt did not care about that either. Nobody could know all the trees in the Murkowydir, except Shangar Shaark Ayen, who had lived so long and possessed the guile of nine serpents.

"Mik . . . Shini . . . Gita," Shangar's sibilant voice said. "Shame . . . fire . . . fear . . . kill soul . . . kill . . . soul."

305

Kitt knew the old man was talking about him, he knew what Mik Shini meant, the shameful death, death without honour at the hands of the women and children, a death slow, hard and disgraceful. But he did not think that his soul was in Shangar Shaark Ayen's hands.

After some time orange firelight filled his vision and he felt the heat on his skin. He was standing upright, arms bound behind him around a stake. The bonds that tied him to the pole were hard and inflexible, cutting painfully into arms and legs. Tightly woven bark strips he thought, drying in the fire crackling near him.

It was very quiet as if he was alone.

He raised his head.

Out of slowly focusing eyes, he saw the fires burning near him, and the Feen, standing in a ring around the stake. All were watching him, women and children, behind them the men, a ring of eyes, black with no whites in it. The women and children held bone needles and sharp stones for the scraping of the skins in their hands. As he regained awareness, they stirred.

A light wind sprang up, driving the flames toward the stake, forcing Kitt to breathe smoke, and he suppressed the urge to cough.

Two men came forward to throw more dry wood onto the fires, so that the flames leapt high, burning hot on his shoulders. Hot air streamed into his lungs.

Then they piled on green wood so that smoke billowed up and engulfed the stake.

Kitt's eyes burned, his tongue cleaved to his palate, and his head hurt. The smoke parted, and the faces wavered. All he saw clearly were a pair of big eyes looking at him. It was the little woods-girl, whom he had met years ago when fleeing from Mangan Sorkera. She had grown, but he still knew her by her eyes and the kittenish face. She held a long bone scraper. Kitt smiled at her, and she smiled back shyly.

Behind the little woods-girl stood another figure that Kitt knew, a tall warrior, with finely cut features, and long blue-black hair falling down his back. His only adornment was a hand-long curved tooth, gleaming white on the deeply tanned, broad chest. Exuding an air of extraordinary strength and quiet authority, he watched Kitt impassively, his eyes shining a metallic blue in the firelight.

"Mangan Sorkera!" Kitt called in a hoarse voice between laughter and a cough. "Kra-Tini Feen bad hunt? Fry Gawthrin Lye eat?"

A deep dusky flush welled up under Mangan Sorkera's tanned face, noticeable even in the red glow of the fire.

Kitt grinned, knowing full well that to call a Feen an eater of human flesh was one of the worst insults possible.

"Dshooka!" A young warrior sprang between the fires with his arm raised.

"Djanadir Thomiat," said Mangan Sorkera lowly, savagely.

The young Feen stopped and withdrew, looking mortified.

Glask was one of several young warriors who had meddled with Gawthrin Lye in the solitude of the Sreedok.

Each had been struck down ignominiously. For his heavy fist, Gawthrin Lye had been given a second name, Djanadir, Hammerer. He never killed any of those he struck down, making the insult infinitely worse. This was the way a strong warrior, Thomiat, showed his contempt for a weaker enemy. Mangan's words threw this shame into Glask's face, and the young man faded to the back of the crowd, where the proper place was for an untried warrior.

Mangan Sorkera, Singing Bear, watched the big, young man at the stake. The Feen war leader had another end in mind for the long-standing feud between him and Gawthrin Lye. This youth had killed Mangan's blood-brother Agetool A Shushei in a fair fight, and defied the war leader himself for years. Mangan Sorkera wanted to give him the terrible death of a brave enemy among the sacred red Tini trees. He had been overruled.

Feen warriors owed their war leader obedience only in war; at home in the village in peacetime, he was a man like all others. The last word lay with the Ludoshini, Shangar Shaark Ayen, who had confirmed the majority decision that Gawthrin Lye, Djanadir Thomiat, would die the Mik Shini, the shameful death.

The women and children would tear and beat and trample him to death; what was left of him would be thrown out in the offal place for the scavengers to devour. Mangan Sorkera would never devour

Gawthrin Lye's heart and never drink his blood from the cup made of his skull, taken as he was still alive. Agetool A Shushei would never know that his friend had avenged his death and honoured his slayer.

The fires burned already low, and the ring of the women and children tightened.

Two young warriors stepped forward to throw armfuls of dry wood on the fires. The flames shot high, and the circle of women and children retreated.

With wooden lances, the young warriors pushed the burning embers nearer to the stake.

The heat of the flames singed Kitt's hair, the skin on his shoulders and arms blistered and cracked, a shower of sparks enveloped the stake, and he jerked at his bonds.

The Feen jeered at this flinching from pain. Their mocking voices drowned the cracking sound of drying fibres breaking. The bark ropes were becoming brittle in the heat, but they still held. Kitt did not try a second time. His lungs fought the smoke, and his will fought the slowing heartbeat.

Outside the ring of fire, a drum began beating in a slow rhythm.

The two young warriors continued feeding the fires, and shoving them nearer to the stake.

A flame tongue licked Kitt's shoulder, and indescribable pain shot through his arm like lightning, but he did not move, knowing that any attempt to avoid one fire would only bring him into the other, and then the pain would overwhelm him, his courage would break, and he would be lost.

The firelight glittered in his deep-set eyes as Mangan Sorkera regarded Gawthrin Lye.

More warriors began appearing at the edge of the circle, coming in out of the wood where they had taken position, to apprehend any attempt at escape. Now they judged that the victim was weakened enough, and came to watch the end.

Tadir and Shaluwa brought more dry wood. Despite their youth, they were seasoned warriors, who knew the worth of a valiant enemy as only brave men can. They wanted to oblige their war leader by giving his enemy a good death, even defying Shangar Shaark Ayen's verdict.

Mangan Sorkera listened to the drumming that came from the hut, low and menacing. Soon the Ludoshini would come out, and then it would be too late. Nobody disobeyed Shangar Shaark Ayen to his face.

Kutcher neared the fires, carrying Gawthrin Lye's long knife. It was a Dshooka weapon, made of the grey metal that no fire in the Sreedok could smelt.

Kutcher held the blade into the flames until the tip glowed red-hot, then stepped between the fires, braving the heat.

The glowing metal neared Gawthrin Lye's hairless chest, just beside the Graykhol Rere tooth. Kutcher looked at his war leader for approval.

Mangan Sorkera folded his arms, a faint smile playing over his lips. Kutcher had never had any sense, quite unlike the tree cat that he claimed had appeared in his dream of initiation, and after which he was named. Mangan thought sardonically that maybe it hadn't been a tree cat, but another far less intelligent animal.

The hot steel's radiating heat blistered Kitt's bare skin.

He tensed, and every muscle and sinew of his body stood out in sharp relief in a play of red light and black shadow. A gusty sigh went up around the fire.

There was a sharp crack, and then another as the bark ropes broke. Kitt wrought the sword from the young Feen's hand, and knocked him out with the pommel, as his foot lashed out to kick another Feen in the stomach. His fist landed squarely before the third warrior's chest, sending him sprawling into the fire.

A warrior came at him with a knife, and Kitt avoided his slash once, twice, three times with the ease of a dancer, before a contemptuous knock on the head sent him falling towards the flames with flailing arms.

Deep laughter boomed. "Good, Gawthrin Lye, good!" It was his old enemy Mangan Sorkera, still standing there with his arms folded.

Kitt brought down another man with a quick play of feet, jumped high over the head of the little woods-girl, and disappeared into the cool darkness of the wood.

His eyes blinded from the firelight, he could not see, and his head and lungs were full of smoke. Twice he swung his sword blindly, the broad of the blade connecting with flesh. With fist and feet he lashed out at warriors he heard and felt more than he saw them.

He won the oak thicket and reached for a thick ember, swarmed up and crouched in the tree motionless, his arms around the trunk as the fresh night air filled his chest, clearing his sight.

Below, he heard soft steps, a breaking sound, a low call, and then another, louder call, at more distance. They thought that he was still running. Didn't they think of the trees? The war leader would. But he had allowed Kitt to break the bonds, hadn't joined the scrimmage before the stake -had let him get away, he made no mistake about that.

Kitt ran along the bow and was in the next tree, then another, moving away from the Feen village, farther into the wood without a leaf stirring on his path.

The Feen were left looking at an empty stake, while five warriors were scrabbling on the ground, trying to get up. Four were severely burned, having been tossed into the fires.

Mangan Sorkera didn't uncross his arms even now.

Shangar Shaark Ayen appeared outside his hut. The glare of his unhooded eyes went from the empty stake to the war leader.

The Singing Bear smiled. "Mangan Sorkera goes now, fight Gawthrin Lye."

"Mangan Sorkera dies," Shangar Shaark Ayen said.

Kitt woke from a fitful half-sleep filled with black thorns and glowing knives, the fevered images still floating through his pounding head.

The paling sky heralded the hour when according to Shangar Shaark Ayen's will Kitt should have died at the stake.

Before the faint light, the trees stood out stark and black.

When the sun stood high above the wood, and the summer heat set in, Kitt was far south-west from the Feen village, and the calls of pursuit had faded behind him.

He curled up in the crown of a giant oak and slept through most of the day, to wake at sunset, feeling stiff, with the skin on arms and shoulders burning hot and blistering. Around him was nothing but the rustling of leaves, the evening song of the birds and the buzz of insects.

Kitt continued to climb from one big oak tree into another until he came to a brook. With smarting eyes, he looked down on the water which was running over white sand, clear and fast. For a moment, he was aware of nothing but his overwhelming thirst. To survey his surrounds cost him an impossible effort, before he lowered himself into the middle of the cold water, agonizingly slowly. To kneel down and thrust his hands into the cold water seemed to take an eternity, until he felt the indescribable relief when his lips touched the clear water. Then he forgot everything while drinking.

He had taken four deep draughts before he raised his head again to look around in haste. For a vulnerable moment, he had not been aware of his surroundings. No enemy, no beast had approached during this short time of careless bliss.

He bent down to the water again to take smaller sips now; all senses on his surroundings, he cooled his eyes and sloshed the cold water over his still sore head and burning skin.

Then, with undiminished caution, he took to the trees again. Kitt was almost sure that the pursuing Feen warriors would expect him to have doubled back and be on the run to the seashore, to Latunsrigo, to repeat his successful escape from years ago. They would not think of him going in the almost opposite direction, deeper into the wood that they called Sreedok, with the dangerous exception of Shangar Shaark Ayen who knew what Kitt wanted, and the Feen war leader.

The only question was whether Mangan Sorkera would bring along his warriors, or if he decided to settle their feud one on one. Kitt thought that the Singing Bear would come alone. He was convinced that Mangan Sorkera had anticipated his escape, had let him do it because the war leader and the Ludoshini, Shangar Shaark Ayen, disagreed about the way Kitt was to be brought to death. Mangan Sorkera wanted Kitt's heart and skull, and he wished to take them in a way that was honourable to Kitt, and even more painful than what Shangar Shaark Ayen had in mind. If Mangan Sorkera caught up with him, then one of them would die. There was no other outcome possible.

After three days of fleeing through the Murkowydir wood, Kitt still made every effort to hide his track, and took to the trees whenever he could.

#

On the morning of the fourth day, Kitt espied Mangan Sorkera trotting along under the oaks, not bothering to hide.

"Come down, Gawthrin Lye!" he called in the language of the north. "No more running! Come and fight!"

"How did Mangan Sorkera find Gawthrin Lye?" Kitt murmured a little louder than the wind in the oak leaves.

"Willow tree," Mangan said briefly, facing the oak in the sure knowledge that Kitt had neither bow nor spear. "Mistake," he added.

Stung, Kitt cursed inwardly as he remembered the few willow leaves and a small piece of bark which he had taken, very carefully as he had thought, to chew against the headache and help quicken his blood after the long thirst.

"Come down, Gawthrin Lye," the war leader demanded. "Mangan Sorkera is alone."

"Mangan Sorkera is mistaken," Kitt said nearly inaudibly.

From his vantage point, he suddenly saw something, that Mangan could not see from down below. Noiselessly, shadowy figures were drifting through the underbrush.

Mangan Sorkera stiffened, and then he whirled around.

Twenty men at least surrounded the war leader, signalling to each other with claw-like hands that ended in long, black, curving nails. Their faces appeared inhuman masks; the short hair covering their round heads was like fur, short and of a deep, velvety black, like charcoal. Their skin was pale like frog bellies, covered with black tattoos, which resembled the patterns of light and shadow among the

312

trees, and made them nearly invisible.

About to drop down from his oak tree, Kitt checked the impulse.

More were still coming.

With a rush like a gust of wind, shadows flew like autumn leaves, long leather thongs shot out, and wrapped around the war leader's arms, body and legs. The thin ropes ended in sharp thorns that clawed into his skin, ripping it bloody. Heedless of the gashing wounds that caused him, Mangan used all his strength to try and break away, slashing at the thongs with his knife.

The men at the other end of the ropes held him in place; they tightened and pulled in the thongs, thereby drawing themselves towards the bleeding Feen war leader, and making the thorns dig still further into his flesh.

"Meder!" cried Mangan Sorkera, fury and loathing in his voice, and unimaginable in the Feen war leader, panic and fear.

Meder meant devils, Kitt remembered Shangar Shaark Ayen's words. The Shakro-Shork, the black thorn tree, must be near. Cunning as nine serpents, the old man can't lose. That last thought was dedicated to the Ludoshini, the Wise Man of the Feen.

The Meder did not speak; they did not call out to each other, even as they had their prey secure.

Kitt counted thirty tattooed, silent men surrounding Mangan Sorkera and then stopped counting, for still more were coming to cluster around the war leader. He did not move. None of the Meder looked up into the crown of the oak.

Jerking on the thongs, they brought the war leader down. Their black talons dug into his limbs, further tearing flesh and skin.

One Meder came too near Mangan's knife, while the Feen could still move his hand a little. Kitt could see that the Meder blood gushing from the neck was darker than that of other humans and of a deep-purple colour.

After that, the fight was truly over. Wrapped in thongs and biting thorns, Mangan Sorkera was a captive, unable to move hand or foot.

Kitt watched as the Meder dragged his old enemy away, and left a broad track of broken bushes and thick blood drops.

After careful scrutiny of his surroundings, Kitt dropped down from his tree to follow the bloody spoor.

Mangan Sorkera sat with his back to a stake, facing the Shakro-Shork.

The black thorn tree grew over the crowns of oaks and beeches as a black mound which rose like a dome bigger than anything built by the Dshooka. Within one summer, the Shakro-Shork had overgrown the heart of the Sreedok wood. Apart from its overwhelming dimensions, the black, malignant growth was like a bramble or hawthorn bush, bare as in winter.

No Feen had realised the danger, not even the Ludoshini, until spring, when it became clear that the Shakro-Shork would never grow a single green leaf. Its black thorns devoured everything living, trees, animals and people. The Shakro-Shork was not of the Sreedok; it was something that lived on the Sreedok. Only the Meder could live under the black thorn-bows.

Mangan Sorkera was unable to move. Long leather thongs were wrapped around his body and limbs several times, and at the slightest movement, the sharp claws bit into his flesh. He could only turn his head and see the Meder silently passing in and out of the tunnels that opened in the spiky mound. The black patterns which covered their skin made them nearly invisible.

There was no talk, no laughter, only thorn branches stirring, hands gesturing, and a constant noise like wind. That was how they talked, but it was entirely different from the sign language the people of the Sreedok used.

The Meder had another prisoner, a Graansha, tied to a stake that stood nearer to the black thorns than Mangan's. The Graansha was naked, and long, bloody slashes crisscrossed his white skin. Thin red thorn creepers were growing into the wounds like ivy into cracks in a rock, enveloping the Graansha's body; one creeper lay across his forehead, pulling the head back against the stake. His green eyes rested on Mangan and were entirely devoid of the customary contempt between the two neighbouring tribes.

Mangan Sorkera knew that the same trapped look was in his own eyes, the same despairing terror.

314

The creepers fastened upon the Graansha's skin were growing thicker and longer before Mangan's eyes, as their red colour changed to black, with the Graansha's already pale skin turning chalk white. Where the thorns grew deeper and deeper into the wounds, the flesh took on a blue colouration. Impaled as he was on many black spikes, the Graansha had not cried out once, had moved no muscle of his face.

The Meder went in and out of their tunnels, their faces unreadable masks, never looking upon the sacrifice. For them the Graansha was not a man, only meat to feed the Shakro-Shork. This was an annihilation as not even criminals condemned to die the Mik Shini, the shameful death, had to suffer, a death without witnesses, honour and redemption. Almost bloodless in the embrace of the black thorns, the Graansha was dying. Only Mangan looked at the victim, saw his courage, and knew of his death.

Nobody would see Mangan Sorkera die.

"Graansha brave man," Mangan spoke the words customary to acknowledge the honourable death of an enemy at the stake among the Tini trees.

"Royopit," the Graansha said, nearly inaudibly.

Mangan Sorkera nodded once, to show he had heard the name.

And then, suddenly, the thorny net began to vibrate, shaking and tearing the Graansha's body. Fresh blood poured from the countless wounds, until a red twisted thing hung at the stake, still held up by the thorns piercing it. Only now did the Graansha scream, as Mangan had never heard a man of that tribe scream, not even at a Feen stake.

Mangan felt the fear rise in him that he too would have to end his life screaming. Then he was glad that nobody would see him die.

No merciful faint came to the Graansha's rescue in the long time it took life to leave the torn body. At last, he stopped screaming. The thorn bush wrenched apart the bones; it sounded like a Graykhol Rere feeding.

Then the black thorn tree began to flower, fleshy blossoms red as blood and white as bone emerged among the torn remains of the Graansha sticking on the thorns.

On the blossoms followed fruits, red and spiky like chestnuts, hanging on long stalks. Before Mangan's eyes, they grew to the size of a man's head, turning from red to black with a purple shimmer.

Then the Meder came for Mangan Sorkera. Two Meder attached long leather thongs to the bonds on his hands and drew him up the stake to which he was bound, high enough to place a bowl under his feet, a black, spiky thing made from a thorn bush fruit.

There they left him hanging, with his hands growing numb until he could feel them no more, only the pain in his wrists and arms, a pain that a Feen was expected to endure without a sign that he felt it. To Mangan, it seemed like a reprieve, knowing what was yet to come.

The Meder went their ways past the Feen leader, never looking at him.

Suddenly, Mangan felt eyes upon him, cold, alien. A shapeless figure emerged from one of the tunnels in the Shakro-Shork, tattooed so heavily that there was more black than pale skin.

The figure approached, and Mangan saw that it was an old man, the tattooed skin hanging in folds from bones thin like sticks. His movements were strong and assured, and seemed too forceful for the frail frame that it should break at each step, but did not break. The thin black lips drew back from pointy black teeth in a mocking smile as he cocked his head to look up into the face of the hanging Feen war leader out of malevolent, purple-rimmed black eyes.

With revulsion, Mangan Sorkera looked down into the inhuman mask. This was the Gree Meder, the guardian of the foul Meder magic that was eating the heart of the Sreedok. In his clawed hand the Gree Meder held a coal-black stone knife; it was long as a man's hand, and shaped like a willow leaf, with sharp edges of dusky light and rainbow colours.

The Gree Meder slowly approached, the black stone knife held high above his head, until he stood before the war leader. He reached up and set the edge of the stone knife on the hanging man's collarbone to drag it across his chest. The knife slit the flesh cleanly, and the hurt was subtle and deep. Mangan felt blood running down his belly and legs and heard it drip into the spiky bowl at his feet.

The black stone knife made two more long shallow cuts in Mangan's chest, and then the Gree Meder cut his arms and legs, drawing the knife edges over the wounds caused during Mangan's capture. This was a pain that a Feen was expected to endure, and he endured it without move or sound, although the Meder knew no honour and therefore did not count as witnesses. It mattered to Mangan himself.

Two Meder carried a limp figure before the stake; it was the creature Mangan's knife had hit before he had finally been overcome.

With the black stone knife, the Gree Meder cut the long stalk of one of the black fruits which grew on the thorn bush after the Graansha's death. From the cut surface trickled a purple liquid, and the Gree Meder carefully bound up both cut ends of the stalk, just as the women did when cutting the cord between the womb and the newborn babe.

The Gree Meder set the edge of the stone knife to the fruit, and it split open upon the touch. A carrion smell struck Mangan's nose.

Next, the Gree Meder moved the stone knife over the heart and head of the dead man; although the edge barely touched the corpse, it was slashed apart piece by piece. These pieces the Gree Meder placed into the cut in the fruit. Although the body was much larger, it fitted into the fruit entirely. When the corpse had all disappeared, the spiky globe lay there whole, as if it had never been split.

The Gree Meder trotted over to Mangan's stake, and took away the blood-filled bowl from under his feet, to empty it over the fruit. Through a great wave of dizziness, Mangan saw the fruit burst, and a soft red stalk with thin, red thorns emerged, like a young bramble.

The Gree Meder returned into the Shakro-Shork, leaving the Meder to crowd in around the young thorn bush, caressing and talking to it with their hands. The red bramble branched out into five soft, thorny stalks, that began waving and twitching in a way that seemed familiar to Mangan Sorkera until he recognised the hand talk of the Meder.

The young thorny branches grew longer, while the first stalk began to grow thicker and darker in colour. At the base, it was already black like the Shakro-Shork. One by one, the Meder left the circle to disperse into the tunnels and archways in the thorny black brush.

Mangan Sorkera felt a light touch on his foot and saw that one of the red branches from the thorn fruit had reached him.

There was another touch on his side. At first, it hurt little when the thorns pressed into the cut on his foot. Then the first branch grew thicker, the thorns longer, to pierce skin and flesh to the bones. The pain was as if a bear bit his foot.

A thorny whip lashed towards Mangan's face and fastened across his forehead, that he could not move his head.

Another sharp pain bit into his side like a wolf's maw. Dizziness swapped over him in waves as he felt the thorns drain his blood, growing thicker and darker all the time, he knew without being able to see it. That was how the Shakro-Shork spread, he thought. The Ludoshini needed to know, but Mangan Sorkera could not bring him this knowledge. One day the great wood Sreedok would be gone, the Feen would be gone, and there would be only the Shakro-Shork -and the Meder.

Mangan Sorkera felt another touch on his feet. He could not look down, and did not try; he was too tired, too dizzy. He had given up.

Suddenly his feet were hanging free. He jerked his head, and the thorns pressed into his forehead; he could move just enough to see a thatch of thistle-coloured hair.

His brain worked only slowly to realise that it was Gawthrin Lye who had just cut the bonds on his legs. Mangan had forgotten about Gawthrin Lye. The youth straightened up and severed the thongs binding Mangan's wrists. The war leader fell, tearing the thorns out of his flesh by the weight of his body, and his feet struck the ground.

He went down to his knees, spots swimming before his eyes, and between them he saw Gawthrin Lye move away from him, towards the Shakro-Shork, and disappear into one of the black thorny tunnels.

Mangan Sorkera crawled away from the pole, tearing off the last creeper that still held his foot, while the pain of the blood returning to his hands joined the pain of the wounds the thorns had torn into his body. He crawled on all fours until he met an obstacle, the body of a Meder, groaning and trying to rise, his taloned hand scrambling for a greenstone knife lying on the ground. Gawthrin Lye's fist felled this one, Mangan thought woozily, Djanadir Thomiat.

As his hands were still useless, Mangan gripped the knife with his mouth, and threw himself against the Meder, knocking him back so that he lay across its body and pinned it down. He strained to reach the Meder's neck and slit its jugular with the knife clenched between his teeth. Dark purple blood spurted over him in a high arc, and he crawled over the twitching body, away from the black thorn tree Shakro-Shork, into the Sreedok, to die there a death that he understood.

Kitt struck down two more Meder with his fist and went into the tunnel, where he had seen the Gree Meder disappear, moving swiftly, while red and purple thorns snapped for him.

The older, darker thorns were stiffer and slower than the young red ones; they only stirred and rustled venomously, as the youth glided further into the black thorny tunnel.

As Kitt followed the shambling shadow of the Gree Meder into the Shakro-Shork, he passed stake after stake stuck within the thorns. He knew what they meant, had seen the Graansha die. It had cost him all he had not to rush in at that moment. He knew that had been prudent, considering how many Meder had been about at that moment -as he knew that this death would haunt him.

White bone fragments gleamed in the half-light among the black thorns, the skulls of humans, wolves, bears, stags. He came past dead tree trunks pierced by the black thorns like nails. Shakro-Shork eats the heart of the wood, Shangar Shaark Ayen had said.

Behind Kitt, the tunnel began twisting like the gullet of a giant trying to swallow the intruder, and the youth felt as if he was deep in the maw of a predator full of malicious intelligence, hungry to devour him. He went deeper and deeper into it instead of fleeing, as all his senses told him he should.

The Gree Meder seemed oblivious to the pursuit, never once looking back, but Kitt was convinced that the old man was leading him to a place in the Shakro-Shork where he could be dealt with. The Gree Meder reminded Kitt of Shangar Shaark Ayen, both wise old men, who could not be overcome by mere strength.

The tunnel behind Kitt contracted faster, forcing him into a run. A black thorn branch whistled like a whip; he encountered it with his sword just in time, but the keen iron could not cut the thick creeper. A thorn left a long burning slash across his chest. If all the barbs of the branch had hit, it would have flayed him.

To avoid several more thorny whips, Kitt ran faster still.

Before him, the tunnel opened into a dome. In the centre, a twisted black trunk was rooted with a circumference larger than ten men could span. The Gree Meder went towards it and laid both hands on the thick black trunk. He turned his head to look back at Kitt with gloating triumph; then he melted into the trunk as if he was sinking in a pool of tar.

Before Kitt could reach him, the Gree Meder had disappeared. He spotted the stone knife left lying at the foot of the black trunk among the gnarled roots, and picked it up to stow in his belt. Kaulra Gooth, this was what he had come for.

The entire thorn dome began contracting, and black branches and creepers worked loose and lashed towards Kitt. He deflected them with his sword and followed through slashing at the trunk. The steel sprang back without causing a scratch to the dully gleaming, skin-like bark. Soon Kitt would be caught in a thorny net, and his blood would wet the gnarled black roots of the Shakro-Shork.

Kaulra Gooth cut Shakro Shork, Kitt thought, a cold sweat breaking out. He gripped the hilt of the black stone knife and dived to draw it across the black trunk.

The mere touch of the stone edge caused the huge trunk to split open like swollen flesh. A purple liquid ran from the deep cut, and a scream shook the whole Shakro-Shork. Kitt cut at the trunk again. Branches whipped towards him, and he whirled around, holding out the stone knife. The embers flinched away like living limbs.

Holding Kaulra Gooth high, Kitt started towards a tunnel opening. The net of thorns parted before him, shuddering, the tunnel opened wide, and Kitt bounded into it. As he ran, the thorns quailed before the black stone knife.

A whiplash thick as an arm with hand-long thorns whistled out at him and did not catch him by surprise; Kaulra Gooth split it with a wet sound. The cut ends fell to the ground gushing streams of purple liquid like a cut artery. The tunnel strained open wider to let him pass.

Suddenly Kitt was among a group of Meder who shrank from the black stone blade in his hand. A few spiked leather thongs whistled and missed Kitt's back as he stormed on with undiminished speed.

As Kitt emerged from the thorn mound, sunlight shone on the knife-edge of Kaulra Gooth and burst with rainbow fire, and the great thorn dome behind him was convulsing.

#

When Mangan Sorkera became too weak to crawl on all fours, he dragged himself along on his belly, and when he grew too weak to move, he hid under the roots of a fallen tree, with the last spark of his conscience holding on to his only weapon, the greenstone knife taken from the Meder. His fading awareness told him that something was on his track, coming after him. Pressing his back against roots and earth, he kept still, waiting for that which was approaching. Maybe it would not see him and pass.

It did not pass. Feeling a shadow fall on him, Mangan Sorkera struggled to open his eyes. Gawthrin Lye was standing over the war leader's hiding place. A deep red scratch ran across his chest, and the black stone knife Kaulra Gooth stuck in his belt.

Mangan had hoped that it would be Gawthrin Lye who got to him first, and not the filthy Meder. He managed to raise the hand clutching the knife a little, prepared to fight, yet knowing that weakened from blood loss and pain he had not the least chance to kill his enemy. That did not matter, what mattered was that he would die fighting. Just as Mangan Sorkera had allowed Gawthrin Lye to escape from the Mik Shini, the shameful death, Gawthrin Lye gave him the chance to end his life honourably.

Gawthrin Lye bent down with an outstretched hand.

Mangan Sorkera tried to lash out with the knife, but his hand fell back, the knife hilt slipping from useless fingers. He was too weak to defend himself from the shame of his enemy's touch. He would have to die a weak man's death.

Gawthrin Lye straightened, seemed about to speak, to taunt him, Mangan thought.

321

The youth said nothing, fixing Mangan Sorkera with searching grey eyes for what seemed an eternity of burning shame.

Then, Gawthrin Lye averted his eyes, and for a moment he hesitated, to look back briefly again with a slight shake of his head. Then he turned and melted into the wood without noise, resembling the Mooankayit, his real shape in the real world.

Mangan Sorkera fell back exhausted, thinking that he had never understood Gawthrin Lye, and didn't understand him now -and that the black thorns of the Shakro-Shork would grow no more, as long as Kaulra Gooth, the black stone knife, did not return to the Sreedok. Gawthrin Lye had Kaulra Gooth now.

Mangan Sorkera fainted.

#

"Shakro-Shork three days Mukine-Kad-Nidyas. Shangar Shaark Ayen know?"

"Not know." The old Ludoshini sat hunched over the fire.

"Meder Mirril, magic," Mangan Sorkera said. "Gree Meder more strong Shangar Shaark Ayen?" That was the right question to ask, and by brutally asking it, Mangan Sorkera proved that he had been the right choice to lead the Feen in war, and of that, the Ludoshini was glad at a time like this, when the answer was, "Shangar Shaark Ayen not know."

"Gawthrin Lye Kaulra Gooth." That was the news Mangan Sorkera had needed to bring to his Ludoshini, even at the price that the warriors and the women had seen him stumble with shaking knees across the village place, covered in his own dried blood.

"Djanadir Thomiat Kaulra Gooth foolish Dshooka."

"Gawthrin Lye warrior Sreedok."

To one who knew the Feen language, the conflicting ideas of the war leader and the Ludoshini were clearly expressed by the different names each used to describe one and the same youth. Mangan called him Gawthrin Lye, a fox cub, clever child, a name for a friend, a younger brother, a beloved enemy. Although Mangan did not understand how the youth thought, he knew the soul of a man who moved with the wood, bent to it, was it. But Shangar Shaark Ayen called Kitt Djanadir Thomiat, the name the other Feen warriors had

322

given the youth because of his heavy fists, and his contemptuous treatment of unsuccessful attackers, a name for a dangerous enemy.

"Djanadir Thomiat enemy. Not Feen. Gita."

Gita. The fearful name. Once its sound had set Mangan Sorkera and his friend Agetool A Shushei on the trail of the boy. Now Agetool was dead, by Gawthrin Lye's hand, and Mangan Sorkera was alive, and could not understand why Gawthrin Lye had not killed him. Shangar Shaark Ayen knew the place of all things in the world behind the fire, the real world, knew Gawthrin Lye's true shape. But why he acted as he did, the Ludoshini didn't know either.

"Gree Meder comes," Shangar said. "Hide Gita trail." That was bitter for the old man. To keep the black stone knife Kaulra Gooth from the Gree Meder the Gita must be protected.

#

In the swaying bluegrass of the real world Nyedasya-Dyarve, the world behind the fire, stood the coal-black bear, a long-legged sinewy animal.

Beside him writhed the nine serpents, in a knot of black and white.

In Nyedasya-Aurayskahan-Ashyalish, the dream world of illusion and lies, the world the people inhabited, Gawthrin Lye never left a track. But in the real world, a being like the Mooankayit could not hide.

The nine serpents flitted away, searching for the trail of the Gita. It was the black bear who found it, bright like a path of lightning.

The nine serpents changed shape into the Ludoshini. The old man gathered up the bright spoor like a thread, cut it, and wound it up into a gleaming ball.

###

Kitt timed his arrival on Isenkliff for nightfall.

His parents would be sitting in the kitchen for dinner, his mother feeding little Swantje. That was the time when her attention would be engaged, and distracted even from the arrival of the knife Kaulra Gooth, which Kitt knew to be a magic thing.

On the southern side of the island, the sea reached to the top of Brynnir's anvil where Kitt made fast the boat. He climbed up the steep path used by the goats and their hunter in the light of the moon

323

three days after full, and still very bright. He came up to the ledge with the deep recess behind it, where the Moonlight Girl, the Lady of the Silver Sword, was looking out to the sea, waiting. Kitt hadn't been this near her since she had fought him in the hall of Isenkliff. He was wary, ready for the attack.

She didn't move.

From his belt, Kitt took Kaulra Gooth, the black stone blade, won so hard. He had no idea what to do with it; ought he to cut the air, or the sea, or the rock? Until this moment, everything had been clear. Go to the Murkowydir, corner the Ludoshini Shangar Shaark Ayen, find out where Kaulra Gooth was, bring it back without killing any Feen Woodstalkers. That had been clear enough - the easy part. Now he felt defeated and stupid.

The Lady of the Silver Sword said nothing. Her silver-black eyes remained on the distance. Waiting.

Without relaxing his vigilance on her, Kitt also waited, for something to occur to him, recapitulating what his friend Gweronell had told him about the Ska-Muni shadow wall and the Nedye-Muni world divide, and how the Gree Meder had used the black stone knife.

Then, far out in the sea, a wave rose, gigantic, something golden glittering in it.

The sea brought back Malan Jian and laid him at the feet of the Lady of the Silver Sword, like a dead fish, with moonlight glittering on golden brocade and on the seawater moving the dark red strands like seaweed, and enveloping each copper hair like glass. The moonlight shimmered on dead flesh with the dull sheen of a fish belly and nested in the elongated dark eyes that were not dead, but full of despair.

The wave sank back. Water ran off the cliff in thin, gurgling streams.

The Lady of the Silver Sword knelt to kiss the Golden Warrior.

Kitt had read about True Love's Kiss, and in the tales it brought back the dead lover without fail.

Nothing happened.

Her silver-black eyes boring into Kitt's were terrible.

For the first time, Kitt heard the lady of the sword speak in her voice like broken crystal; he recognised words in the language of Luxin Shoo that Malan Jian had taught him, and understood what she said. "Help him!"

He had to do something, anything. Experimentally Kitt moved the knife before him.

A thunderclap sounded.

With half-formed ideas running through his mind, Kitt took his sword. It was the last he had forged; impressed with the Golden Warrior's fighting skill, he had made it similar to the silver sword.

He unsheathed the slightly curved blade and laid it beside the Golden Warrior's corpse.

Then, he set the edge of Kaulra Gooth to the steel.

A deep metallic boom sounded, and ripples appeared on the surface of the blade, opening wider than the blade was broad, and the steel began to glow as in the forge.

Encouraged by that, Kitt took Kaulra Gooth and dragged the stone edge along the corpse from the left temple to the right foot, and then crosswise, as he had seen the Gree Meder do. It was not the same as cutting real flesh and bone, but there was a result. He strove to make the exact same movements to shift the cut bits. Bit by bit, the corpse disappeared into the glowing opening which closed over the last piece with metallic tolling, and the steel was cool.

Was that a good thing? Or had he made everything worse? Kitt looked down on the two swords lying side by side, and didn't know.

Suddenly, the recess lit up with gold and silver light. The Golden Warrior and the Silver Woman stood face to face, looking into each other's eyes. Their hands rose, and touched – entwined.

Quietly, Kitt lowered himself down from the ledge. Kaulra Gooth he left lying in the recess with the two swords.

With a deep feeling of relief, he took the boat around to the western bay. The melancholy fate of Malan Jian and his woman Niluba had been at the back of his mind for a long time. Now it was all good, he thought with exhausted happiness.

The flood was still reaching up to the grass line. The moon was shining bright in the west, lighting up the valley. High on the southern promontory, the bright light shone still, silver and golden.

By the time Kitt came up to the hall, it was dark. Back in his room, he could not sleep, despite his exhaustion and relief. New worries began to raise their heads like a knot of serpents.

As long as Kaulra Gooth was on Isenkliff, the Shakro-Shork, the black thorn tree, would not grow. Could magical things be hidden at all? Such objects had their own life, their own laws, however deep they were hidden. Such will always come to light again, for good or bad. Could the Gree Meder cross the sea to reach Isenkliff? Nobody would get past Malan Jian and his woman, not even the Gree Meder, of that he was sure. The sea was another matter; giant waves did reach up to the promontory. Where did giant waves originate? Was it possible to destroy a magical thing of such Seidar power? Should something like that be destroyed even if it were possible?

The Ludoshini of the Kra-Tini Feen would know what to do with the thing that threatened his people directly. Was Shangar Shaark Ayen able to cross the sea? Kitt never wanted to see the old man again.

Maybe his mother could answer his questions, but would she? Kitt didn't regret that he had finally helped his friend. But he didn't look forward to tell her what he had done to accomplish it.

He got up, lit a lamp and went out to the west side gallery. The shelf there contained books which his mother had forbidden him to even touch -books, scrolls and tablets dealing with Seidar and Zaubar magic.

Kitt scanned through the books for something that could help him. Direct mention of the black stone knife Kaulra Gooth was too much to hope for. He set aside the books that seemed to refer to world divides. The magic works were hard to read, very different from the travel accounts and treatises on steel or the planting of crops which he usually read. He knew that to find answers he had as long as it took his mother to notice what he was doing.

The light of morning came through the glass windows, first pale, growing brighter. Kitt extinguished the lamp he was reading by. He heard his mother clatter about in the kitchen; she had come down first in the morning, as she did every day. Did she know that he had returned?

The kitchen door opened. Across the hall table covered with the forbidden books, they faced each other, Aslaug and Kitt, as they had so often in the past when he had returned from the Dark Wood Murkowydir.

In the pale morning light, Aslaug noticed the singed hair, a fiery burn at the base of the neck that ran under the shirt, the line of exhaustion beside the mouth.

"What have you done again, Kitt?"

"I did nothing wrong, mother." Kitt's reply was that of a boy caught out, as usual.

"You brought a thing of power, and you used it!"

Of course, his mother knew. How could he think she would not?

"I needed the black stone knife Kaulra Gooth to help Malan Jian. I didn't know how to use it. Somehow, I must have done it right." He felt sudden anxiety that his mother would tell him that the respite for Malan Jian and Niluba was only temporary, and that he had made it infinitely worse.

"What do you seek in these books then?"

"What to do with Kaulra Gooth? I cannot find anything about it in the books. Can I leave it where it is now? I don't want to take it back to the Murkowydir. Shangar Shaark Ayen, his name means nine serpents, he tricked me and - I broke free. I didn't kill any of the Woodstalkers, you need not worry."

"First, I must dress your wounds," Aslaug said. "The burns must hurt you badly. Why did you put on your shirt, you know better! It's stuck to your wounds now! I can see what shape you are in, you can't hide this from me. And I insist that you eat breakfast and then sleep!"

Kitt let his mother treat his wounds and drank what she gave him.

#

Angry with herself, Aslaug stood before the shelves on the gallery.

How often had she been on the point to give in to the pleasure of teaching Kitt's quick mind, lured by the satisfaction of quenching his thirst for knowledge? He had always wanted to learn about Seidar and Zaubar, the magic inherent in the world and its application. His hunger for knowledge seemed without bounds. She had often considered giving in; trying to fool herself that if she gave him at least Seidar learning, he would leave the way of the sword. What a monster might she have created, if she had added the slightest knowledge of magic to this inhuman strength, to this innate killing instinct? And now he had acquired a powerful magic tool and used it, and then had taken down those books himself, against her categorical ban. She was losing control of him.

All these magic writings had come to the island with the ships of men who wanted weapons. She reached up, again and again, dragged down the books, scrolls and tablets, and threw them over the balustrade until everything lay in a heap on the floor below.

She went down and carried everything to the fire-place. Throwing armfuls of books and scrolls onto the earth fire, she almost stifled the flames. A red tongue sneaked out from under the heap and licked at a papyrus. With both arms she gathered up the books which Kitt had already piled onto the hall table.

Aslaug watched the written matter burn in green and blue and bright yellow flames, watched the pages curl, their letters and runes crumbling into the ashes, watched without remorse.

Suddenly, she heard Kitt exclaim.

She turned to see him half-naked, bandaged up and dazed with the sleep mixture she had given him.

"Why aren't you asleep?"

"I heard the noise."

Kitt crossed the hall and reached into the flames with his bare hands to pull out the whole heap, patting out the flames eating at the papyri. His hands full of soot, he looked up to the gallery at the empty spaces gaping on the shelves; and then he looked at Aslaug, with a face like a child feeling vaguely guilty because it was being punished but did not understand why. "You always said to leave these for reading last – for when I had read all the other books. You said you wanted to give me explanations when I was ready."

"You do not need this kind of knowledge. Words and runes of power can protect and heal, but they can also bring about destruction and death. They are too dangerous, uncontrollable, if they fall into the wrong hands."

"Mine are the wrong hands?"

"You already know too much about dealing death."

It unexpectedly pained her to see Kitt labouring to make his face into a mask that would not show his hurt; it pained her, even more, to see him succeed. She realised with a pang that suddenly the child was gone and that Kitt had grown up.

"Nobody should read those books!" she said. "They shouldn't even have been written."

"I won't read them then. Just don't burn them! Some of these have no other copy anywhere in the world!"

"It is good that you are passionate about something besides weapons. But you give too much importance to things! Knowledge written down is an indulgence, for those with weak memories, just as weapons are an indulgence for a weak soul."

"Mother, people write these books by the shine of a candle, losing their eyesight because they cannot bear to wait until the light of the next day. People have spent their whole lives to write the one book, paint the pictures in it. So many books burn in sieges and wars and because somebody doesn't like what's written in them. And then they are lost! A book cannot be bad any more than a sword can, it's what a man makes of them. I promise I won't open them again." He swallowed. "I won't even look at them anymore. If you don't trust me - you can hide them somewhere, and I won't search, but promise that you won't destroy them!"

She sighed. "Let me look at your hands. You have burned yourself again."

A great thorny monster, with paws ending in innumerable talons, and a long snout studded with spiky black teeth, ran on the lightning spoor the lion Mooankayit left, to recover the stone knife, for without it the black thorn could not grow and the Meder died.

Dark gore dribbled from two gashes in the Gree Meder's side. From time to time, he emitted a noise between a scream and a snarl.

The lightning spoor ended, cut off.

The Hardening Line

A ship was coming to Isenkliff with the western wind.

It was a three-master with Tolonian rigging and had all sails set. A hundred yards from the shore it turned about and moored.

Kitt thought that the captain must know the depth of the bay; he manoeuvred as if he had steered a ship into this natural harbour before.

On the last mast, the black and red pendant of the Red Lily Knights unfolded. A boat was lowered over the side.

The Swordmaster Diorlin do Consabura et Vesac came alone, leaving his knights back on the ship. Kitt thought he knew what the old man wanted.

The Swordmaster of Eliberre sat in the same seat by the fire-place, and Eckehart sat in his, while Kitt perched on the big chest between two doorways.

Diorlin was telling a tale of intrigue and strife. "Sisebut the Good fell ill, and as the doctors despaired for his life, the king called the nobles of Tolosa around his sickbed and bid them to elect his successor in the old way. They elected duke Gesalon, a – bastard-who claims to be a direct descendant of Alaron I, the first king on the Saddle Throne of Avanton. After the election the king's health took a turn for the worse, and thinking his life at an end, Sisebut abdicated in favour of Gesalon. Miraculously, after his abdication, Sisebut recovered fully."

On her gallery where she had retreated, Aslaug looked up sharply.

"Poison?" Kitt asked breathlessly. In his mind, he ran over the plants and minerals which might have been used. Nightshade perhaps or Hela's ashes, by the sound of the symptoms.

Diorlin grinned wryly. "You are quick, Kitt. Yes, rumours began flying about that the king had been slowly poisoned over the years. Although proof was never found, many suspect the sorcerer Zinnober and his master, Gesalon's strongest ally and son in law, whom Sisenand foolishly, inexplicably trusted. Count Hugo do Zafra et Tuixen." At the mention of that name the old swordmaster's face distorted, and he breathed deeply before he continued in the same ironic voice as before.

"Sisebut tried to revoke his abdication, and many seconded his claim, although few dared do so openly. Gesalon and Hugo were too strong.

"One night, Sisebut disappeared and was never seen again. His party then declared crown prince Sisenand as successor. In the last days of his illness, Queen Teodora had retired to her estates of Talavera, with the two younger royal princes and the infant princess, where Sisenand joined her. She fortified Talavera castle, and after the king's abdication she closed the gates against Gesalon, and drew men loyal to king Sisebut around the prince."

Diorlin paused for a moment as if thinking about how to continue. Kitt watched his face, and the Swordmaster seemed to resent the searching look. The smith was seemingly observing the blue sparks crawling over the glowing stones in the fire.

It was all very much like the first time Diorlin had visited, as if two years had not passed.

"After Sisebut's abdication, I took my School of Knights to Talavera. On the way, we heard that Prince Sisenand, Queen Teodora and her younger children had disappeared without a trace. We continued, or you might as well say we fled, to Port Roian and took ship to the seaport of Moleto in Luzitan. There I had already sent my nephew, Ramiro, to stay with the Count of Fera. He is of your age Kitt, fourteen."

"The change of dynasty he talked about last time, it has happened," Kitt answered a question of his father's. "There is a sorcerer, but maybe he is only a mere poisoner."

"You must teach your brothers in arms how to express the heartbreak of thousands and the toppling of a world in only two sentences," Diorlin remarked, drawing his eyebrows together. "Gesalon however, surprisingly, turned out to be an unexpected champion of the renewed Order of Red Lily Knights." Here, the black eyebrows did their fantastic dance. "He expressed his supreme displeasure that the best sword school was now in Luzitan, and that Tolosan nobles had to go to the court of Fera to study the way of the knightly sword. He sent several emissaries, offering me gold and guarantees. I returned to Tolosa and re-established the School in the old compound in Eliberre."

At that point of the tale, Diorlin became acutely conscious of the grey eyes steady look into his face, so direct and scrutinising that it could hardly be considered polite any more.

"You wonder why I heeded the call of the usurper?" he challenged. "To the Order, it matters not who sits the Saddle Throne of Avanton. Did I tell you the tale about the Tyrant Slayer?"

"I read it. I never understood that tale," Kitt said. "Couldn't Sir Damon see the sun? Isn't it always sunny in Tolosa? Or if it was cloudy, wasn't there moss on the trees, or-?"

"You can't imagine that not everyone moves like a panther in the woods, or an otter in the water," Eckehart said. "Or a hawk in the air."

Kitt made a face. "There are so many possible signs to know precisely where one is."

"Well, Kitt, Sir Damon did not know quite so precisely where he was. He knew what it meant to live by the code," Diorlin said, with the emphasis on he. "Where the sun stands or the moss grows is a side issue, and I wish that was all which you don't understand about the tale. The Lily Knights guard the Way of the Sword, only loyal to the Code of Knightly Honour. You remember the six words?"

"Purity, Poverty, Mercy. Help, Save, Serve."

"Exactly. It matters not how a king took a throne unless his deeds bring him in conflict with the code. So far, Gesalon has behaved honourably towards the order and kept every promise. I suspect that by now he has become, well, not afraid, Gesalon is not scared of anyone, but just a little wary of his allies, many of them born to magical power. That may be the reason why he likes the idea of a New Order built on knightly principles and loyal to the throne. If he does, he is mistaken. The Lily Knights were never loyal to any king, and only conditionally to their Grandmaster. As I keep repeating, Lily Knights are loyal to their code. But against count Hugo and his sorcerer Zinnober," Diorlin's lips sneered at the mention of those names, "the order stands with Gesalon. It is a long, secret struggle,

332

for on the surface Tolosa is at peace. But under that surface knights disappear, knights die, and against this stealthy persecution, not even Gesalon can protect us. You remember Sigerian do Lallin et Arosa?"

Kitt remembered the older knight, quiet, scrupulously polite, a competent fighter. He felt an unexpected pang of regret.

"Apparently he challenged for a duel which he lost," Diorlin said. "I consider the story highly unlikely. In fact, there is everything wrong with it. We also lost Erevid do Alkotor et Belver and Amaris do Frades et Osuna, gangrene and fever. Erevid's cousin and Amaris' and Sigerian's brothers took their places. You will see new faces and miss old acquaintances."

"Have you come for your metal bones, Diorlin?"

The Swordmaster's head jerked up at Eckehart's direct question in hard, accented Tolosan. "The time you and your wife gave me, it is not enough for what lies ahead. The last time I shirked and shied from what must be undergone."

Eckehart looked up to Aslaug, and she looked down to him.

"It must be done," she said.

"All is ready," Eckehart said. "Your iron bones have been waiting for you, Diorlin."

"Maybe one day the minstrels will sing ballads of the less refined about how a blacksmith tricked the Swordmaster Diorlin into lying down to be slaughtered like a lamb. What a joke!" he tittered with a hysterical note in his voice. "They will laugh a good deal at the old fool."

"They won't," Kitt said.

The old swordmaster relaxed. "You'll not hear that often, Sir Kitt, but you are a sweet boy. True courage – it is demanded of me now."

#

The steel bones had been ready since the last visit of the Red Lily Knights.

This time Kitt didn't ask by what methods his father meant to fuse them to Diorlin's living flesh, how his mother would heal such wounds. He didn't ask any questions that came too near to Seidar and Zaubar, too near to magic.

Kitt looked in on his little sister Swantje Birla, in her bed, fast asleep. The swallows flitted around the room to and from their nests with the second brood of that year. Three young birds were sitting by Swantje's blonde little head, emitting their chirping, whining and gurgling. Kitt thought it was the most peaceful sound in the world.

He went outside to receive the Red Lily Knights. Twenty young men came along the jetty in their black cloaks, led by Leonin do Almorox et Mohorte. "Well, here we are again, Sir Kitt," Leonin said. "I didn't miss you. This is going to get painful and irritating again."

"I didn't miss you either," Kitt returned the compliment. He left the knights to erect their pavilion in the same place, protected from the western wind, in some distance of the hall.

Leonin stayed beside Kitt and they went to the hall. The beautiful knight looked disconsolate. "Sigerian, Erevid and Amaris didn't come."

"Sigerian was no fool. A good fighter."

"Better than me."

"More experienced."

"He liked you too, thought the world of you. I don't know how he came to challenge. There was no way he could have lost against that adversary, and therefore, he wouldn't have challenged, far too decent, and he couldn't be provoked. It makes no sense. I told you we are under attack."

Kitt nodded.

"It all went so well after we returned from Isenkliff. Diorlin was so full of strength after your mother treated him the last time. Gesalon proved unexpectedly reasonable. We had count Vitiza's records, and Diorlin executed a roll-call that was followed. There were about two hundred Lily Knights with us in our compound at the School in Eliberre and three hundred more in the town. Then we began losing knights. When Diorlin said he had left something undone on Isenkliff, we came with him, the seven of us left, and the ones Diorlin considers most at risk. Geraldo, Sigerian's kid brother, is with us. It would be fine if we only came for swords. But the old man clings so to this legend, he doesn't see another way before him. I don't know what to do."

"Nothing," Kitt said.

"You are oddly comforting, you know that?"

"What I'm here for," Kitt muttered.

"Now I beg that you don't get mad. Those who haven't been here before and don't know better, asked if the Swordmaster would really put himself into the hands of a blacksmith and a hedgewitch? It has been hard to explain. I warned them not to talk any nonsense, but if they do, please don't knock them on the head. As a particular favour to me. I'll make them sorry for it, that's my function of a Senior Pupil."

Kitt shrugged.

"If this goes wrong, I am to lead our knights back to Tolosa, to stand with Ramiro against Hugo. Do you think this can go wrong?"

"I don't know. My parents don't trust me with this sort of - knowledge."

"I'm sorry," Leonin said with a look at Kitt's face. "Really sorry, man. Your parents, they are formidable. It is just that I'm so worried.

Kitt shrugged again. "Now I have work to do. Diorlin wants swords for all of you."

"I have my Aurora blade."

"That one my father made for me. Now you'll have one made exactly for you."

"Jay, another insult coming my way. I can't wait," Leonin muttered.

#

After a day of hunting and working Kitt was dreaming.

The big water-driven hammer was working behind as Kitt stood before the ironbound door of the dome inside the mountain. It was open a crack, and light came through, a harsh cold glare.

The last time he had heard but not seen things in the dome. This time it was different.

The huge iron cauldron that hung high up in the big fireplace was let down, and Eckehart was bending over it, in each hand a long thin tool the kind of which Kitt had never seen, uttering verses as Kitt never heard him say.

Aslaug stood beside him, saying words of her own.

335

A black froth began boiling over the rim of the cauldron, running into the fire and up again in endless convolutions.

It took Kitt some time to realise that what appeared like froth was the small gargoyles shaping the friezes which he had always thought to be the cauldrons ornaments. Their pinpoint eyes blazed red. Although the cauldron was now suspended directly over the flames of the earth-fire, the metal did not glow and stayed deep black. From inside the cauldron, a tinkering as from very tiny hammers sounded.

On a table lay an undefined heap of white and red.

The Swordmaster Diorlin was nowhere to be seen.

Kitt tried to catch Eckehart's words. Even as he recapitulated them in his mind, a sudden disturbance rose among the gargoyles. The little iron heads turned around and they began flowing off the cauldron's sides.

Eckehart spoke louder, in a tone of firm command, forcing the metallic creatures back. The gargoyles resumed their rhythmic movements, but their heads kept turning, and so did Aslaug's, trying to pierce the gloom.

Kitt retreated carefully, his curiosity unsatisfied again.

When he reached the mountain passage, he moved more rapidly, striving not to speak Eckehart's words in his mind, but as that was naturally impossible, he fairly ran.

Where the passage forked between hall and smithy, he saw the blocky form of Gullo. The Jarnmantsje looked at him steadily.

"I owe you, Gullo," Kitt said.

The Jarnmantsje sniffed loudly.

Kitt went to stop the big hammer. What lay on the anvil wasn't the alibi iron, pounded into a shapeless lump. It was Diorlin's body.

Kitt awoke feeling confused between dream and reality. Did he owe a goat to Gullo, or didn't he?

#

This time of year the garden gave green beans, spinach and onions.

Since he had done so the year before, on his mother's instruction, Kitt brought the day's harvest to the pavilion. It was a bigger affair than the first time, a small castle of cloth and rope with four twelve-

336

foot-high masts.

The school's cook, a small, wiry Tolosan named Avarik looked harassed. "I suppose you can't give them permission to hunt? The last time you didn't allow it, and you said that there were dangers on this island? Might you have said that only to tease the young gentlemen?"

"Nobody must wander about," Kitt said firmly, with the Jarnmantsjes in mind. "They wouldn't catch anything, hunting with lances. There is no game for that here, no deer, no stag, or boar."

"It's just that there is a big dinner tonight and now we have the greens, which I thank you for very much in the name of the Order. And we have the bread, cheese and the sweets and the captain sent the fish. But I don't know what to serve as the main course. Twenty knights to feed, every day, and they complain if there's only fish. Talking about cheese . . ." he dropped a cloth-wrapped wedge into Kitt's empty basket.

Kitt liked cheese very much and appreciated that Avarik remembered. "We'll feed them," he promised.

Two young knights Kitt didn't know came into the kitchen section, looked at him with wide eyes and sat down to peel the onions and slice the beans. The Swordmaster and the Senior Pupil both believed in lessons in humility.

Leonin appeared as Kitt left the tent. "You are hereby invited to dinner tonight."

"No," Kitt said.

"As a Lily Knight, you have to attend two dinners per month, unless you have a valid excuse, such as being absent on a mission. Or dying."

"If I don't come, you'll take away that coat?"

"Oh, do come," Leonin said. "Don't forget your coat. I will call on you tonight."

"I know you will," Kitt muttered under his breath.

"Will it kill you to behave graciously just for once?" Leonin muttered under his.

#

True to his word, Leonin called at the hall by nightfall.

"I have to bring my sister," Kitt announced.

Swantje Birla had slept all day, which had allowed for Kitt to hunt geese and then begin preparations for the forging of seven swords. Now the toddler was sitting up in her little bed bright as a sparrow requiring attendance. "My mother hasn't returned yet."

"Is everything – well?" Leonin asked anxiously.

Kitt thought of his dream. "Yes," he said. If it weren't, his parents would be back.

"The Lily Knights will be honoured by the presence of Lady Swantje Birla at their dinner table," Leonin bowed.

The table was set with candles in porcelain holders, silver cutlery and glass plates, brightly patterned earthen bowls and glass goblets. The younger knights acted as stewards, one behind every chair, with serious faces.

"I can serve myself," Kitt objected. Having somebody standing behind him went against all his instincts.

"You will be served, Sir Kitt," Leonin retorted. "Or Sir Severo do Belver et Alkotor will want to know what objection you have against him."

The young knight in question looked serious.

Biting back a retort Kitt sat down.

"I deem it an honour, Sir Kitt," Sir Severo do Belver et Alkotor said and filled his goblet with red wine from a glass carafe.

"That's how it's done Sir Kitt," Leonin said. "I'll agree with you that these forms don't have any value as such – intrinsic is the word I was searching for. These formalities exist to organise and facilitate as they are something agreed upon by knights hailing from many places. Much like dance steps. Or fencing figures. Know them, and you will fit into good society wherever these customs are observed, Tolosa, Daguilaria, Luzitan, Bohemia, and any of the independent castles. If you were to ask Diorlin, he'd tell you the same. Because he did tell me, at the time, much the same words too."

Leonin had the right of it, Kitt admitted to himself, and he had been in the wrong. "I deem it a favour, Sir Severo," he said.

"You are learning," Leonin remarked with satisfaction. "A good sign, the Swordmaster would say."

Kitt sat between Swantje and Leonin. Little Swantje Birla had been placed at the head of the table in the Swordmaster's chair on a pile of cushions and was eating angel cakes and drinking orange juice with the doting attendance of Geraldo do Lallin et Arosa, Sigerian's younger brother.

The first toast was proposed by Leonin for the lady at the table. The wine was deep red and tasted of raspberry.

"Swordmaster Diorlin will thoroughly approve Lady Swantje's health being drunk with his old Madiran," Leonin remarked. "The Swordmaster!" The glasses were refilled for this second toast.

After the two toasts, all applied themselves to the roasted geese.

The meal was declared a success by all participants. Enough food remained for consumption by the attendant knights, after they cleared the table. Bottles of wine made their appearance.

"A toast to Ramiro!" Sir Terence proposed.

Knowing Ramiro only from what Diorlin had told him Kitt considered a sip from his glass sufficient. The wine was strong, and after this third toast, the knights' eyes began glittering in the candlelight.

"Did the adoption business come to anything?" Wallia asked. "Did I miss something?"

"You didn't."

"Gesalon the Pretender, as I will call him until he makes good his word," Wallia cried. Confusion to him!"

"Confusion!"

Not knowing King Gesalon either Kitt took a cautious sip to his confusion. He noticed that Leonin also drank prudently. The other knights were too merry to notice.

"Diorlin demanded that Gesalon adopt Ramiro as the condition to move the school back to Tolosa," Leonin explained for Kitt's benefit. "And Gesalon surprised everyone by saying that he would grant this request. After all, Ramiro's mother was a born Vesac. If the Saddle Throne had a hereditary king, that adoption would bring Ramiro past Hugo's wife and their offspring with a flying jump, right after Gesalon's two legitimate sons."

"But if not . . ." Sir Wallia scowled.

"I know, what with the adoption business dragging itself out due to thin pretexts."

"Not pretexts. Excellent reasons, as Ramiro is a Vesac, you said it yourself," Viterin remarked cryptically. "In the meantime, the Proclamation of Succession to the Saddle Throne is still in force."

"Just so," Leonin said. "Not to mention that people keep coming forward explaining that they are the lost crown prince or that they have seen Sisenand or that they know somebody who has seen him. The Olive Throne is still standing empty in the palace of Lutetia. As a Vesac Ramiro has sort of a claim to it."

"Sort of. But once Ramiro is not only legitimate but a member of the Royal House he qualifies to become the Grandmaster of the Order," Viterin pronounced.

"You sum it up concisely as usual," Leonin said. "A cup of wine with you, Sir Viterin! Hugo moves to become Grandmaster himself, Diorlin blocks any Grandmaster at all until Ramiro is ready, and Gesalon probably wishes by now that he hadn't sat down on the Saddle Throne. He is a sensible sort of cove, really.

"Confusion to the Pretender!"

"Just so. As you can appreciate, it is a pretty kettle of fish for us to be in the middle of. A cup of wine with you, Sir Kitt!"

Addressed thus directly Kitt found himself obliged to drink up his newly filled glass.

"In the meantime, every young noble wants to enter the School. Diorlin turns away very few, only those who are really hopeless." Leonin pursued. "He formed an inner circle. Those who are not invited to swear, don't even know there are such oaths. Or anyway they shouldn't know. But somebody does know."

"So that's behind the trouble?"

"The surface of it, my dear Sir Kitt, I merely skimmed the surface of very turbid waters. Another glass of wine with you!" This time Leonin only sipped from his and Kitt followed his example.

"Yes, a glass of wine with you, Sir Kitt," Wallia called from his side of the table. You are looking at us too sharply still."

"Recalling the details. I have the making of your blades."

"So Diorlin really wants us to have Auroras?"

"I want you to have swords made exactly for your hands, each one of you."

"You said something very gracious there," Sir Terence remarked. "A glass of wine with you, Sir Kitt."

The lady Swantje Birla officially retired from the table. Kitt carried her to her room, fast asleep, accompanied by all the Lily Knights with torches. He warmed towards them for their scrupulous courtesy and care towards his little sister.

The swallows were in their nests, chirping and gurgling quietly. The young wolf hound looked at Kitt reproachfully.

"There you have her back." Kitt laid Swantje into her bed without waking her, and then scratched the big animal's massive red head, the pelt there so much softer than the grey and black of his body.

The older knights outside the hall insisted that some more drinking had to be done. Kitt felt that they had the right of it, but he didn't want to leave Swantje alone in the house. She might have a dream. Therefore, his fellow knights proposed to help Kitt watch over the lady's sleep. More bottles made their appearance, as the knights spoke in low tones suited to their mission.

"Once Diorlin had a sister too," Leonin told Kitt," a half-sister, much younger than he, whom he adored with a passion."

"Sonnica. She was beautiful by all accounts," Sintilian observed from Leonin's other side.

"So, she was. Well when King Sisebut the Good called Diorlin to Lutetia and persuaded him to move the School there, he left his sister in Eliberre. Thought the court of Lutetia wasn't a good place for a young girl, degenerate and violent and all that."

"He was right of course, only it turned out that Eliberre wasn't safe for her either."

"Nobody knows how Hugo got at her, the girl never told."

"I can guess," the youngest knight said.

"Keep your speculations to yourself forever, Sir Gundemar, do!" Leonin requested. "The lady may have retired to her chambers, but it is unfitting at any time."

The young knight scowled and averted his face from Leonin's

furious stare to look into the round of disapproving faces.

"One day, news came from Eliberre of Sonnica's illness," Leonin pursued. "Diorlin got there just on the day when count Hugo celebrated his wedding with Gesalon's daughter up in the castle."

"Count Gesalon, as he was then."

"Gesalon the Pretender, confusion to him!"

"While the town illuminated Sonnica died in childbed. The child lived, Ramiro, he is your age now."

"Sisebut the Good did nothing to punish Hugo; he was by then ill."

"He trusted Hugo and if sorcery was not at the bottom of that-"

"A change of subject is indicated," Leonin requested. "One involving less heartbreak if you please."

"That stern Grandmaster of Alkantara in the Dragon Slayer's tale, he was Diorlin's ancestor," Sir Terence said.

"This story is an allegory, to teach you something, if possible. Which I increasingly doubt," Wallia said acidly.

"Why shouldn't the story have happened like this?" Leonin said philosophically. "Without the dragon, of course. Some dangerous creature that became a dragon over the centuries of telling."

"Why are you so sure that dragons don't exist?" Kitt objected. "In the great wood Murkowydir live animals that everywhere else are a legend. I have seen them."

"Are you saying that you saw a dragon in that unpronounceable wood of yours?" Sir Wallia laughed. He hiccupped when Kitt turned around. "I beg pardon I'm sure Sir Kitt, but this seems incredible."

"Not a dragon as such," Kitt elaborated. "But I have seen a white serpent as long as your ship. The Graansha - some Woodstalkers - worship it. It has white skin and green eyes just like them. Each midsummer night they feed it three war captives, which the white serpent swallows whole, like mice, and then sleeps another year."

"A hundred-foot man-eating serpent? White? Come on, man! Maybe it was something else you saw."

"Are you saying I don't see well?" Kitt inquired. "Or even that I lie?"

"Why shouldn't there be a serpent a hundred feet long. And why shouldn't it be white and eat people?" Leonin said peaceably. "But it surely does not spit fire, or does it, Kitt?"

"No, it doesn't," Kitt admitted.

"See, and that is the point on which everything hinges," Leonin said patiently. "No living flesh, however fantastically shaped, can contain fire, and therefore white serpents may exist, and dragons cannot."

And no living flesh can be welded to steel, that is just another myth, Kitt thought, but even drunk he still had enough wit about him to keep quiet about that.

#

The next morning brought a headache and a dry mouth and general disgust with himself.

Kitt drank water until his insides felt less parched and brewed himself a draught of willow-bark, which was bitter like punishment. Swantje was chirping with her swallows and looking as rosy as one could who had indulged in no worse than orange juice.

Kitt went to the smithy to work the memory of having talked far too much out of his system. By the time the bleary-eyed Senior Pupil came to the smithy door, Kitt was in an offensively good condition again. He treated Leonin to the rest of the willow bark.

"I always knew that you hated me," the beautiful knight complained. "It is bitter, bitter, bitter!"

#

All eyes were on the old swordmaster, as he come down to the practice place.

Diorlin walked with a spring in his step, a hint of the tireless effort his limbs were now capable of. The knights all sensed a change in their old swordmaster, renewed hope, that was an expression on the tame side to describe this new air about him.

Kitt stared at the old fighter's legs in fascination, trying to imagine that the bones of these legs were now reinforced with steel, that there were steel ligaments welded to the muscles and sinews. He failed. The mending of wounds took ten days even in the best of circumstances, but the healing process could not happen so completely in such a short time?

"I had fewer. Dreamed that somebody was cutting and drawing out

343

every bone of my body. Better now." Diorlin caught Kitt's puzzled look. "Oh yes, I can stand on these," he said cryptically. "Will we try out the swordarm?"

"Allow me, Swordmaster!" Leonin stepped forward.

"No, I want Kitt."

They crossed arms; carefully at first on Kitt's side.

Diorlin was fast, and he did not tire. The Lily Knights' applause for their Swordmaster grew louder with every passage of arms.

Finally, Kitt had to break free with a brutal blow on the Swordmaster's weapon that would have broken the old Diorlin's shoulder. It was as if he hit a steel wall - a steel wall moving in on him, inexorably. He saved himself by a long jump back, which was essentially a flight. The Lily Knights' delight knew no bounds at seeing this. Kitt watched the old Swordmaster carefully. He couldn't allow himself being cornered by this new Diorlin.

"Now you know how we feel opposite you," Leonin remarked. The beautiful knight looked thoroughly entranced. "He didn't exactly knock you about. Nobody ever really could. But he came close. I loved seeing you thinking so hard."

"Well, do you agree now that I taught you all, my dear Sir Kitt?" Diorlin demanded. "And I will say that you paid attention."

"If I hadn't, you'd have taken my head off."

"Deservedly so, deservedly so," Diorlin said coolly. "The sword you made for me suits me even now."

#

The new swords had been presented; all had the hay-wagon punched in at the base.

Once more, Eckehart had rejected Diorlin's gold but asked for every book and paper, the only exception being Sir Vitiza's copy of the Order Statutes of the Lily Knights, which now accompanied them always. Accordingly, the table in the hall was covered with assorted books, treatises, leaflets and maps.

Eckehart, Kitt and Aslaug stood above the shore watching Diorlin step into the boat.

"Don't you regret that again you are not going with them?" Eckehart asked.

"Not any more than Diorlin regrets it," Kitt said soberly. "He invited me the first time, when he shied away from . . . what you proposed. Then he didn't like me seeing his weakness and fear either. But he thought he could make use of me."

"So," Eckehart said only.

"But he hasn't spoken of my coming to Tolosa anymore. He thinks he is strong enough himself now. And he can't want to have a witness to his transformation coming to Tolosa with him. "

"No," the smith agreed.

"I will always bear him a grudge."

"Grudge for not inviting you?"

"No. Not for trying to kill me either. But if he had succeeded, I think . . . I'm convinced . . . that he would have attempted yours and mother's life too. Ungrateful. Graceless. Not what he told me a Lily Knight was."

"You have taken a very hard look at Diorlin, son. Not fitting for a youth of your age -it's hardly respectful. He is your teacher, and you could learn from him. What he told you is still valid, even if he falls short of it himself."

There was a shout from the ship. One of the Tolonian sailors up in the main-mast called out pointed and to a silver speck, which had appeared in the south, glittering in the morning sun.

The Knights ran to the rail; shading their eyes with their hands, they looked across the sea. On the shore, Kitt watched the silver speck grow, saw beating wings.

"Not a bird. It's far too big for that. Wingspan thirty feet at the very least. And it's coming fast. I'll get my bow," Kitt said.

"Yes. Quickly!" Eckehart had gone deathly pale. "Come away from the ship!" he shouted, running down to the shore, waving his arms. "Come back to land! Hurry!"

The men did not head him. The sailors went about their work, and the knights were pointing and speculating at the top of their voices.

"A silver bird!" Wallia shouted. "A good omen for our venture?"

"Omen yes, good no," Leonin said. He was the only one paying attention to Eckehart's waving and shouting on the shore.

"Is it a pelican?"

"A pelican, this far north?"

"By the Trifold Sky Lord, what is it?"

The flying thing had come near enough to see that it had features of both bird and lizard - narrow, ribbed wings, a long snout rimmed with a saw tooth border so broad that it didn't close completely, and taloned legs drawn up under the smooth silver belly were now discernible. The long neck moved from side to side, as if searching.

"They're doomed," Eckehart panted. "Stay inside, Aslaug! Something dangerous is coming through the air. From the south."

Kitt was already running out of the hall again with his Kirgis bow in one hand, and a quiver full of arrows in the other.

"Come back!" Eckehart shouted. "You can't fight it! Come back! Damn the boy!"

Aslaug took up a glass mirror hanging from her girdle and looked into it. The mirror didn't show her face, but the blue sky and a silver speck, which was growing in size.

She came down from the gallery, to set an iron kettle filled with water over the earth flames in the fire-place.

"Hurry up!" Eckehart muttered and ran after Kitt.

The metal bird-lizard circled over the ship, and the men below were running here and there on the deck. The metal snout opened wide, and a long flame roared towards the ship, enveloping it in a fire ball. The sails were burning; the high-pitched screams of men rent the air. Knights and sailors were swimming in the water beside the burning ship, with the monstrous metallic creature circling above.

One of the young knights had reached the mole and drew himself up dripping. The flying monster swooped towards him, and a long orange fire tongue lashed down. The knight died with a scream that had nothing human left in it.

Stunned, the men in the water stopped moving, as all stared towards the smoking huddle on the mole, that once had been a Lily Knight.

The bird dived in the manner of a pelican, snapped up one of the Tolonian sailors and carried him up into the air, screaming and with kicking legs. The other men looked on with horror as the saw tooth jaws closed, and bit the man through in the middle. The two body halves fell into the water in a shower of blood and entrails.

Kitt began shooting. His arrows thudded into the wings with a metallic boom, making round dents as the iron tips hit the smooth metal of body and head and glanced off.

The monster rose slightly, veered, dipped down again, and a second sailor was carried into the air.

"I don't know the vulnerable spots!" Eckehart shouted. "I didn't build the thing. Try the eyes! And see can you can shatter the wing bones, Kitt, or at least bend them."

"Yes father," Kitt said calmly, drawing the bow and aiming, the cool, grey eyes estimating, calculating. "I'll soon be out of arrows. Go back and hide in the mountain with mother!"

The old smith looked at his son, shuddered, and ran inland again.

The circling monster opened its snout wide and spit a long flame into the water where a group of men were swimming. Steam and screams rose into the air.

One of Kitt's arrows hit a big, silvery eye, but was deflected without visible effect. Kitt's shooting had so far done little to impair the bird's flying abilities, but the youth noticed that the bird had begun to react to each arrow-hit with a mechanic veering manoeuvre. He made use of that in his attempts to distract the monster from the helpless men in the water.

From somewhere Kitt heard a long high whistle piercing the air. The sound flew out to the sea. Suddenly, clouds swelled up and towered into the clear sky, first on the western horizon, then fast darkening the whole sky.

Abruptly, the silver bird abandoned the men struggling in the water and took course towards the beach with metallic maws gaping wide. Another of Kitt's arrows went up the beast's long snout, rattling like a pebble in a drainpipe, and was bitten in two by the row of teeth. Kitt noticed a net of fine white cracks covering the right eye, showing that the arrows had caused some damage after all.

He loosed his last arrow at the left eye. A net of fine cracks sprung up in the glassy round.

Kitt jumped towards the water. An orange flame hit the shore where he had stood, turning the pebbles into a boiling glassy mass. The bird circled hesitantly, the head swinging from side to side, searching for Kitt from the damaged eyes.

Just at this moment a sudden wind gusted in from the sea, caught the wings of the silver beast, and whirled it high into the air. The metal wings spread out wide and strained against the force of the howling air. The metal bird spun around its axis once, and then with a shattering noise, like an ironmonger's market stall toppling over, it clashed against the cliff face, and exploded in a ball of fire and black smoke.

The sudden storm had knocked Kitt back in midjump. He lay on the ground, shielding his face from the wind that snatched the breath away from mouth and nose, and tore up the valley, driving brown leaves, dry grass and even small stones before it.

The sea was first flattened by the force of the wind, and then came into motion. High waves rolled to the beach, carrying exhausted men to the shore, then running out, dragging back to the sea those too weak to hold on to the land.

Kitt waded into the sea to help Leonin, who was holding Sir Gundemar above water.

Diorlin came walking through the water without the least sign of fatigue, the wet cloak slapping around his bony figure.

One after the other, the survivors crawled out of the sea and stumbled onto the beach, standing, sitting, and lying there panting and retching.

"Have you no bows?" Kitt demanded of Leonin.

"Bows are weapons for knaves," the youngest knight hugging his arms to his sodden tunic said with chattering teeth.

Kitt rounded on him. "Are you glad to be alive, Sir Gundemar? Better learn shooting real fast!"

"Or swimming," Leonin laughed unkindly, drawing his sword, emptying the sheath and setting to drying the blade.

The young knight's eyes were dark smudges in a chalky white face. "The fact remains that bows are the weapons of . . ." he paused, and went on doggedly "assassins and barbarian mercenaries."

Shrugging ever so slightly Kitt turned his back on the youth.

Leonin rounded on the young knight savagely. "You are most tiresome, Sir Gundemar! I have no patience with you! I urgently suggest you revise first your behaviour and then your ideas!"

"But...!"

"Shut the fuck up you blithering young ass!"

The young knight broke down sobbing. Leonin slapped his face hard. Sir Gundemar hiccupped twice and sat down in the sand. Leonin knelt beside him, laying an arm around the shaking shoulders. "Shock," he explained to Kitt. "The lad is only fifteen. Come to think of it, so are you, aren't you Kitt?"

"Yes."

"But you've been in some action already. Sir Gundemar has never seen a battle. He's far from home, and all because of a bunch of cyclamens."

Leonin laughed at Kitt's blank face. "That's flower talk. Don't tell me I finally hit on the one language you don't speak? Don't you have a treatise about the language of flowers in your substantial library? Well, most likely you have now, for I think at least one of the lads was cherishing such a booklet. Essential reading for a man of the world. Well, Gundemar gave a Lily of the Valley to a girl, thereby declaring undying love and devotion to her. In return, she gave him a bunch of cyclamens, which is the polite way for a lady to say that she doesn't give a damn for his feelings. It was the first time that happened to him, and so it threw him completely. He'll get used to cyclamen. Dahlias are also bad; for their meaning is that she loves another. Red carnations, on the other hand, or even bluebells, are a sign of promise, and then you give her a red rose to see what she makes of that."

"Y-y-y-y-you c-c-c-can t-t-talk," Gundemar stuttered. "No woman ever gave cyclamens to you, or even Dahlias."

"And sometimes that's worse, Sir Gundemar," the beautiful knight said darkly.

"Let's get him up to the house," Kitt said. "If he isn't able to walk, I can carry him."

"Not sure that I can walk myself, but a roof to hide under does sound attractive." Leonin scrambled to his feet. "What was that thing, Kitt? If this was a dragon after I've just proven so very conclusively that dragons don't exist, I shall be disgusted. Small mercy that I didn't bet on it."

"Dragons don't exist," Kitt said. "Why didn't you tell the thing it couldn't spit fire? Maybe it just didn't know."

"Damn you, Kitt!" Leonin said with some passion. "Such crude barbarian humour is singularly unsuitable for endearing you under any circumstances. Right now, it is particularly annoying. Quoting my very words back to me too. No gentleman would ever do a thing like that, and I believe there is a passage to that effect in Diorlin's manual for budding knights."

As Kitt helped both knights to the house, he saw Aslaug walking among the men lying and sitting on the shore, and whenever she bent down over one of them, the groaning and shaking stopped, the wounded man's eyes closed, and Aslaug passed on to the next wounded. She could at least teach me how to do that, he thought with renewed bitterness.

Kitt lowered the sagging Gundemar onto a footstool in the hall, bending him over, so that his face rested on his knees. "Some wine will do you good."

"Wine? Did you really say wine? You must have some civilisation hidden inside you, I'm sure, if only anyone dares to dig down really, really deep, with a spade, it's certain to be found. I always said so. You know, when I was floundering in the cold water with that monster circling over me, and which I categorically refuse to call a dragon, it was just good to see you planted on the beach like a damn catapult battery, loosing one arrow after the other."

Leonin took the bottle Kitt offered him to Gundemar. When the young knight had drunk some wine, a little colour returned to his face. His eyes wandered around the hall, dazedly as if nothing made any sense to him. After taking a deep draught himself, Leonin held the bottle to the youth's mouth, who drank mechanically, until his eyes closed, the wine running in a thin red stream down his chin.

"Yes, that's right, sleep!" the beautiful knight said, for once without the usual mockery in his voice, and set the bottle to his lips.

Kitt opened Aslaug's medicine cupboard. There were the remains of the medicines she had prepared for Diorlin, extracts of Bilsenkraut and poppy to induce deep sleep, an extract of the dangerous blue foxglove, which sustained the heart in smallest doses, or stopped it if given by unskilled or murderous hands. Her wound medicine now consisted of seventeen ingredients, the seventeenth being an extract of the death-defying purple flower from the Dodlak cave, which Kitt had found in the dark wood Murkowydir.

Kitt already knew the medicines wouldn't be enough for this emergency. He took out dried chamomile, ribwort and woundwort. A kettle was boiling in the fire-place. Kitt put measured quantities of the herbs into it and then rooted in the cupboard again for the cherished bottle of olive oil.

"What are you doing, Kitt? Cooking soup?" Leonin demanded. "Can I help?"

"Good idea. Start chopping vegetables, they're in there." Kitt pointed to the second doorway. "A plucked goose is hanging by the door in the scullery. Use the kitchen hearth!"

Leonin rose to go to the kitchen. "Add a bit more salt than you usually would," Kitt instructed before he left the hall with the medicine he had found ready-made in the cupboard. "There's more in the store."

"Yes, sir, at your order sir," Leonin murmured and chopped onions, with his habitual superciliousness absent, probably hiding under the table shivering with fright, the knight thought grimly, tears running from his eyes, solely due to the stinging smell of the onions of course.

Returning to the beach, Kitt found Aslaug tending to the captain of the ship whose skin was burned and boiled off his face. One eye was milky and crumpled, like a boiled gooseberry; the other eye was brown and wide with terror.

Aslaug took the fresh linen Kitt handed her. "Have you brought more poppy? You have! You thought of everything."

He helped her binding up the burns, and the terrible eye disappeared under the bandages for the time being. Kitt and Aslaug looked at each other in perfect understanding. The boiled eye would have to come out eventually, but not now. The first task at this moment was to contain the pain and shock.

The next was Avarik, the cook, white-faced and staring. There was no wound on him. Kitt was worried about him enough to apply a tiny dose of the heart medicine, and Avarik's colour improved. "The poor boys!" he cried. "The vile persecution! It is terrible! It is unjust! How will we get home?"

Kitt looked over to where the ship lay still burning in the bay. No hope there.

The more lightly wounded were able to walk up to the house by themselves, the severely injured ones Kitt carried; he lifted fully grown men in his arms like children.

Aslaug retreated to the surgery. There, the wounded were brought to her by Kitt, one after the other, the captain first. Aslaug gave him a lot of poppy extract in wine spirits until he fell into a deep sleep. Kitt cut off the bandages and excised the dead eye without any instruction from Aslaug, and filled the cave with a compress soaked in the extract of chamomile and the purple flower of the Murkowydir. That was the only thing to do.

Aslaug watched the big blackened hands, the hands of a smith, and a warrior, moving over the wounded flesh as lightly as her own, and she suddenly felt dizzy with the thought of how many choices these hands had, and how much power. She laid her hands over them. For a very brief moment, both sat very still.

Then they went on working together, not speaking beyond the necessity of their task, but feeling comfortable in each other's company as they hadn't for a long time.

Kitt was bedding the captain down in the hall when Gundemar advanced on him. He still had a downy, unfledged look, like a young bird, and he also looked hung over.

"I have come to beg your forgiveness, Sir Kitt." The young knight was deathly pale except for two red spots burning on his cheeks. "My words to you were quite inappropriate."

"I forgive you readily, Sir Gundemar," Kitt replied in what he hoped was the same vain.

"You are very generous, Sir Kitt. For that, I remain doubly in your debt."

"I beg you not to mention it, Sir Gundemar," Kitt said hastily, desperate to close a scene that was beginning to embarrass him. Leonin nearby looked highly amused at this exchange, and the other knights began to look in their direction. From the corner of his eye, he saw Diorlin approaching.

"Sir!" The young knight insisted earnestly. "I . . ."

Realising that the polite exchange in the formal Tolosan speech might go on a long time, Kitt abandoned his newly acquired finesse for the young knight's sake, feeling that the stern old Swordmaster did not need to know about this incident. "Just forget it!" he said roughly. "I have already. And now excuse me, I have work to do."

The young knight's face clouded, and he was about to flare up, but then remembered that he was apologising to Kitt, so he bowed stiffly, turned on his heel smartly, and marched away.

Leonin chortled, his superciliousness back with a vengeance. "Do you know you just made a lifelong enemy Kitt? You saved his life, and now deprived him of making a song and dance about it, so he could feel better. He will always hate you for it. Quite naturally, too. You sure make it easy for men to resent you, my dear Sir blacksmith."

"Anybody could have panicked."

"Not you, Kitt, that sort of thing could never happen to you. That's rather the point, you see."

"Oh me, that's different."

Leonin burst out in laughter. "Really Sir Kitt, you are the limit! All the same, I'll miss that crude humour of yours."

"I won't miss your cooking," Kitt retorted. "That soup was vile. How you can spoil such simple food - luckily Avarik is unhurt and will recover."

Leonin directed a knock at Kitt's chin which the latter parried. "Cook survived? Thank the Gods. We were the targets. That's fine, we are knights. Others shouldn't suffer. It's beastly." The beautiful knight looked stern and forbidding.

Kitt agreed with him.

"Son!" Eckehart was standing in the door of the hall, beckoning with a worried face. "I need you to go up to the cliff, bring back an accurate description of the thing, and a piece or two if you can get them down."

"Can it wait?" Kitt thought of the patients he had to bring in and out of the surgery.

"It can't. I will help your mother."

"Allow me to assist you, my lord Eckehart," Leonin said. "And you Kitt, if you see another dragon give it hell. If it's two, give me a shout."

The metal bird had hit the southern promontory, and the steep rockface where the monstrous bird had foundered was now marred by a black, smoky spot, below and to the left where Malan Jian had sat.

Kitt climbed down the cliff. Twisted metal pieces were wedged into the cracks and lay on a ledge where gulls roosted. The white and grey birds were dipping and diving, but none landed. A smell of burnt flesh hung over everything, intermingling with the corrupted note of beginning decay.

Most debris had rained down on a ledge below into a colony of Blaupoot, foot-high birds with bright blue feet. The young birds weren't able to fly yet, and the gulls had taken advantage.

Kitt picked up a hand-long, light-grey piece of metal with jagged edges, and noted the dull silvery colour of the metal, almost like steel, but not quite - compared to steel this was an extraordinarily light material. It had been a wingtip. He found more pieces of the wings, with hollow bones formed exactly like those of a bird, if such a big bird existed, and the upper jaw. The saw-edge row of teeth was steel, with a razor edge that had Kitt's full appreciation. Eagerly he looked for the head and didn't see it.

He found a leg, made of the light metal unknown to him, ending in a long steel razor claw, and inside the leg was bleeding flesh, clinging to the metal, fused to it. It was like his father thought -the monster bird had been made of metal and living flesh. He continued his search, but he found no trace of the body itself, and no entrails. He found the lower jaw, but the head was still missing.

Kitt brought the wingtip, the claw, the leg and the jaws into the smithy and laid all on the table in the second room.

"Had a good look, Kitt?"

"No. I promised mother that I would not try to learn about Seidar or Zaubar."

Eckehart looked sharply at Kitt's face showing nothing. "You fought this, you better know about it. I'm saying it, and I'll take it up with mother."

The old smith lifted the leg, from which something disagreeable black and red hung limply; impervious to the smell of unnatural decay rising from it, he scraped at it with a knife. "He made the bones and the skin from metal, and also enforced the sinews and muscles." He spent some time scrutinising the tissue closely, tracing fine wires deep into the torn muscles. "You see?"

"I see."

Kitt turned the wingtip in his hands, tried it with a rasp. "What metal is this? Not iron, not copper, not steel or bronze. I never saw this before!"

"It is a metal that requires the heat of lightning to burn out of the earth. Once won it is easy enough to work. No use for blades though. Doesn't hold a proper edge. That's why he made the teeth from steel so they could cut a man in half."

"Who did make this bird? Who can do something like this?"

The smith chewed his beard angrily. "Maybe Diorlin can enlighten us," he said in a hard voice. "Go and find him, tell him I want to see him at once."

Kitt did not couch Eckehart's request to view the monster bird in polite words, but for once the old Swordmaster made no comment on that, as he followed the smith's summons. He looked at the pieces of the bird with lively interest.

"This - thing - came for you, Diorlin?"

Eckehart's bluntness lost nothing in Kitt's translation.

"I should definitely think so, oh, yes. Who else could it be meant for?" Diorlin's harsh laugh sounded misplaced.

"Maybe one of your knights, or the sailors, is not who he seems."

Diorlin snorted. "They are all exactly what they seem, bless them, poor innocents. I'm the only one meriting a sorcerous honour of such magnitude. As you'll surely agree."

The smith spoke rapidly and at some length in the language of the north, which the Tolosan swordmaster still did not understand beyond a few words, making a pause at what seemed a knotty point, then continuing rapidly, now and again interrupted by a curt question from Kitt. Diorlin had not heard the boy speak this sharply to his father before.

Finally, Kitt turned to Diorlin with a dissatisfied air. "Maybe it came for my father, not you."

"For your father?" Diorlin looked genuinely surprised. "Why should he feel that the monster came for him?"

"Professional jealousy. My father says he hasn't applied this art of welding steel to living flesh for . . . a long time. The first time he uses it again, the monster comes."

"Well, I suppose that the monster and myself have, shall we say, much in common."

"Do you know then who sent the metal bird?"
"I have the perfect idea. That just stinks like a machination of Zinnober's, that devil Hugo's tame sorcerer. Although I had devoutly hoped that not even he would be able to track us this far."

"You came twice. Ample opportunity to track you."

Eckehart spoke in his own language again. When he finished, Kitt translated.

"My father says that he knows one other man who can build this sort of creature. But he is no Tolosan, and his name is not Zinnober."

"Oh, I dare say. Zinnober is just a mercenary spell-mumbler and poisoner, not in the same class as whoever built this thing. But he is certainly doing much damage because he gets hold of people, you know. He must have got hold of somebody with the skill. A smith like yourself. And that means there may be another of these monster birds."

Eckehart talked again. This time Kitt did not interrupt, and his face was stony.

"My father does not believe that there is another bird. Creatures like this can't be built in a day. You know. The bird that came was built beforehand. Somebody suspected why you came."

"Yes, maybe Zinnober suspects my secret. But he can't know for certain, unless by dissecting my body, dead, or maybe alive." Diorlin rose, shook his head slightly, and sat down again. "The only ones who do know are the excellent smith Eckehart and the incomparable lady Aslaug. And you, my dear brilliant boy, who has been watching me lately in a way that I never in a hundred years could teach to my more civilised knights."

"Don't bother about us, Swordmaster. Better concentrate on that sorcerer. How he tracked you."

Diorlin smiled thinly. "You fought a great battle on the beach, Sir Kitt. But that is no reason for arrogance. No justification for forgetting the respect a Knight of the School owes to his elders and his teacher."

"I'm not arrogant. I'm tired of the evasions and half-truths my elders feed me. I'm young, but I'm not dumb." With a glare divided impartially between the two older men, he walked out of the smithy. Eckehart looked after his son with a worried frown creasing his face still further.

"They can get so very angry so very quickly at that age," Diorlin remarked mildly. "The young are so absolute. Everything to them is black or white, good or evil, the truth or a lie. It's really what makes them so endearing. How awkward that our translator has just stalked off in a huff. I would have liked to ask you which knowledge you have denied him." He smiled at the unresponsive smith and continued pronouncing carefully. "Kitt saved us without a thought for his own danger. For such a great fighter, he is so sweet-natured." He wondered if he still believed that himself. But as the swordmaster had expected, the smith brightened at these words.

"Three knights dead, Turin do Alvorge et Mondego, Orrin do Frades et Osuna, Tulga do Arosa et Manresa. Two won't live through the night, Wamba do Rasqera et Sousel, and Wallia do Galera et Orce. And almost half of the ship's crew unfit," Diorlin said in a resume. "Incredible as it seems, it could have been even worse. Madame, you have been an angel of mercy." He bowed to Aslaug. "Excuse the state of my attire, lady. It could have been worse if it hadn't been for that very timely wind. Is it a seasonal phenomenon of these isles?"

"A fall wind," Aslaug said placidly. "They start this time of year, making way for the snow."

"How extremely convenient."

"I need to continue the care of the wounded," Aslaug said through Kitt's translation. "I only could do very little on the shore."

"Certainly. And we others must see what we can do with the ship."

"Watch your men, Swordmaster Diorlin. There may be those walking about unaware of broken bones, or of some internal bleeding, due to the shock, or the medicine I gave them, which takes away the pain, but also awareness."

"Why that will be all the better. Need every hand, however shaky. We must get under sail as quickly as we can."

"The ship is burning down to the waterline," Kitt said. "You won't sail in that. The question is how you were tracked here?"

Diorlin turned on his heel, his wet black coat flapping.

"Do you delight in brutal truths, Sir Kitt?"

"Not particularly."

"Good. It's not an attractive character trait."

Aslaug spoke, and Kitt translated. "We must know how the metal bird could find you, and guard against it. Or something else may easily find you on your back journey. My mother must see all your possessions, each knight, including you, and every seaman."

"That is easy. We only have our cloaks and swords."

"She must see everything, every little thing you have on you."

"So that's what she thinks? And she thinks she can find out by some sort of sorc . . . magic?"

"Don't waste time on useless questions, Swordmaster," Kitt said without translating. "Of course, my mother means exactly what she says. And she has the right of it. Always. As you should know by now."

"It's quite clear who you inherited that iron determination from, to have your will in everything, Sir Kitt," Diorlin said sourly. "You needn't translate that either. Just tell the lady Aslaug, that we are in her hands, and glad to be."

Each knight and each sailor stood naked beside his possessions, while Aslaug went through every little thing.

In the little heap at the feet of Rintilian do Caspe et Fraga Aslaug found a small book of the verses of Gabrel Gades with a love knot woven out of glossy brown hair marking the page with *The Song of Roses*. She turned the hair between her fingers carefully, fingering each loop and knot. "And you also gave her a lock of your own hair." By her tone, it was clear that she merely asked for confirmation.

The knight looked very pink and mortified.

"Answer the lady Aslaug," Diorlin demanded, with a face like thunder.

"Yes," Sir Rintilian mumbled.

"So that's how they found us," Diorlin said, his voice soft and cold, his hand on his sword.

"The boy and the girl both did not know anything about it," Aslaug said. "The man who tied the thread," here her hand moved as if she was tracing an invisible thread that reached across sea and land, "spied on them and diverted the bond a gesture like this creates between two people, however far they may be apart. It is easily done."

"Anyone else who has anything of this nature hidden on his person, better speak out at once," Diorlin demanded sternly. His request met with silence and shrugging at which Diorlin cocked a sardonic eyebrow. Before the sarcastic comment all saw hovering on his lips could be delivered, the young knight spoke. He was near to tears. "I swore to her that I would never part with it, to take it to my grave."

"You may find your grave here on Isenkliff, Sir Rintilian," Leonin said softly; he also had his hand on his sword, and it was one of the rare moments which did not find the beautiful knight smiling. "I promise you to see to it myself, should we have any more of this from you. And you leave the book too. Were you the only one not to hear what was said concerning books? Anything with words written on it was to be given up and left here. If you had succeeded cheating the lord Eckehart out of his full payment, another monster bird or worse might have caught us on the high seas, without Kitt and his bow anywhere near."

"Sir Rintilian do Caspe et Fraga, I will believe that you were innocent if only stupid, by guiding Zinnober's malice to us," Diorlin said in a voice ringing with suppressed rage. "But to keep back the book is a very different matter. By this dishonest act, you have brought incalculable danger, and worse, dishonour to the School. You can be a Red Lily Knight no longer."

Sir Rintilian shot Kitt a look of pure hatred. They all knew by now who really wanted the books.

Kitt didn't particularly desire another edition of verses, and although he had learned enough to know better, he ventured to say so. "Wish one of you had carried a book on mathematics, or astronomy or a dictionary," he added.

Diorlin flew into the expected rage. "Whether you wanted the book or not is immaterial!" he yelled. "You are going to have it! Because that was the agreement!"

"I have already managed to make several enemies in the land of Tolosa before even seeing it. I really must visit there one day," Kitt murmured to Leonin, on whose face the old grin reappeared.

"Do come and you shall have the run of our school library. We only keep it as a matter form anyway. Nobody of us ever reads a book. Comfortable armchairs though, and I sometimes go in there to have an undisturbed snooze. You will just have to be careful when taking down the scrolls, as any might have a wine bottle concealed in it."

The ship had burned down to the waterline, the sails and rigging were ash, the masts charred.

The sailors, desperate to leave, had dragged the blackened, barely floating shell into lower water and were now crawling all over it intending to build a smaller ship and rig it with the spare sails which had been kept down in the lower hold, so that only the top layers and borders were singed. Ship-building tools and the order's gold were also found, dropped through the burning decks into the hold. The newly built ship would be crowded with all the survivors.

Sir Viterin was drying the pages of the Code, which he had not released, almost drowning until Kitt pulled him out of the sea.

The shock about the sorcerous attack was sitting deep, yet only eight men were lost, the three knights and five sailors who had been killed directly by the metal bird. The wounded men were walking about; Diorlin had been wrong about those knights, Wallia and Wamba, who he had pronounced as almost dead. Not only had they lived through the night, but they would have to live with the deep scars of that fateful day.

The captain -somebody had sewn up a padded leather patch which he wore over his empty eye-socket- reckoned that the makeshift vessel could take them to a Rilante port in the west. There Diorlin's gold would enable them to buy passage or a new vessel, if available.

All had only what they had stood up in at the time of the attack. The hall of Isenkliff gave them shelter and even a modicum of comfort. Leonin remarked with amazement upon the hot and cold water coming out of the wall of kitchen and bathroom. "In Tolosa, you'll find that only in the noble houses." He checked himself. "Of course, yours is a noble house. I was only saying . . ."

Kitt laughed at him.

All knights were helping to build the ship. All scanned the sky anxiously every day for flying silver monsters.

Kitt and Leonin had been shooting two goats every day to feed the crowd, as all stores were burnt or spoiled by seawater. The beautiful knight had learned to shoot quite well, and Kitt remarked upon that.

"Oh, don't tell anyone," Leonin begged. "A bow is no weapon for a knight. And anyway it's a small bow compared to yours. Did you have that when you were ten?"

"Horse riders' bow. Skolotian. You really don't know anything about bows."

"Naturally not, as I was explaining. You can get away with it, because you get away with anything, even work. When we work, it is always a lesson in humility, not taking pride in it as you do. Exotic. But nobody minds you. It's only Sir Kitt, they say. If anyone knew that I actually shot a bow, I would never live it down."

"What do they think you're doing, coming to the hunt?"

"Abusing my position as Senior Pupil to gad about, and shirk work."

"And that is better?"

"Infinitely."

Looking out over the sea from the mountaintop, Kitt noticed that the wind changed from the western breeze to an easterly direction. He saw sails unfolding on the eastern horizon and recognised the Birlinn Yehan, returning from Abalus.

"You know a ship by its sails from afar? Know just about everything, don't you?"

"I'd always recognise this ship. She has a steel skeleton, two hundred and eighty feet long without the beam which is thirty-six feet more. Three and a half masts, the main is a hundred and fifty feet. She has just set sail because . . ." his mother Aslaug had seen her come. "The wind changed. But she can run straight into the wind with steam. I don't know any other such ship. The hull is wooden, but everything else is steel."

"I can see how this appeals to you. Do you think it will call here and there would be space on it for us?"

Kitt hoped so. Brynnir's Herd decimated by the Witlyns was not yet numerous again, and soon it would be difficult to feed everyone.

\#

The crew of the Birlinn Yehan lined the rail to comment on the shipbuilding activities on the shore.

Captain Lodemar saw the hall of Isenkliff converted into a camp and understood the situation at once.

"Better not tarry," he agreed.

"We have no luggage," Diorlin said. "Only our knightly code. We are ready to go at once. Farewell lord Eckehart and lady Aslaug, I cannot hope to ever repay you."

"Maybe you will, Diorlin, one day," Aslaug said in a brittle voice.

Eckehart looked at her curiously, a new line of worry appearing on his craggy forehead.

Diorlin performed another of his ornate bows. "Then, I shall pray to the gods for such an occasion to arise."

The old swordmaster and the old master smith bowed to each other formally.

"But the wise never prays to the gods for anything," Aslaug said

362

sometime later.

Almost all the knights had many nice words to say to Kitt.
Sir Sintilian do Caspe et Fraga pointedly ignored everyone, and Sir
Gundemar do Esmoric et Ilaskas bowed to him stiffly, turned on his
heels without a word, and marched along the mole to the ship.

Leonin embraced Kitt; the elegant Tolosan knight was sincerely
moved.

Diorlin's handshake was like a clasp of iron. Kitt still watched him
warily, not letting him out of his sight until the old swordmaster went
away along the mole and stepped into the boat with the springy step
of a young man. He swarmed up the ladder to the Birlinn Yehan's
upper deck without a pause. Kitt heard his shrill laughter blown away
in the wind.

The Birlinn Yehan moved briskly out of the bay, driven by the
eastern wind. Kitt watched the sail on the horizon for a long time. He
did not go back to the house at once. There was so much to think
about, before he faced his parents alone, in the newfound silence of
Isenkliff.

His father Eckehart would not teach him the art of welding steel to
living flesh, and his mother Aslaug would never teach him how to
call up the winds and how to end pain with a touch and a word.
There even was his own promise not to touch the books of Seidar,
magic, Zaubar. Would all roads of accomplishment be barred to him
in this way, before he could reach their end? Or was there just one
road for every man? If so, which would be his? The warrior's way
seemed the only road left, and Diorlin alone had not held anything
back. "Maybe I should have gone with them after all."

The solitude of autumn fell like a veil drawn between Isenkliff and
the world. It was as if the island receded, until the roads on the sea
and to land no longer reached there. An opalescent mist hid it from
all sight.

Library

Documents in a dossier concerning the Kri in the office of Count Grigion Potaerea, adviser to Veterikus Keiter III Emperor of Daguilaria

The Kri appeared in Nordheim six years ago.

They appear to be a kind of northern people with light-coloured hair and eyes, yet taller than the tallest Nordheim warrior. They are built to proportions of perfect symmetry and resemble each other like brothers.

In fact, they are unrelated by blood to any other tribe.

Their numbers are small, not more than five thousand warriors, both men and women. This is not likely to increase due to their constant fighting among themselves and refusal to water down their blood by mating with women of other tribes.

They hire their sword to anyone who pays their price.

They know no other trade.

This price is six to ten times higher than the going rates for ordinary mercenaries. They have proved worth it.

I have it from reliable sources that they use all their pay to buy weapons and armour of iron and steel, which they value far above copper and bronze. There are rumours of a steel hoard on Kullen Tor in Tridden Moor, which is a place in Lalland.

The Kri's strength and skill at arms surpass that of even the best Northern warriors. Only Kri can fight Kri efficiently. They have no inhibition to do so. It is thought that they do this to keep strong their race. I have not been able to ascertain this information first hand. The Kri seldom deign to speak to anyone not of their blood, being by nature a very surely and superior race.

The strangest thing about the Kri is that their females are also warriors and that they have to be hired for the same price. Many Kri will take service only in pairs, one man and his woman, or not at all.

The lords of Burgenland now often use Kri to bring about the death of rival lords in challenges. They were also used to dispatch hostile chieftains by this means, breaking the courage of the tribes' warriors by the humiliation of their leaders. Recently the Judges of Irmin Prono ended this practice by declaring the Kri unfit to challenge, citing their alien blood.

Although single fighters by inclination the Kri have also proved capable line fighters and have been used with spectacular success to break shield walls. The formation called boar's head, with the Nordheim champions fighting in front, could as yet never break a Kri line. These the Kri despatch without fail, leaving the retainers and thralls to the onslaught of the ordinary troops.

It is rumoured that several local rulers and merchants have used Kri mercenaries as assassins, though this has not yet been proven, as the Kri is capable of great stealth.

However, the Kri are a weapon too sharp and heavy for puny hands, as the lords of Burgenwald are beginning to find. The mere presence of Kri mercenaries in any fief kindles mistrust, destroying old alliances. The substantial financial outlay their hiring involves does strain the fortunes, requiring ever more looting to recover the cost of war. Feuds that have been smouldering for long years are now spreading like oil on water. Lands are laid waste and Burgenland is bleeding out.

Soon the Kri will have to come south in search of new employ. It is imperative to take measures that no Kri shall be hired by another power or person, be it ally or enemy. Your humble servant considers the Kri a perfect instrument for the furthering of Imperial interests in Nordheim. And once their strange reticence to outbreed is overcome – the world.

Letter by Mauran Neveokki, merchant

Cannot this lecturing renegade Theusten lout at least make pretence of begging your lordship's indulgence for pronouncing so strongly? However, despite his rambling, crude, presumptuous manner he is entirely correct. Your Excellency's most obedient servant F L.

Note attached by Frenz Linkerhand, Personal Secretary to Count Grigion Potaerea

All Kri mercenaries must either be bound to the exclusive service of the Invincible Light of Murom or destroyed by any means whatsoever.

Copy of a written order from Vladimir Highking of Murom to Iliya, First Overlord of the Muromian Host

From the Chronicles of Castle Waninge

When the Kri warriors saw that Swatgrim was a blacksmith, they did not kill him.

And so, it came to pass that this smith discovered one of the greatest secrets, and lived to tell it. Which is where the Kri warriors go to at every winter from the full moon before winter Equinox to the full moon after, and will not heed commands nor give reasons or consider entreaties.

It is to Kullen Tor they go, a mountain rising out of the dread Tridden Moor in the land called Lalland.

From all the lands where Kri serve as mercenaries they come, even the kingdom of Nyrshany and the empire of Murom, to prove their Right to Live in their sacred challenges when they fight each other one on one, every man backed by his woman.

Come winter solstice those who have survived, return to their place of service. The losers of those fights never return. No Kri gives quarter to another Kri.

On Kullen Tor remain the children and the fledgeling warriors in the care and teaching of the venerable old Kri.

I Maneck, servant of Threefold Divarmitris the One and Only God set this down at the behest of my Lord Bernward as it was told me by the blacksmith Svatgrim of Nordheim when he was allowed shelter in my lord's domain of Waninge.

Shangar Shaark Ayen's song of the Wrong World

Nineteen sun squares
Gita
Feen fight
Feen die
Shadow die
Tini Trees thirsty
Feen fear
Feen hungry
Feen shame
Gita.
Thirteen sun squares
Gita die.
Two sun squares
Gita return Sreedok.

Tales told by the bard Marek the Konoveler: The Eisenstein in the Graumeer

The Eisenstein is an island in the Graumeer, the grey northern sea.

It is the top of a sunken land. Metal ores of rare purity thread the inside of the rocks, and depots of coal repose in the dank depth of the earth. The people on the mainland of Nordheim, Ferys, Gesatoi, Teoden and Theusten, shun the Eisenstein.

But a brave fisherman who dared approach by boat and left corn, or charcoal or a sack of slaked lime on Devil's Anvil, the great flat stone on the South coast, would find a gold coin on it when he returned the other day. And if he laid two pieces of iron on the stone, and returned after seven days had passed, there would be a knife, or an axe, a lance or a hoe or a hammer lying on the flat stone. One could never foresee what it would be. That weapon or tool would never break, the edge never dull. The second piece of iron is payment for the smith.

Few men of Nordheim have ever seen the blacksmith who tends Brynnir's Forge, nor wished to meet him. They say he is in league with beings from the beginning of time and not quite human, the Lütte Jotun, eaters of human flesh.

Few northern men dare to come to the Eisenstein, for fear of passing the island of Wittewal whose lord abides no evil. And who could be sure of themselves?

Those who come to Isenkliff are heroes. They come in ships sailing up north the coasts of Cladith Culuris and Rilante, turn east at Kallasness, sail through the Scattered Islands. There they are hunted by the ships of the Nordmänner of Asringholm, with their high prows ending in serpent's or bird's heads.

Then, where the sea washes the roots of Dark wood called the Bacenis, come long slim canoes full with wild redhaired men who have snake eyes.

Or they take the land way, through the lands of the Polabi and Ferys, whose villages lay like islands in the bogs and woods, and who do not like strangers. When they reach the coast of the Sea of Graumeer, they can pay a gold bribe, escape to have their throats cut and be sailed to Isenkliff, made to jump hip-deep into the ice-cold water and wade to the stony beach, for all Nordheim men refuse to approach nearer than that.

When the warrior finally reaches the Eisenstein, he has to fight an invincible giant, and only those who stand this final test are rewarded by the Eternal Smith with a blade or armour made from indestructible steel, hard, supple and murderously keen, that never notches or breaks - the Aurora Steel. And they pay the earth for it. It is worth every single heavy cold coin. The cream of the fighters swears by Aurora steel, they can afford to pay the price.

Such swords are a mark of excellence. The Eternal Smith sees the innermost of every man, and he can do many things that surpass even the forging of the Aurora Steel.

Itinerant smith's song of Brynnir's Forge

There always is a smith on Isenkliff.
Take up Brynnir's hammer, take the wow.
Learn Brynnir's songs and earn much gold.
Sit in Brynnir's hall and never leave,
Until another grips Brynnir's hammer,
Another lays his hand on Brynnir's forge.
Then one may leave, and one must stay.
There always is a smith on Isenkliff.

Nordland Sagas: The Smith of Isenkliff

Brynnir was a Swaterf	In the mountain of Isenkliff
Smelted iron silver gold	Hammered fog and ice and air
Forged Niflhelm and Isabrünne,	
	Gullenbrand, Grimger and Hartshield.

Wollhand was a smith	Came to Brynnir's forge
Hammered Gullbaugen,	From clay he forged the Screaming
	Wings.

Swatsollig was a smith	Took Wollhand's place.
Spread Screaming Wings	Wollhand flew from Isenkliff.

Orm was a smith	Took Swatsollig's place.
Sigurd came to Isenkliff	Asked of Orm a sword
The hero slew Orm	Slew Brynnir in the mountain
Far away from Isenkliff	Brynnir's spear slew Sigurd.

Wittig was a smith	Came to Isenkliff
To Brynnir's living curse	Took up Brynnir's hammer
Forged the sword	of ice and quicksilver
Forged the sword	of flesh and bone.

Eckehart is a smith	There always is smith on Isenkliff.

Book Asruna, Fragments

The island of Isenkliff lies in the cold seas of the Graumeer. Veins of pure metal ores thread the inside of Isenkliff, sleeping swords for warriors unborn.

Beds of rock coal repose in the wet hot darkness of the earth, to feed Brynnir's Forge.

Hidden powers work day and night where fires glow deep down in the kingdom of Erzkuning, lord over the Lütte Jotun folk.

On Isenkliff stands Brynnir's forge.

There always is a smith on Isenkliff.

###

A white island lies in the Graumeer.

The Swaterf Finsterkuning lives on Wittewal. The Dark King abides no evil.

To find the truth of a man send him to Wittewal alone from Sunrise to Sunset.

###

No one knows whence the Kri came.

They broke out of the north-eastern ice fields in Jotunheim, from where all things bad come.

Some say that they were the spawn of the Isjotun, Ice Giants.

Some say that Thurym the Giant King created the Kri from water drops out of the Bitter Fountain at the depth of Hollgard to fight against Donner and destroy Nordheim, the land under the Defender's protection.

Some say that as Slitur River runs out of the Poisoned Valley, the bloody waters carry knives in their waves and carry the Kri above them.

But wise men know a forgotten tale about an ancient people in Strakenland, driven out of Nordheim for their coldness of heart and of a thousand warriors' march over the Western Rim. The Thousand went around the world in pursuit of red deeds, and the Kri were the ones who returned from that march.

We still do not know to this day.

They made their settlement in Lalland, at Kullen Tor in Tridden Moor, and sold their swords to the enemies of the Gods and the People for gold and iron.

Tainted in their origins and nature, these bought Kri made war on Nordheim, slaying kings and champions, fouling the ancient customs of battle, leaving leaderless and hopeless the people, full of fear and prey to foreign lords and to the Empire.

It was in the summerless year at the Allting of Iloe that Modi's Urloghorn was sounded east, south, west and north, and the Thirteen Judges of Irmin Prono called the Allfriede that all feuds and enmity might cease among the peoples of Nordheim until the Kri were destroyed to the last.

At Winter Solstice Svalinir's spear was cast over the Kri. This happened on the Sixth Winter Solstice after the Kri had appeared in Nordheim.

Chronicles of the Order of Red Lily Knights of Eliberre

In the old times, it was the custom that the Tolosan kings were elected by all swordbearing men from among their midst.

In that time a man's honour was his most valuable possession.

As Tolosa became a powerful and rich land, the privilege to elect the King became the reserve of the nobles who spoke for the men of their following.

Amalrin, son of Alaron I attempted to found a dynasty and took the throne. Not to be denied their privilege the nobles elected Luvin according to custom.

King Luvin, capable and ruthless, with the support of all the noble lords behind him, destroyed Amalrin, and all who had taken his party. There was more blood than wine drunk in Tolosa in that time, and thus the Code was restored.

Soon after he had taken the reins of Tolosa with an iron hand, like that of a bucking steed, King Luvin passed the Law of Lese Majeste. Hence he always was surrounded by his guards. Many knights denounced as betrayal this behaviour among equals who lived by of the Code of Knights.

Luvin forced Tolosa into law, order and prosperity. So great a ruler was Luvin considered, that his son Luvigin was proclaimed his father's successor. Thus, it came to pass that Tolosa had a dynasty after all. This breach of the old custom seemed to remain without adverse consequences, because Luvigin continued the great work of his father. It was in that time, that Tolosa waxed rich through trade and artisanship, and became famous for it's wine, glass, lace, stonecutting, and not last for the serpent blades.

Finally, the breach of the old customs bore in itself its own vengeance.

Luvigin's sons were weak, and a long time of degeneration began. The lords fought the King and each other for power and the Saddle Throne was won by poison and black magic.

Since then the Knights of the Order of the Red Lily obey the King only if the King obeys the Code. Each must choose his allegiance and once chosen, there is no turning back.

Betra Hyerote, the Iron Rock, is the mountaintop of a submerged ancient land rising from the bottom of the Graumeer.

In the language of the northern barbarians beyond whose bleak realms it lies, it is named Isenkliff and held in awe.

For a warrior to cross the vast lands of the Northern barbarians, have a blade made to measure on the Iron Rock, and make it back is an adventure worthy of a Knight.

The warrior desirous of Aurora steel must traverse the lands of the northern barbarians to the end of the world, where the Eternal Smith lives on a fiery island in the Graumeer, the Grey Northern Sea.

There he must fight an invincible giant, and only those who fight the giant well may ask the Eternal Smith for a sword, a battle axe or armour.

It is said that the Eternal Smith of the Iron Rock can see into a warrior's heart and that sometimes he will tell him the outcome of future battles, and if the knight asks it, the smith can tell him the manner of his death.

It is better not to ask.

It is said that the Eternal Smith can fulfil all wishes a warrior may have.

It is better not to ask.

The instructive tale of the dragon under the Castle of Alkantara

Once upon a time when the world was pure, the dragon Viboron awoke under the Castle of Alkantara after a hundred years of sleep.

Viboron was a True Dragon with four legs and two wings, and in his sleep, he had grown. Big as he was, he still favoured the cow's milk. When it came into the stables to drink its track in the sand was molten glass, setting the straw afire where it passed, and eating the cattle that perished in the fires.

Five of the best and bravest Red Lily Knights had already paid their courage with their lives when the Grandmaster of the Order forbade to attempt battle with the dragon.

The people of Alkantara grew very disappointed with the Order and even refused to supply the Dining Hall with food, but the Grandmaster would not allow to confront the dragon.

One day all folks celebrated in the street of Alkantara, and there was great jubilation.

"Free is the city of the dragon!"

And before the Grandmaster in the Hall came Sir Isidor, the youngest knight, and spoke: "I have fulfilled the knight's duty, to save and succour, free the world of trouble and harm. The dragon that wasted the land lies slain. Peace returns for the farmer in the valley, the herder on the hill, the traveller on the road."

"You have done what none could do before you, like a true hero," said the Grandmaster. "But say, what is the very first duty of a knight of the School?" The knight bowed his head. "Obedience to the Code is the first duty."

"And this duty, my son, you have failed by undertaking a battle that has been forbidden to all the knights."

"I took no unnecessary risk. I remembered that strength must be guided by wisdom, and guile must conquer brutish power. From a wise man, I learned that the call of gold is all-powerful for the dragon; it is a smell in his nose, the shine of gold blinding to his eyes, a song in the dragon's soul.

"And so, I made a dragon image and plated it in gold. Inside I hid a great crossbow with an iron arrow six feet long.

"Then I drove a herd of cattle near the hill of Alkantara. When the beast had gorged, it retired into his cave to sleep. Viboron did not hear me bring the golden image until I was before the cave.

"Then the call of gold woke Viboron, and out he came, the horrible monster, like a grey mountain. When it saw the golden dragon, it stood still to gaze upon it. I shot my arrow, piercing through the beast. And I took my good sword and ran in to finish, striking under the belly, where all creatures are soft.

"The long tail knocked me from my feet, and I saw into the great gaping maw studded with teeth, and I thought my days were over. But Viboron's wounds were mortal, and the dragon fell, burying me under his bulk. My followers came, the brave souls, to free me and not a scratch had I sustained."

At hearing this story, there was a great cheering, and all present, including the other knights, demanded that the young hero be crowned with laurels.

But the Grandmaster called for Order and spoke.

"The dragon that wasted the land you slew with your strong hand. A demi-god are you now for the world. But to your Order, you return as a renegade. A more poisonous dragon has been born in your own heart, the wilful mind that brings discontent, disobedience and disorder. That is the true dragon that destroys the world. Even a barbarian can have courage, but it is the Vow of Obedience that makes a Red Lily Knight, to harness his own will in the service of the Order. Lay down the cloak with the Red Lily and go out of my sight, for you have disregarded the Code."

A storm of protest broke out in the Hall of the School.

Sir Isidor alone did not protest. The knight lay down his cloak at the Grandmaster's feet, kissed his hand and turned to leave the Hall.

When he was by the door, the Grandmaster called him back, for he had now shown true humility.

The School of the Order of the Red Lily moved to Eliberre, for the people of Alkantara had showed themselves unworthy. It is a shame to this day.

The instructive tale of the Knight and Tyrant slayer

Once upon the time when the Capital was still in Eliberre, it came to pass that King Luvin the Ruthless rode to hunt with his entourage.

A white stag sprang up before them.

The hunters followed this rare animal through woods and heather, but they could not catch up to it.

One by one the king's attendants fell back until only one knight held pace with the King, Sir Damon.

At last, the King brought down the white stag with his spear.

And across the body of the white stag, Sir Damon challenged his King to battle.

King Luvin reminded the knight of a new law, the Law of Lese Majeste, the inviolability of kings.

"And if you will not fight as a knight, you will be killed as a dog."

The King answered, "I will face you in battle, Sir Damon, but I do so to preserve my life against criminal assault, and not because I recognise the Knight's Code for which you stand."

They drew their swords and began fighting, King Luvin and Sir Damon.

But the knight had not realised that in pursuit of the stag they had not ridden straight, and the king's followers were far nearer than he had thought. Had the knight known how near the king's men were already, he would have challenged all the same for hatred of the tyrant who slew so many valiant men in the Battle of a Thousand Knights.

The fight drew on long enough for the king's followers to catch up, and they took Sir Damon prisoner.

King Luvin condemned the rebellious knight to death according to the new law.

Sir Damon pleaded a six-day stay of execution until he had given his sister in marriage. As a guarantee for his return, he offered his best friend Sir Carlon as a hostage.

The King granted Sir Damon the six days stay, stipulating that if he had not returned on the morning of the sixth day, his friend Sir Carlon would be executed in his place, but the knight would be free of the sentence if he never set foot in the king's city again.

Sir Damon gave his sister in marriage and set out to return to the King. His journey stood under an unlucky star.

About to cross a river, robbers set on him. He pleaded with them to let him go, as he had only his life, and that was forfeit to the King. But the robbers would not desist, and so he smote them, and when three of them lay dead, the rest fled.

Then he called across the river for the ferryman, but the ferryman had seen the battle, was scared and would not come. The knight jumped into the river and swam across, but the current carried him far downriver.

It was already noon of the sixth day when he saw the towers of Eliberre. On the road, Sir Damon met a man who knew him, and called to him to flee, as his friend Sir Carlon had already been executed.

Upon hearing that dire news, the knight cried out. "And is it too late and I cannot come as saviour, death shall unite us, and the tyrant will not mock the Honour of Knights!"

At last, Sir Damon reached the place of execution; his friend knelt on the scaffold, and the executioner raised his sword.

The knight pushed through the crowd calling loud to the executioner to stay his hand, that he, Sir Damon, was the one convicted to death.

The execution was halted, and there was a tear in many an eye, even veterans of battle were not ashamed to cry.

The story sung ever since is how King Luvin granted both loyal friends their lives, begging them to accept his friendship as the third in their allegiance.

But the true story is that both friends were brought before the King, and many pleaded for them. And king Luvin judged that as the knight had been too late, and as he had returned to Eliberre, both Sir Damon and Sir Carlon had forfeited their lives. He granted Sir Carlon a pardon, banning him from Tolosa under the loss of all his possession, to never return.

Sir Damon was executed.

Printed in Great Britain
by Amazon